RUINS

THE SOVEREIGNS SERIES BOOK ONE

AMANDA ZUELO

MIDNIGHT REIGN PUBLISHING LLC

First Draft Edit by H. Sawyer

Editing by Renzo DeLuca

First edition 2025

CONTENTS

Dedication   VII

Epigraph   IX

Trigger Warning   XI

1. Santo   1

2. Santo   6

3. Santo   13

4. Vasilisa   20

5. Vasilisa   31

6. Santo   41

7. Vasilisa   48

8. Vasilisa   54

9. Santo   60

10. Santo   67

11. Vasilisa   75

12. Santo   83

13. Vasilisa   92

14. Santo   98

15.	Santo	103
16.	Vasilisa	113
17.	Santo	125
18.	Vasilisa	131
19.	Vasilisa	142
20.	Santo	149
21.	Vasilisa	158
22.	Santo	163
23.	Vasilisa	172
24.	Santo	178
25.	Vasilisa	189
26.	Santo	196
27.	Vasilisa	204
28.	Santo	214
29.	Vasilisa	222
30.	Vasilisa	230
31.	Santo	238
32.	Vasilisa	252
33.	Santo	261
34.	Vasilisa	268
35.	Santo	279
36.	Vasilisa	283
37.	Santo	291
38.	Vasilisa	300

39. Santo   310

40. Vasilisa   319

41. Santo   326

42. Vasilisa   338

43. Santo   345

44. Santo   355

45. Vasilisa   362

46. Santo   367

47. Vasilisa   375

48. Santo   384

49. Vasilisa   393

50. Santo   403

51. Vasilisa   412

52. Santo   419

53. Vasilisa   425

54. Santo   435

55. Vasilisa   444

56. Santo   454

57. Vasilisa   456

58. Santo   460

59. Vasilisa   468

60. Santo   474

Epilogue One   485

Epilogue Two   488

Acknowledgements 491

About the Author 493

For anyone who has ever feared their darkness was too much
to love. May you find someone who not only embraces it,
but sees your shadows as beautiful.

This is for you.

"The endurance of darkness can bring forth your own light."
Harper Sawyer

TRIGGER WARNING

This book contains mature themes and content that may be triggering
to some readers. Topics include:
Violence
Murder
Graphic descriptions of death
PTSD and mental health struggles
Emotional manipulation
Attempted abduction
Attempted sexual assault
Power imbalances in relationships
Blood play
Explicit sexual content.
Please read at your discretion.

CHAPTER 1

SANTO

17 YEARS OLD

I t was my mother's hand.

Over a week ago, my father, brother, and I all received pieces of my mother's mutilated body.

I received her hand.

The one that held mine for seventeen years, that scuffled my hair when I was happy and wiped my tears when I scraped a knee.

There it laid, severed from her body, with her wedding ring still glittering on her finger.

My father gave it to her when he proposed and declared that she was the most beautiful woman he had ever seen.

Their love, in this kind of life, belonged in the books I read growing up, a love fit for fairytales rather than the nightmare it has become.

I spend the night hacking every surveillance camera in the area for an inkling of which one of our enemies did this to her.

That's my job now.

It's my time to join Cosa Nostra, work for my father, the Don, and find my mother's murderer.

My stomach lurches as I imagine what she must have endured, the fear she must have felt.

The computer pings.

I found it.

I found surveillance from a traffic camera of the men in question.

I send off the footage to my father's email and I continue to search for anything closer to her home.

Her home.

That was his biggest mistake.

If the great Marcello Amato made any mistake in his life, it was separating my mother, from our family home. In his fear for her safety, he did the one thing that caused her demise.

Another ping thrills through the computer as it pulls up footage from the broken camera I salvaged from the front of her estate, but I can't watch it.

I *won't* watch it.

I refuse to watch as they take my mother from the front steps of her home.

Instead, I send the footage to my father.

I blow up their images from the traffic camera and put them through the facial recognition software I built last year.

Grabbing what's left of my energy drink, I chug it down as I wait.

I'm supposed to start Stanford next week. I graduated high school early and I'm ready to get away from this shit. I don't want to be a consigliere, or an underboss, or a soldier.

I want to invent; I want to make my genius ideas tangible and help people.

I don't want to kill, fight, steal or maim.

I want to be me. I want to read; I want to build.

I want to be the son that makes my mother proud whether or not she's here.

Another ping.

A hit.

The screen pulls up two photos of the men who took her. Their names… they're Armenian.

That doesn't make sense.

As far as I know, Vartan Sarkisian, head of the Armenian mob, doesn't have an issue with us. We aren't friendly, but we aren't enemies.

His men wouldn't do this unprovoked.

I send over the photos and intel to my father's email, and I finally leave my computer, throw myself on my bed and rest.

***

With a jolt, I'm ripped from sleep by the forceful hands of my older brother. His grip is tight and urgent, adrenaline snapping through me as he shoves a pair of rumpled jeans at my chest.

"We have to get ready," Angelo seethes, his normally smooth voice rough and strained. "We found those fuckers."

My mind struggles to catch up with his intense energy. "Where are *we* going? Who is Dad sending?"

Angelo's jaw clenches, the muscles jumping beneath his skin. "Who is he *sending*? He's sending us!" He bellows, spittle flying from his lips. "We are spearheading this shit, it's about *our* mother. You want anyone else avenging her death?"

Sitting on the edge of my bed, I run a shaky hand through my hair. "Angelo, I don't want to do this."

He shoves me roughly, grabbing the collar of my shirt and lifting me until our faces are inches apart. "You don't *want* to?" he scoffs. "You don't have a choice, little brother." He pushes me back onto the bed forcefully.

I bounce slightly but steady myself, bracing for a punch that never comes. "I can't do it, Angelo. I'm not like you."

He turns away quickly, but then whirls back around to throw a shirt at me before getting in my face again. "Like *me*?" He locks his darkened gaze onto mine, his voice filled with venom and self-loathing. "A monster like me, you mean?"

I shake my head and try to speak, but he cuts me off.

"No, you think that don't you? Because you were sheltered under mommy's protection while I had to struggle and fight for Dad's approval."

He sneers at me.

"While you buried your nose in books and hid away with your little trinkets, building foolish gadgets like a child, I was getting my hands dirty and preparing for a battle like this."

He spreads his arms wide, manic. "And this, little brother, is the biggest fight of our lives. So, you're going to have to pull your head out of the clouds, close your fairy tale books, and get your ass up because tonight will be your first kill."

His words hang in the air, heavy with tension and the weight of our family's vendetta.

My heart races even faster, thumping against my chest like a wild animal trying to escape its cage. My breaths come in sharp gasps, each one harder to catch than the last. The room feels smaller; the walls closing in on me as I struggle to breathe.

"Angelo, please. I can't do it."

"You can!" he shouts, grabbing me by the shoulders, his fingers dig in painfully. "When we spar, you- you get angry and strong. Use whatever you feel then to your advantage now."

"That's just adrenaline, I—"

"Then use it!" He shakes me, his eyes blazing with a ferocity I've never seen before. "Remember how you felt when you found Ma's hand in that box? Think about her begging for help and no one coming. Use that anger," he grits, pushing me away.

My vision blackens around the edges.

And when it clears, I find myself standing over a sniveling man; the same man from the photos I sent my father.

He's one of the men who took my mother.

In one trembling hand, I hold a sharp knife, while in the other, a pair of plyers clamps down on a severed tongue.

My heart is pounding so hard it feels as if it will burst out of my chest.

The man before me sobs uncontrollably, blood spilling from his mouth in a constant stream.

Another man is tied to a chair as Angelo beats him mercilessly. Knuckles cracking against bone. Wet, sick sounds.

A sharp ringing overtakes everything.

The knife is still in my hand. My fingers won't let go.

The man isn't screaming anymore. Blood drips from my grip, warm and thick.

I don't know if I want to vomit or if I feel nothing at all.

Then—darkness.

When my vision returns, I'm standing in the foyer of my father's home. The weight of his hand hitting my shoulder feels like a heavy boulder pushing me under waves. My shirt is stiff with dried blood, the metallic tang still clinging to my skin. My muscles ache—*how long have I been running on adrenaline?* The sudden stillness of the house feels foreign, like I've stepped into a place I no longer belong.

"I'm proud of you; we got them," he says with a beaming smile. "You've made names for yourselves, Scythe and Sinner. Your mother would be proud."

My gaze falls on my brother, noticing how worn he looks.

How long has it been since I last saw him?

His eyes meet mine and he places a heavy arm on my shoulder, leading me up the stairs.

"We did it, Scythe," he says with a sense of triumph in his voice. "We avenged her."

"Scythe?" I question, confused by the use of this nickname.

He chuckles darkly.

"We did good," he repeats, emphasizing each word. "It was a long and difficult month, but we did it."

My mind reels trying to piece together what happened.

A month?

Memories flood back to me in disjointed fragments, bringing with them a whirlwind of emotions; relief, grief, dread.

It all feels like a distant dream now that we've achieved our goal, but at what cost?

5

CHAPTER 2

SANTO

29 YEARS OLD

When my father's call comes through, I'm elbow-deep in wiring Athena, my latest surveillance system, into every inch of my estate.

The last perimeter is nearly secured when his name slashes across my screen, cutting through the silence like a blade.

Tension tightens down my spine. My teeth clench.

I *hate* being interrupted.

But when the Don calls, you answer.

I exhale, swallowing the irritation burning beneath my skin. It's not just the interruption—it's the disruption of control. Athena isn't just a project; it's a fortress, a statement. Proof of my strength. My legacy. Built with my own hands.

Leaving it unfinished feels like leaving my doors wide open, inviting enemies inside.

The weight of it undone sits heavy in my ribs as I pull up to my father's estate. The place looms, all excess and power, a monument to the life carved out for me before I ever had a say in it.

I park at the front, already mapping out my exit.

In and out. Keep the old man satisfied so I can get back to things that actually matter.

Then I see it.

Angelo's Ferrari. Gleaming beneath the afternoon sun like a coiled serpent.

That changes everything.

This isn't a routine check-in.

This is business.

And in our world, business means blood.

One of the guards moves to open the heavy oak doors, barely glancing at me.

He's new.

I don't acknowledge him. He won't last long enough for it to matter.

My steps echo against the cold stone, each click deliberate, each movement weighted with purpose. The house feels darker than usual. *Colder.*

The kind of cold that doesn't leave. The kind that seeps into your bones and stays there.

This house raised us in shadows, molding us into what we are. My brother and I grew up here, our childhood etched into these walls.

Then our mother left, and with her went the only light we'd ever known. Summers at her estate were the closest thing we had to warmth.

But in this family, light never lasts long.

Our father shapes us with iron and fire, carving away every soft edge until only sharpness remains. Reverence. Fear.

He demands both.

I approach his study, every step a reminder of the man he made me. A man forged in his image, still walking willingly into the lion's den.

I knock, braced for the usual grunt.

Instead—

"Come in."

Not his usual bark. *Too light.* Too damn cheerful.

I push open the door, and the thick stench of cigar smoke wraps around me, suffocating and dense. It clings to everything, settling in the air like a warning. Familiar, but heavier.

At his desk, my father grins. *Too wide. Too satisfied.*

Like he's already won a game I haven't even realized we're playing.

"Santo, my boy!" My father's voice booms through the room, arms spread in mock warmth as he gestures to the seat beside Angelo.

Angelo sits stiffly, legs spread, hands folded. Black-on-black suit, severe against the mahogany. His gaze meets mine, then drops.

Angelo *never* looks away.

Unless he's hiding something.

Warning bells set off in my head. The energy in the room shifts, settling into my bones like lead

This is *not* a check-in.

I move toward the empty chair, slow and measured, lowering myself into it without breaking eye contact with my father.

"What's this about?" My voice is neutral, but the tightness in my gut says I won't like the answer.

My father leans back, exhaling a thick stream of smoke as he taps his cigar against the edge of a crystal ashtray.

"It's a celebration," he says, smugness curling at the edges of his mouth.

I don't blink.

My gaze flicks to Angelo.

His expression stone still , fixed on our father.

"And what exactly are we celebrating?"

"Your impending marriage," my father announces, grin widening.

The words slam into me.

I freeze.

Silence stretches, too thin, too heavy, broken only by the slow tick of the clock.

I exhale. "I must have misheard. Did you just say *marriage?*"

"I did." His eyes gleam. "Your marriage will solidify our alliance with the Russians."

I drag a hand over my jaw, biting back the surge of heat threatening to rise. It's no secret that Angelo and Maksim Korsakov, the Pakhan of the Bratva, have been close since childhood.

A decade ago, Maksim's father stepped down, passing the reins to his son—something our father should have done years ago.

He didn't.

And now, this is the leash he's tightening around *my* neck.

"Why not Angelo?" My voice is low, sharp. "He's next in line to lead."

My father's expression doesn't change, but his eyes go colder. "I have other plans for Angelo."

The vagueness grates.

He reaches into his desk, pulls out a thick manila folder, and slides it toward me.

I don't touch it.

Instead, I inhale slowly, forcing the tension from my neck and shoulders before snatching the folder off the desk in one sharp, deliberate motion. The rough edge scrapes against my fingertips as I flip it open.

The first thing I see is a photograph.

A young woman stares back at me—golden hair cascading in soft waves, framing a face too light for the weight of the world she comes from. Crystal blue eyes shine with an untouched brightness, out of place in the darkness we swim in.

Delicate features make her almost ethereal.

She's smiling. *Genuinely* smiling.

It's disarming.

She wears a fitted black turtleneck tucked into a dark plaid skirt that hits mid-thigh, the bare stretch of skin between the hem and her ankle boots adding an edge of playfulness to an otherwise composed appearance. The juxtaposition feels intentional—elegance laced with subtle rebellion.

Her full lips curve with that soft smile.

Like she doesn't know anything about the life waiting for her.

She looks *kind*. Fragile. *Breakable.*

"Your bride," my father announces, his voice slicing through my thoughts. He gestures toward the photo with that same smug satisfaction. "The cousin of the Pakhan."

I lift an eyebrow, letting the folder drift shut under my fingers as I lean back in the chair.

"She looks young." The words fall flat, emotionless, but the implication is clear.

"She's twenty," he replies, casual.

I set the folder down, sliding it across the desk without breaking eye contact. "She's *too* young. I'm not marrying her."

The leather creaks as I straighten—a deliberate end to the conversation.

It doesn't end.

"Nonsense." His tone hardens, warmth gone. "Your mother and I had more years between us than that."

I hold his gaze, letting the silence stretch between us, thickening the air, making it heavier than the smoke curling between us.

"That's exactly my point," I say, cold.

Beside me, Angelo cracks open the folder, his interest obvious as his gaze lingers on the photo. His lips quirk in amusement.

"I'll marry her."

He leans back with a lazy chuckle, just enough bite to rile me.

Our father shakes his head, a grin tugging at the corner of his mouth. "No, she's for Santo," he says, gesturing toward me without missing a beat.

His eyes flick to Angelo. "Besides, once he marries her, you get what you want."

My attention snaps to Angelo.

His grin falters. Something unreadable flashes behind his eyes. I catch the slight dip of his head—shame, maybe regret, but it's gone as quickly as it came.

"And what exactly do you get, Angelo?" My voice is sharp, cutting through the smoke.

Angelo flushes, his easygoing façade cracking. He surges forward, hands slicing the air as he fires off rapid Italian, reminding our father he was supposed to *wait* before telling me.

They launch into their usual argument, voices rising and falling, colliding in a tangle of frustration and unspoken resentment. I don't bother stepping in. Let them argue. Let them exhaust themselves in their back-and-forth.

Their voices fade into the background as I refocus on the folder in front of me. I flip through the details, every line meticulously typed out like a résumé, like a fucking sales pitch, for a girl who doesn't yet realize the weight of the life she's being sold into.

Vasilisa Popov.

Twenty years old.

One younger sister.

Likes dogs, lilies, music, and baking.

I skim over the trivial list. None of it matters. She could collect stamps for all I care.

But as my eyes drift lower, the next paragraph pulls me up short.

Her father owns NovaRael—the largest tech and surveillance company in the city.

"*There* it is."

My father's voice slices through the noise, shushing Angelo with a raised hand. His grin stretches wider as he gestures toward the page in my grip.

"You see that, Santo? Her father only has daughters. He's stepping down, and when he does, Vasilisa will inherit the company—one she knows nothing about. She'll need someone to handle things for her."

His eyes flash with satisfaction as he leans back. "And who better than her husband?"

I let the weight of the proposition sink in.

NovaRael. A tech empire. Access to every cutting-edge surveillance system that could rival, or dismantle, my own.

ZEUS.

I built ZEUS from nothing. It's more than a company; it's the foundation of my power within Cosa Nostra. But merging NovaRael with ZEUS? That would shift everything.

Possibilities unfold in front of me.

And all I have to do is marry the girl.

A sheltered tech heiress. Naïve. Easy to steer.

Keep her comfortable, keep her distracted, and quietly build something far greater.

I snap the folder shut and set it on the desk. The tap of my ring against wood is the only sound as both men look at me.

"I'll do it," I say finally, my voice steady, cool. "No lavish ceremony. Just papers signed."

My father's expression softens at my agreement, but I can already see the stipulation forming in his mind. He doesn't waste time voicing it.

"We need a ceremony and reception to bring the families together," he says, measured but firm. "It can be small."

I nod once. Our world runs on perception. Alliances have to be seen.

Beside me, Angelo's shoulders relax slightly, but I catch the flicker of tension he hides behind his mask of composure.

Our father offers a quick smile, sensing the shift in the room.

"Under one condition," I add, letting the words settle in the space between us.

Angelo stiffens. My father chuckles, low and knowing.

"Tell me," I continue, gaze locked on my father's, "what Angelo gets in return for my favor to the family."

A slow, satisfied smile spreads across his face, like he's been waiting for me to ask.

"He gets to be the Don."

The words hang in the air.

I turn to Angelo, reading the flicker of restraint in his eyes. He's braced for a fight that isn't coming.

Instead, I grin.

I rise, pulling Angelo into a tight embrace. There's a brief hesitation in his stance, tension in his muscles, before he claps me hard on the back.

"Good," I say, meaning it. "It's about time."

Angelo steps back, watching me like he's still trying to figure out if I'm fucking with him.

Our father moves to the bar, retrieving three glasses. The quiet clink of crystal echoes through the room as he pours whiskey, amber liquid swirling in each glass.

"We celebrate," he declares, passing one to each of us.

We raise them.

The soft chime of glass striking glass fills the air, a toast to a future neither of us truly chose.

The whiskey burns down my throat, settling warm in my chest, but it doesn't wash away the truth.

A strange sense of victory lingers. Bittersweet. *Inevitable.*

Angelo will take the throne he's spent years preparing for. I will marry Vasilisa—a girl I haven't met, whose name I only learned minutes ago.

Not exactly a *fair* trade.

But fairness doesn't interest me. *Opportunity* does.

NovaRael isn't just a dowry—it's a *crown jewel* wrapped in ignorance. Vasilisa knows nothing about the empire she's meant to inherit, and if I move fast, play this right, I'll have control long before she even realizes what's slipping through her fingers.

I take another sip, already calculating.

Merging NovaRael with ZEUS would transform our operations overnight. Angelo at the helm, my hand on the technology—we could outpace every rival. Expand our reach into territories no one else has dared to touch.

Still, a thin thread of unease coils beneath the surface.

What will Vasilisa think?

The thought flickers—unwelcome, irrelevant.

It doesn't matter.

She won't have a say. None of us did.

And if I were a better man, maybe I'd pity her.

But I'm not.

I tip back the rest of my whiskey, swallowing the lingering doubt along with it.

Maksim is reckless to let this slip through his fingers. The alliance feels too simple, almost *careless* on his part. The thought nags at me, but I push it aside.

His loss. My advantage.

Before I leave, I fire off a quick text to one of my men.

Vasilisa Popov. Cousin of Korsakov. Tail her.

I want eyes on my future wife long before she realizes I exist.

CHAPTER 3

SANTO

In my home office, plans to take over NovaRael are already in motion.

The wedding is still weeks away, but the contract?

That can be signed now.

I call Maksim to set up a meeting with Miroslav Popov, ready to push the deal through. He doesn't hesitate.

"Popov can be at your estate within the hour," he says.

Good.

I hang up and the door swings open without a knock.

Mrs. Keen, my housekeeper, steps in, a pitcher of iced tea in her hands, the same way she has for the last fifteen years. I barely glance at her before making a mental note to install the Athena lock system once the surveillance data finishes uploading.

She moves through the room like she owns it.

Maybe, in her own way, she does.

There's something grounding about her presence—soft, familiar.

Always here. Always steady.

A part of my life.

The tea is homemade, just like my mother used to make when I was a boy.

She hesitates. Just for a second. But I don't miss it.

I lean back in my chair, raising an eyebrow, waiting.

She sets the pitcher down at the office bar, pours me a glass, then finally meets my gaze.

I exhale, already knowing.

"Who told you?"

She lowers her head slightly.

"Luca," she admits. "But don't be upset with him. I overheard him… something about ordering a tail on your—"

She pauses, careful not to overstep.

Doesn't matter. I already know who she means.

"I'm not upset," I say. "You'd have found out soon enough. I'm getting married in two weeks. She'll be living here."

Mrs. Keen's entire face lights up, her joy so *genuine* that it almost catches me off guard.

"Oh, Santo, this is wonderful!" she exclaims, hands clasping together. "I can't wait to meet her."

She starts pacing, rattling off ideas—changes to the house, dinner menus, accommodations, already planning for a bride she's never met. Her excitement is relentless, spilling into every word until, mid-sentence, she freezes, brows knitting together.

"I leave for vacation next week," she says, disappointment heavy. "I won't be here for the ceremony, and I won't meet your wife until after… I can reschedule—"

I raise a hand, cutting her off. "You deserve your break. Lila can assist my wife with anything while you're away."

The word *wife* lingers on my tongue, feeling foreign in a way I hadn't expected.

Mrs. Keen nods but hesitates, her fingers twitching like she's debating whether to say more. "But I *can't* miss your wedding," she says softly.

"It's supposed to be a small ceremony." I keep my voice even, neutral. "Nothing extravagant."

She sighs, but the spark in her eyes doesn't dim. "Very well." I can already see her mind spinning, filing away ways to make a "small" wedding feel like something. "Do you have a photo of her? What's her name?"

Something tugs at the corner of my mouth. I ignore it, pull the folder from my desk and hand her the picture inside.

"Her name is Vasilisa."

Mrs. Keen gasps the second she sees the picture. "A beautiful name for a beautiful woman," she beams. "She'll fit in perfectly here."

I say nothing.

Because for the first time, I wonder if she's right.

I shut the thought down.

Mrs. Keen disappears from the room, only to return minutes later—this time, with the photo framed. Without asking, she sets it on my desk like it belongs there.

"You should always have a photo of your wife in your office," she says with a satisfied nod before shutting the door softly behind her.

I exhale through my nose, leaning back in my chair.

The framed photo sits there, unassuming, yet impossible to ignore.

Vasilisa's bright smile stares back at me—*unfamiliar* yet… strangely settling. I let the image sit with me, fingers absently tracing the rim of my glass before I take a slow sip.

The moment doesn't last.

The rare calm shatters as my phone rings.

Miroslav Popov has arrived.

I answer briskly, instructing the front gate to let him through.

Moments later, a knock sounds at the door. Romeo, our newest recruit, steps in, leading Miroslav into the office.

Popov steps inside—a short, unassuming man with neatly combed white hair and a stern expression. His dark suit is crisp, a sleek black briefcase hanging at his side. His handshake is firm, stronger than expected.

"The Pakhan says you're eager to start your ownership of *my* company," he says, voice edged with quiet disdain.

I remain composed. "That's the stipulation your Pakhan set for our alliance, is it not?"

His eyes narrow, his mouth tightening. "Not everyone is fortunate enough to walk into power so easily."

I hold his gaze, let silence stretch. "If you have an issue with the arrangement, take it up with Korsakov. I can call him now, if you'd like."

I reach for my phone.

Popov's hand snaps up, stopping me. A flicker of irritation wrinkles his features. He sets the briefcase on my desk, pulls out paperwork, and slides it toward me.

"I've signed my part," he says. "We just need yours. My office was informed of your potential arrival weeks ago, as per the Pakhan's instructions."

I absorb this new information in silence.

Korsakov and my father expected a yes. Assumed I'd fall in line.

As if I ever had a choice.

My jaw tightens, but I push it aside.

A twinge of anger prickles through me, settling deep.

I shut it down.

I pick up the pen.

I skim the contract, eyes catching on a particular clause.

"I can't change the name?" I ask, glancing up.

Popov straightens, his expression unwavering. "NovaRael is named after my daughters. Vasilisa's middle name is Nova. I ask that it not be erased."

I consider this.

I had planned to merge ZEUS and NovaRael under one brand, a single entity under my control. But sentimentality isn't worth interfering with. Not now.

Not when the goal is *ownership*.

It's not worth the time.

I'll have NovaRael. That's what matters. If keeping the name is the price, then so be it.

"Fine," I say, signing the papers. "I'll have copies sent to you later in the week."

Popov rises, smoothing his jacket. At the door, he pauses.

"Will you be visiting Vasilisa soon?"

"There's no need."

He lifts a brow but says nothing. Just offers a brief nod before exiting, leaving the room steeped in quiet once more—save for the faint ticking of the clock.

And the framed photo now occupying my desk.

Vasilisa *Nova.*

★★★

NovaRael is a masterpiece.

The sleek, modern building stands tall, cutting into the restless city skyline like it was built to rule over it. Its glass panels reflect the chaos of the streets below, untouched by it. Unbothered.

I step inside, firing off a quick text to Luca.

Keep me updated on Vasilisa's whereabouts.

The office hums with quiet *luxury*—polished marble, glass accents, meticulously curated décor that doesn't just whisper wealth, it demands acknowledgment.

Employees move through the space, but I don't miss the way heads subtly turn as I pass. They know exactly who I am.

Or at least, they *think* they do.

Miroslav Popov's name is still etched into the glass of his corner office, but not for long. My fingers twitch at the thought, already anticipating the sight of my own name in its place.

Stepping inside, I take my time.

The panoramic windows stretch wide, framing the city like a painting. A reminder of what's mine.

My city.
The office is expansive. Every detail deliberate. Artifacts, records, relics of Popov's reign clutter the space. Most of it will go.
A large wooden desk anchors the room—grand, but *outdated.*
I can already see the replacement.
Glass. Sleek. Modern.
My eyes drift to the plush chairs circling the space. Comfortable, but not too comfortable.
Inviting, but not *welcoming.*
I settle behind the desk, leaning back in the chair as if it's already mine.
It fits.
The knock at the door comes sooner than expected.
Popov steps inside, wearing a calm, polite smile. His eyes flick briefly to me, seated in *his* chair.
"Powerful feeling, isn't it?" he asks, gesturing toward the office with an easy familiarity.
"It is," I reply, watching him carefully.
He lowers himself into the chair across from me, sliding a thick folder across the desk.
"Everything you need is here." His tone remains even. "Passwords, protocols, schedules—I've sent copies to your email. I have no doubt you'll lead NovaRael well."
Not a flicker of regret. No sadness in passing over his empire. No reluctance.
Only *calm resignation.*
Odd.
"I look forward to it."
"I'm sure." His smile is tight-lipped, unreadable. "Sandra will serve as your secretary until you hire a replacement."
I lift an eyebrow. "You didn't have one before?"
"I did. He left recently. Maksim requested my retirement before I could hire someone new." A flicker of irritation edges his voice, but he smooths it out as quickly as it appears. "This is all yours now. I'll clear out my personal belongings, but you're welcome to keep anything else."
My gaze sweeps over the artifacts again.
The remnants of his reign.
"I won't need them."
Popov studies me before nodding. "It will all be out by noon. Congratulations again, Mr. Amato."
I stand as he does, shaking his hand. His grip is firm, his demeanor polite, but there's no warmth in it.
Just a transaction.

A man handing over the keys to something he no longer owns.

At the door, he hesitates.

"My retirement party is coming up. You're welcome to join."

I offer a nod. "I'll be here."

A lie.

His celebration is irrelevant to me.

Once he's gone, I sink back into the chair, letting my gaze sweep over the office again.

Mine.

The thought of reshaping NovaRael into something distinctly *mine* fuels me. Since the name must remain, ZEUS will fall under it as a subsidiary. Salvatore, my managing partner, can oversee day-to-day operations. He'll appreciate the promotion—especially with his wife about to give birth.

I press the call button.

Sandra steps in almost immediately.

Her hair is neatly braided, glasses perfectly positioned on the bridge of her nose, but I don't miss the faint tremble in her hands as she stands before me.

"Popov said you'll be filling in temporarily," I note, studying her closely.

"Yes. I'm in product management on the fourteenth floor, but I can coordinate interviews for your secretary position," she replies, voice soft but professional.

"The fourteenth floor," I muse, filing the detail away. "There's plenty I need to learn about this place."

"That's true, Mr. Amato," Sandra agrees, her gaze flicking subtly toward the desk. "Would you like me to arrange for the moving company?"

I shake my head. "They'll be here."

She hesitates.

Her fingers twitch at the edge of her glasses, something weighing on her. I wait, silent, watching as she debates whether to speak.

Finally, she does.

"I know Mr. Popov had… other business interests outside of this company," she says carefully, her voice dropping to a near whisper. "Do you share those… interests?"

I smirk, leaning forward just slightly.

"Why do you ask?"

She exhales, lowering her gaze. "There's a separate list of candidates for… men in your specific line of work."

A quiet chuckle escapes me.

"Yes, Sandra. I'll need that list."

Her eyes widen briefly, but she recovers quickly, giving a small nod before excusing herself.

I lean back, the smirk still lingering as my gaze drifts to the city skyline.

NovaRael is my kingdom now.

Chapter 4

VASILISA

After our last class, Luna and I head straight to our favorite café.

Our little ritual since we started university. No matter how insane life gets, once a month, we carve out time to sit, sip overpriced lattes, and spill every last bit of gossip we've collected.

Between our packed schedules and completely different courses, it's the one chance we get to catch up properly.

Luna's been my best friend since seventh grade. She knows me better than anyone, probably even better than I know myself sometimes.

When the whole school found out I was Maksim Korsakov's cousin, that I came from *Bratva* blood, people started treating me like I was carrying a loaded gun.

Not Luna.

She never flinched, never looked at me differently. If anything, she leaned in closer, like she *enjoyed* the chaos. She loves my family, reputation and all.

We slide into our usual booth by the window, lattes steaming between us, a plate of food already half-demolished as we talk and laugh.

Luna's brown eyes glint with mischief as she leans in, her voice dropping into a conspiratorial whisper.

"Can you get us into Exile?"

I pause mid-bite, my panini hovering in front of me. "You know Maks doesn't like us going to his club without him knowing," I murmur, avoiding her gaze.

Luna groans, stabbing at her salad with unnecessary force. "Please, Vasi."

Then come the puppy-dog eyes.

"I'll even ask Maks myself if you give me his number." She wiggles her eyebrows, grinning.

I snort. "You'd love that, wouldn't you?"

"Obviously." Luna grins, all confidence and mischief.

"But no," I say, my tone softening at her persistence. "You don't know Maksim like I do."

She shrugs, smirking. "He's always been sweet around me."

I huff a laugh. "That's because you're *my* friend." I lean in, lowering my voice. "It's a different story for the women he… dates." I grimace.

Luna rolls her eyes. "I'm sure I can handle it. What about him?" She nods toward someone behind me.

I don't have to turn around. I already know who she's talking about. *Pietro.*

My guard. Maksim's soldier. A shadow that follows me everywhere. "No."

Luna sighs dramatically. "Why not? Do you still have a *little* crush?"

Heat crawls up my neck.

"No. I'm with Jude."

Luna fake gags, loud enough that the couple at the next table side-eyes us. It only takes a second before we both dissolve into giggles.

No one likes Jude.

Not even me anymore.

I swallow the thought before it can go anywhere, before I have to acknowledge what it really means.

I'd end it if I could.

But Maksim wouldn't *allow* it.

I sigh, checking the time.

Obligation calls.

Maksim expects me at the charity event with Jude, and there's no getting out of it.

We gather our things. I steal a glance at Pietro.

Maybe I can convince him to talk to Maksim. Maybe, just *maybe*, I can get permission for Luna and me to go to Exile soon.

A night out with her might be exactly what I need.

⋆⋆⋆

Jude is *rambling,* his voice too loud, too eager, filling the back of his father's town car like an unwelcome echo.

The city lights blur past the windows, streaks of gold and red cutting through the dark.

The stench of alcohol rolls off him, thick and nauseating, making my stomach twist.

His words slur together, tangling into one long, incoherent mess. I stop trying to follow, letting his voice fade into the background. Instead, I focus on the steady hum of the engine beneath us, the familiar rhythm grounding me.

We've been together for a couple of years now, though *together* feels like a stretch. Ever since he moved away for grad school, it's been more of a long-distance *obligation* than a relationship.

His father, *the mayor,* is in the middle of a re-election campaign, and Jude?

Well… he's just Jude.

Handsome in his designer suit, sure, but that novelty faded fast when I realized we have nothing in common. His entitled, shallow worldview grates against everything I believe in, everything I know to be true.

But I never chose this.

Maksim asked me to date Jude back in my freshman year—as a favor to the family. And I agreed.

Because that's what's expected of me.

My sister and I have always been pawns, groomed for arranged marriages that would strengthen the Bratva's alliances.

I just never imagined I'd end up as the wife of a future politician.

That's all Jude talks about these days—politics, strategy, his grand plan to one day be president. The thought of *him* at the helm of an entire country sends a shiver down my spine.

I barely register the question he's just asked, nodding out of habit as the car rolls to a stop.

Finally.

I reach for the door, eager to escape, but before I can, Jude moves closer, his lips crashing against mine. His tongue is sloppy, pushing against my lips, demanding entrance.

The taste of vodka and desperation turns my stomach.

I press my hands to his chest, pushing him away gently.

I hate when he drinks.

"I should get inside," I say softly, hoping he'll take the hint.

"Of course." Jude nods sharply, unbuckling himself and stepping out to open my door.

The second I step into the cool night air, his hands are on me—pressing me back against the car, his arms caging me in.

Too close.

"I'm sorry," he murmurs, his breath thick with alcohol. "I just miss you so much, and every time I'm home, we have to make these appearances for my family. Move to Seattle. Live with me."

His lips find my cheek, trailing downward along my jaw.

I turn away, trying to maneuver out of his hold, but all that does is give him access to my neck.

I place my hands firmly on his chest, pushing slightly. "I have two years left of school. And my family—you know they have opinions."

Jude pulls back just enough to look at me, his brow furrowing.

"But they arranged this, they arranged us." His voice is quieter now, edged with frustration. "Why would they have a problem with us being together? With you moving in with me?"

His eyes darken, searching mine for something I *can't* give him.

I exhale slowly.

Jude only knows *half* the truth when it comes to my family.

He doesn't know about the *real* reason Maksim picked him. Doesn't know about the clandestine dealings, the hidden alliances, the unspoken expectations that come with being Bratva.

And he *never* will.

I press harder against his chest, and this time, he finally steps back.

"Let's discuss this another time," I say, avoiding Jude's intense gaze. "It's not as simple as you think. I need time."

His brow furrows, confusion flickering across his face. "What do you mean? You know how much I care about you."

I take a step back, trying to put distance between us. "I know. But please, I just... I need time to sort things out."

Jude's expression shifts in an instant—his frustration flaring as he closes the space I just created.

"Is there someone else?"

I shake my head quickly. "No, it's not that. I just need space to *breathe.*"

But even as the words leave my mouth, I know they aren't entirely true.

Jude exhales sharply. "Fine then."

He steps aside, finally letting me pass. I don't look back as I walk up the driveway.

This is always how it ends—with Jude dropping me off at the gate, leaving without a second glance.

I greet the guards with a forced smile, relieved by their presence as they push open the gates.

As Jude's town car pulls away, another set of headlights rolls up—an SUV with its engine rumbling low and steady.

Pietro.

He's late.

He must've made a detour with that pretty brunette from the charity event.

The window on the passenger side slides down, revealing his lopsided grin.

"Get in, gorgeous."

"Pietro!" I scold, climbing into the vehicle. The familiar scent of his cologne wraps around me, soothing in a way I don't question. "The other guards can *hear* you. And Maksim would not like you calling me that."

Pietro chuckles, the sound easy, familiar. "What? Maksim knows I adore you. We're close in age. And it's all platonic… *unless you don't want it to be.*"

I roll my eyes, but a smile tugs at my lips.

I slap his arm playfully, and he gives me a gentle shove back. The easy familiarity between us lingers as he drives down the long, winding driveway toward my home.

Comfortable silence settles between us.

He parks in front of the house.

But doesn't move.

The ignition stays on, his hands gripping the wheel tighter than usual. He doesn't reach for the door, doesn't throw out another teasing remark.

One look at his face puts me on edge.

Something is wrong.

"What is it?"

Pietro exhales slowly, a few strands of blonde hair slipping from his top knot, framing his sharp jaw. His hand lifts, cupping my face so gently it makes my chest tighten.

His eyes lock onto mine.

"I've been reassigned."

His thumb brushes my cheek, his touch lingering like he knows what this means for me, like he knows I'll hate what comes next.

I shake his hand off, my pulse hammering. "No. You can't. I'll call Maksim, this isn't fair—"

I fumble for my phone, but my clutch is missing.

Of course, Pietro already thought of that. He reaches into the back seat and hands it to me. "Maksim is the reason I was late to meet you."

My stomach drops.

"When you go in there," he continues, pointing toward the front door, "your father will have news for you. You will take it. And you will make us proud."

I know what that means.

I've *always* known.

This moment has been looming over me for years, and yet, somehow, I thought I'd have more time.

But knowing doesn't make it easier.

The sting behind my eyes comes fast, the lump in my throat growing thick, impossible to swallow. I force it down anyway, willing the tears to *stay put*.

This must be it.

They're making me marry Jude. *They're making me a politician's wife.*

This *can't* be happening.

Despite my efforts, a single tear escapes.

Pietro catches it before it can fall, his hands framing my face again. He presses a firm kiss to my forehead, the warmth of it steadying me, even as my world shifts beneath me.

Then, just as quickly, he releases me.

He steps out, walks around, and opens my door.

I take a few short, sharp breaths, trying to push down the emotions clawing their way to the surface.

Shoulders back. Chin up.

I unbuckle myself, stepping out of the car, nodding at Pietro in silent thanks.

Then I turn toward the house.

Toward my fate.

As I step inside my home, I pause, taking in the inviting golden glow of the interior. The walls, adorned with precious family portraits, paint a picture of warmth, of love, of home.

But it's all a lie.

A carefully curated illusion meant to hide the truth.

I was born into this world not as a daughter, not as a sister, but as a pawn—another piece in the high-stakes game of power and control. My sole purpose? To marry into a powerful family, to secure alliances that would strengthen the Bratva.

I always knew marriage was inevitable.

But this soon?

To someone I didn't even like?

And worst of all—to lose Pietro in the process?

Maksim always kept me in the loop, or at least let me believe I had some say. When he wanted me to date Jude, he told me himself, assured me it was just a means to an end. That I was helping the family, that it was *temporary.*

This?

This feels *different.*

Rushed.

Like a door slamming shut before I even realized I was walking toward it.

There is no love, no passion, nothing between Jude and me except his selfish desires and his relentless hunger for power. He will do *anything* to get ahead, to climb higher, and he expects me to be his stepping stone.

That doesn't bode well for a marriage.

With a heavy heart, I reach my father's study and knock.

"Come in." His voice is steady, familiar.

I push open the door to find him sitting behind his desk, a folder in hand.

His smile is practiced, polite, but I sense it immediately—*something is off.*

I close the door behind me, forcing my shoulders back, my expression composed as I lower myself into the chair across from him.

Without a word, he slides the folder across the desk.

"Congratulations, Vasilisa." His voice carries no warmth, only finality. "Maksim has found you a husband. This will be a powerful alliance for our family, one that you should be proud of."

I nod stiffly, my fingers curling around the folder.

"I know. Jude mentioned it."

I open it, bracing myself for what I expect; a contract, a marriage certificate, a one-way ticket to *Seattle.*

Instead—

I'm greeted by a photograph.

A man.

Handsome. Sharp features. Dark hair. Dressed in a perfectly tailored three-piece suit.

He doesn't look like a politician.

Doesn't look like a *Jude.*

He looks like he belongs on the cover of a magazine.

Not in an *arranged* marriage.

"Jude mentioned what?" My father's eyebrows furrow in confusion.

I tear my eyes away from the photo, my pulse quickening as I try to find the right words. "He mentioned… me possibly moving to Seattle."

The second the words leave my mouth, my father's expression hardens.

"Well, that's certainly not going to happen." His voice is firm, absolute. "You can take your folder now and go. Everything you need to know is in there."

I barely hear him. My fingers tighten around the edges of the folder as I scan the name printed on the page.

Santo Amato.

Cosa Nostra.

Not Jude. Not a politician.

But something worse. Something *far more* dangerous.

This isn't just an arranged marriage. This is a power move—an alliance between two of the most powerful crime syndicates in the world.

My stomach turns.

I wasn't ready to *belong* to Jude, but at least I knew him. Knew his selfishness, his ambition. His hunger for power was predictable.

Santo Amato?

He could be anyone.

And the unknown is far more terrifying than the familiar.

"Wait," I breathe out. The walls feel like they're closing in around me. "I don't think I'm ready."

My father doesn't even blink. "There is no waiting, Vasilisa. Maksim has arranged this, and you will do it."

I linger, hoping for something.

Anything.

A moment of hesitation, a shred of warmth. A sign that this *matters* to him beyond the business of it.

But there's nothing.

Just the dismissive wave of his hand, as if marrying me off is no different than finalizing a deal.

Like I'm an *asset.* A transaction.

I swallow hard and rise from my chair, clutching the folder like it might ground me.

Without another word, I leave the office, my heels clicking against the marble as I make my way up the stairs.

I hold the tears back until I reach my room.

The second the door closes behind me, I let them fall.

I *hate* this.

I know my duty. I know what's expected of me. But that doesn't make it easier.

I toss my clutch onto the dresser and collapse onto my bed, my fingers still gripping the folder like it holds the answers to a future I *never* wanted.

With a shaky breath, I open it again.

My eyes fall back to the photo.

Santo Amato.

The man I'm supposed to marry.

He is *strikingly* handsome.

The kind of man who looks like he was sculpted for power—broad shoulders, sharp angles, deep gray eyes that seem to see right through me. His jawline is strong, defined, a silent promise of determination.

His dark hair is a perfect balance of control and chaos; the sides neatly trimmed while the top is left just a little longer, styled in a way that looks both deliberate and carelessly tousled.

It's unfair, really. The kind of effortless suaveness that makes it look like he never has to try at anything.

The expression in the photo is blank.

Not warm. Not cold. Just *composed*.

I wonder what kind of man he is behind that stoic façade.

He looks perfect. *Too perfect.*

Men like him don't need arranged marriages.

Whatever reason Maksim had for choosing him, it wasn't because he lacked options.

My gaze flickers to the information sheet beside his picture; details about his family, his education, his career in *technology*.

That explains the alliance.

A man in search of power.

Just like every other man in my world.

A sharp knock at my door pulls me from my thoughts.

I blink, wiping at my cheeks, forcing myself to breathe as I straighten. "Come in."

The door creaks open.

Mimi.

She lingers in the doorway, her expression hovering somewhere between concern and curiosity.

Dressed in sleep shorts and an oversized shirt, she looks even *younger* than fifteen—especially when she smiles, her braces flashing, making her seem more like the kid she used to be.

She steps inside, shutting the door quietly before padding over to me.

I sit up, the folder still clutched in my hands.

Mimi doesn't hesitate. She never does.

She just hops onto my bed, like always, giving me a small, apologetic smile.

"I heard Mom and Dad talking… are you okay?"

Mimi's voice is quiet, hesitant, and it cracks something inside me.

She still has *time.*

A year, maybe less, before Maksim starts arranging her future; lining up potential matches, setting her up with the sons of powerful men.

I envy her for it.

For the short-lived freedom she doesn't even realize she has.

Wordlessly, I hand her the folder. She flips it open, her eyes widening as a long, low whistle escapes her lips.

A blush creeps up her neck, blooming across her cheeks.

"Wow, Vasi. He is really hot. You lucked out."

I chuckle, shoving her playfully before snatching the folder back. "He's handsome, but he's a *stranger*."

Mimi shrugs. "Did you want to marry Jude instead?"

I grimace. "Definitely not."

"So what's the problem?"

I exhale, setting the folder on my nightstand. "I just... I wanted to know the man first."

Mimi tilts her head, her gaze turning knowing. "The way you know Pietro?"

I freeze for half a second.

"There's *nothing* between Pietro and me. He's just my friend."

"A friend that you *had* a crush on." Her smirk is infuriating.

"Had. Past tense."

Mimi sighs, studying me for a moment before her voice drops. "He's here, you know."

My stomach tightens. "Pietro?" I shake my head. "No, he said he was reassigned..." I trail off as she bites her lip, suddenly avoiding my gaze.

"Yeah. He did." Her eyes flick toward my bedroom door.

A sudden, urgent pull drags me forward.

I rush to the door, yanking it open.

And there he is.

Pietro.

His gaze meets mine, heavy with something I don't want to hear.

An apology.

"I was told to let Mimi know, so I came back," he says, voice quieter than usual. "But I'm leaving for the night. I just wanted to let you know as well."

I don't think.

I move.

Throwing my arms around his waist with enough force that he lets out a quiet grunt before wrapping me up in return.

"I thought you were reassigned to another family!"

I pull back just enough to swat at his firm chest.

His lips curl into a smirk. "Ow, Vasi."

"In my defense, Maksim didn't tell me who I was assigned to until after I dropped you off," he says, glancing toward Mimi, who now stands beside us, watching the exchange.

"See you tomorrow, Pietro."

She flashes him a quick smile before darting off to her room.

Pietro's eyes don't leave her until she's safely inside. He turn his attention back to me.

"You okay?"

I exhale slowly, my grip tightening around the folder still in my hand. "I don't know. I'm apparently marrying Santo Amato."

His eyebrows shoot up. "I knew you were arranged, but I didn't know who to." His head tilts slightly, expression shifting. "He's a big deal, Vasi. A powerful man like him, in a powerful family… no wonder I was reassigned. You're going to need more security."

My stomach twists. *"More security?"*

Pietro immediately softens, shaking his head. "Hey, don't worry, Vasi. This is good for you. And for the Bratva."

His hands find my shoulders, grounding me, steadying me. They slide up slowly one resting against my cheek, fingers tilting my chin up until I have no choice but to look at him.

"Breathe."

I inhale shakily, focusing on the quiet intensity in his gaze—filled with concern and something more, something unspoken yet palpable.

Pietro has been my protector, my confidant, the one person I can count on when everything else feels like it's spinning out of my control.

He knows me better than anyone.

Knows my fears. Knows my hopes. Knows *me.*

And right now, standing in the dim glow of the hallway, with an arranged marriage hanging over my head and an uncertain future waiting for me, he's the only thing that feels familiar.

A rush of emotions crashes through me, gratitude for his unwavering loyalty, anxiety over what lies ahead with Santo Amato, and something else.

Something I can't place.

Pietro's thumb brushes against my cheek, a silent reassurance.

A promise.

No matter what happens, we're in this together.

"You'll be fine, Vasi," he says, his voice a soothing balm to my frayed nerves. "I'll make sure of it."

A sense of calm settles over me. "Thank you, Pietro," I whisper.

For a second, I let myself lean into his touch, wishing, irrationally, that it could be him. But wishing is dangerous, and in this life, it's useless.

"Goodnight."

Pietro makes his leave as I go back to my room and prepare myself for what's to come.

CHAPTER 5

VASILISA

I wake up to my blanket being ripped off me, followed by the sharp clatter of blinds being yanked open.

Sunlight floods my room, merciless and unforgiving.

With a groan, I bury my face into my pillow, clinging to the last remnants of sleep.

It doesn't last.

A firm grip wraps around my ankle, pulling.

"Mom, I'm tired." I grumble into the mattress.

My mother stands over me, unimpressed, arms crossed as she watches my pathetic attempt at resistance.

"You need to be up and ready," she says, her tone clipped. "There's no time for lounging. We have shopping to do, dresses to look at. Your future husband has made *many* arrangements."

My stomach twists.

Future husband.

Reluctantly, I drag myself out of bed.

My mother doesn't just expect obedience. She expects perfection.

She lingers, eyes sharp as I get ready, ensuring that every detail of my appearance is flawless.

The way my hair falls.

The precision of my concealer.

My posture.

Her gaze follows me as I reach for a skirt and sweater from my closet.

I don't even get the chance to pull them out before her hand clamps around my wrist.

I meet her eyes that mirror mine only colder, harsher, more unyielding.

I *expected* pushback from my mother.

No matter how hard I try, I will never be good enough for Vera Popov.

She wants a daughter like her—poised, elegant, dutiful without question or emotion.

To her, I'm *too* much.

Too emotional. Too inquisitive. Too *bright*.

'Men don't like women with their noses in books.'

One of many mantras from Vera Popov.

I've never been able to stop myself from reaching for more than what she's willing to give.

My sister, on the other hand, my mother will have a much harder time taming her.

I pull my arm away with a sigh.

"You cannot wear that," she spits, disgust dripping from her tone.

I lift a brow. "And what would you have me wear, *Mother?*"

"Anything but those awful, matronly atrocities you claim to be clothes." She waves a dismissive hand toward my closet. "You look like a librarian."

A flicker of amusement tugs at my lips.

She ignores me.

"The only thing I can appreciate in your wardrobe are your heels. The higher, the better—especially given your height."

Her eyes trail over me, assessing, *judging.*

I already know what's coming before she even turns toward my closet.

She rummages through it like it belongs to her, fingers brushing past my sweaters, my skirts, my carefully chosen pieces, before she reaches the back.

The hidden section.

The place where I shoved all the dresses she bought me, hoping she'd forget.

I cringe internally, bracing myself as she lets out a triumphant squeal. "This one!"

She pulls a blue silk dress from the hanger, clutching it like a prize.

I hate that dress.

"Put this on. It's perfect." Her smile is almost loving. "All the shops we're visiting today know who you're engaged to. We need to be sure you look the part—lest they say something to Mr. Amato."

The way she says his name sends a cold shiver down my spine.

I don't argue. It's pointless.

Instead, I slip into the delicate silk, the fabric clinging tightly to my frame.

Uncomfortable.

A glance in the mirror, barely recognizing myself.

Gone is the girl who cried herself to sleep just hours ago.

Today, I am Vasilisa Popov—poised, primed, and ready to fulfill my duty.

A favor to my family. A transaction to strengthen an alliance.

Today, I play the role I was born into.

Behind me, my mother watches through the mirror, pride gleaming in her reflection.

I force myself to turn, tugging in vain at the hem of the dress, trying to lengthen it. "When is the wedding? Can't we take our time?"

She doesn't answer right away, and I push further. "I have class later. I don't have much time for shopping."

She clears her throat gently before hurling the bomb.

"In two weeks. Mr. Amato has requested not to meet before then. As for class, I've sent in a deferment so you can focus on being a wife."

My head snaps to her so fast my vision blurs.

"What?"

The word scrapes past my throat.

A *deferment.*

The word alone sends a jolt of fear down my spine.

My stomach twists violently.

That was *mine. My future.* The one thing I had control over. And now, it's slipping away like everything else.

"For how long?" My voice barely above a whisper.

I clutch the fabric of the dress tighter, as if physically holding onto something will keep the rest from slipping through my fingers.

"You can't—what about finals? My degree? I'm not ready to get married, I—"

The words choke out of me, sharp and frantic, as my mother's earlier statement settles deep in my bones.

Two weeks.

An icy shiver spreads through me, curling around my spine, sinking into my gut.

This isn't how I imagined my future.

Not like this.

Not hastily thrown into a marriage with a stranger. Not being forced to put my education—*my dreams*—on pause.

What if he won't let me go back?

The panic surges higher, clawing at my throat, at my lungs. I take sharp, shallow breaths, trying to steady myself, but my mother's gaze pins me in place. Expecting compliance. *Expecting* obedience.

On the surface, I force calm. But inside—inside, a storm rages.

Fear.

Uncertainty.

And something dangerous.

Something that tastes like rebellion.

"I need time." My voice trembles despite my best efforts. "Time to prepare myself."

My mother's expression hardens in an instant. Cold. Unyielding.

"This isn't about readiness, Vasilisa."

Her tone is sharp, slicing through any argument before I can form one.

"This is about loyalty. You *will* marry him. And in doing so, you will secure our family's future. There is *nothing* more important than that."

The words press hard against my chest, suffocating the refusal burning on my tongue.

I want to tell her no. That I won't do this.

But I swallow it down.

Tears blur my vision. They spill, hot and heavy down my cheeks.

There's no way out.

I am a pawn.

A sacrifice.

Another transaction in the name of the Bratva.

"But, Mama, please, I can't—" My breath shudders, coming in short, erratic bursts.

"You can, and you *will*, Vasilisa!"

The room tilts.

My vision narrows.

A ringing takes over my ears, drowning out everything—my mother's voice, the walls closing in, the crushing weight of expectation.

I can't breathe.

I can't breathe.

Soft hands grip my shoulders. I barely register the touch, the quiet voice cutting through the suffocating haze.

Mimi.

She's holding me as I crumble, as my knees hit the floor, as the fabric of the dress chokes the air from my lungs.

She strokes my hair, whispering to me.

Her voice reaches me in fragments. Echoes of calm, of comfort, but they're distant.

"You're okay. You *can* do this."

Mimi's voice is soft, steady, a lifeline in the middle of the storm.

I blink up at her sweet, concerned face and force myself to take a breath, mimicking the rise and fall of her own.

My mother throws her hands in the air. "This is ridiculous," she mutters, turning on her heel. "You have ten minutes."

The door slams behind her.

Mimi wipes away the last of my tears, grounding me back into the harsh reality I have to face.

"Let's fix your makeup," she says gently, guiding me toward my vanity.

I nod, following without protest.

My reflection stares back at me, red-rimmed eyes, shaky breaths, the ghost of panic still lingering behind my carefully reconstructed mask.

Mimi dabs on blush, sets everything in place with a dusting of powder, but the weight pressing down on my chest doesn't fully lift.

I don't want to move.

I don't want to *leave this room.*

Mimi's voice cuts through the silence, unexpected but thoughtful.

"You know," she says, putting the brush away and moving toward my bed, "you're the one who gave me hope for getting married. Even an arranged marriage."

I blink. "What?"

She ignores my confusion, crawling under my bed and pulling out a small shoebox. She dusts it off with the sleeve of her sweater before settling onto the floor, lifting the lid with careful fingers.

Curious, I abandon my vanity and sit beside her, peering inside.

The box is filled with torn pages—fragments of old romance novels, stories I used to collect like stolen treasures.

Love, passion, stolen kisses, and sword fights in the name of honor.

Mimi plucks out a worn scrap of paper, smoothing it out between her fingers before reading aloud.

"He was a stranger that became the beginning and end of my world, his touch bringing forth the brightest of gold from my once cold heart."

She sighs dreamily, then giggles, handing me the faded excerpt.

I take it, tracing the jagged edges, the ink smudged from years of handling. The paper feels fragile in my hands—just like the hope it once held.

I had forgotten about this. About how much I loved the idea of love blossoming from nothing but stolen glances, subtle touches, a *desire* stronger than thirst in the desert.

Mimi nudges me lightly. "He could be that for you."

Santo Amato.

The thought lingers.

He could be the man who changes everything. Who turns the impossible into something *golden.*

Or…

He could be nothing more than another name in a long line of expectations.

I tuck the box away, letting the thought settle—not rejecting it, but not *embracing* it either.

Not yet.

But just for now… *I let it exist.*

***

The luxurious bridal boutique is dripping in opulence.

Gold-trimmed mirrors, chandeliers casting a warm glow, silk curtains cascading over pristine white walls.

And then there's her.

Cassandra.

A stunning stylist, handpicked by my soon-to-be husband.

Her chestnut hair cascades in soft waves down her back, and her moss-green eyes glimmer under the boutique's golden light. The dress she wears—skin-tight, perfectly tailored—hugs every inch of her curvaceous frame, exuding confidence.

I shift uncomfortably, feeling plain in comparison.

My mother sits beside her, laughing—*laughing*—like they've been friends for years.

Cassandra's boisterous laughter rings through the boutique, bouncing off the walls, effortless and bright.

I sink further into my chair beside Mimi, resisting the urge to fidget under the weight of it all.

Across the room, Pietro leans casually against the wall beside my mother's guard.

He catches my eye, winking mischievously like this is all some kind of inside joke.

I almost smile. *Almost.*

With a deep breath, I force myself up, joining my mother and Cassandra as she launches into a monologue about how she's styled Santo for years.

"He's a delight to style," she says, voice lilting with familiarity.

I try to picture it—Santo Amato standing in front of a mirror, allowing this woman to adjust his tie, smooth out his suit jacket.

I can't.

Because I *don't know him.*

Not really.

Cassandra's eyes land on me, her smile warm, genuine.

"I'm very excited to extend my business toward his soon-to-be wife."

Something *bubbles* up inside me at the words.

Something I can't name.

Because she knows him.

Really knows him.

Cassandra leads me into a spacious dressing room, where an entire rack of pristine white gowns waits for me. The air is thick with the faint scent of expensive fabric and roses.

The door clicks shut behind us.

I glance over my shoulder just as Cassandra glides pass me.

"You're going to try these on with me," she says, voice smooth as silk.

I blink, taken aback. "In here? *With you?*"

She tilts her head, smiling.

"Of course. Full service. Just the way Mr. Amato prefers."

I nod, swallowing my hesitation.

Cassandra gestures at me, her manicured fingers poised midair. "Over or down?"

I frown. "What?"

"Your dress," she clarifies, tapping the thin strap on my shoulder. "Does it come off over your head or down?"

Heat rushes to my cheeks. "Down."

Before I can even react, her fingers slide under the straps, guiding them down with practiced ease.

The silk pools at my feet, leaving me standing in nothing but blue lace panties and heels.

My arms snap across my chest instinctively.

Cassandra smirks. "Step out."

Her tone is confident, commanding—like she's done this a hundred times before.

Like she's undressed women for Santo before.

I step out of the dress, my skin burning under her assessing gaze.

She folds the fabric neatly, setting it aside on the bench before turning back to me with an easy smile.

"No need to be shy, Vasilisa." She chuckles. "We'll be working closely together to perfect your entire wardrobe. This is just the beginning."

The words linger in the air.

Heavy.

I force myself to meet her gaze, my arms still locked tightly around myself.

Cassandra grabs a gown, unzipping it with ease before bending slightly so I can step in.

The fabric whispers against my skin as she pulls it up, my arms falling uselessly to my sides.

The dress is stunning.

Strapless, the lace bodice shimmers under the golden light, intricate embroidery catching in the mirror. The tulle skirt flares out from my hips, cascading in soft waves to the floor.

As Cassandra zips me in, my gaze flickers to the mirror.

And for a moment—just a moment, I hesitate.

Because I almost don't recognize the woman staring back at me.

She looks ready.

I do *not*.

Click.

The sound is quiet, but unmistakable.

My head snaps toward Cassandra just as she lowers her phone.

She doesn't look the least bit apologetic.

"Photos for Santo," she says smoothly, fingers dancing across the screen. "He'll want to see you in the dress, even if he pretends he doesn't."

Her words settle in my chest like a stone.

I don't *know* him.

But already, he's *seeing* me before I ever see him.

Cassandra tucks the phone between her breasts and gestures for me to follow. Her voice washes over me in an effortless stream of dress specifications—details I barely register as we step out of the dressing room.

Mimi and my mother are waiting.

I step onto the podium, my heart hammering in my chest as their eyes land on me.

Mimi's smile bursts across her face. "You look gorgeous!" she exclaims, eyes shining with admiration.

Relief flutters through me, but I turn to my mother hesitantly.

"Mama? What do you think?"

She scrutinizes me for a long second before offering an approving smile. "It's beautiful."

Relief floods through me.

I shift just enough to meet Pietro's gaze.

His mouth is slightly ajar, his eyes dragging over me.

He blinks. Once. Twice.

Then clears his throat and gives me a sharp, almost forced nod.

Cassandra has been watching the exchange silently.

But I don't miss the way her eyes flick to Pietro. How her expression sharpens—just slightly before she turns back to me, her smile never faltering.

"Ready for dress number two?" she asks brightly.

I nod, stepping off the podium.

She leads me back to the dressing room, closing the door behind us.

I barely have time to brace myself before she's unzipping the gown.

The dress falls before I can cover myself.

I suck in a breath, suddenly hyperaware of my exposed skin.

Cassandra doesn't seem to notice—or care.

She keeps her eyes locked on mine through the mirror as she gathers the dress.

Then, casually, almost *too* casually, she asks, "Who is that boy out there? The blonde one."

I blink, confused. "Pietro?"

"Yes, him."

Cassandra's eyes narrow slightly, her expression shifting—sharp, accusatory.

"Who is he to you?"

I blink at her tone, caught off guard.

"My sister's guard."

The words feel stiff, unnatural under the weight of her stare. "He used to be mine… my guard, I mean."

A quiet hum slips from Cassandra's lips as she watches me in the mirror, considering my words carefully.

"Were you two ever together?"

I shake my head. "No. Never. We're just friends."

Her lips press into a thin line, unimpressed. "The way he looks at you says otherwise."

A flicker of unease crawls down my spine.

"Does Santo have concerns about him?" she asks, her voice deceptively light.

I hesitate.

Not because I have something to hide, but because I don't know how much to say.

"No… I don't think so."

Cassandra scoffs, the sound dismissive, disbelieving.

"I find it hard to believe Santo didn't ask about your guard." She studies me through the mirror, eyes sharp. "Has he met him?"

"*We* haven't even met yet."

The words slip out quieter than I mean them to, but she hears them anyway.

Surprise flickers in her gaze. "You haven't met Santo?"

I shake my head. "It's an arranged marriage."

For the first time, her perfectly poised demeanor cracks. Her jaw drops slightly, lips parting in disbelief before she lets out a laugh—dry, knowing.

"An *arranged* marriage?" She shakes her head, amusement dancing across her features. "That makes sense now."

The words sink deep, twisting something inside me.

Shame and confusion wash over me, tightening around my ribs.

Why does that make sense?

I *need* to know.

Cassandra notices my expression, but doesn't soften.

Instead, she kneels slightly so I can step into the next gown, her movements measured, intentional

"How does that make sense?" I ask, anger rising in my chest.

She doesn't answer right away.

I struggle to keep my composure as she pulls the dress up, slipping my arms through the delicate lace sleeves. The fabric feels heavier than before, pressing down on me in ways it shouldn't.

Cassandra steps behind me, fingers working deliberately as she fastens the buttons.

Our eyes meet in the mirror.

And I see it.

The pity.

The quiet, almost apologetic glance before she delivers the final blow.

"He tends to go for a… *fuller* figure."

Her voice is light, almost thoughtful, but it cuts deep.

"You're not his usual type."

I shatter.

Any lingering hope I didn't even know I had—*gone.*

Chapter 6

SANTO

A couple days at NovaRael, and I'm already in my element.

I've met with every department head.

Development, security, finance, engineering, all the way down to sales.

The cybersecurity and finance departments are the only ones privy to the *actual* business operations.

The rest? Just a front for the successful empire that is NovaRael.

With WesTech as our only real competitor, I have little to worry about as I settle into my newly decorated office.

I insisted that the large wooden desk be removed before my first day.

Now, sitting behind my sleek glass desk with multiple monitors perched on top, I go over the finances and operations of NovaRael.

As I dig deeper into the files, one stands out.

QUEEN.

A single word, locked behind a firewall I can't crack.

My attempts to access it are denied.

Irritation flickers through me.

I don't like secrets.

I search through Miroslav's email for a hint.

Nothing.

No mentions. No passwords.

No explanation.

I don't like that.

I grab my phone and call the head of cyber security.

"Find out what the hell 'QUEEN' is," I order. "I want answers before the week is out."

He assures me that his team will have answers soon.

A sly smile creeps across my face.

I have everything I want.

Angelo gets the title he wants, I don't have to run Cosa Nostra.

I throw a credit card at my vapid bride, and I run surveillance intel for both Cosa Nostra and the Bratva.

Perfect.

A knock breaks through my concentration.

"Come in."

Luca walks into my office, a folder in his hand.

"I got the information you wanted on Vasilisa," he says, handing me the folder.

He takes a seat and kicks his feet up onto my desk. "We followed her to a charity event, she went with Jude Olsen, the son of the standing mayor. Apparently, they have been together for a couple of years."

I open the folder. It's filled with photos and phone records.

I quickly scan the first photo.

Vasilisa, trapped between a car and Jude Olsen, wearing a black dress that looks uncomfortable on her petite frame.

The next photo shows her getting into an SUV.

"Who's driving the SUV?"

"Pietro Ivanov, her former guard," Luca answers. "He was reassigned to her sister that night according to Korsakov."

I flip through more photos, each one showing Vasilisa with either Jude or Pietro by her side.

In one photo, Pietro even has his lips pressed against her forehead.

A tingle of unfamiliarity ripples through me.

"What *exactly* is their relationship?"

Luca chuckles, "As far as I know, just a guard. But he did escort them to the bridal store."

I raise an eyebrow and move on to the next photo.

Pietro admiring *my wife* as she tries on wedding dresses.

A flash of anger washes over me.

I take a deep breath, steady myself and continue flipping through the folder.

There are more photos of Vasilisa, shopping with Cassandra, some with her family. Nothing out of the ordinary, but the ones of her alone with Ivanov give me pause.

Some show them holding hands.

I slam the folder shut.

"Is she always this close with her guard?" I grit out.

Luca removes his feet from my desk and studies me. "I thought this was just an arrangement."

"It is, but I don't want my wife still entangled with other men after our marriage," I state firmly.

Luca nods in understanding. "From what I've seen, she only goes for his hand when her mother is around. She looks comfortable around him, probably because they're close in age, but there's no evidence of anything physical between them."

"What else is in here?"

"The photos hacked from her cellphone and taken from her socials, contact information and text transcripts too. As you can see, the texts with Pietro are mostly him asking for her location. No personal topics discussed between them."

I open the folder again and take in the photos, all of them are selfies or photos of Vasilisa and who I assume is her sister, the others are photos of her and that *Jude*.

I flip through the text transcripts. Luca's right, the messages with Pietro are harmless.

But my attention is drawn to the texts between Vasilisa and Jude, specifically the final one where he asks about her arranged marriage. Her response is a simple confirmation.

Satisfaction fills me as I close the folder and set it on my desk. A photo slips out, fluttering to the ground. I grab it, flipping it over—

And pause.

Vasilisa. A soft yellow dress. Sunlight framing her golden hair. She's smiling—bright, open, untouched by the world I live in.

Something unfamiliar settles in my chest. I don't know what to call it.

But I do know one thing.

She is stunning.

Luca clears his throat, interrupting my thoughts. "Anything else, boss?" he asks, smirk widening as he glances from my face to the photo in my hand.

"I want her phone. I need you to deliver her a new one that doesn't have access to her socials *or* the photos of her and the mayor's son. The only contacts she needs to keep are familial, add my number and yours."

I wave a hand dismissing him.

He chuckles knowingly before leaving without another word.

I'm left alone with Vasilisa's photo in my hand.

I wonder how she feels about our arrangement.

My work phone buzzes on the desk, snapping me out of my thoughts.

"Mr. Amato, I have a list of potential candidates for the secretary position," Sandra's voice rings out through the speaker.

"Thank you Sandra, please email me the list."

"Of course, sir," she responds before hanging up.

I make a mental note to schedule interviews for a later date.

Tonight, I have a meeting with Angelo at Exile, Maksim should be there, and I can ask him about *Pietro.*

Despite the innocent texts I've seen, Cassandra mentioned the way he looks at Vasilisa.

If Maksim is there, I'll make sure to arrange a meeting with Pietro to clear up any misunderstandings about who Vasilisa now belongs to.

As her husband, I expect a certain level of respect when it comes to what's mine.

★★★

Exile is busy most Friday evenings, but tonight seems especially crowded.

I sit in VIP, high above the dance floor, with Angelo and Maksim.

They're three drinks in, the bottle service girls draped across them like ornaments. Their laughter blends with the bass thumping below.

My patience wearing thin, I finally speak up.

"Do you think you could dismiss the girls so we can get down to business?"

Maksim smirks, tipping his glass toward me lazily. "Why don't you lighten Santo up, Ana? He's about to be a married man. Show him a good time."

Before I can react, the redhead slides onto my lap, her perfume clinging to the back of my throat.

"No." I stand abruptly, catching her waist to steady her.

Maksim and Angelo's laughter follows me as I descend into the crowd, weaving through bodies moving to the pulse of the music. Their sweat and perfume mix in the air, but I filter it out as I approach the bar.

"Santo!" The bartender greets me before I can speak, pouring whiskey without waiting for an order.

"Busy night?" I ask, glancing at the dance floor.

"Busier than usual." He gestures toward the entrance, and my gaze follows instinctively.

There she is.

Vasilisa glides into the club, and suddenly, everything around her fades. Golden hair bouncing with each step, framing her delicate features in soft, loose waves.

And that dress.

Midnight blue, clinging to her like it was made for her, dipping low in a sharp, daring V that catches my breath.

It hugs her slender frame, tracing every subtle curve, and the way it catches the light makes it hard to look away.

It's the kind of dress that turns heads. The kind that invites attention, lingering stares, and thoughts that men shouldn't have about *my* wife.

A slow heat curls in my chest.

Possessiveness, sharp and sudden.

She's supposed to be mine.

No one else should be looking.

She chats with the brunette she walked in with, her face lighting with a bright smile that's impossible to ignore.

Pietro follows closely, a silent shadow at her side.

My eyes narrow.

I thought he was her sister's guard now.

I take a slow sip of whiskey, but the taste barely registers.

Without thinking, I head back to the booth, sinking into the seat next to Maksim. My eyes never stray far from her.

She's found a table to sit at directly in my eye line, she wears a neon blue band on her wrist indicating she's underage to drink.

Despite that, Pietro brings them both drinks as the two women continue to talk.

She laughs and the air around me stills, her beauty triples the brighter her smile is.

I wonder what was said that evoked that laugh.

I want it to happen *again.*

"So, I send the girls away just for you to sit here in silence while you watch *your* girl?" Maksim teases beside me breaking me from my thoughts.

My girl.

I remove my gaze from Vasilisa and shift my attention to Maksim and Angelo. "I didn't expect her to be here."

"She's not supposed to be," Maksim says passing a sharp look in Vasilisa's direction, I notice then that Pietro is staring up at Maksim. "She should be at home preparing for her upcoming nuptials, but you know women these days. I'll allow her to have the night."

Angelo watches her too, and the way his gaze lingers makes me tense.

"She's even more beautiful in person," Angelo comments.

My grip tightens on the glass.

"She's my favorite cousin," Maksim says with pride. "She's built for this life."

"Built for it?" I murmur, eyes fixed on her.

Maksim leans back, tipping his drink toward the ceiling, finishing it before answering. "She'll be the perfect wife. Knows how to keep quiet and stand by her man. She respects the business, understands what it means to belong to it. She'll be whatever you need her to be."

His words leave a bitter taste behind.

I expected a wife with no strings; a woman content with luxuries, happy to stay out of my affairs. Not someone Maksim crafted to be a mirror of this life.

Angelo lifts his glass. "Lucky man."

"I wouldn't say that."

But I can't stop watching her.

She's now dancing with her friend, their bodies swaying in sync with the pulsating beat.

Maksim chuckles at my response. "Don't be an ass Santo," he retorts.

"My cousin is a good woman. She has a kind temperament *and* she's smart, You'll get along well."

I scoff at his words, nursing my drink as I watch her. Vasilisa sways, her body moving in perfect sync with the music. There's nothing rehearsed about the way she carries herself.

Confidence.

The kind that feels rare. It pulls at me, making it harder to look away.

She stops suddenly, scanning the club.

Her gaze locks with mine from across the room.

Everything else fades.

Recognition flickers in her eyes, widening just slightly as realization sets in.

She *knows* who I am.

And she doesn't look away.

Neither do I.

For a fleeting moment, I see something in her expression—curiosity? Uncertainty?

We hold each other's gaze for longer than necessary.

Longer than I should allow.

She turns, the spell breaking as if it never happened.

I swivel my attention back to Maksim and Angelo and lean forward, resting my forearms on the table.

"Pietro Ivanov," I say, not bothering to mask the edge in my voice.

Maksim's brow lifts. "What about him?"

"Will he be an issue when it comes to Vasilisa?"

Maksim chuckles, "No need to be jealous Santo, he's a family friend and uninterested in Vasilisa."

"As far as *you* know."

The amusement flickers in Maksim's eyes before fading. His expression hardens slightly.

"He knows better. He owes me, and he's more useful alive than dead. There's no need to concern yourself."

I nod, setting the thought aside.

For now.

"Fine, let's get back to business."

The night wears on, we delve into deep discussions about our next strategic moves in acquiring valuable territory. I'm tasked with spearheading the campaign to acquire buildings owned by the wealthy Beaumont brothers. One of them happens to be my biggest competition, but I agree to set up a meeting at their enterprise. Maksim shares his struggles with dealing with the Turkish mob, who have been encroaching on his territory and selling knock-off versions of his highly coveted drugs. Angelo offers his men to aid Maksim's in locating, capturing, and interrogating one of the interlopers in hopes of obtaining information on their source.

But even as the conversation shifts, I feel her.

When I leave, Vasilisa's gaze finds me again. This time, she smiles.

It's subtle, small and soft, but it unsettles me more than I expect.

I walk out into the night, the image of her lingering longer than I'd like.

CHAPTER 7

VASILISA

S anto is intimidating.

In person, he's magnanimous, besides his size, his presence takes up a lot of space, even in the expansive club, I could feel him every-where.

I sensed his eyes on me before I saw him and recognized him instantly.

For the past week I have stared at his photo, and those intense eyes, more times than I can count.

I could pick those eyes out in a lineup.

But last night those eyes stared into me as if I were prey and he was hunting my every move.

A chill rolls up my spine.

My husband to be is a force of a man.

If just being in his company in a room full of people stifled me, I can't fathom being alone with him.

I look down at his photo again; Santo Amato is handsome in a way that feels dangerous—like a man who could unravel you with a glance but wouldn't care enough to piece you back together.

There's nothing in his eyes that gives away who he really is.

But after seeing him, I should count myself lucky. I could have been arranged to Jude or, worse, someone older, less fit, hateful.

I hope Santo isn't hateful.

I trace my fingertip over his photo and startle at a knock on my door. Mimi pokes her head inside.

"Someone is here to see you," she says quietly.

"Who?"

My heart stutters in my chest. I place the photo down and smooth out my skirt.

"I don't know, some hot guy," Mimi says her eyes lighting up.

Confused, I follow her to our front door where my mother stands with a man I haven't seen before.

He's well built, his red shirt stretching over his chest, he's wearing a harness with his guns strapped securely.

His dark hair is gelled keeping his curls neat, his warm brown eyes meet mine, and he gives me a kind smile. "Vasilisa?"

I nod and my mother steps away giving me some space with the stranger in our foyer.

"My name's Luca Cattaneo, I work for Santo," he says simply, and I notice a plain brown box in his hands my heart thrums.

A gift?

"Nice to meet you," I say extending my hand, but instead of taking it, he places the box in mine.

"Santo wanted you to have this, I'm supposed to collect your old one while I'm here."

His gaze lands on Mimi.

"Hi," she giggles.

"Hey, kid," he replies.

I open the box to find a cellphone. Hesitantly, I remove it and hand the box back.

"Why? I have a phone."

"You need a new one," Luca explains, "and this one has Santo's number in it and mine, just in case you can't reach him."

I stare at him, uncertain. "Is that all?"

"If you could just get your old phone, I can be out of your hair."

My eyes widen, but I say nothing, my brain unable to compute what is happening, I glance at my mother who furrows her brow at me and nods vigorously, shooing me to go.

I nod and head back upstairs to retrieve my old phone, my fingers tightening around the new one.

It's sleek, expensive.

Beautiful.

But it's also a leash, isn't it?

A way to control what I see, what I say, who I can talk to.

And yet, I go through the motions, handing over my old one without protest.

Because that's what's expected.

I return shortly to where Mimi is doing cartwheels in front of an unimpressed Luca.

"And that's how easy it is," Mimi says breathlessly, "you just have to practice."

"Mimi, leave him alone," my mother scolds from the other room and Mimi reluctantly leaves.

I hand Luca my old phone. "Is he going to… *keep* it?"

Luca shrugs. "I don't know. I just do my job."

I nod. "I guess I'll see you at the wedding?"

Luca smiles, "Of course, text me if you need me."

He leaves and I lock the door behind him.

Still bewildered, I turn to Mimi hiding in the hall. She grins, eyes sparkling.

"Well, he was *charming*," she says. "Think he'll come back?"

I roll my eyes and head back to my room, the new phone clutched tightly in my hand.

It gleams under the sunlight spilling through my bedroom window. I switch it on, and sure enough, his number is there.

A sudden surge of anxiety floods me. I'm marrying into a world far more intense than mine.

I keep staring at the blank screen, the reality of it all sinking in.

I try to distract myself by tidying up my room, but the new phone buzzes. A text message. My heart skips a beat when I see his name.

Santo

> Vasilisa, hope you're settling well with your new phone. Just wanted you to be able to reach me directly if needed.

I read it several times, unsure how to respond.

What do I even say to a man who just *took* my phone?

I type out a simple thank you, my thumb hovering over the send button.

The blank screen stares back at me, taunting me. A plain thank-you feels too impersonal, too stiff for the man I'm about to marry.

Before I can overthink it, I switch to the camera, aim it at myself, and snap a quick photo. Nothing fancy—just me sitting at my vanity, sunlight spilling through the window, my hair loose around my shoulders.

I hesitate.

Staring at the picture for a long moment.

Would he even want this?

But I send it anyway.

A leap of faith.

The message shows as delivered.

I wait, my heart thrumming in my chest.

But nothing comes.

No response.
Minutes stretch into hours.
Then into an entire evening.
Still, nothing.
I shouldn't care. *It's just a text.*
A simple photo.
But when I finally set the phone down for the night, something in me deflates.
Foolish girl.

***

The weekend passes in a blur of fittings, final touches on the wedding dress, and endless back-and-forth with my mother about traditions I'm apparently supposed to uphold as Santo Amato's wife.

I try not to think about the selfie.

Or the fact that I followed it up with more photos; every dress, every accessory, even the simple pink heels I picked out.

He doesn't respond to any of them.

Each photo disappears into silence, met with nothing but a read receipt. No acknowledgment, no reaction, just a blank void.

I tell myself it doesn't matter. That I shouldn't care.

But when my phone buzzes Sunday night, the single word on my screen nearly steals my breath.

Santo

Beautiful.

I stare at the screen, my heart doing an embarrassing little flip.
That's it.
One word.
And yet, it feels like so much more.
From that point on, I find myself sending him more photos—another dress, a set of earrings, a bouquet my mother insists on.
Sometimes, his responses come hours later.

Santo

Perfect. It suits you.

Sometimes, they're immediate.

Elegant.

Always brief.

That's stunning.

But with each reply, a warm and unfamiliar feeling sparks inside me. Like maybe this isn't just about tradition and duty. As if maybe, just *maybe,* we're beginning to find a way to meet in the middle.

The phone buzzes, breaking me out of my thoughts. I grab it off my nightstand, a small smile sneaking onto my face.

Sleep well.

It's the first time he's texted me unprompted.

This is strange territory, planning to marry someone I barely know, wrestling with the idea of sharing a life with him.

But each text from Santo feels like an outreached hand, a small gesture telling me it's alright to take the leap.

And with each day that passes, I find myself more willing to grab onto it.

I decide to take a leap when my father mentions the retirement party set for this morning.

Santo is certain to be there.

Maybe we can talk in person, even if he doesn't want to see me before the wedding.

His texts say otherwise.

They have sparked something in me, a small hope that maybe he wouldn't mind seeing me there after all.

I choose an off-the-shoulder pink dress, one of my favorites.

The skirt flows with every step.

It feels like me, soft and a little romantic, a far cry from the tight dress and smoky makeup Luna coaxed me into at the club.

It was bold, *sexy,* but today I want Santo to see me as I am.

I pin my hair half up and go lighter on makeup—I want him to see my face today, not one hidden under layers.

Finally, I slip on my highest heels.

Given how tall Santo is.

I'll need it.

With a steadying breath, I smooth my dress and glance at my reflection one last time.

My heart thrums with nerves, but I push them aside.

It's just a meeting.

A conversation.

And yet, as I reach for the door, my fingers tighten around the handle, the weight of what I'm about to do settling deep in my chest.

I exhale slowly. *I'm ready for this.* I have to be.

I head downstairs, determined to speak with my groom face-to-face.

CHAPTER 8

VASILISA

The office shouts a group greeting as we walk in, everyone happy to see my father, clapping his back and shaking his hand.

I ignore it all. I scan the room for Santo, but I don't see him anywhere.

Slipping away from the crowd, I trail through the halls, toward my father's old office—only now, the name on the door isn't his.

Santo Amato.

I should knock.

I shake away the thought and just open the door.

Santo is seated behind a sleek, large glass desk with metal drawers attached.

The city skyline forms a striking backdrop behind him.

He's focused on something he's scribbling on a notepad and doesn't notice me enter.

His shirt sleeves are rolled up, and his tie is loosened.

A tendril of hair falls into his face from his otherwise perfectly tousled style, and his strong jaw is shadowed with stubble.

My eyes linger.

"Are you going to keep staring, or do you plan to say something?" Santo's voice rumbles through the silence.

His eyes don't leave the notepad.

I freeze.

"I just wanted to get away from the crowd. I didn't think anyone would be in here," I lie.

His stormy gray eyes flick up to meet mine.

My breath catches.

A smirk tugs at his lips.

"Well, *surprise.* I'm here."

I feel like prey under a predator's gaze, but I refuse to let him see that.

Keeping my movements unhurried, I walk toward the bookcase, running my fingers over the spines.

I recognize quite a few titles.

"You have an extensive collection," I murmur, tilting my head slightly. "Do you actually read them?"

Santo leans back in his chair, his eyes following me, "I do."

His voice is so smooth.

Deep.

"Tolstoy is a favorite of mine," I say, sliding the book from the shelf.

"One loves because one loves. To reason about it is to destroy everything," Santo says quietly.

A smile spreads across my face as my fingers brush over the worn book. "You read Anna Karenina?"

"I have," he replies, his gaze never wavering. "You seem surprised."

"I'm not surprised," I manage, my voice softer than I intend. "Just… impressed."

He leans forward, resting his elbows on the desk, his face a mixture of curiosity and amusement. "Why?"

"The characters," I say, tracing the book's worn spine as I gather my thoughts. "They're flawed. Messy. Real. Tolstoy makes you feel them—their desires, their regrets. It's tragic and beautiful all at once."

Santo studies me for a moment. "I appreciate the complexities," he says at last. "But to me, it's a story about *passion,* and how it destroys."

His words linger in the air, heavier than I expect.

We're no longer talking about the story, but something deeper.

Something closer.

"And you?" he asks abruptly, interrupting my thoughts. "What is it about Tolstoy that brings you back to this book?"

The question hangs between us.

Charged.

I glance down at the book in my hands, searching for the right words.

"The honesty," I answer truthfully. "Tolstoy doesn't shy away from showing us the brutal truth of human nature. The flaws, the pain, the moments of redemption, even when they're fleeting."

His gaze sharpens, as if he's dissecting my response, peeling it back layer by layer.

"Brutal truths," he murmurs, almost to himself. "Not everyone can face those."

I look up, catching the faintest flicker of something raw in his expression, and I know, without him saying another word, that we're no longer talking about Tolstoy at all.

I place the book back on the shelf, desperate to shift the energy in the room, and turn toward the painting hanging on the wall. "Is this an original Monet?"

His eyebrows lift slightly.

"You know art."

He doesn't phrase it as a question, just a simple statement.

I flush under his gaze, my fingers fidgeting at my sides. "I… I like to paint from time to time," I admit softly.

"Do you?"

He rises from his chair, moving toward me with an unhurried grace that makes the space between us shrink too fast.

His presence is everywhere; suffocating, magnetic, inescapable.

"I do," I breathe.

He's too close now, his heat wrapping around me, unraveling my thoughts before I can catch them.

Santo doesn't say anything at first. His gaze lingers on my face, then trails deliberately down to my now clasped hands.

"I would love to see your work," he says, his voice quiet, but certain.

Like it's already decided.

The honesty surprises me, catching me off guard.

"Sure," I manage, the word trembling with a mixture of nerves and something warmer, softer.

The air between us shifts, the heavy tension giving way to something quieter, more familiar.

And yet, his presence still weighs on me, impossible to ignore, impossible to escape.

He tucks a loose strand of hair behind my ear.

His touch is feather-light, sending tremors through me.

The height difference apparent even with my heels, makes me feel insecure.

I step out of his orbit and toward his desk spreading my hands across the top.

"My father got rid of it," I say, the words tumbling out.

Anything to fill the silence between us, *anything* to shake off the lingering heat of his touch.

I feel Santo behind me, "The desk?"

"Yes, I'm surprised he let it go," I turn around and Santo is still in my space, his eyes roam over my face, slow and deliberate, as if he's memorizing every detail.

I resist the urge to shift under his gaze.

The weight of it making me feel exposed, unsure if he sees too much. His eyes lock back onto mine, steady.

"I didn't see a use for it, I prefer the glass desk over wooden," he states calmly.

The tension in the room is choking me.

He seems unfazed.

"It's nothing," I say quickly. "When I was little, my father used to tell me a story—that the desk was carved from a tree where a princess and a prince etched their initials into the bark. Their love became part of the wood, immortalized forever."

I stammer the last bit and chuckle nervously.

Shut up Vasi.

My cheeks burn, his eyes are on me quiet and assessing, but my mouth won't stop, "I carved my initials under the desk while I was hiding one day as a child. I don't think he ever knew about it."

Santo pulls back and takes a seat.

I've spoken myself into a corner and embarrassed myself in front of him.

For what seems like an eternity, Santo remains silent, his gaze fixed on a distant point over my shoulder.

A multitude of questions dance in his eyes, and for a moment I wonder if I've overstepped some unspoken boundary.

He glances down at his glass desk, his fingers drumming a rhythmic pattern against the smooth surface.

Finally, he looks at me, a newfound curiosity etching his features.

"Vasilisa," he says, his voice smooth, like melting chocolate as he tastes my name, "that's quite a story."

"It's just a silly fairy tale my father used to tell," I reply hastily.

It seems too immature, too *personal* now that the words had been said out loud.

There's a brief flicker of something in Santo's eyes—recognition? Empathy?

But it's gone as quickly as it came.

"Fairy tales can tell us much more about ourselves than we think," he says thoughtfully.

His eyes meet mine once again, and this time they're softer, less the predator on the hunt and more... *human.*

He leans back into his chair and folds his arms across his broad chest.

"It shows," he begins slowly, "that you are an optimist. That you believe in love and magic."

A blush involuntarily heats my cheeks.

I lower my gaze.

He's so overwhelming.

The room falls silent once more, save for the distant hum of the party outside and the *tick-tick-tick* of an old clock mounted on the wall behind me.

"Were you waiting for your prince to find it?" Santo's voice is low, almost like he's asking a question he doesn't want the answer to.

I look up and my breath catches.

His gaze is so intense that my heart starts racing again.

"I—I don't know," I admit. "I suppose part of me always hoped so."

"Silly girl," Santo murmurs.

There's no mockery, just warmth, edged with something else.

Something that makes my pulse trip over itself.

Even with his eyes boring into mine, I find comfort in his gaze.

Maybe Santo isn't a cold, distant man like I feared he might be, but I could be just another naïve girl swept away by a handsome face.

"I can't offer you a desk made from enchanted wood," Santo says, his voice measured as he pulls open a drawer.

From inside, he retrieves a slender metal tool, its tip gleaming under the low light.

I watch, curiosity prickling at my skin as he leans forward and begins carving something into the glass desk with deliberate, steady strokes.

"I don't have fairy tale trees or immortalized love stories," he murmurs, his focus still on the desk. "But maybe, *we* could make our own."

With a final swipe of his hand, he brushes away the lingering dust and places the tool back in the drawer.

He motions for me to come closer.

I hesitate for only a moment before stepping forward, standing beside his chair.

When I look down, a gasp escapes my lips.

Two initials, intertwined on the glass surface.

V & S.

My heart stumbles at the sight, warmth blooming in my chest and spreading outward until I can feel the heat creeping into my face.

Slowly, I lift my gaze to his.

He's watching me closely, his expression neutral.

"I—" I begin, but the words tangle on my tongue.

He's taken my childhood story, and turned it into something *real.*

Santo rises, the space between us closing in an instant.

Towering over me, his presence is undeniable.

The tension from before still lingers, but there's something softer now, something quieter.

He stands there in silence, waiting for me to speak.

But I don't know what to say. All I can hear is my own heartbeat, its pounding echoing through my ears, filling the silence between us.

Desperate to focus on something—*anything*—else, I glance down at his desk, my eyes sweeping over the surface.

And then I see it.

A framed photo.

Of me.

Dressed in my favorite yellow dress.

My breath stills.

That photo was on my phone.

I school my expression quickly, but it's too late. Santo catches my reaction.

His throat bobs as he clears it, a fraction too late.

"Your father left that behind," he says.

He's lying.

The photo was *never* printed.

Never shared.

"Oh. Okay," I murmur, stepping back—from the desk, from *him*.

Santo watches me for a moment longer before lowering himself back into his chair.

He picks up his pen and returns to his notes.

Moment gone.

"I should get back to work."

I nod, hesitating at the door even though I've clearly been dismissed.

I *should* leave.

And yet, something in me lingers.

I steal one last glance over my shoulder, but Santo doesn't look up.

His focus remains on his notepad, his pen moving in smooth, practiced strokes.

My future husband is a contradiction.

A man who carves initials into glass like a lover and steals photos like a thief.

I'll unravel the mysteries of Santo Amato after the wedding.

CHAPTER 9

SANTO

G rand gestures are not my thing.

I don't date women; I don't bring them home to meet family. I'm *never* exclusive.

I meet a woman, we fuck and I move on.

Keeping a woman is a liability, a responsibility and a weakness, one that my enemies would use against me.

Now, I'm forced to take a wife, one that I thought I could easily keep in my fortress of a home, and that I could have followed by guards if she wanted to go out.

We would make appearances when needed and she would then be safely tucked away, no affection, no love, no fairy tales.

Safe and distant.

Instead, I get *Vasilisa.*

I read her file.

She's young, trained, dutiful and knows the rules of being part of this life.

What *wasn't* in the file is that she and I have things in common.

She's *smart,* she likes books, art and she's *breathtakingly* beautiful up close.

But she lacks the softness of rounded curves that line a woman's body with a fuller figure; one that could handle a man like me and knows it's nothing more than physical, no love, no expectations, no marriage, *no happily ever after.*

Vasilisa is the opposite.

She's small, breakable, vulnerable, and full of *hope.*

Those eyes, like ice shimmering under sunlight, searing into mine with interest and an unspoken longing for a prince.

I wanted her.

I *want* her.

Her texts replay in my mind. The endless stream of photos—dresses, bouquets, shoes, each one paired with a quiet hope that I'd respond.

And I did, against my better judgment.

Just a few words here and there.

But it meant nothing.

I was humoring her, keeping things civil.

But it wasn't nothing.

Each photo was a glimpse into her world, a world I'd soon be a part of, whether I wanted to or not.

She's supposed to be just a name on a contract, but now she's becoming real—*too real*.

I lean back in my chair, the faint trace of her perfume lingering long after she's gone.

Vasilisa.

She's as delicate as I imagined, but she's also somehow… *strong.*

Strong enough to walk into my office without hesitation.

To smile, despite the weight of what this life means for her.

I thought my biggest fear would be wanting her.

But now, that's not what eats at me.

No, the real fear coils deep inside me—what happens when she meets Scythe?

She'll fear him.

She should.

Maybe that would make this easier.

Maybe it would stop whatever this is inside me from turning into something I can't control.

I scoff at the idea, but in that moment, in this room with her and her intoxicating scent of sweet cashmere—a warm, amber softness that wraps around me like a forbidden caress filling my senses, all I wanted was to give her exactly what she needed and everything that she desired.

That's dangerous for a man like me, *wanting* her.

It would be one thing to just want her body, consummate the marriage and play our roles, but Vasilisa managed, in a *moment,* what other women could never achieve in weeks.

She stirred in me a desire, an equal longing.

I hate it.

This should be simple.

Physical. Monetary.

No, this… this feels like something else.

Something harder to walk away from.

Vasilisa isn't supposed to matter.

I drag a finger along the edge of the glass desk, stopping at the rough curve of the initials I carved.

I shouldn't have done it.

I don't do things like this.

My phone buzzes.

Sandra's voice crackles through. "You have a visitor."

The wedding planner.

A woman steps in hesitantly, clutching a tablet, her shoulders stiff like she's preparing for war. She lingers near the entrance, nerves practically radiating off her.

I glance up, barely masking my irritation.

"Mr. Amato," she starts, shifting the tablet nervously in her hands. "I just have a few questions regarding the wedding."

I sigh quietly, leaning back in the chair.

"Make it quick."

She nods, pressing the tablet closer to her chest. "Do you know if your bride has a preference for flowers or food?"

"Julian can deal with the food," I reply, brushing it off. "Talk to him. He knows what I like."

Her stylus glides across the screen, but she pauses again. "And the flowers?"

"Lilies," I say without hesitation. "And roses."

I glance up to find her staring at me, waiting for more.

"Small ones," I add, watching as confusion flickers across her face.

"For the tables?"

"No." I drum my fingers against the glass. *"For her hair."*

Her eyes widen slightly. "Real roses?"

I let the silence stretch just long enough for her to realize it wasn't a suggestion.

"Why would I ask for fake ones?" I reply flatly.

"Oh—" she stammers, eyes flicking down to the screen. "It's just... sometimes faux flowers are easier for styling. They stay in place longer."

I level her with a look. *"Real* ones."

She nods quickly, scribbling the note. "I'll have them sent to the estate."

"Send them to Cassandra."

The stylus halts mid-stroke.

"Cassandra?"

"Her team is styling Vasilisa's hair."

The planner nods again, lips pressing together as if that should've been obvious.

She writes, her brows pull slightly together in thought, "Vasilisa... beautiful name."

I still.

Her name hangs there, soft but heavy, cutting through the space in a way I wasn't prepared for.

It shouldn't matter. It shouldn't affect me.

But hearing her name said aloud by someone else settles wrong in my chest.

"Yes," I say quietly. "It is."

The planner seems oblivious to the shift, tapping notes into her screen.

"Thank you, Mr. Amato," she says, offering a tight smile. "I'll handle the arrangements."

I give a brief nod, eyes fixed on the edge of the desk.

She starts to leave, but before she reaches the door, I add, "Make sure the roses are white."

Her head bobs in agreement before the door clicks softly behind her.

The room falls silent once more, but the weight of Vasilisa's name lingers like an echo I can't quite shake.

I press my thumb to the carved initials.

They're deeper than they should be.

Permanent.

I don't do things like this.

This wasn't supposed to happen.

And yet, she's everywhere, even when she's not here.

★★★

Sandra lines up potential secretaries for me to interview.

The process goes seamlessly, with three candidates surpassing my expectations.

Any of them could be a permanent fixture in my office. I'll take the week to decide.

Just as I am about to call Marcus, the head of the cyber department, for an update on our progress with the QUEEN file, a loud commotion erupts outside my door.

Without warning, a woman bursts through the door, her chestnut curls are disheveled, the papers in her hand wrinkled.

She's dress in business attire for sure, but the way the pencil skirt and blouse cling to her curves should be a crime.

This woman is a sexy, curvy, brunette, with big brown eyes and cherry red lips, but I can't find it in myself to stir any sort of desire as my mind travels to the svelte golden ray of light that was in my office earlier.

Sandra follows behind the woman with a deep scowl on her face.

"I'm sorry Mr. Amato, I told her the interviews were *over*."

I lift my hand and gesture for Sandra to give us a moment.

She hesitates, but leaves.

The brunette steps forward.

"I'm so sorry I'm late, my name is Olivia. Olivia Baker."

She extends her hand and I ignore it.

"You're late Ms. Baker, and the position has been filled, thank you."

Her eyes widen and she deflates, "Already?"

"Yes already, you're over fifteen minutes late, do you *always* lack punctuality?"

She sighs defeated, "Are there any other positions? I would do *anything*, and I mean anything."

I raise an eyebrow in disbelief.

A wave of shock rolls over her face.

"No!" She says her face turning mauve, "Not like that, I meant I would clean toilets if it meant I could have a job."

"Unfortunately, Ms. Baker this was the only position, and it *has been filled.*"

She takes a deep breath, squares her shoulders.

"Thank you for your time," with a polite smile Olivia Baker gathers herself and leaves promptly.

The rest of the day passes in a whirl of emails, phone calls, and meetings.

As the sun begins to dip below the horizon, I lean back in my chair, pinching the bridge of my nose to stave off an impending headache.

From the corner of my office, I hear a soft knock.

Sandra peeks around the door. "Mr. Amato, your six o'clock canceled. Your evening is free."

"Thank you, Sandra."

The relief in my voice unsettles me.

The door closes behind her, I stand, turning to the window.

Hands in my pockets, my gaze sweeps over the city.

I shouldn't be thinking about her.

I shouldn't still feel the ghost of her presence in my office; the way her soft perfume lingered in the air, the way her gorgeous, hopeful eyes searched mine like I was something *more* than I am.

I shouldn't do this.

Before I can stop myself, I pick up my phone and dial.

It rings twice before she answers.

"Hello?"

"Vasilisa," I mutter.

My voice should be steady. *It isn't.* "It's Santo."

There's a slight pause before she replies, soft, almost teasing. "I know. Your number is saved, remember?"

I falter.

I *don't* falter.

Apparently, I do now.

Something shifts inside me, something I don't know how to name.

My fingers tighten around the phone, my jaw locking, my body suddenly too warm, too aware.

Why did I call her?

I *shouldn't* be doing this.

"Right." The word is clipped, an attempt to regain footing. "Good."

It's *not* good.

None of this is good.

And yet—

"Join me for dinner tonight."

The words are out before I can think them through, before I can measure or weigh or anticipate.

Another pause.

I almost expect hesitation, resistance.

"I'd love to."

I exhale.

I shouldn't feel satisfaction. I shouldn't feel anything.

"I'll send a car in fifteen minutes."

"Fifteen?" Her voice is quiet.

"Do you need more time?"

I can almost hear her smile. "No, I can be ready."

The ease of her acceptance settles something in me, even as it unravels everything else.

"Excellent. I'll see you soon."

I end the call, already texting Marco to pick her up.

Then I text Vincenzo, my restaurant manager.

Shut down La Serenata for the night. Only one reservation... for two

Vincenzo

Understood, Mr. Amato.

I open my desk drawer, fingers automatically reaching for the small velvet box.

It was meant to be delivered through Miroslav or Luca.

That plan doesn't sit right with me anymore.
Tonight, I'll give it to her myself.
I slip it into my breast pocket, straighten my jacket, and head for the door—before I can talk myself out of this.

Chapter 10

SANTO

I take in the restaurant with a single sweep of my gaze.

Immaculate, as it should be.

Vincenzo runs a tight ship.

Spotless floors, polished silverware, crisp white tablecloths.

The faint scent of fresh flowers softens the richer aromas of seared steak and aged wine.

He leads me to a perfectly set table; chilled drinks, mouthwatering appetizers, lighting dimmed just enough to cast everything in a warm, intimate glow.

A romantic touch; unnecessary, intentional, and *entirely* something Vincenzo would do.

Vincenzo greets me, takes my jacket, and I stop him, pulling the box from the pocket before letting him fold the fabric over his arm.

His eyes catch on it, a smirk tugging at his mouth.

"I heard about the arrangement," he says, amusement laced in his voice. "Didn't think you'd actually propose."

"I'm not," I reply flatly. "I'm giving it to her to formalize the arrangement. Nothing more."

His smirk falters slightly, but he doesn't push. Smart man.

"We won't be long," I say, shifting the conversation. "I won't keep you late—I know Arturo and the baby are waiting."

Vincenzo waves me off.

"I called him after you texted. He's fine if I'm late, and the baby's already asleep."

There's a quiet pride in his voice, one that softens the usual edge.

Vincenzo and I have known each other since college. He stayed in the closet for longer than I expected, but once he burst through, he went all in. Within a year, he had a husband and most recently, a baby. He is a trusted and loyal friend, though *far* too invested in my romantic life. I'm sure that if anyone in my circle would take to Vasilisa kindly, it would be him.

I take a seat as he leaves to put my jacket away; I place the box on the table and sip my glass of wine.

Everything is perfect.

Yet—

My fingers tighten around the glass.

Ridiculous. I don't get nervous.

I push the feeling down. She's already mine, whether either of us wanted it or not.

The contracts are signed.

There's no turning down this ring.

My phone buzzes. A text from one of my men I had pick her up.

Marco

She's here.

I stand, my gaze locked onto the entrance.

There she is.

Vasilisa steps inside, eyes wide as she takes in La Serenata, the candle-light catching in the crisp blue of her irises. Vincenzo says something that earns a small smile, but I barely register it.

Her eyes meet mine, and in an instant, the fluttering in my chest ceases.

She smiles, and something inside me stutters.

A brief, sharp halt—like the world just changed, and I was the last to notice.

The flush on her cheeks, the curve of her lips; innocent, utterly unaware of the hold she already has.

My gaze trails.

The emerald green dress clings to her like it was made for her, cinching at the waist, the low-cut neckline daring me to imagine how it would look pooled at her feet.

It flares at her hips, moving with an effortless grace, teasing with every step.

Short. Showcasing legs that deserve to be worshipped. Four-inch heels lengthen them, accentuating every perfect line.

Heels *again.*

I wonder if it's insecurity, if she resents the height difference between us.

She doesn't need them.

With or without, she carries herself like a queen.

And I, despite the arrangement, am nothing more than a man caught in her orbit.

She is *breathtaking*.

I go to her, extending my hand.

Her touch is light, but her grip is steady and firm. She lets me lead her to the table, moving with that same effortless grace that commands attention without trying.

When I pull out her chair, she sinks into it with perfect poise, pure class in every movement.

I take my seat across from her, watching as her gaze sweeps over the restaurant in quiet wonder. Then her eyes meet mine again, and she gives me a soft smile.

"This place is beautiful," she says quietly.

I let a slow smile tug at my lips. La Serenata was the first of many businesses my brother and I built, and while I rarely allow sentimentality, pride settles in my chest at her approval.

"I'm glad you like it." I keep my voice warm, easy.

I want her to stay comfortable.

A soft blush dusts her cheeks before she drops her gaze, scanning the spread of food between us. Then, she giggles—a sound so light, so effortlessly sweet, my heart thuds.

"You have enough food on this table for four grown men."

I glance down.

Bruschetta, arancini, caponata, and an antipasto platter of olives, meats, and cheeses—just a few of my favorites.

Nothing excessive.

"This would barely feed my brother and me," I smirk.

She giggles again, and my chest tightens. I loosen my tie, clearing my throat before I do something stupid.

She opens her napkin and places it on her lap then takes bruschetta and places it on her plate delicately.

"Your brother is the Don?" she asks innocently enough, but her mention of Angelo gives me that unfamiliar tinge again.

"Yes, Angelo is now the head of Cosa Nostra," I say dismissively.

I take a few olives from the platter before I say more.

She nods and lifts the bread, taking a bite, her full lips close around it, her tongue darting out to catch any stray crumbs.

My eyes follow her tongue and trail over her face, mesmerized by the way she enjoys the food.

A small moan escapes her lips, sending a shiver down my spine.

I want her.

I shake my head, clearing the thoughts and motion for Vincenzo to come closer.

"That is undoubtedly the best bruschetta I've ever tasted," she says, placing the remaining piece down with a satisfied sigh.

"I'll be sure to let the chef keep his job," I say jokingly.

Her eyebrows raise, "You own this restaurant?"

Before I can answer Vincenzo approaches,

"Mr. Amato, Ms. Popov would you like to have your entrees brought out now?"

"Oh no, there's more than enough food on this table to last me a lifetime," Vasilisa says with a small laugh.

Dio, that laugh.

"Nonsense. If anything, you should eat more," The words are light, teasing, meant to coax another smile out of her, but something shifts.

Her eyes widen.

She blinks, glancing down at her plate, the laughter gone from her lips.

I turn to Vincenzo, covering the moment with an easy command. "The entrees can come out in fifteen minutes. I called you over to ask if you could bring me the book."

Vincenzo's brows rise slightly before understanding clicks into place.

He nods and steps away.

I turn back to Vasilisa. She's still looking at her half-eaten bruschetta, lost in thought.

My fingers tighten around my glass. "Everything alright?"

She looks up at me, her eyes momentarily forlorn.

It's barely there, just a flicker of something fragile, before she masks it with a smile, straightening her shoulders, slipping back into the effortless poise she wears like armor.

"Yes, of course. Everything is so... beautiful here," she says. But her voice is softer now, and her eyes don't quite match her words.

Before I can press, Vincenzo returns, holding my mother's book.

"Vita Nuova," Vasilisa gasps reaching for the book, but she catches herself and clasps her hands together, returning to her poised state.

"Yes, Vita Nuova," I say, taking the book from Vincenzo and dismissing him. I let my fingertips graze the worn cover for a brief moment before extending it to her.

She hesitates, then takes it, running her palm reverently down the aged leather.

"It's my mother's, and now it's yours."

Vasilisa's beautiful mouth forms a small *o*, and she flushes, her gorgeous face glowing.

"I couldn't possibly," she starts, lifting the book to return it.

I stop her with a raised hand.

"It's yours. You'll be bringing it to our home soon enough anyway."

She exhales softly and places the book down, delicate in the way she handles it, as if it's something sacred.

"Thank you."

"You're welcome."

Usually, I wouldn't part with anything that belonged to my mother, but Vasilisa likes books, she will treat it well.

I take a sip of wine, my gaze lingering on her. I could get used to this—her presence, the quiet grace that draws me in when I least expect it. She's warm in a way I hadn't anticipated.

Her fingers trail absently along the worn edges of the book, her expression softening, eyes filled with a silent appreciation, it makes my chest ache.

"Have you read it before?" I ask her, eager to delve into a conversation that would lay bare more of her personality.

Her lips curve into a smile as she lifts her gaze. "Partially, for one of my literature classes. Dante's story of love and devotion is... moving..."

Her voice drifts off.

Her smile fades, replaced by a distant look.

I'm tempted to ask what's hidden behind those soulful eyes. I wonder if it's the arranged marriage that makes her sad or something else entirely. I doubt she will tell me if I ask.

It's too soon to gamble so instead, I take another sip of wine and lean back into my chair.

"Tell me about the art you make. Should I expect our home to be adorned with your pieces?"

Her expression flickers, something sorrowful flashing in her eyes before she quickly drops her gaze, shaking her head.

"No," she says quietly. "None of my pieces will be coming with me."

Before I can question that, the waiters move in to clear the appetizers, and Vincenzo sets down our entrees—linguine with salmon, cooked to perfection.

"This is perfect," she says, her voice lighter, picking up her fork and twirling it through the pasta.

"Why can't you bring your pieces?"

She chews, her hand coming up to cover her mouth, blushing slightly as she tries to finish quickly to respond.

"My father didn't find them suitable for the house," she finally says with a small shrug. "So he had me leave them in the garage, and they got ruined. I didn't even get to see them before he tossed them."

She pauses.

"He thinks it's a waste of a hobby anyway."

A slow, seething heat creeps up my spine.

I set my fork down.

"Your art isn't a waste." My voice is low, firm. "You'll make more. In our home, you'll make more."

Her eyes widen slightly, caught off guard. "You... want me to paint in the *house?*"

"Where else would you paint?"

She hesitates.

"I don't know, my father doesn't like paint in the house, so I usually painted outside, but one time it rained, and all my supplies got destroyed so I just stopped painting."

My jaw flexes.

"That won't happen again."

The words come out hard, final.

"You'll paint inside. You'll have a room with natural light. You'll hang your work wherever you want."

She stares at me, her fork stilling against her plate.

"Okay," she says softly, hesitant.

Perhaps I pushed too far.

But, we eat comfortably and our conversation drifts between art and literature. Vasilisa is an engaging speaker—intelligent, passionate, effortless. When she talks about *The Divine Comedy* or a painting she once admired at an exhibition, her eyes glow with something rare, something *alive*.

I'm drawn to her, not just to her beauty, but to the way she speaks, the way she sees the world.

We finish our meal, and Vasilisa looks up, thoughtful.

"I don't think I've ever met anyone quite like you, Santo."

Her words hit deeper than they should.

I chuckle. A strange mix of pride and something heavier ripples through me, something I can't name.

"And you, Vasilisa, are not like any woman I've known before."

She tilts her head slightly.

"Is that a good thing?" A hint of vulnerability slips into her voice, barely there but unmistakable.

"I believe it's the best thing."

The words leave me before I can think twice.

I reach for the velvet box, taking a slow breath before flipping it open.

The ring gleams—my mother's ring, heavy with history. *The same ring that was on her hand.*

My throat tightens. For a brief, painful second, I can still see it on her finger, delicate yet firm, a symbol of a love that once held the weight of the world.

I shake the thought away, focusing on the woman in front of me.

I slide the box across the table.

Her eyes widen. "Santo, I—"

"It's just a formality," I cut in, too quickly. "To solidify our arrangement."

The second the words leave my mouth, I regret them.

Her face falls. It's just a flicker—so quick she almost hides it.

But I see it. I *feel* it.

Then, just as swiftly, she replaces it with a small, practiced smile.

A nod. "Thank you."

She removes the ring from the box, her movements graceful, careful.

Before she can slip it on, I reach out, grasping her hand.

"Allow me." My voice is softer now.

She watches as I slide the ring onto her finger.

It fits perfectly.

I glance up, searching for her gaze, but she doesn't meet my eyes. Instead, she stares at our hands, her teeth catching her bottom lip, lost in thought.

The sight sparks something dangerous in me.

The urge to kiss her—*to claim her*, to wipe away that sadness lingering in her eyes; claws at me with unbearable intensity.

Instead, I force myself to let go, pulling my hand back as I close the box.

"That looks beautiful on you," I murmur, the words slipping out unbidden.

Her eyes snap up to mine, startled. For a moment, I expect her to dismiss the compliment, to brush it off the way she did my blunder.

But slowly, carefully a smile spreads across her lips, radiant, breathtaking.

And just for a second, it feels like catching a glimpse of *paradise.*

"It's getting late."

"Yes, it is," she replies, but there's hesitation laced in her tone—an unspoken agreement. Neither of us is quite ready to leave this moment behind.

We rise, and Vincenzo appears with my jacket. I shrug it on, then reach for Vasilisa's hand.

My eyes catch on the ring now gracing her slender finger.

My mother's ring.

It fits her perfectly, so effortlessly, that the thought settles deep in my chest—as if it was *always* meant to be hers.

Under a sky full of stars, I walk Vasilisa to my car.

The night air is crisp, the twinkling lights above reflecting in her eyes, making them shine even brighter.

She looks ethereal.

I open the door for her, guiding her inside. My fingers brush against hers—just a fleeting touch, nothing more—yet it sends something dark and possessive curling low in my gut.

I shut the door before I can dwell on it.

Sliding into the driver's seat, I take the wheel, the car cutting through the quiet streets toward her family's estate.

A sense of contentment settles over me, unexpected but steady.

For the first time in years, the past doesn't haunt me.

My mind isn't clouded by old ghosts or unfinished wars.

And I find myself looking forward.

To the possibilities. To the unknown. To the future.

And all I can see in that future...

is *her*.

CHAPTER 11

VASILISA

The date with Santo went better than expected.

At lunch, I glance down at the ring on my finger. It's beautiful and heavier than I thought it would be.

An unshakable reminder of the responsibility I carry for my family.

Santo's comment about how I should eat more lingers in my mind throughout the day.

I stare at the plate in front of me, barely touched. He'd expect more, but I've always been picky when it comes to food.

I'm more of a snacker. The salmon linguine yesterday was perfect—one of my favorites, but the beef stroganoff served at Maksim's penthouse? Not so much.

I'd much rather have pelmeni or kasha, but asking for that would earn me one of my mother's looks of disappointment.

Embarrassing her in front of Maksim would be a near death sentence.

Not that she'd actually strike me with my wedding so close.

But there are other ways she could make me miserable.

I push the food around with my fork, making it look like I've eaten something.

My mother sits to my left, Mimi to my right, devouring everything on her plate.

Across from her, Pietro catches my gaze, his eyes flicking to my barely touched meal before settling back on me with silent curiosity.

I offer him a passive smile.

My mother and father's animated conversation with Maksim pulls me from my thoughts. My cousin has changed his hair color yet again.

At the club, his platinum hair had been dyed a cool blue to match his icy eyes, but now it's dark purple.

He smiles at my mother as he speaks. Maksim is an intimidating presence—tall, fit, and always looking slightly furious—it could just be the tattoos and piercings he wears that give him that vibe.

But to me, he's just my *mishka*—the affectionate name I gave him when I was little.

He was always kind to me.

Right up until I became useful.

His gaze locks onto mine, and the corner of his mouth tilts into a smirk.

"Kisa! I heard about your date with Santo. How'd it go?" Maksim asks smoothly, using the childhood nickname he gave me.

His tone is casual, but his gaze is sharp, always reading between the lines.

"It went well," I say quietly.

The ring catches the light, gleaming like it has a life of its own.

My mother lifts my left hand.

"She's being modest," she interjects, turning my hand toward Maksim.

His eyes flick to the ring, lighting up with recognition.

He nods, resting his elbows on the table and folding his hands under his chin, studying me with something close to amusement. "His mother's ring."

I shift under his gaze.

"Yes. He said it was hers," I answer, even though he never actually asked.

Maksim smirks, reaching for his glass and raising it. "A toast—to your union and our alliance. Thank you, Kisa, for your *support* to the Bratva."

Glasses clink around me, and I take a sip of the clear liquid, swallowing before I can even think.

It burns down my throat, settling in my stomach, sour and unforgiving.

★★★

I watch Mimi and Pietro walk the grounds of our estate.

They move side by side, talking, their silhouettes shifting under the dimming light. A sharp pang of jealousy bites at me. Pietro hasn't spoken to me in a while. He saw the ring this morning and said nothing.

Maybe our friendship really is over. Or maybe it never was a friendship, just duty disguised as something more.

My phone vibrates. I glance down.

Santo.

My heart leaps. I stare at his name, debating whether to answer.

Why is he calling me?

Taking a slow, steady breath, I answer and bring the phone to my ear. "Vasilisa."

My name rolls off his tongue like a slow pull of velvet, and despite myself, a thrill races down my spine.

"I hope I'm not interrupting anything important," he adds smoothly.

"No, you're not." My voice is quiet as I glance out the window again, watching Pietro and Mimi move together.

"Good," Santo murmurs. "I heard you had lunch with Maksim. Did you enjoy your time with family?"

"I did." I hesitate for a beat, then add honestly, "Well... aside from the beef stroganoff. Not a favorite of mine."

He chuckles, a rich, low sound that does something strange to my chest.

"No stroganoff for our wedding then," he notes, his amusement evident.

The casual mention of our *wedding* makes heat rise up my neck. And yet, the thought of it—*of him*—sends an unbidden flutter through my stomach.

"Can I steal you away for the rest of the day?" he asks, his tone deceptively light, but there's something underneath it.

Something intent.

"Steal me away?"

"You're right," he concedes smoothly. "It wouldn't be stealing, considering you're set to be mine soon enough."

His words send a shiver through me. *Mine.*

"Alright," I whisper. "When?"

"I'll send a car again. See you soon."

The line clicks dead.

I exhale slowly, looking down at myself. I'm still in my sundress from lunch, the same one from the photo on Santo's desk.

My fingers brush over the fabric as I consider changing, but I don't.

He likes this dress.

And a part of me, one I don't want to name yet, wants to see his reaction.

★★★

Santo meets me in the lobby of NovaRael, and despite a flicker of worry that he might be here to work, my heart races at the sight of him.

His eyes light up when his gaze lands on me, a broad grin lighting his features, those gorgeous gray eyes look lighter today.

"Vasilisa," he says, my name rich and warm. He takes my hand, pressing a chaste kiss to my knuckles, lingering just a second too long. "Thank you for coming."

"Of course," I murmur, squeezing his hand in return.

His thumb strokes along my knuckles in a slow, unhurried caress before he leads me toward the elevator.

We ascend in silence, hand in hand, but it's not the awkward kind.

It's easy, natural.

The elevator doors glide open, and Santo guides me through a maze of corridors until we reach an open-plan office.

The space is alive with movement—groups huddled around screens, whiteboards filled with sketches, design concepts, algorithms. The pulse of innovation is tangible.

But it's Santo who commands my attention.

He glitters here.

There's something seamless in the way he moves, his confidence effortless as he introduces me to his colleagues. Some of them have known me since I was a child, but now they look at him not just as their new boss, but as someone they admire.

A visionary.

NovaRael was always my escape. As a child, I spent summers in these halls when my mother had grown tired of me and Mimi. I loved the noise, the ideas constantly in motion. I loved curling up in my father's office, eavesdropping on meetings, soaking in the thrill of creation.

Now, I watch Santo in it. A place that had always felt like mine.

It feels like he belongs here too.

Santo leads me toward his office, bypassing a beautiful blonde seated at the desk near Sandra.

The woman's gaze flicks to me, her perfectly sculpted brow arching just slightly before she shifts her attention to Santo, her smile polite, but assessing.

"Hello, Mr. Amato. I don't see anyone listed for an appointment today," she says smoothly, her eyes drifting over me.

"That's his wife," Sandra cuts in sharply before Santo can answer.

Her voice carries the kind of familiarity that makes warmth bloom in my chest.

Sandra has known me for years, even before she transferred floors. When I was little, she used to sneak me cookies from the bakery near her house.

"*And* the former boss's daughter," she adds, winking at me.

I can't hold back my smirk.

The blonde's eyes widen slightly, her posture stiffening.

"I'm so sorry, Mr. Amato, I didn't know—I just—" She gestures hesitantly toward Santo's hand. "I didn't see a ring."

"If you learned to keep your tongue before speaking, you wouldn't embarrass yourself," Santo says sharply.

A chill settles over the room.

His tone isn't cruel, but it's firm, *final.*

"This is Vasilisa," he continues. "Don't forget her face. Don't forget her name. Or you won't have a job."

The woman—*Evie,* her nameplate reads—nods quickly, dropping her gaze. "Yes, Mr. Amato."

Santo doesn't spare her another glance. "Make sure no one disturbs us, Sandra," he says before leading me inside his office, closing the door behind us.

My heart flutters.

Santo can command a room.

His protectiveness is so instinctual it feels almost *possessive.*

He releases my hand and strides behind his desk, his movements fluid, precise.

"We had to meet here since a meeting came up, then we can head out," he explains, his tone shifting to something softer. "I didn't want to postpone your visit. I hope you don't mind."

There's something about the way he says it. *Like he wouldn't have let work come before me.*

I swallow, my fingers brushing over my palm where his hand had been moments ago.

"I don't mind," I say softly.

He takes a seat behind the desk, his fingers moving effortlessly over the keyboard. For a moment, he's absorbed in his work, but then his gaze lifts—darkening as it trails over my body.

The air between us shifts.

Thickens.

He inhales, slow and measured, before gesturing for me to come behind the desk.

My heart pounds as I step forward, anticipation curling through me.

Two large screens glow in front of us, displaying what looks like surveillance footage. My brows furrow as he pulls up more feeds, clicking through them with ease until he stops.

"This is my home. *Our* home."

He turns slightly in his chair, his eyes locking onto mine, and pats his leg, beckoning me to sit.

I hesitate. His hand, warm and firm, presses gently against my lower back, guiding me forward. My legs slip between his, and I perch on his muscular thigh, my skin heating at our sudden closeness.

The scent of his cologne—warm, dark, laced with spicy vanilla, wraps around me, intoxicating. My pulse flutters as his arms move to cage me in, pressing against the desk on either side of me.

I'm trapped.

Yet, I don't *want* to escape.

His fingers dance over the keyboard, the glow of the screens casting soft shadows across his sharp features.

"I want you to choose a room to paint in," he murmurs, his breath teasing the sensitive skin near my ear.

I blink, momentarily thrown.

I turn my head slightly, my gaze colliding with his. His eyes flicker down to my lips, and my heart stutters.

"A room to paint in?" I repeat.

A small smile tugs at the corner of his mouth. His focus remains fixed on my lips.

"Yes."

I force myself to look away, trying to steady my thoughts.

"You brought me in here to pick a studio for my art?" I muse.

"I also expected you to join my meeting, so you wouldn't be cooped up in here alone," he replies, his voice deceptively casual, though there's an underlying tension beneath it.

"Unless you'd rather help yourself to some books," he adds with a slight chuckle.

I try to focus on the various rooms displayed on the screen, but it's nearly impossible with his warmth pressed against me, his scent clouding my thoughts.

My fingers twitch at my sides, restless, but after a few moments, something catches my eye; a large room bathed in natural light, the windows stretching wide and tall.

"Can I see that one bigger?" I ask, pointing.

He clicks on the image, expanding it, and my breath catches.

A library.

"That's my library," he states nonchalantly, as if it isn't one of the most beautiful things I've ever seen.

His hand leaves the mouse, settling on my lower back, fingers pressing lightly.

I lean in, captivated by the endless rows of shelves, the dark mahogany desks, the cozy lounge chairs nestled in corners. It's everything I could dream of—warm, inviting, perfect.

"It's beautiful," I breathe.

Turning toward him in excitement, I barely register how close we are until I realize our faces are mere inches apart.

The tension snaps tight.

"Can I paint in there?"

His gaze hangs heavy.

His hand moves from my back to the nape of my neck.

His fingers curl slightly, a slow, deliberate caress. The air between us is thick, electric.

"Yes," he whispers.

"Thank you." My voice comes out softer than I intend.

He studies me, his gaze piercing. He leans in, and for a brief moment, I think he's going to kiss me. My breath catches, anticipation coiling in my stomach—

The phone on his desk buzzes.

Sandra's voice fills the room, shattering the moment. "Mr. Amato, the team is ready for you."

Santo exhales through his nose, a flicker of annoyance crossing his face before he turns his chair slightly, giving me space to stand.

"Would you like to come with me to my meeting?"

"Yes, I want to go with you," I say eagerly.

Heat rushes to my face, embarrassment creeping in.

Santo chuckles, the sound low and indulgent, and takes my hand. His fingers envelop mine, warm and steady, his grip firm yet gentle.

It feels natural, effortless. I'm caught in the quiet pull of his presence.

His fingers squeeze lightly, a silent reassurance, steadying the nervous energy thrumming beneath my skin.

He leads me through familiar hallways until we get to a conference room I recognize from my youth. The long table is lined with six men, their curious gazes flicking to me as we enter. Santo doesn't release my hand until he pulls out a chair for me, and I sit. He sits beside me.

"What progress have we made?" Santo asks, his tone edged with authority.

"Still no luck opening the file, sir," a man in wide-brimmed glasses reports. "We might get further in the upcoming weeks. Is this urgent?"

"As urgent as anything here. I want to know what's being hidden as soon as possible."

Santo's patience thins.

"Of course," the man replies smoothly, unfazed. "The six of us will work overnight if we have to."

"Even on weekends," another man chimes in.

"What have you tried so far?" Santo presses.

"We've attempted brute-force attacks, decryption algorithms, even rainbow tables, but nothing is working. The encryption is rock solid," the first man explains.

"An encryption?" I echo under my breath, recalling the cybersecurity training I had during my summers at NovaRael.

An idea forms in my mind, and before I can stop myself, the words slip out.

"Have you tried a social engineering approach?" I suggest. "Sometimes it's easier to exploit human error than to crack the encryption directly."

A brief silence falls over the room. Seven pairs of eyes swivel toward me. I can feel Santo's gaze settle on me, sharper than before.

I shift in my seat.

"Or… what about a zero-day exploit?" I add quickly, my confidence faltering under the weight of their scrutiny. "There might be a vulnerability that hasn't been patched."

Another pause.

Slowly, I lift my eyes to meet Santo's. His expression is inscrutable, his gaze lingering, assessing.

I should have stayed quiet.

CHAPTER 12

SANTO

My future wife is a brilliant enigma.

Watching Vasilisa command the room with an ease she doesn't appear to know she has. She speaks, and every man at the table hangs onto her words, drawn in without even realizing it.

Her words ignite a hunger to know more about her.

And then, I feel it; that quiet hum in my chest.

Not jealousy. Something deeper.

Possessiveness.

Around the table, brows furrow, lips part in astonishment, their eyes fixed on Vasilisa as if she holds the key to some profound mystery.

One man leans forward, eyes lingering longer than necessary. My grip tightens on the armrest.

She fidgets with the hem of her skirt, unaware of the effect she has, not just on them, but on me.

Fire licks at my throat.

I'm overcome with the simple need to remind *everyone* who she belongs to.

Vasilisa's shoulders stiffen slightly under the weight of their gaze. I reach for her hand, brushing my thumb over her knuckles, a silent tether, pulling her back to me.

A warning to them.

"I believe we have a new strategy, gentlemen." My voice is smooth but cuts sharp through the murmurs.

Marcus shifts in his seat. "Yes, yes, of course."

He adjusts his glasses, clearing his throat.

Good.

"Thank you for your invaluable input," I continue, casting a glance at Vasilisa.

Amusement tugs at the corner of my mouth, but the flicker of pride outweighs it. "I'll let you all get back to work."

Rising, I pull out her chair. My hand rests lightly at the small of her back as we step into the hall.

"You were incredible in there," I tell her sincerely making our way back to my office.

Vasilisa looks up at me, her doubt evident in her eyes.

"I just said what came to mind," she replies modestly.

"And that's *exactly* what we needed," I assure her. "I'm proud to have you, Vasilisa."

A spark of joy lights up Vasilisa's eyes, and once again, I'm captivated by the woman who walks by my side.

Her cheeks burn a rosy red.

"Thank you," she responds, biting her lip, a small smile playing at the corners of her mouth.

Back in my office, Vasilisa drifts toward the large windows behind my desk, her fingers trailing lightly along the edge as if committing the space to memory.

"I've always loved this view," she says, her voice touched with nostalgia.

I watch her, the sunset wrapping around her like she was made for it.

I could tell her that the view means nothing without her standing in front of it.

Instead, I just smile. "I'm happy to share it with you whenever you'd like to visit."

She lingers by the glass, her silhouette cutting against the golden light.

It's mesmerizing... *too mesmerizing.*

I move behind her, hands finding her shoulders. Her body stiffens beneath my touch.

There.

That.

That flash of hesitation.

It makes me pause, waiting until she slowly relaxes into me.

Darkness stirs within me.

No.

Something else.

A need to eliminate the space between us.

"Thank you," she murmurs, without turning away from the window.

"For what?"

"For allowing me to be a part of this..."

She waves her hand vaguely around. "It's all the happy parts of my childhood."

Her words are simple, but they land harder than they should.

I swallow the unexpected weight pressing at my chest. "I want you here."

She turns, and as the sun dips lower, it sets her in an ethereal glow.

I've seen beautiful things in my life.

None of them compare.

There's something about this woman, something elusive, something profoundly personal about her presence that demands to be respected and *cherished.*

That, is the most endearing thing about Vasilisa.

I cup her cheek, thumb grazing over soft skin.

She leans into it.

That's it.

I lower my head, close enough to feel her breath warm against my lips. Her eyes flutter shut, and for a second, recognition stirs.

She's everything I shouldn't want.

Yet, I do.

Her scent, warm, sweet, familiar, threatens to ruin every wall I've ever built.

My lips inches from hers.

This goddess of a woman is mine.

The shrill chime of my phone shatters the moment.

Vasilisa's eyes fly open, and she steps back, as if grounding herself.

I clear my throat, biting down the urge to snap the damn phone in half as I pull it from my pocket.

Whoever it is better have a damn good reason for calling right now.

Nico's name flashes across the screen.

Lucky bastard.

"Excuse me," I say to Vasilisa stepping away from her.

Nico is my brother's consigliere, and he wouldn't call unless there was an emergency.

I swipe to answer, "Go for Santo."

"Sinner's live, meet us at the town house," Nico says giving me a name that's laid dormant for over a year now.

I turn back to Vasilisa and her expectant gorgeous face. "I have to cut our day short; I have some business to attend to."

Her brow furrows. "Business?" She looks around the office.

"*Family* business," I allude and watch as her brows raise in understanding.

"Of course," she nods.

"I'll walk you out and Marco will take you home," I say leading her out of the office and toward the elevator as I text him.

"His name is Marco?" She asks. "That's good to know, he doesn't speak so I just sit in silence."

She chuckles, but a fire ignites in my chest at Marco ignoring her.

I walk her out to the car, where Marco stands waiting. Before he can reach for the door, I beat him to it, opening it myself and guiding her inside.

She settles into the seat, I reach for the belt, my face hovering just inches from hers. My fingers graze the soft fabric of her dress as I carefully pull the strap across her, clicking it into place.

Our eyes meet—hers wide, searching.

In their depths, I see every color, every unspoken emotion, clear as crystal.

For a brief moment, her gaze drops to my lips. Then, just as quickly, she looks back into my eyes.

"Marco will let me know when he drops you off, but I would appreciate a text from you letting me know that you've arrived safely."

"Okay," she replies with a soft smile.

I shut the door and turn to Marco.

He catches the look on my face and takes a step back.

Not fast enough.

I grab him by the collar, yanking him close. "If my wife speaks to you, you *answer* her." My voice is low, controlled. Deadly.

I shove him off. "Get her home safe."

Marco nods quickly. "Will do, boss."

He scrambles into the car, wasting no time as he peels away.

I don't wait to watch them leave. I'm already in my car, dialing Nico as I tear out onto the road.

He picks up on the first ring.

"Talk."

"Someone tried to take Elena this morning," Nico says, voice clipped. "Riot got the guy. Put him on a flight here. Angelo's been working on him."

Pressure clamps down in my chest at the mention of my sister's name.

My hands tighten around the wheel.

"Elena okay?"

"She's rattled, but Riot's got her. She's safe."

"I want her back home."

"Angelo said the same. She's refusing."

"We'll handle that later," I grit out, ending the call and pressing harder on the gas.

The ride is a blur—just speed, headlights, and the steady pulse of rage in my veins.

When I finally pull up to the abandoned house, I don't hesitate.

Memories hit me as I step out.

Scythe and Sinner.

Me and my brother, carving our way through the lessons our father drilled into us.

Rebellion. Violence. *Blood.*

Nico's already waiting on the front steps as I screech to a stop.

I kill the engine, shrug off my suit jacket, and slam the door shut.

I stride toward him, unbuttoning my cuffs, rolling up my sleeves.

Time to get to work.

"Everything's set. Angelo's made a bloody mess," Nico mutters.

We step inside, the old floorboards groaning under our weight as we head toward the basement.

Since the day we avenged our mother, Angelo and I have been known as Scythe and Sinner.

Torturers. Judges. Executioners.

We don't show mercy. Not for men like this.

The second we descend the stairs, the stench of burning flesh hits me like a punch to the gut.

My body reacts before my mind does—Santo disappears, and *Scythe* takes over.

Down in the basement, Sinner's already in his element.

Shirtless. Covered in sweat. His pupils blown wide, his grin sharp and wild as he works.

A butane torch in his grip, flame roaring to life as he presses it to the bastard's stomach.

The man screams, a raw, agonized sound that echoes off the walls.

Angelo just laughs.

The man is strapped to the metal table, his head encased in a steel box with nothing but a narrow slit for air and speech.

His wrists and ankles are cuffed, but Sinner went the extra mile—barbed wire coils around each limb, slicing into raw flesh, ensuring that even the slightest movement shreds him further.

Nico was right.

It's a fucking mess.

Blood drips off the table in thick rivulets, pooling on the cement floor before trailing toward the nearest drain.

I step forward, placing a steady hand on Sinner's shoulder.

He stills. A deep inhale.

Then, slowly, he turns to face me, a manic, sweat-slick grin splitting his face.

His pupils shrink slightly, focus sharpening as consciousness returns to his eyes.

"Welcome back, brother," I murmur, my own grin mirroring his.

Sinner chuckles, wiping a smear of blood from his chest. With a grand gesture, he extends his arm toward his work of art—the burned, mangled, twitching mess sprawled out before us.

"My masterpiece," he announces, pride lacing his voice as he finally sets the torch down.

I take in the sight, admiring the meticulous destruction.

Brutal. *Effective.*

I knock twice on the metal box covering the man's head.

Clang. Clang.

He whimpers, body jerking. The barbed wire bites deeper.

More blood spills.

A slow smile spreads across my face. "Your best work yet."

The man cries out, gasping through the slit in the steel.

"Tell me," I say, voice calm, collected—deadly. "Who sent you to take Elena Amato?"

A choked sob. "Just kill me."

His body shifts, fresh blood gushing from his torn limbs.

I tilt my head, watching. "If you tell me who sent you, I'll make it quick. A bullet between the eyes."

He lets out a broken, shuddering breath.

"If I tell you," he whimpers, "will you bring my body to my family?"

I consider it, letting the silence stretch.

Finally, I agree. "Your family will receive you." My voice is devoid of warmth. "Now, who *sent* you?"

"Gabriel Kaya." The words tumble from his lips, breathless and desperate.

I flick a glance at Nico.

He nods, already typing on his phone.

"And your name?" I ask, voice casual—like we're old friends catching up.

"Baris…" he wheezes, barely getting the name out. "My name is Baris."

"Please… just kill me."

I grip the metal box and yank it off his head. His face is a mess—red, battered, nose broken, one eye already swelling shut. I steal a questioning look at my brother who smirks.

Reaching for the scalpel and clamp from the table beside the butane tank, I motion for Sinner to join me.

He doesn't hesitate.

Baris senses it now; the shift in the air, the finality of it.

Sinner grips both sides of his jaw, forcing his mouth open as Baris thrashes wildly.

The barbed wire digs in deeper, ripping more flesh, more blood.

I lean in close, my breath hot against his skin.

His body stills.

His eyes widen.

Terror seeps into him as he realizes the truth—

He's not getting out of this.

I smile, slow and cruel.

"I lied," I whisper.

Then, with one swift motion, I clamp down on his tongue, yank it forward, and slice clean through with the scalpel.

A wet, gurgling scream rips from his throat.

Blood floods his mouth, choking him, drowning his own cries.

His body convulses, the barbed wire shredding him further as his own suffering becomes his executioner.

I watch, savoring the moment.

His tongue, slick and useless now, I place it on the table next to the rest of our tools, a grotesque trophy in a collection of nightmares.

The scent of blood thickens the air. Metallic. Warm.

I inhale deeply.

Power.

A rush surges through me, sharp and electric, coiling in my veins like fire.

I snap back to myself as Nico steps into the basement.

I never saw him leave, but now he's back, phone in hand.

"Maksim's on the way. He thinks we should deliver Baris's body to Kaya—says the Turks have been pushing into his territory. Sending it back will make a statement. Show solidarity in our alliance."

Nico glances at the mess behind us. "I'm guessing you took his tongue?"

A ghost of a smirk tugs at my lips. "Of course."

"Good." Nico exhales, rubbing a hand over his jaw. "Maks wants to be the one to gift-wrap it for Kaya."

I nod, barely hearing him now.

The high is fading.

"Got it from here, boss, if you're good," Nico adds.

Angelo picks up his shirt from the tool table, sliding it on.

I follow him up the stairs and out into the night air.

"That was invigorating," Angelo says, clapping me on the back, his voice buzzing with residual energy. "You did excellent work."

"Thank you," I say heading to my car.

The words feel distant, mechanical.

The blood is still drying on my skin.

"I heard Elena doesn't want to come home," I say, changing the subject.

Angelo stiffens. His jaw ticks. "She doesn't have a choice now. I'll get on a flight and drag her back if I have to."

I nod, but my mind is barely registering his response. My thoughts are still tangled in the remnants of adrenaline and violence, my body still buzzing with the aftermath.

The rage, the power—it burns out, leaving a hollow, sinking weight in its place.

Then Angelo speaks again, and the hollow ache twists into something else.

"What about Vasilisa? You moving her in before the wedding? Just in case."

Vasilisa.

Her name slams into me like a wrecking ball.

The image of her flickers to life; her face, bathed in golden light, the sunset casting a halo around her.

The way her skin felt beneath my fingertips.

The warmth of her breath against mine.

How close I was to tasting her.

How fucking pure she is.

A punch of shame coils tight in my gut. I had forgotten her.

Forgotten her completely in the sea of blood I spilled.

Her angelic face erased beneath the carnage, the screams, the warmth of torn flesh under my hands.

Sick.

I'm sick.

She doesn't belong in this world. She doesn't belong with *me.*

I almost let myself believe I could have her. That I could hold onto something normal, something untouched by death and destruction.

But I'm not a normal man.

And nothing in my life is fair.

I meet Angelo's gaze. His eyes reflect the same emptiness as mine—the same hollowed-out grief, the same silent rage that's been carved into us since the night our mother was murdered.

Vasilisa could end up just like her.

I shove the thought down, bury it deep, and lock it away with the rest of my weaknesses.

"No," I say, my voice flat. "She's just an arrangement. She's not a target."

"Not a target *yet*," Angelo responds as he leaves my side for his car.

I reach for my door, grabbing my jacket off the driver's seat to toss onto the passenger side when my phone slips from the pocket, landing with a soft thud.

I pick it up. The screen lights up.

A text.

Vasilisa

I'm home safe.

Just as I asked.

Sweet, obedient Vasilisa.

Shame washes over me like ice water, cutting through the last remnants of bloodlust.

My grip tightens around the phone as I text her back, each letter feeling heavier than it should.

I look up. Angelo is just about to slide into his car.

"Hey!" I call out.

He pauses, glancing over the roof.

"You want to go to Opulent?"

A slow, knowing smirk spreads across his face.

"*You*, of all people, want to go to our strip club?" He lets out a short laugh, shaking his head. "Hell yes."

He gets in his car, still chuckling as he drives off, his headlights cutting through the darkness.

Shame grips me tighter.

I sink into my seat, exhaling sharply as I hang my head.

I had *her*.

Just hours ago, Vasilisa was in my hands, her scent in my lungs, her warmth curling around me like something I could keep.

She was light, soft, pure—everything I've never had, everything I don't deserve.

But Scythe doesn't care about light.

Scythe doesn't care about *anything* except the rush—violence and power, the only gods I have ever worshipped.

And with every drop of blood I spill, I stain the pieces of her that have already begun to cling to me.

She deserves more.

More than a man who forgets her in a sea of red.

More than the shadow of death waiting to swallow her whole.

If she's ever going to have a *good* life, it sure as hell won't be with me.

Chapter 13

VASILISA

The rest of the week flies by, and I haven't heard from Santo since the night he sent me home. All he left me with was a simple text—

Santo

Glad you're home safe.

After that, nothing. No calls. No messages.

Silence.

I tried reaching out, sent him a good morning text with a selfie, something light, something that might make him smile. But it was left unread.

The distance between us stretches like an empty, endless sea.

Every time my phone lights up, my stomach twists. Hope flutters, only to collapse under the weight of disappointment when it's never him.

He's turning into a ghost before he's even mine.

He had been so tender, so careful with me, and for a moment, I let myself believe. I let myself *hope*.

But the more I think about it, the more distressing it becomes, like thorny vines coiling around my heart, squeezing tighter with every passing second.

Now, standing in front of the mirror in my bridal gown for the final fitting, I barely recognize the woman staring back at me.

The lace is delicate, the embroidery perfect. The veil catches the light just right.

And yet, my reflection looks hollow. Like a bride on a music box—beautiful, elegant, and trapped behind the glass.

She's beautiful, yes. But sad.

I don't feel like a dutiful daughter securing an alliance for my family and the Bratva.

I feel naïve.
Hoodwinked.
Foolish.
Falling for him in a matter of days, like a child still believing in fairy tales and dreams.

Cassandra circles me, beaming.

She gushes about how stunning I look in the off-shoulder lace gown, how it hugs my waist before flowing into a cloud of ivory tulle.

But all I can think about is how I'm a lamb being led to slaughter—adorned for a fate that now brings me no joy.

"He's smitten with you, I see," Cassandra says, pulling me from my thoughts.

"What?" I blink, confused.

She smiles knowingly and lifts my left hand. "His mother's ring."

"Oh… yeah." I gently pull my hand back, cradling it in the other. "He gave it to me at dinner with her book—for formalities."

Cassandra's eyes widen. "What book?"

"Vita Nuova."

I say it softly, my gaze dropping to the ring as it glitters under the boutique's lights, casting fractured reflections against my skin.

"Vasilisa!" Cassandra all but shouts, grabbing me by the shoulders. Before she can say another word, the door swings open, and my mother and Mimi step inside, dressed for the wedding.

"You look phenomenal, Vasi!" Mimi exclaims, eyes bright with excitement. "Like a real princess! Can you picture it? With the flowers in your hair?"

"What flowers?" my mother asks, her tone clipped with thinly veiled disapproval.

"We're weaving in small white roses," Cassandra says, fussing over my gown. "She's going to be breathtaking."

"Is that necessary?" my mother counters, her voice a delicate dagger.

Cassandra's expression hardens as she glances at her. "It's what Santo requested."

My heart stutters.

Santo *requested* it.

The sound of his name coils around me, unexpected and suffocating in the best and worst way.

My mother, stiff and poised, presses her lips into a thin line before giving a curt nod. She steps onto the podium, letting an attendant work on the final touches of her dress.

Cassandra doesn't wait. She takes my hand, guiding me off the platform and through the boutique to the dressing room.

Once the door clicks shut behind us, she studies me through the mirror, arms crossed.

"What's going on with you?"

"I'm fine," I say, meeting Cassandra's gaze in the mirror.

She narrows her eyes, unconvinced. "Liar. What's wrong?"

I hesitate, glancing away. "Why did you say that earlier? About him being smitten? And why were you so excited about the book?"

She gives me a look like I should already know the answer. "Vasilisa, he gave you his mother's ring *and* her favorite book."

I frown, confusion knitting my brows. "What does that mean?"

Cassandra huffs, rolling her eyes. "He never gives away his mother's things. *Ever.* He treasures them—they're his last mementos of her."

The weight of her words crashes into me. My knees buckle, and I sink onto the velvet bench, a lump rising in my throat.

"She passed away?" My voice is barely audible.

Cassandra nods solemnly.

My hand presses over my heart.

Poor Santo.

My mother and I aren't particularly close, but losing her… it would wound me.

I can't imagine what it's done to him.

"So," Cassandra sits beside me, giving me a pointed look, "if he gave you those things, he sees something in you. Otherwise, he would never part with them."

I swallow hard.

"But… he's been distant lately." The words feel fragile as they leave me.

She chuckles, shrugging. "He's second-in-command now. He has businesses to run, both legal and otherwise."

She smirks. "It comes with the territory."

I sigh in relief.

Cassandra gives my hand a comforting squeeze before standing up from the bench, but says nothing as she clips in my veil behind me in silence. Her face is expressionless in the mirror's reflection as she folds her arms across her chest and tilts her head assessing me.

"You'll learn to navigate his world," she says finally. "It may seem daunting, but it's always been part of *your* world. You're just in the thick of it now."

I nod, feeling lighter. Squaring my shoulders, I inhale deeply, pushing aside the uncertainty. Whatever comes next, I will face it.

For my family. For the Bratva.

***

After a long, warm shower I prepare for bed, and pack away the last of my things.

The designer outfits Cassandra picked out for me are neatly folded in my suitcase, though she assured me the rest have already been sent to Santo's estate.

My mother packed a few boxes with my books, jewelry, and toiletries, making the transition feel real.

Tomorrow is my wedding day.

The thought settles over me like a heavy weight, curling in my stomach as I check my phone. Still nothing. No calls, no messages.

The silence from Santo is suffocating, stretching on like an endless void.

I exhale sharply, staring at the neatly folded clothes, the carefully packed books. Everything is in order, just as it should be.

And yet, as I reach for the zipper, my hands hesitate.

Just for a second.

Before I can think twice, I seal my fate shut.

Placing the suitcase on the ground, a sharp knock sounds at my door.

"Need some help, Vasi?"

Pietro peeks in, his lopsided grin familiar, comforting.

"No, thank you, Pietro," I manage a small smile, shaking my head.

He steps inside anyway, his gaze sweeping over the packed boxes and neatly folded clothes before settling on me.

"Excited for tomorrow?"

I hesitate. "I'm nervous."

I stare at my suitcase, as if it holds the answers I need.

"That's natural," he assures me, leaning lazily against the doorframe.

Pietro has always had a way of making everything seem lighter, as if life itself was something to be laughed at.

I've always envied that about him.

"You're about to step into a new phase of life."

"I know." I bite my lower lip. "It's just… a lot to take in."

Pietro nods, pushing off the doorframe and wandering toward a box filled with books.

He picks one up, flipping it open, his fingers skimming over the pages.

"Change can be scary," he murmurs, more to himself than to me.

He lifts his gaze, his expression uncharacteristically serious.

"But you're not alone, Vasi. You've got people who care about you... people who will always have your back."

I give him a weak smile. "Like you?"

Pietro chuckles, placing the book back in the box. "Well, of course."

"I know." My voice wavers, uncertainty pressing down on me like a weight I can't shake.

He must sense it, because he steps closer, gently takes my hand in his and raises it to his lips for a gentle kiss.

The tenderness of it sends a fresh wave of emotion crashing through me, burning at the backs of my eyes.

"Hey now," he murmurs, pulling me into his arms. His scent wraps around me like a safety net, so familiar it aches.

And that's what breaks me.

A quiet sob slips free, muffled against his chest.

He holds me tighter, his broad shoulders absorbing the weight of my fear, my doubts, my quiet desperation.

I clutch at his shirt, my fingers digging into the fabric as the tears finally spill over.

"I'm scared, Pietro," I whisper, my voice barely more than a breath.

"There's nothing to be scared of, Vasi." His voice is low, soothing, as he rubs slow circles against my back. "Santo's a good man. He'll take care of you."

His words should be a balm, but they only deepen the ache inside me.

I'm losing my grip on everything that once felt solid.

Pietro keeps speaking, his voice a gentle hum in my ear, but I barely hear him over my own thoughts.

Santo *is* a good man.

I felt that.

Before he stopped speaking to me.

But Pietro...

Pietro has been my constant.

My best friend. And the thought of losing him—*of stepping into this new life without him*—feels like stepping off a ledge into the unknown.

"Pietro..." I tilt my head up, blinking through my tears.

My heart feels like it's lodged in my throat, making it impossible to speak, but I force the words out anyway.

"Promise me you won't leave me."

He stills, surprise flashing in his eyes before he schools his expression. His grip on me tightens.

"I..." He hesitates, but only for a second before nodding. "I promise, Vasi." His voice is firm, unwavering. "I will always be here for you. Just a call away."

His promise settles the storm inside me; if only for a fleeting moment.

Swallowing hard, I wipe at my tear-streaked face and take a careful step back, putting distance between us.

"This is just a job to you, isn't it?" I ask, my breath steadying. "You work for Maks to pay off a debt."

Pietro's eyes narrow slightly, a flicker of hurt crossing his face before he masks it with indifference.

"My family's debt is paid. Maksim is helping me with something more… personal."

Guilt knots in my stomach.

"I'm sorry," I say quickly, shame washing over me. "I didn't know. I misspoke—I shouldn't have pried."

He grips my shoulder gently, reassuring.

"It's okay. You didn't know." A beat of hesitation passes before he adds, "He's helping me find someone."

"Who?" The question slips out before I can stop it.

His jaw tightens.

"A childhood friend. She ran away… and you know where most runaways end up."

His voice is low, heavy with something haunted, something broken.

A chill settles over me. I know exactly what he means.

Maksim doesn't believe in selling flesh. When he finds women who have been taken, he helps them. If Pietro's friend is among them, it makes sense why he needs Maksim's help.

"Thank you for explaining Pietro. I hope you find her," I say quietly.

His gaze lingers on me before he gives a small nod and exits the room.

The door clicks shut behind him, and I stare at it, my heart twisting with a tangle of emotions I don't fully understand.

Then, my phone buzzes on the bedside table.

Santo.

I reach for it, my breath catching as I read his message.

Santo

> **Sleep well, I'll see you tomorrow.**

Simple. Direct.

His words ease something in me.

Exhaling softly, I switch off the light and slip beneath the covers.

Tomorrow, everything changes.

CHAPTER 14

SANTO

Vasilisa didn't respond.

I don't blame her.

I spent the rest of the week bathing in self-loathing.

Days at NovaRael. Nights at Opulent.

Pretending she didn't exist, as if that would erase the taste of her name from my mouth or the scent of her skin from my memory.

It didn't.

Tomorrow, I'm supposed to stand beside the most innocent woman I've ever met, look into her eyes, those goddamn eyes and let them strip me bare. She doesn't know it yet, but she's staring straight into the abyss.

She wants a prince. A fairy tale.

I can't give her that. I can't give her anything but the weight of my shadow.

Scythe.

She belongs to me and yet every time I look at her, I feel him.

He stirs when I see her, claws at the surface of my skin like he's ready to break free, to take and consume.

Being near her makes me feel the same as when I pull the trigger, or carve a knife into skin, like the world slows and sharpens, like the kill is inevitable.

But she isn't a target.

She's *everything* else.

I watched her anyway. Watched the little blue dot on the tracker app drift across the city.

Luca trailed her, invisible but close. I couldn't keep away, not even from a distance.

Obsessed.

That's what I am. A man infatuated with something fragile and beautiful, something that will shatter the second I lay my hands on it.

So, I won't.

A glass slams onto the table, shattering the thought.

Angelo laughs, leaning back against the leather of the booth.

"Another round!" He shouts over the music at Opulent.

Opulent was my father's vision of a gentlemen's club. Angelo, ever the blunt one, calls it a strip club with taste.

Our bottle service girls wear what they please, as long as it's black or red.

The dancers on stage don't just spin around poles—they command attention, dictate their own performances, and walk away with their own money.

The golden rule? *No touching.* Anyone who lays so much as a fingertip on them takes a one-way trip to the basement.

That is where I've spent my nights here, in the basement serving punishment to those that dare to break our rule.

Tonight, though, Angelo convinced me to stay above ground. Let my knuckles heal before the wedding.

So here I sit, Luca to my right, Angelo to my left, and Nico beside him—a makeshift bachelor party I never asked for.

I drain the last of my whiskey and set the glass down with a dull thud.

"No more rounds. I'm heading home," I say, giving Luca a nod to let me out of the booth.

Luca stands, but before I can move, Rachel slides in, pressing herself against my side like she belongs there. Her fingers toy with the lapel of my jacket, a slow, teasing drag. "Don't go," she purrs, her voice soft and honeyed. "I've been waiting to get you alone all night."

Rachel is a beautiful girl, fiery red hair, hazel eyes, but that's never mattered to me.

She's been through hell. We found her in a shipping container meant to carry only weapons. Smuggled in, dehydrated, battered, and discarded like cargo. We gave her a choice—help to start fresh, a ticket to school, or work at one of our establishments.

She picked *this* life, took a job as a bottle service girl, and now shares a luxury apartment with another survivor—one who went on to become a nurse at our hospital.

"Not happening."

I gently pry her hands off of me and help her out of the booth with me.

She pouts, her eyes scanning my face for any crack in my resolve. She won't find one.

"My shift ends in thirty minutes," she tries again, her voice softer this time. "We could leave *together*."

Across the table, Angelo snickers, clearly enjoying the show. I shoot him a sharp look before turning back to Rachel.

"Still a no. Luca will take you home."

Luca gives a curt nod, already used to this routine.

"I'll see you tomorrow. Don't get so fucked up you can't be coherent at the wedding," I say to my brother and Nico as I head for the exit.

"No promises brother," he shouts.

"Don't go," Rachel whines from behind me.

I'm starting to get irritated. I turn to her trying to keep my cool as I tell her in no uncertain terms to fuck off, but she hands me a card instead. "Call me if you change your mind."

I glance down. Her number scrawled across the top, her name beneath it, finished off with a kiss mark in that bold red lipstick of hers.

I huff out a quiet laugh.

Rachel never quits. I pocket the card and walk out, not bothering to look back.

This fucking wedding can't come soon enough.

★★★

My head pounds from lack of sleep.

I spent the night dreading today, knowing that by nightfall, my home won't be mine anymore. She will be here. Vasilisa. A permanent presence I won't be able to ignore.

The thought unsettles me.

I toss off the covers and sit up, rubbing my temples. This arrangement is a business move, nothing more. An alliance. I get NovaRael out of it.

I wanted NovaRael.

That's what matters.

At least, that's what I keep telling myself.

I think of Evie Mitchell, my new secretary, and how dismissive she was of Vasilisa. I didn't like it. In fact, I may have to replace her.

I exhale sharply and shake my head.

This—this impulse to remove anyone who so much as looks at Vasilisa the wrong way—is the real problem.

I can't let this infatuation turn into something deeper. If it does, it'll make her a target.

They already tried to take Elena.

She refuses to leave university, despite Angelo and I threatening to drag her home.

She has a final exam, so we allowed her to stay under strict protection.

Riot, her guard, hasn't left her side.

Before, she was our *only* weakness.

Now? Vasilisa is another.

And if I let myself *care*—if I get *attached*—it will cost me.

Cost *her*. And I know what price we tend to pay.

I push the thought down and step into the master bathroom, seeing it now from a different perspective—hers.

This will be her space.

It's grand but not excessive, classic but not suffocating.

My gaze drags over the mirrored wall, the marble countertop with two sinks, my grooming products still neatly arranged beside a vase of fresh flowers from the garden.

The scent is subtle, trailing in the air like a whisper.

The rich chocolate-brown ottoman sits in the center of the room, a striking contrast to the lighter marble tones. A functional piece, yet something about it feels indulgent, an invitation to linger.

I exhale in relief. It isn't too much. She'll like it.

Then my gaze catches on the soaking tub beneath the window, and that's where the problem starts.

I see her there.

Hair damp, cascading down her back, water beading against her skin. Her eyes closed, her body half-submerged, exuding a kind of serenity that is entirely out of reach for a man like me.

I drag a hand down my face and clench my jaw.

No. No, no, no.

The image refuses to fade.

I turn the shower on, the rush of water breaking the silence. Steam rises, curling against the mirrors, but my thoughts remain tangled. *I can see her here,* feel her presence in a space she hasn't even set foot in yet. Walking barefoot across the mosaic tiles, trailing delicate fingers along the marble counter.

I hate that she's affecting me like this.

I hate that I want her to.

My fists tighten, nails pressing into my palms as I force myself to breathe through it.

This arrangement is *strategic.* Necessary.

Nothing more.

But as I strip off my clothes and step under the hot spray, I can't deny the truth, no matter how much I try to bury it.

Vasilisa is already slipping past my walls.
I tilt my head back, letting the water burn away the weakness.
At least, I try.

CHAPTER 15

SANTO

The wedding being held at my father's estate was Maksim's idea. The property has its own ballroom. That was my mother's favorite place to entertain before my father sent her away.

The drive doesn't take long.

The new doorman barely gets a word out before I'm led inside. My father greets me with open arms, Angelo standing beside him, looking surprisingly well-rested for a man who spent the night drinking.

"Santo, today's the big day, how do you feel?" My father claps me on the back, throwing an arm around my shoulders as best he can given my height.

"I'm ready."

He steers me toward the ballroom, Angelo following in our wake.

As we make our way through the grand foyer, I can't shake the feeling of apprehension that gnaws at me.

The marble floors gleam under the soft glow of the chandeliers, but my steps feel heavy, weighed down by the burden of my impending marriage.

The ballroom doors swing open, revealing a controlled chaos of final touches. Servers move swiftly, adjusting linens, setting out crystal, perfecting every detail.

The air is thick with the scent of lilies—Vasilisa's favorite. I'd chosen them to appease her, but now, they serve as a reminder of what's coming.

Of what I'm about to step into.

My father gestures toward the scene with a satisfied smile. "Isn't it magnificent, Santo? Your mother would've been proud."

I nod, but my mind is elsewhere. The grandeur of it all only sharpens the unease clawing at my gut.

Vasilisa may be young, beautiful, the perfect bride on paper, but she'll be a target, just like my mother was. Just like *every* woman tied to men like us.

A cold thought settles in my chest.

This could be a mistake.

We step into the gardens, where the greenery stretches wide, lush and endless.

The aisle is laid out before us, dressed in satin ribbons and scattered with petals from my mother's favorite roses, leading straight to the ornate gazebo where I'll be exchanging vows.

The sight of it is... *daunting.*

"Your bride's here already," my father says, voice laced with amusement. "Her mother and sister are getting her ready in your room."

My room.

The thought of her being in there stirs something in me.

Before I can dwell on it, my father waves down a gardener and leaves me with Angelo.

"Maksim and her father are in the office," Angelo says, eyeing me. "You wanna have a drink with them before we get ready in my old room?"

I exhale slowly, trying to shake the feeling sitting heavy in my gut.

"Where's Luca?" Angelo asks as we head back inside.

"He'll be here soon," I say, shooting off a quick text to confirm. "Let's get that drink."

We make our way to my father's office, the sound of our shoes echoing off the paneled walls.

Memories creep in, ghosts of a time when this house was full of laughter, before my mother was sent away.

Now, the grandeur feels hollow, an empty shell that mirrors how I feel right now.

I step in to my fathers office; Maksim and Miroslav are deep in conversation, their sharp profiles outlined against the mahogany bookshelves.

"The groom arrives," Maksim announces, a faint smirk playing on his lips. He extends his hand. "Congratulations, Santo."

I clasp it firmly, nodding. "Appreciate it, Maksim."

Angelo moves to the bar, pouring himself a whiskey before offering me one.

The amber liquid swirls hypnotically in the cut crystal glass as he hands it over. I exhale, taking the drink with a nod before bringing it to my lips.

"How's business?" Miroslav asks, his tone casual, but I don't trust casual—especially not with him. Given the QUEEN file, I hesitate, but this is a chance to gauge his reaction.

"Good," I say, then tilt my glass slightly. "Except for a file that's been causing some issues."

His brow furrows. "What file?"

"It's labeled *Queen*."

For the briefest second, he stills. Then, he shrugs.

"No clue. Never seen it before."

A lie.

Before I can press, Maksim cuts in. "No more shop talk. We have a wedding to get ready for."

He stands just as my father steps inside.

"Miroslav," my father greets with a nod. "If the boys are leaving, we can finish our conversation from earlier."

Maksim gives Miroslav a questioning look, but doesn't push.

Instead, he heads for the door, Angelo trailing behind. I place my glass on the bar and follow, even though every instinct tells me to stay and press Miroslav further.

Once we step into Angelo's room, I find my suit laid out neatly on his bed—shoes, cufflinks, the whole ensemble. The sight of it sends another sharp pang through me.

It still doesn't feel real, like I'm walking through a moment meant for someone else.

"No cold feet, little brother?" Angelo teases, pulling open a drawer and threading a tie around his collar with practiced ease.

I let out a low grunt in response.

Cold feet would mean I wanted to run.

That's not it. It's not that I don't want to marry Vasilisa—I made this choice.

But the uncertainty of it, of *us*, sits in the back of my mind, steady and unshakable.

Angelo must pick up on it because he stops halfway through tying his knot and steps over, clapping a hand on my shoulder. "Don't overthink it."

"Kisa's stronger than she looks, if that's what's got you wound up," Maksim adds, sounding sure.

"Of course she is," I say. "She's survived *you* so far, hasn't she?"

Maksim chuckles, shaking his head as he grabs his suit pants. "That she has."

The tension inside me loosens, just a little.

The easy back-and-forth, the casual ribbing—it shifts the moment, turning it from an obligation into something else.

A ritual, a rite of passage, something shared.

A knock on the door interrupts us, and Luca steps inside. He pauses, his sharp gaze flicking between us, taking in our polished appearances.

"Well, don't you all clean up nicely," Luca remarks, a smirk tugging at the corner of his mouth.

"Thanks, Luca," I reply, adjusting my cufflinks. "You, on the other hand, look like the best man at a funeral."

Maksim snorts.

Luca rolls his eyes, straightening his tie. "Funny. I'll make sure to wear black when I'm putting you in the ground."

The laughter lingers, shaking off the last bit of unease in the air. But as it fades, Luca shifts, his smirk dimming into something more serious.

"You ready?" he asks, tone steady now.

I nod and step into the hall where my men are lined up.

The weight of their stares settles over me, but another, more pressing need rises in my chest—a sudden, unshakable urge to see Vasilisa before the ceremony.

"I'll meet you in the garden," I announce, already moving toward my old room, where I know she'll be.

With each step, the knot in my stomach tightens. The hallways feel longer than I remember, the polished floors stretching endlessly ahead.

Servants glance my way as they rush between their tasks, their eyes flickering to me with a mix of curiosity and unease.

My pulse thrums in my ears, growing louder with every step.

Finally, I reach the door.

My pulse hammers in my ears as I raise my hand, hesitating for a fraction of a second before knocking.

A muffled noise comes from inside, followed by the soft creak of the door opening.

Mimi stands in the doorway, her wide eyes blinking in surprise, fingers still curled around the doorknob.

"Santo?" she gasps, her voice pitching higher in shock. "You *shouldn't* be here."

I know.

I know I shouldn't be here, shouldn't have left the others, shouldn't have let this *pull* drag me down these hallways like a man possessed.

But knowing doesn't stop me.

"You're right," I reply, forcing a small, apologetic smile that doesn't quite reach my eyes. "But I need to speak to Vasilisa."

Mimi hesitates, lips pressing together, weighing the risk.

Then, a mischievous grin tugs at her mouth. "Where's Luca?"

I almost laugh. Her not-so-subtle crush on him reminds me of Elena at her age; awkwardly transparent, endearing.

"He just went downstairs," I say, lowering my voice like I'm letting her in on a secret. "If you hurry, you might catch him."

Her cheeks flush a delicate pink, and in a blur of soft fabric and barely concealed excitement, she's gone.

The moment she disappears, the humor fades.

I push open the door, stepping inside.

Soft whispers fill the space, accompanied by the rustle of fabric, the quiet hum of final preparations. My sitting room has been transformed—delicate touches, elegant details, a place no longer mine but hers. But none of it matters.

Because there she is.

Vasilisa stands in front of a full-length mirror, bathed in the golden glow of the afternoon sun filtering through the window. Her gown cascades around her in soft waves of ivory, and Isabella, Cassandra's hired help, carefully pins small white roses into her golden waves—exactly as I had requested.

It shouldn't knock the air from my lungs.

Behind her, Cassandra fluffs the layers of her gown with quiet precision. Across the room, her mother, Vera, sits stiffly on the leather couch.

The second I enter, her sharp gaze snaps to mine.

"Mr. Amato," she says quickly, standing. "You shouldn't be in here." There's a rush to her words, a flustered sort of urgency. "I mean… superstition and all that."

I arch a brow, unimpressed.

She flounders for another excuse, but before she can find one, she mutters something under her breath and makes a quick exit.

Vasilisa turns.

Our eyes meet and just like that, I forget how to breathe.

Everything else vanishes.

The noise, the nerves, the weight of the past—*gone.*

All that's left is her

I've looked at her photo a thousand times. I *know* her face.

But standing here, draped in ivory, glowing like something out of a dream—something I can't touch, *shouldn't* touch—she is something else entirely.

A vision.

A temptation.

A reminder of everything I swore I wouldn't want.

Yet here I am.

Drawn to her like I have no other choice.

Cassandra and Isabella linger for a beat too long, eyes darting between us like they can feel the shift in the air, the weight pressing in around us.

Then, with a quiet exchange, they start toward the door.

Before leaving, Cassandra stops beside me, placing a hand on my shoulder. She leans in, her voice barely above a whisper.

"*Don't* ruin her dress or makeup."

A wink. A giggle. Then she's gone.

The door clicks shut behind them. And suddenly, we're alone.

The silence stretches, taut and heavy. I can't remember why I came here.

I don't think it matters.

Because all I can think about is how much I *missed* her.

How much I *craved* her.

It hits me all at once, knocking the breath from my lungs. A hunger so deep it feels like it's been starving inside me these past few weeks.

I drink her in—the fabric of her dress catching the faint light, the delicate flush of her lips, the way her gorgeous eyes search mine, wide, unsure.

She's looking at me like I'm a man.

I'm *not*.

I'm something darker, something raw and restless. The thing inside me, the thing that belongs to her alone, stirs, sharp and unrelenting.

Scythe.

I want to take.

Claim.

Leave my mark on every inch of her skin.

I swallow hard, forcing air into my lungs, forcing some semblance of control into my body.

But the way she watches me—like she can feel the war raging inside me—undoes me.

She moves.

A slow, careful glide, the soft rustle of her dress filling the space between us.

Then she touches me.

Her fingertips graze my cheek, cool against the heat burning beneath my skin.

It's the softest of touches, hesitant, like she's learning me.

I stand there, rigid, breathing through my nose like I can regulate the storm inside me, like I can force myself to just be in this moment.

Her eyes never leave mine. They shine with something I don't deserve—wonder, curiosity… a quiet sort of trust.

She should be afraid.

She *isn't*.

And that, more than anything else, unravels me.

"Santo," she whispers, her voice barely audible, yet it crashes through me like a storm.

There's a tremor in her words, a hesitance that mirrors the chaos inside me.

Her fingers drop, tracing an aimless path over the lapel of my jacket, a soft, lingering touch that sends fire licking up my spine.

"You... you look stunning," I confess, my voice rough, raw. I capture her wandering hand, gripping it tighter than I mean to, feeling the delicate pulse beneath my thumb—rapid, uneven. *Mine.*

I bring her hand to my lips, pressing a slow, reverent kiss against her knuckles. Her breath stutters, but when she smiles at me, it's radiant—something warm and blinding that threatens to undo me completely.

She's *too* close.

"I came here because…" I hesitate, swallowing hard. "Because our first kiss shouldn't be in front of everyone."

Her lips part, a soft inhale, her lashes fluttering as she searches my face. I don't give her a chance to respond.

I lean in, closing the space between us.

Her breath hitches the instant our lips brush, the slightest contact setting my body on fire. It's soft at first—hesitant, cautious, a delicate testing of boundaries. But then she exhales against my mouth, a quiet surrender, and I lose the fragile grip on my restraint.

The kiss deepens.

I thread my fingers through her hair, tangling in the soft golden strands, heedless of the roses slipping free and tumbling to the floor.

She clings to my lapel, her grip tightening, a quiet moan slipping from her lips as she kisses me back with more fervor, more need.

Her tongue skims my bottom lip, a deliberate, seeking touch, and I part for her without hesitation.

The moment her tongue slides against mine, a sharp jolt rips through me, something electric, primal.

My heart drops, and suddenly, I have to take control.

I *devour* her.

Without breaking the kiss, I lift her effortlessly onto the nearby dresser.

She gasps, the sudden movement catching her off guard, but it only takes a second before she melts back into me, her legs wrapping around my waist, the delicate silk of her gown wrinkling between us.

I break away just enough to look at her.

Her crystal blue eyes are darkened, heavy-lidded with lust.

Her lips, swollen and glistening, part slightly as she tries to catch her breath.

She swallows, her chest rising and falling in sharp, desperate movements.

I'm a madman.

Every part of me is unraveling, barely holding Scythe back by a thread.

I grip the nape of her neck, pulling her in, capturing her lips again, this time with none of the hesitation from before.

I nip at her bottom lip, sharp enough to make her gasp.

The sound goes straight to my cock, hard and aching against the layers of her gown.

I need more.

I leave her lips, trailing down the delicate column of her throat, sucking, teasing, tasting.

She moans again, breathless and soft, her fingers threading through my hair, tugging—desperate, *pleading.*

I could have her right here.

I *will* have her.

My fingers find the zipper of her gown, and I yank it down in one swift motion.

The silk falls away, revealing white lace hugging the curves of her breasts, soft and inviting.

I barely take a second to breathe before my lips are on her skin, pressing open-mouthed kisses down her collarbone, across her shoulder, down to the valley between her breasts.

She clings to me, nails digging into my shoulders as though she needs me to keep her tethered to the earth.

I am *intoxicated.*

By her scent. By the warmth of her body against mine. By the soft, needy sounds spilling from her lips with every touch.

I lift my head, meeting her gaze—questioning, asking, *begging* for permission.

She swallows hard, lips parting, and I already know she's going to say yes.

A sharp knock shatters the moment.

The air is ripped from the room, from my lungs, from us.

Vasilisa stiffens against me, breath caught in her throat, eyes wide with realization.

I could kill whoever is standing on the other side.

"What?" I bark, my frustration spilling over before I can rein it in.

"It's almost time. We've got to go," comes Luca's voice, calm but insistent.

A growl of frustration rumbles in my chest as I pull away from Vasilisa, my hands lingering for just a moment longer than they should.

"Go away, Luca," I grind out, my voice low and sharp.

Of course, he'd choose *now* to interrupt.

"No can do, boss. Maksim's looking antsy."

His tone carries the usual teasing lilt, but the urgency beneath it is clear.

I exhale sharply, dragging a hand down my face.

Fuck.

My eyes drift back to Vasilisa. Her lips are slightly parted, her eyes still heavy with desire.

A soft blush blooms across her cheeks, and her dress is deliciously rumpled.

The roses that once adorned her golden locks now lay scattered on the floor, a testament to what almost happened.

She slowly slips off the dresser, her movements hesitant, her fingers pulling up the bodice of her gown in a futile attempt to erase what we just did.

"I'll send Cassandra and Isabella to fix your hair," I say, forcing a small, regretful smile.

Her gaze flickers toward the door, then back to me, her blush deepening.

Wordlessly, I move behind her, zipping up her gown with slow, deliberate care.

My fingers linger at the small of her back, adjusting the fabric, smoothing it into place when I know damn well it's already perfect.

She bends to pick up the fallen roses, hands trembling slightly, movements delicate and careful.

I crouch beside her, sweeping up scattered petals, and before I can stop myself, I reach for a single bloom, tucking it gently back into her hair.

She looks up at me.

Her eyes shine with something fragile—a quiet hope that grips me by the throat.

A promise.

The desperation to kiss her again is almost unbearable, an ache that settles deep in my chest, but I force myself to step back.

There's no more time.

Outside, hundreds of people are waiting.

Our families.

Our responsibilities.

She's mine. But I can't have her.

Not yet.

I swallow the need threatening to consume me and brush my lips over her flushed cheek—a fleeting, restrained touch.

"I'll see you at the altar," I murmur.

Then, before I can change my mind, before I can ruin everything, I turn and walk away.

As I leave the room, only one thought remains, echoing in my mind.

Vasilisa is perfect and pure and good.

I cannot let my darkness consume her.

CHAPTER 16

VASILISA

H e kissed me.

Consumed me.

That kiss was like coming up for air after drowning, like finally drinking after dying of thirst. It was passionate, magnetic, breathta king... perfect.

Maybe Mimi was right. Maybe this could be more than duty. More than an arrangement.

Santo leaves, and I reach for my swollen lips, still tingling from his touch.

That kiss—it was intense, filled with passion, with unbridled need. I've never *felt* anything like it.

I exhale shakily, placing the fallen roses onto the dresser and gathering what's left of my breath.

My skin still burns where his lips touched, a phantom heat I ache to feel again. I wanted more.

I want more.

His scent lingers in the air, in my hair, wrapping around me like a whisper of what just happened.

I turn to the mirror, and the sight makes me blush.

Anyone would think something far more scandalous happened in this room.

The door swings open, and Cassandra and Isabella return.

The moment their eyes land on me, my cheeks ignite.

Isabella giggles.

Cassandra sighs, rolling her eyes.

"I told him not to *ruin* you," she says exasperated. "I hope you two had fun, it's going to cost him double to fix this."

"We—I didn't—" I stammer, but Isabella just giggles harder, meeting my gaze in the mirror as she re-pins my hair and tucks the roses back into place.

"Sure," Cassandra drawls, shaking her head in disbelief.

She kneels, fluffing out my dress. "Did he at least leave your underwear intact?"

My eyebrows shoot up, and if my cheeks get any pinker, I might actually combust.

"Good," Cassandra chuckles. "Let's get you decent again."

Isabella finishes securing my hair, then drapes the low veil over it before moving on to my makeup. She smirks as she sweeps on shimmering shadow, then soft lipstick.

"So… is he as good as they say?"

Cassandra swats her arm. "Bella, she does not want to hear what his exes say."

"He doesn't have exes, Cass. More like flings," Isabella giggles, but I find nothing funny about it at all.

My stomach twists.

Of course, I expected Santo to have a past. But hearing it out loud—*casually*—turns expectation into reality, and reality stings.

"Enough," Cassandra scolds, shooting Isabella a withering look.

She immediately lowers her gaze, mumbling an apology. The air shifts, quieter now, as she brushes some highlight onto the tip of my nose and wordlessly packs up her things.

I inhale deeply, forcing the sour weight in my stomach to settle.

"Santo's past doesn't matter." My voice is even, though the words are more for myself than anyone else. "What's important is the present. The future we will share together."

Cassandra offers me a small, knowing smile. Isabella stays silent.

When they finish, I smooth my dress and turn to admire my reflection.

My heart flutters, a delicate mix of excitement and anxiety. I take a steadying breath.

I am fulfilling my duty.

Needing a distraction, I reach for my veil, fidgeting with the delicate lace.

"How do I look?" I ask, shifting slightly to view myself from all angles.

Cassandra steps back, her critical eye sweeping over me with approval before she dusts off her hands.

"You look breathtaking," she says sincerely.

Isabella finally lifts her gaze, whatever tension from before forgotten as she takes me in.

"Like a true princess," she whispers, awed.

A knock at the door cuts through the moment. My breath hitches in anticipation as Isabella steps forward to open it.

It's not Santo, as I half-expected.

Instead, Mimi stands in the doorway, eyes shining with excitement, a stunning bouquet of lilies and roses clutched in her hands.

She gasps as she takes me in fully.

"Oh, Vasilisa," she breathes, holding the bouquet out to me. "You are going to take everyone's breath away."

I accept it gratefully, pressing the flowers close to my chest.

Santo may have had flings.

Meaningless. Forgettable.

But I am the one he is marrying. Arranged or not, this is *ours now*. And I am determined to make it work—to build something real, something lasting.

Steeling myself one last time, I meet my own gaze in the mirror.

"Here goes," I whisper.

I turn and follow Mimi out of the room.

My father waits in the hall, adjusting a cufflink, the smallest sign of nervous energy from a man who rarely falters.

"Everyone is outside and ready," he starts, but when his eyes finally land on me, he stills. His breath catches, and something shifts in his gaze—something warm.

"You are a vision, dochen'ka," he murmurs, the words thick with affection.

The tenderness in his voice surprises me.

"Thank you, Papa," I say softly, tucking my hand into the crook of his arm as he leads me downstairs, Mimi trailing behind.

The weight of the moment settles over me with every step.

At the double doors leading to the garden, Mimi slips ahead, stepping into the soft serenade of music as she takes her place as my maid of honor.

The garden is magical. The air is thick with the scent of roses, and the soft hum of anticipation ripples through the crowd like an overfilled champagne flute ready to spill over.

And there—at the end of the aisle, beneath the ornate gazebo—stands Santo.

Not a hair out of place. His suit tailored to perfection. A man carved from discipline and control.

But his eyes—his dark, stormy gaze, is locked onto me.

Only me.

A shiver rolls down my spine.

My father guides me forward, his grip steady, grounding. I can feel the weight of every gaze, hear the hushed whispers carried on the warm breeze.

But none of it matters.

Because Santo's eyes never leave mine.

He doesn't move, doesn't so much as blink, but as we approach, a muscle in his jaw twitches.

Maybe he feels this too.

"Are you ready?" My father's whisper pulls me from my thoughts as we reach the altar.

A wave of unexpected calm settles over me.

"I am," I reply, steady, certain.

He presses a kiss to my forehead before offering my hand to Santo.

Santo steps forward.

The moment his fingers brush mine, a slow, unfamiliar tingle spreads through my palm.

Electric. Undeniable.

He holds my hand—not too tight, not too soft, but with a quiet claiming.

His eyes search mine, a thousand emotions swirling beneath the surface.

The officiant clears his throat, shattering the silence.

"Ladies and gentlemen, we are gathered here today..."

As he continues with the traditional opening of the vows, I find myself studying Santo's face.

Wondering if he will be faithful in this marriage, if he feels the same nervous excitement as I do.

His gaze softens as he watches me.

Just slightly.

The vulnerability flickers there, fleeting but real, and somehow, *that* reassures me more than any vow could.

This is just as new for him as it is for me.

"Do you, Vasilisa Nova Popov, take Santo Dante Amato to be your lawfully wedded husband?"

The officiant's words pull me back to the moment.

Santo's gaze holds mine, expectant. Waiting.

And I know—there's only one answer.

"I do."

★★★

The ballroom is stunning,

Lilies bloom across every surface, their delicate fragrance wrapping around me like a promise.

Santo chose them.

The thought lingers, softening the tight knot of nerves in my stomach. I want to believe it means *something*.

That maybe, despite the distance he's kept between us these past weeks, there's hope.

Music hums in the background, a soft, steady rhythm beneath the murmur of conversation. Laughter ripples somewhere nearby.

Familiar faces drift in and out of my periphery, but it all feels distant, like I'm watching through glass.

Until Santo's hand finds mine.

His grip is firm. *Grounding*. A quiet claim in a sea of uncertainty.

His thumb brushes over my knuckles, absently, *effortlessly*, but the touch sends a slow, heat curling through me.

My breath hitches.

"Ready?"

His voice is low, intimate. A thread of warmth in the cool distance between us.

I nod.

Though I'm not sure I am.

He leads me to the center of the ballroom, where the first dance waits like a spotlight.

A hush settles over the room.

I feel every gaze pressing against my skin, a silent weight of expectation, but Santo doesn't seem to notice.

His focus remains locked on me.

His hand finds my waist, and *heat* seeps through the delicate fabric of my gown, spreading in slow waves.

His other hand closes around mine, steady, guiding, his touch impossibly sure.

"You're trembling," he murmurs, leaning in just enough that his breath grazes my temple.

A shiver rolls down my spine.

"I'm not used to dancing in front of an audience," I admit softly, willing my voice to stay even.

His lips twitch at the corner, the ghost of something amused, something almost *affectionate*.

"You'll be fine." His grip shifts, subtle but firm. "Just follow me."

The music swells, and Santo moves slow, deliberate, effortless.

I stumble slightly, my body stiff with hesitation.

His hold tightens—not rough, not forceful, but unshakable.

"Relax," he says, voice lower now, something intimate threading through it. "No one's watching as closely as you think."

But he is.

I lift my gaze, and the intensity in his nearly steals the breath from my lungs.

The world around us blurs, the grand ballroom softening into nothing but movement and warmth. His steps are smooth, surprisingly graceful for someone so imposing.

We move as one, the space between us narrowing with every turn, every breath. The faint brush of his jacket against the bodice of my dress sets my skin alight.

His fingertips press into the small of my back.

I burn beneath his touch.

"Better?" he murmurs, his lips just beside my ear.

I nod, but words feel distant.

Fragile.

As if speaking might shatter whatever delicate thing lingers between us.

His thumb strokes a slow, absent pattern along my waist. A touch that feels less like reassurance and more like possession. I wonder if he even realizes he's doing it. Or if it's instinct.

By the time the music fades, I'm almost disappointed.

Applause ripples through the ballroom, pulling me back to the present.

Santo leads me back toward our table, his hand slipping from mine too soon.

But the warmth of it remains, ghosting over my skin.

I hesitate, then reach beneath the table, slipping my fingers through his—just to hold onto the moment for a little longer.

For a while, everything feels… easier.

I sip champagne, let the murmured congratulations wash over me, and lean into the quiet comfort of Santo's presence beside me.

It's not perfect. But it's something.

Maksim appears, his hair an unmistakable flash of teal as he strides toward us with a crooked grin.

"I'm borrowing him," Maksim says by way of greeting, already tugging Santo to his feet. "Don't worry, Kisa, I'll bring him back in one piece."

There's a teasing lilt to his voice, but the weight of his title is heavy beneath the humor.

The Pakhan doesn't really ask.

Santo exhales quietly but doesn't resist.

I smile politely—because what else can I do?

Still, as he walks away, he glances back.

For just a moment, our eyes meet across the room.

And something passes between us; something unspoken, something I can't quite name.

My gaze drifts through the ballroom, catching on my cousins—Maksim's siblings, Katya and Kostya.

Katya is wildly beautiful, her white-blonde hair cut into a sleek bob, a form-fitting dress hugging her figure perfectly. She sits with effortless poise, long legs crossed, engaged in quiet conversation with her brother.

Kostya is her contrast in every way—where she is polished, he is careless. His crumpled button-down and leather jacket make him look more suited for a bar than a wedding.

Yet, despite the heinous choice of attire, his face remains striking, deceptively soft against the hard edges of his demeanor.

I'm still studying them when a shadow overtakes my table.

Tall. Commanding.

I look up and meet a pair of brooding, familiar eyes.

A slow, mischievous smile spreads across his face, dark hair cropped low, tattoos peeking from beneath the crisp edges of his all-black suit.

There's an edge to him, something sharp and unreadable.

But his eyes—light gray, where Santo's are dark—give him away.

Santo's brother.

The Don.

I rise to my feet, smoothing my expression into something polite.

"Don Amato," I say extending my hand.

He chuckles, clasping my hand in his and bringing it to his lips, pressing a light kiss to my knuckles.

"You can just call me Angelo," he says smoothly.

But he doesn't let go.

Instead, he guides me around the table until I'm standing at his side, still holding my hand.

"You are a beauty."

"Thank you," I mutter, trying to pull away.

He squeezes gently before finally releasing me.

"I wanted to welcome you to the family, Piccola," he says, his gaze trailing down my body, slow, assessing.

"Piccola?"

"Tiny," he smirks, licking his lips. "You are rather *small*—even with those heels."

Heat prickles across my skin.

"I can't really help my height," I say, a little defensively.

Angelo moves in closer, lowering himself until his breath grazes my ear. "I never said it was a bad thing."

A shiver runs down my spine. His voice, his proximity, the implication in his tone—it's enough to make my stomach twist with unease.

He straightens, gaze never leaving mine.

"Now, let's find my brother," he murmurs, brushing his knuckles across my cheek in a slow, deliberate caress.

I tense.

Before I can process the moment further, a loud commotion draws our attention.

We both turn—*Santo.*

He's striding toward us, his face set in a deep, unrelenting frown.

"Angelo," he growls, his voice dangerously cool.

Angelo grins, slow and taunting. "There he is."

He throws his hands up in mock surrender.

"Relax, fratello," he says smoothly. "I was just admiring your wife."

Santo's gaze flickers to me, then back to Angelo.

In one swift motion, he's at my side, his arm locking around my waist, pulling me against him.

The tension thickens.

"If you're finished making introductions," Santo says icily, "we have other guests waiting."

Angelo smirks but keeps his hands up, backing away at an infuriatingly slow pace.

He nods at me.

"Piccola," he regards in parting, before turning and disappearing into the crowd.

Santo's grip on me tightens.

"Are you okay?" His voice is softer now, edged with concern.

I nod.

"Yes. Yes, I am. He's your brother, right? I wouldn't be in any danger?"

Santo exhales, his hold firm but reassuring. "Correct. He's just a pain in the ass."

The rest of the night passes in a flurry of warm wishes and heartfelt toasts. Laughter and music swirl around us, a blur of celebration.

Through it all, Santo never leaves my side. His arm stays firm around my waist—not just a show of unity, but something possessive, protective. The earlier tension has faded, replaced by something lighter, something almost comforting.

But when the reception ends and we step outside, reality crashes in.

Hand in hand, we walk toward the waiting limo—toward my new life.

My belongings are already at Santo's estate. My home now.

This is real.

Sitting in the back of the limo beside him, my nerves unravel all at once.

I have a duty to fulfill.

I'm a wife now.

I belong to the Bratva *and* the Cosa Nostra.

I've created an *alliance*—there's no going back. Not to university. Not to my childhood home.

I will live with Santo. Share a bed. *Become a mother.*

The weight of it closes in, suffocating.

My chest tightens, breath coming too fast, thoughts tumbling too quickly.

Santo's hand finds my shoulder, warm and grounding.

"Are you alright?" His voice is steady, but there's genuine concern in his eyes.

I nod, though I'm still struggling to breathe. Santo grabs my hand, intertwining our fingers.

"Vasilisa." A gentle squeeze. "I know it's a lot to take in all at once."

I swallow hard. "Is it... will it always feel this chaotic?"

I don't know why I'm surprised. I knew what I was agreeing to—the merging of two powerful families, the life I was stepping into. And yet...

"Life can be chaotic sometimes," he admits, "especially when you're part of families like ours."

There's something in his gaze, honesty, maybe even understanding, that eases the worst of my fear.

But it doesn't erase it completely.

"I will miss my home," I whisper, mostly to myself, staring out at the city lights rushing past.

"You can always visit them," he says, pressing a hand to his chest.

Then, more solemnly, "And you will make new memories in our home."

His words are meant to be a comfort. And they are.

But the unknown still looms large and daunting before me.

As we pull up to the grand estate, my heart thrums wildly against my ribcage.

The mansion gleams brightly under the moonlight and for a moment it takes my breath away. This is my home now.

The thought claws at my chest.

"We're here," Santo announces, stepping out first before offering me his hand.

I take it, letting him help me from the car. The cool night air rushes over my skin, a sharp contrast to the heat curling in my stomach.

He leads me up the stairs towards the grand entrance and with every step, it sinks in deeper that this is my reality now.

Inside, servants greet us with warm smiles and murmured welcomes, their kindness at odds with the storm of nerves twisting inside me. I respond where I can, polite and composed, but my mind feels elsewhere—spinning, grasping, trying to anchor itself.

Santo's voice pulls me back.

"I'll introduce you to everyone formally tomorrow," he reassures me as we approach a set of ornate double doors.

His thumb rubs gentle circles on my hand, offering silent comfort.

The doors give way under his push, and the air shifts as we step inside.

I am struck silent by the magnificence of the room before me.

The sitting room is grand and elegant, with a cozy nook nestled by the large windows where I can imagine myself spending hours lost in a book.

It's as if a full-sized living room has been seamlessly incorporated into a bedroom, complete with plush couches for lounging.

Santo leads me through the threshold with a firm grip on my hand, never letting go as we enter the bedroom.

My eyes are immediately drawn to the imposing four-poster bed, a stark reminder of what it means to be his wife.

My heart flutters wildly at the thought.

I swallow hard, pushing the feeling down before my nerves can take over.

"Will you unzip me?" I ask softly, turning just enough to expose the zipper at the back of my dress.

"Of course." Santo's hand trails slowly down my spine, a whisper of heat against my skin as he grips the zipper and tugs it down.

The dress pools at my feet in a graceful cascade, leaving me bare save for delicate lace.

My breath catches.

The cool air against my skin. The weight of his gaze. The awareness of what's expected—what I should do, what I *have* to do.

Santo is speaking, but the words don't reach me.

I don't think.

I move.

I throw myself into his arms, pressing my lips to his in a fierce, frantic kiss.

Santo catches me, his hands steady, strong, molding to my body.

He gives in.

He returns it.

His lips move over mine with a heat that slows my desperation, turning it into something deeper, devastatingly controlled. His fingers trace over my bare skin in gentle but unyielding caresses, soothing me, grounding me.

But then he pulls away.

Releases me.

Takes a step back.

"What was that?" His voice is low, unreadable, but there's a furrow in his brow.

I cross my arms over my chest, suddenly feeling exposed, embarrassed. I gesture toward the bed with a shaky hand, words slipping out before I can stop them.

"We have to… consummate."

The moment the word leaves my lips, I regret it.

Why did I use that word?

My cheeks burn.

Santo's gaze darkens before his expression smooths into something carefully controlled.

"We don't have to do anything." His voice is calm, but there's a quiet edge of finality beneath it. "I was just telling you—this is your room. You can run a bath if you'd like. All your things are here, including what Cassandra ordered."

He gestures toward a large door on the left. "In the closet."

I blink.

"*My* room?"

A different kind of heat floods my face.

Disappointment, humiliation, shame.

Santo nods. "Yes. I have the room next door."

I scramble for my wedding dress, trying to cover myself, as if it can shield me from the sharp ache of rejection.

Santo steps forward. He cups my cheek in his strong, warm hand, tilting my face toward him.

His touch sends a shiver straight to my core, melting my resistance, unraveling me.

His lips brush close—his breath warm as he murmurs, "When I take you, I want you to *crave* it. I want you wet, *desperate*, dripping, and begging for an insatiable release."

The words stroke something deep, something dangerous inside me.

"It *won't* be to fulfill a duty."

I tremble. His eyes, intense, dark, searing into mine, hold me captive. "Do you understand, *Mia Dea?*"

My breath hitches. I nod, licking my lips without thinking.

Santo's gaze flickers just slightly before he exhales.

His jaw ticks.

"I have work to attend to. You go unwind and get some rest. We'll see each other in the morning."

He presses a soft kiss to my forehead, releases me and leaves.

The weight of his words, his touch, his promise—*lingers*.

CHAPTER 17

SANTO

I need to get away from her.

Away from her scent. Away from soft, supple skin and the sheer, agonizing temptation of her.

I didn't expect her to let the dress fall. And when it did—*fuck*. My cock begged for escape.

She threw herself at me. Not out of desire. Not out of want. But for *duty*.

And I wanted her.

I *want* her.

I could've had her—pushed her back against the bed, buried myself so deep inside her there'd be nothing left between us but heat and sweat and surrender.

And she would have let me.

But she doesn't *want* me.

I saw it. The vulnerability in her eyes, the way her hands trembled.

I would have *ruined* her.

And if I'm going to claim her, *if I'm going to own her*, it won't be like that.

Not like some transaction, some contract to uphold.

She will come to me willingly.

I need to get miles away from her.

A door isn't enough. These walls aren't enough.

The need to consume her, to possess her, is *too much*.

I need to burn it off.

Before it burns me alive.

Without a second thought, I grab my keys and head for the car parked out front.

The drive is a blur—a mess of streaking city lights and rage curling under my skin, hot and relentless.

I *need* to hurt something.

I need to *punish* someone.

I pull into the familiar back entrance of Opulent, my pulse pounding in my ears.

Alessandro leans against the wall, chatting up Rachel—the redhead who never seems to take a hint. He glances up as I stride past, his expression shifting.

I give him a hard nod.

He excuses himself from his admirer, falling into step beside me.

"Santo! What brings you by tonight?" His voice brims with false cheerfulness.

As if he doesn't *already know.*

"Business."

The single word grates from my throat as I push past him, moving through the club with purpose, with barely leashed fury.

The atmosphere hits like a punch to the gut.

Loud music vibrates through the floors, pounding against my chest, syncing with my restless pulse.

Hazy lights flicker across glittered corsets and bare skin, painted lips and drunken smiles.

Their joy is cheap. Fleeting. Meaningless.

I head straight for the concealed door leading to the basement.

Alessandro keeps up, silent now, smart enough not to ask questions.

Opulent's basement is a world away from the glitter and the glamour above. Upstairs is for pleasure.

Down here is for punishment. It's here that we deal with the men who deserve pain.

The ones who harm the women in our organization.

The ones who think strength is meant for breaking rather than protecting.

Weak men.

Disgraces.

Tonight, it will serve another purpose.

Tonight, this room, these men, will be my outlet.

I roll my shoulders, exhaling slow, steadying myself for what comes next.

The air is thick, damp, stifling. The walls reek of blood, sweat, and fear.

Three men are chained to the concrete wall, their gaunt, frantic eyes flickering under the dim light.

Human waste.

Each of them has their own sob story, their own excuses, their own troubled pasts that stopped mattering a long time ago.

I stop in front of one.

His features are unremarkable—except for the nasty scar slicing down his face.

My doing.

A reminder of what happens when men like him forget their place.

I step into his space, close enough that he has to feel the heat of my presence.

"Remember me?" My voice is low, sharp—a blade sliding under the skin.

His breath catches. His wide, terrified eyes flick to Alessandro, then back to me.

Fear.

Good.

I grip his tattered shirt and yank him upright, his body weak and trembling. "Because I remember you."

Then, I release him. He crumbles.

Pathetic.

"Alessandro." I don't break my stare from the whimpering man in front of me. "Take off the restraints."

There's a beat of hesitation.

Alessandro pulls a key from his pocket. Metal scrapes against metal as the chains unlock, and the man collapses to the floor.

I barely glance at Alessandro before snarling, "Get out."

No hesitation this time.

He nods, stepping back toward the door, but not before lingering. As if second-guessing leaving me alone. The door slams shut behind him. Silence descends—thick, suffocating. The only sounds left are ragged breaths.

His.

Mine.

The man forces himself to stand, but his legs buckle.

He drops again.

He doesn't fight. They never do at this point.

The ones who survive more than a day down here know better.

I crack my knuckles, stepping closer. "Last chance to plead innocence before we get started."

He shakes his head violently, tears already pooling.

Some part of me acknowledges his fear.

Recognizes it as a testament to my own power, but most of me is too far gone to care. I don't waste another second.

I pull back and swing.

Bone cracks under my fist. Pain explodes through my knuckles. A sweet, biting relief. For the first time tonight, I feel something. And it's not *her*.

I swing again. Flesh gives. Blood spatters.

I lose count of the hits.

The roar in my head drowns out the cries. Each punch is a release. Each blow is a distraction.

Each crack of bone is a moment where I don't feel her soft, sweet-scented skin. Her innocent eyes staring up at me.

She deserves more than a man like me.

Or a *monster* like Scythe.

★★★

I pull into the estate, veering toward the underground garage. The car hums to a stop beneath my home, safe from prying eyes.

I pass my gym and indoor pool, moving straight for the elevator.

A quick press of my thumb against the scanner, and the hidden elevator hums to life, carrying me up through the walls of my home. It was installed as a precaution—an escape route if an attack ever came.

Usually, I'd take it all the way up to the master bedroom closet, but that room belongs to Vasilisa now.

The thought of her sends a sharp, unwelcome ache through me.

This house is hers as much as it's mine now, and tomorrow, I'll have to show her around. I push the thought aside and take the stairs up to my new room.

Light spills from under the master bedroom door. It's almost three in the morning.

She should be asleep.

I should keep walking.

Instead, my feet betray me, carrying me to her door before I have a chance to second-guess myself.

My hand moves before my mind does, twisting the knob. The door gives way without resistance.

The dim light casts a soft glow around the sitting room, illuminating Vasilisa perched on the window nook.

In her hand, she holds a book—not just any book, but *Vita Nuova* .

My heart *aches* at the sight of her.

She runs a hand through her glossy hair, the shadows play across her face, accentuating her features.

Light catches on the delicate curve of her jaw, the gentle slope of her neck. Her plush lips move soundlessly as she reads, captivating me in their every movement.

The sight is mesmerizing, but my attention is soon drawn to what she's wearing, or rather, what she's *barely* wearing.

Lingerie.

Sheer white lace clings to her body, teasing, barely concealing anything.

The transparent robe draped over her is open, useless, falling off one shoulder like an afterthought.

The delicate lace bra hugs her breasts perfectly and it's enough to break my resolve.

Her smooth stomach leads down to lace underwear that leaves nothing to the imagination, held on by mere string.

And those legs; smooth and perfect, are crossed provocatively, daring me to touch her.

Heat licks through me, hunger sharp and instant.

She startles, eyes snapping to mine, her breath hitching in a quiet gasp. My need for her coils tighter.

She sets her book aside and slides off the window nook, her steps measured, almost hesitant, as she closes the space between us.

Her small hand reaches for my wrist, tugging gently, urging me to follow.

I let her lead, watching every move she makes, every breath that causes her breasts to rise and fall.

Her eyes flick over me, assessing, studying, and it takes everything in me to stay in control.

She stops in front of the couch, her useless robe still clinging to her frame, I want to *rip* it off.

Her hand presses lightly on my shoulder, guiding me down.

I sit.

She captivates me.

She stands between my legs, close, delicate fingers trailing up the buttons of my shirt. One by one, she works them open, brushing against my skin with every movement.

Her touch is light, but it *burns*.

The subtle scent of her sweet cashmere perfume wraps around me, tightening the hold she already has on me.

I clench my fists to keep from grabbing her, from dragging her against me and tasting every inch of her.

Then she speaks.

"Where are you hurt?"

The words hit like ice water.

She isn't trying to *seduce* me.

My hand grips her wrist before I even register the movement.

She gasps, eyes flicking up to mine, wide with something close to fear.

Only then do I notice the blood splattered across me.

She's trying to *tend* to me.

Realizing my hold has tightened, I release her wrist, guilt pressing down like a weight on my chest.

"It's not mine," I mutter, my voice rough. "I'm not hurt."

Some of the tension in her face eases, but she steps back, pulling the robe around herself, as if shielding herself from me.

"Oh, I'm sorry," she whispers. "I thought—"

I stand abruptly, and she stumbles, nearly losing her balance.

My hand catches her waist instinctively, steadying her.

For a brief moment, our eyes lock, and I'm struck by the compassion shining in hers.

It's disarming, *unfamiliar*, and for the first time in what feels like forever, the darkness inside me ebbs.

Her gaze drops—to my lips.

I rip myself away.

"It's fine," I rasp, my voice unrecognizable. "I'm going to shower. You should get some rest."

I don't wait for a response. I leave, each step heavier than the last.

A part of me wants to turn back, to stay with her, to feel that fleeting humanity she offers.

But I know better. For her sake, I have to keep my distance.

So I force myself forward, shutting the door on her, on this, on whatever dangerous thing she's stirring inside me.

CHAPTER 18

VASILISA

I wake early, the unfamiliar weight of the house settling around me.

I shower in the luxurious bathroom, steam curling against the cool glass.

I take my time getting dressed, reaching for what feels like me.

A silk blouse, a short skirt over sheer tights, soft fabrics that remind me of home.

I'm grateful to Cassandra for picking more designer versions of my usual style, but the closet also holds dresses I wouldn't usually wear.

Tighter, shorter, lower cut. There are silk slips barely longer than my fingertips, delicate lace that leaves nothing to the imagination.

Maybe they were chosen for *his* tastes.

Maybe he prefers his women to show skin.

He may just not be interested in *my* skin showing considering he's abruptly left the room every time I'm in lingerie.

I glance at my reflection, fingers hesitating at the buttons of my blouse. I undo a few more than usual, just enough to let a glimpse of my red lace bra peek through.

My fingers comb through my hair, debating whether to leave it down.

But the air shifts, heavy with the weight of being watched.

I startle slightly as I meet Santo's reflection in the mirror.

He's standing behind me, close but not touching, his broad frame still, stoic.

His eyes lock onto mine, visible just above my head, dark and unwavering.

His gaze lowers trailing down my body, slow, deliberate.

Like he's memorizing.

Like he's teetering on the edge of something dangerous.

I turn to face him, my pulse skipping.

I give him a bright, practiced smile, an attempt to ease the tension that coils between us.

His predatory stare softens.

Just a little, but not enough.

"I didn't expect you to be awake so early," he drawls softly.

"I wanted to get started on our day," I say, brushing past him as I leave the bathroom and head toward the closet.

My pace quickens, but I can feel Santo trailing behind me, his steps steady and deliberate.

I grab a pair of heels from the closet and move toward the bed to put them on.

As I approach, I falter.

His eyes are still following my every move.

My gaze shifts to the sitting room couch, considering my escape, but before I can act, Santo's fingers graze mine.

His touch is light but firm as he takes the shoes from my grasp.

"Allow me." His voice low and smooth.

He nods toward the bed.

Reluctantly, I climb onto the edge, my legs dangling awkwardly over the side.

The ridiculous height of the bed makes it impossible to do anything gracefully, obviously it's designed for him, not me.

A soft chuckle fills the space.

I glance up, my cheeks warming instantly.

Santo watches me, eyes stormy and unwavering.

He kneels.

The sight steals my breath.

Santo Amato, larger than life, dangerous and untouchable, kneeling before me.

He sets the shoes beside me on the bed, his hands moving with an ease that feels far too intimate.

Carefully, deliberately, he lifts one of my feet onto his knee.

He takes the first heel and slips it on, his touch slow, reverent.

His fingers brush against my ankle, lingering just a second longer than necessary.

Fastening the strap into place, the warmth of his skin seeps into mine, sinking deeper than it should.

I bite my lip, stifling a sharp inhale when his thumb drags lightly across my skin.

His gaze flicks up.

A slow smirk tugs at his lips.

"Are you okay?" His voice dips lower, teasing, coaxing.

Like he enjoys unraveling me.

I nod quickly, too quickly.

He knows.

He says nothing, just shifts to my other foot, repeating the process with painstaking attention.

I can't look away.

His hands move with precision, care, reverence. As is this isn't just some simple task—like this is *worship.*

Something deep inside me stirs, and suddenly, the room, the house, the world beyond this moment, all of it fades.

There is only Santo.

His hands. His touch. His presence wrapping around me like silk and steel.

"Thank you." My voice breathier than I mean it to be.

Santo doesn't blink.

"Anything for you, Dea."

His voice is so warm, so sure, it sends a shiver straight through me.

But he doesn't let go.

His thumb lingers, tracing slow circles against my ankle.

The touch is light, unhurried—yet it leaves behind a heat that spreads through me like a secret I shouldn't be keeping.

I want to speak, to say something, anything, but the words never come.

His gaze clashes with mine.

Heavy.

"Shall we go?"

His voice pulls me from my thoughts, smooth and unaffected as if he hasn't just unraveled me without trying.

He releases my foot and rises back to his full height, offering his hand.

A gentlemanly gesture. *Simple.*

Yet somehow, my heart flutters wildly against my ribs.

"Sure," I breathe out, slipping my hand into his.

The moment our fingers intertwine, his grip tightens—just for a second, just enough for me to feel it.

He helps me down from the bed and leads me toward the door.

"You should eat something before we start our day."

I nod, but I barely register the words.

My mind is still tangled in the moment he touched me.

I follow as he leads me down the grand staircase, but I'm barely listening.

He's talking—about the architecture, the security, the household staff, someone named Mrs. Keen, but I hear none of it.

I hear only the sound of my own pulse.

Because my focus is locked on him.

On the way his fingers remain intertwined with mine.

The way his jaw flexes as he speaks, tightening and relaxing like he's holding something back.

An image flashes through my mind without warning. My fingers threading through his hair. The way it felt beneath my touch when he devoured my mouth, when my legs wrapped recklessly around him on the dresser.

Heat floods through me.

I barely catch myself before I stumble.

"This is Julian." Santo's voice snaps me out of it, grounding me.

I blink, realizing we're standing in the kitchen.

It's large and bright—white marble, gleaming steel, expansive windows.

Behind the island stands Julian.

Tall and lean, with chestnut hair that falls carelessly onto his forehead. He looks closer to Santo's age, his warm smile instantly welcoming.

He bows slightly in greeting, a playful glint in his eyes.

"A pleasure to meet you, Mrs. Amato," he says, his voice rich and smooth.

Before I can respond, I feel it.

The slightest shift in Santo.

His hand tightens around mine so faintly, so imperceptibly I almost miss it.

Almost.

"Julian here is one of the most sought-after chefs," Santo continues, his voice smooth—too smooth. There's an edge there now, one that wasn't there before.

His gaze lingers on Julian a beat too long before finally flicking back to me.

"Would you like something specific for breakfast?" His tone is polite, carefully neutral. "Julian can whip up anything you like."

But I can tell his mind is elsewhere.

His eyes keep darting back to Julian.

Like he's watching.

Calculating.

I hesitate, glancing between them.

"I... Um..." I clear my throat. "Maybe a croissant? And a cappuccino?"

"Coming right up." Julian's response is easy, confident, unfazed.

He moves through the kitchen with effortless familiarity, his hands precise as he works. "And for you, boss?"

"My usual omelet." Santo's voice is clipped, cool.

Without another word, he guides me toward the breakfast nook, pulling out a chair for me.

I settle in, murmuring a quiet, "Thank you."

As he sits across from me, something feels... off.

His jaw is locked tight. His posture rigid.

The air thickens.

The smell of fresh coffee fills the kitchen, a welcome distraction, comforting in a way that eases some of the tension.

Julian places a cappuccino and a croissant in front of me, then sets down Santo's omelet.

"Thank you." I say sincerely taking a bite, the croissant warm and flaky, melting on my tongue.

A soft hum of satisfaction slips past my lips.

Santo watches.

He eats slow.

He doesn't speak.

His stormy gaze fixates on me, unblinking.

Something in his face softens—just slightly, just enough for me to notice.

Julian moves to clear the dishes, his presence lingering a second too long.

I can feel his eyes on us.

Santo notices, too.

And just like that, his entire demeanor shifts.

"Vasilisa."

His voice is low, dark, commanding.

It slices through the space.

Even Julian pauses.

Santo stands, his movements controlled, deliberate. "Let's continue. I need to show you the library, where you'll be painting."

I can't help the excited gasp that escapes me. "Now?"

Santo chuckles. "Of course."

He takes my hand. The way his fingers close around mine, firm, warm, certain, makes my breath hitch.

He leads me out of the kitchen, guiding me through the vastness of his home like it's second nature.

We ascend the grand staircase, the wood polished to a gleaming shine. My fingers drift along the intricate carvings of the banister, tracing the silent stories etched into them.

Santo walks with quiet authority, his grip steady, unyielding, yet somehow... gentle.

The route to the library is labyrinthine, winding through halls steeped in history. The walls shimmer with tapestries and gilded frames, bathed in the soft glow of antique chandeliers.

I should be taking it all in.

But it's *him* that holds my focus.

His presence. His touch. The way he commands a room without a word.

"This is the east wing," he finally speaks. "Most of these quarters are reserved for the staff if they choose to stay. Or for guests."

Before I can respond, he pushes open a set of double doors. I step inside—and stop breathing.

The library.

Shelves stretch up high, towering toward a vaulted glass ceiling. Sunlight streams in, filtering through the dust particles dancing in the air. The scent of aged paper, polished wood, and something distinctly Santo wraps around me.

Then, I see them.

The easels.

Near the massive windows, bathed in natural light.

My heart stutters.

This will be my sanctuary.

A place where I can exist.

Create.

Lose myself in color.

Santo's voice pulls me back. "Do you like it?"

His gaze is on me, not the room.

I look up, meeting his stormy eyes, hoping he can see what I feel; the gratitude, the relief.

"Like it?" The words barely leave me. I swallow, breathless. "Santo, it's... it's beautiful."

He squeezes my hand gently.

A small smile plays on his lips, brief and quiet.

He leads me through the space, showing me every detail, every hidden corner, every untouched book.

The silence between us is weighted. *Charged.*

A quiet storm waiting to break, but he says nothing as we leave the library.

Not until we reach the bottom of the stairs, stopping in front of a heavy wooden door.

His home office.

Santo pauses.

"Vasilisa."

His voice is different this time. Calm, but final.

"This is your home now, you are welcome everywhere, except one place."

His gaze flicks to the closed door.

A warning.

And I understand. His world has merged with mine, but not completely.

Some parts remain locked away.

I nod, offering a small smile.

For now, what he's given is enough.

Santo watches me for a moment longer, then his expression shifts. Softer.

He takes my hand again, and this time there's a sense of excitement behind it.

He leads me toward the back of the house, stopping at the large glass sliding doors.

"I want to show you our garden," he says proudly escorting me outside.

My heart leaps at the word.

Our.

Santo leads me down the stone path, his grip steady as he guides me deeper into the garden's embrace. The further we walk, the more I realize this place is a hidden paradise.

The vibrant colors spill out around us in a breathtaking array; fiery reds of the roses, calming blues of the hydrangeas, the soft blush of peonies tucked into the greenery.

Nothing is out of place. Every flower, every vine, every stone in the path feels meticulously placed, a work of art cultivated with care and intention.

I can feel his gaze on me as I take it all in.

At every turn, something new captures my attention.

I pause to admire unfamiliar blooms, inhaling their delicate scents, running my fingers along petals that feel impossibly soft.

Then I spot lilies, my heart flutters.

I glance at Santo, but he says nothing—only watches.

"This is my favorite part of the garden."

His voice is quieter now, almost reverent, as we approach a stone bench nestled between two towering magnolia trees.

I gasp softly.

The blossoms shower down like a cascade of soft pink and white petals, forming a delicate canopy above the bench.

Sunlight filters through the branches, casting golden halos around us, illuminating the space with an almost ethereal glow.

It feels untouched by time.

Sacred.

My fingers slip from his as I step forward, unable to tear my gaze away from the sheer beauty of it all.

I turn back to him, emotions welling in my chest.

A lump forms in my throat, my voice hoarse with emotion. "Santo…" I whisper. "This… this is gorgeous."

His features soften, just slightly, and he walks toward me, reclaiming my hand in his.

"I wanted to share this with you."

He angles himself toward me, his expression wavering.

"My mother loved this garden," he continues, his voice low, weighted. "I continued to build it in her memory."

I blink in surprise, absorbing his words.

I hesitate, not wanting to break whatever fragile thread has formed between us.

"I'm sorry for your loss," I say softly.

He nods once, his gaze distant. "She lived here for her last few years. I visited during summers."

Something about the way he says it, careful, measured, makes me tread lightly.

He's letting me in, but only just enough.

Still, I can't help but ask. "Were your parents divorced?"

The shift is immediate.

Santo releases my hand and steps away.

The absence of his touch is instant, jarring.

I shouldn't have asked that

"No."

His tone is clipped, sharper than before. He turns his back to me, his broad shoulders tense, his posture stiff.

"She lived here because my father thought she would be safer." A bitter pause. "He was wrong."

A chill runs through me.

"We have many enemies in this life." He exhales, slow, controlled. "They look for weaknesses, and they attack."

Finally, he turns to me again.

His gaze locks onto mine, filled with something raw, something restless. "*You* are a weakness."

The words knock the breath from my lungs.

A weakness.

I part my lips, but no words come.

I don't know how to respond to that.

His voice remains steady, detached, but the weight of his meaning is suffocating. "Being my wife makes you a target."

I swallow thickly.

He's not saying it to be cruel. He's stating a fact.

A brutal, irrevocable truth.

I'm a liability to him.

Santo steps closer, his expression unreadable once more. "I will ask that you take guards with you when you leave the house and that you make those ventures out brief and seldom."

I deflate, sinking onto the bench.

The walls are closing in already.

But I nod.

His piercing gaze holds mine, searching.

Seconds stretch, dragging between us like something unspoken, something unbreakable.

I reach out hesitantly, expecting him to pull away.

He doesn't.

Instead, his hand finds mine again.

He lowers himself beside me, his touch firmer this time. More certain.

"I can do as you ask." My voice is softer now. "But I want something."

His brow furrows slightly, intrigued.

A flicker of dark amusement dances through his stormy gaze. "What do you want?"

The word *'you'* is on the tip of my tongue, but instead, I choose something safer. Something easier.

"I want to continue university."

His expression shifts, the tension in his frame coiling tight. His eyebrows rise so fast I almost regret saying it.

But I press on. "Online. I want to take courses *online.*"

For a moment, he doesn't say anything.

Then, relief floods his features. His smirk is back, slow, calculated, something possessive curling at the edges.

"Of course."

His grip on my hand tightens slightly, just for a second, before he relaxes.

"I'll have a laptop brought to you as soon as tomorrow."

"Thank you," I murmur, staring at our joined hands, my fingers brushing over his in a way that feels dangerously natural.

His thumb nudges under my chin, lifting my gaze to his.

"What are you studying?"

"Business," I answer simply.

His smirk deepens. "Smart girl."

His knuckles skim across my cheek, a barely-there touch.

I lean into it.

We spend what feels like hours beneath our pink canopy, sharing stories and laughter as petals fall softly around us.

I tell him about my childhood, about the days spent running through endless fields of sunflowers and tall grass, with nothing but laughter as my guide. He listens, his thumb absently grazing the back of my hand, and when I pause, he speaks.

"My mother loved flowers." His voice is quieter now, softer, as if the memory is something delicate. "She had them everywhere—lining windowsills, filling drawing rooms, even the bathrooms. I used to tease that she was trying to turn the whole house into a garden."

I smile at the thought. The most dangerous man I know was raised in a home overflowing with flowers.

I love it.

He keeps his hold on my hand, his fingers strong, steady.

I lean my head on his shoulder, and he doesn't pull away.

For a long moment, we just sit there. No walls, no expectations, no weight of Cosa Nostra hanging over us.

The heady fragrance of magnolias, the sweet scent of roses, the crisp undertones of fresh greenery wraps around us, it's intoxicating.

A breeze rolls through the garden, shaking the branches above us.

A rain of petals cascades down over us. I gasp, delighted, squealing as I lift my hand to catch them.

Santo laughs.

A real laugh. Deep, rich, unrestrained.

It rings through the garden, echoing around us, bright and rare and so heartbreakingly beautiful I don't realize I'm staring.

My lips pull into a smile, unable to stop it.

He looks so different like this. So alive.

His handsome face softened by the warmth of his laughter, his stormy eyes lighter, unburdened.

My gaze drops to his lips.

The urge is sudden, undeniable.

I want to kiss him.

I want to taste his laughter, to feel it against my own mouth.

Without thinking, I lean in.

Santo moves first.

Abruptly, he stands, tearing his hand from mine.

The loss is so sharp, so jarring, I barely mask my surprise.

My heart stutters as I watch it happen—the walls slamming back into place, the openness in his expression disappearing behind something cold and blank.

Santo is gone.

His jaw tightens. "We should get back inside. You can paint, and I'll call Luca about that laptop."

He doesn't wait for me.

He just turns, heading back up the stone path, putting space between us.

I stare after him for a moment, something heavy settling in my chest.

Then, without a word, I follow.

VASILISA

I nside, Santo introduces me to Lila, a young housekeeper with warm brown eyes and an easy, inviting smile.

She tells me that Mrs. Keen, Santo's favorite employee, will be back in a week.

Lila is a little older than me, but younger than Santo.

There's something gentle about her, something that puts me at ease.

As soon as Santo disappears into his office, she zeroes in on me, linking her arm through mine like we've known each other for years.

"Oh, your outfit is stunning," she gushes, eyes sweeping over me. "And your hair? Your makeup? Seriously, girl, you're gorgeous."

I blink.

Caught off guard by the enthusiasm, the warmth. Compliments aren't foreign to me, but… this feels different.

Like she's *trying* to put me at ease.

My gaze flickers toward Santo's office.

Lila leans in close, her voice lowering conspiratorially.

"Mr. Amato works a lot, but he is totally obsessed with you."

My breath catches.

My head jerks toward her, brows knitting together. "What do you mean?"

She grins, leading me upstairs, her steps light and secretive.

"I like to know about everything that happens in this house," she admits with a mischievous gleam in her eyes. "Mrs. Keen hates it—scolds me all the time for gossiping, but I love it."

I'm not sure what to do with that information, so I just listen as she pulls me along, past grand hallways and polished banisters.

When we reach the master bedroom, she opens the door, then shuts it behind us with a soft click.

"This is the only room in the house without audio."

I freeze. "What?"

Lila laughs lightly, flopping onto the couch like she just told me something as simple as the weather.

"The whole house has cameras inside and out. But this room?" She exhales in relief. "No audio. Just video."

I scan the room, my pulse quickening.

"How do you know that?"

Lila winks, tucking her legs under her. "A pretty face gets a lot of information around here."

She tosses her hair over her shoulder, her voice turning coy. "You flirt a little, they give a little."

I hesitate before sinking onto the couch beside her.

Something about her confidence makes me uneasy.

Not in a bad way.

More like she's… *too* bold for this house.

Lila suddenly turns serious, her tone dropping. "Not you though."

I glance at her. "Excuse me?"

"You shouldn't flirt with the guards. Unless you want Santo to take care of them."

I still.

"Take care of them?"

"Yeah. Get rid of them. Kill them. End their lives."

She says it casually, like it's just a flippant fact.

"Anyway," she sighs, stretching, "I heard Santo had Luca follow you around before you got married. Even took pictures of you."

My stomach lurches.

"What?"

She nods, like it's nothing. "One of the guards said he was pissed about… Peter? Pasco?"

My throat tightens. "…Pietro?"

Lila snaps her fingers.

"Yes! That's the one. And Jude—the mayor's son, right?"

"Yes, Jude and I were together for a bit," I say quietly, avoiding eye contact as I pick at my nails nervously.

Lila's eyes light up. Her lips curve into a devious little smirk.

"I hear he's *big*," she whispers, like she's telling me a scandalous secret. "How was he?"

Heat rushes to my face.

I choke on air.

Lila bursts into laughter, the sound echoing around the room.

"Oh, girl, don't be shy!" she teases. "I didn't mean to pry."

She winks. "I'm just curious."

I blink at her, still mortified.

In my family, no one talks about sex. It isn't a conversation.

The only thing I was ever told was not to have sex—or Maksim would kill me.

And while I never believed he'd actually kill me, I heeded the warning.

Lila must sense my discomfort because the laughter dies down, leaving behind something quieter.

A pause. A shift.

Then, smoothly, she changes the subject.

"Oh, look at us getting all distracted." She pops up from the couch, brushing herself off. "Let me finish showing you around."

I let out a slow breath, grateful for the escape.

We spend the next hour exploring different parts of the house—rooms adorned with exquisite art pieces, hidden corners with lavish décor, and she even tells me about an indoor swimming pool, but to wait until Santo shows me that himself.

She keeps the conversation light, entertaining, regaling me with stories about the house—some outrageous, some believable. I'm not sure which to trust, but I find myself enjoying her company.

Until she slows.

Her laughter dies off, replaced by something quieter, tenser. She glances over her shoulder, checking the hallway behind us.

I'm about to ask what's wrong when I hear it.

A voice.

Santo's voice.

But not the one I know.

"Your incompetence is unacceptable." The words are sharp, precise, and cold enough to make my blood run cold.

Santo's voice… it's different now—darker, harsher.

"Please, Mr. Amato, we didn't—" Another voice stammers, but Santo cuts them off.

"Don't waste my time with excuses. You had one job, and you failed. The Turks are mocking us now, undermining my authority because of you. Do you have any idea what that *means*?"

The silence that follows is deafening. Lila's grip tightens on my arm, her unease almost contagious.

Still, I can't bring myself to walk away.

I take a step closer, leaning just enough to catch a glimpse through the crack in the door.

Santo stands in the center of the room, towering over two men who look like they'd rather disappear into the floor than face him.

His stance is rigid, his hands curled into loose fists at his sides.

The air around him seems almost charged, as if his fury alone could suffocate the room.

His back's to me, but his presence is overwhelming.

"I don't want apologies," he continues, his voice dropping lower, almost a growl. "I want results. Fail me again, and you'll wish the Turks had killed you themselves."

One of the men flinches as if the words are a physical blow. The other stammers out a desperate promise to fix things, but Santo doesn't respond.

He just stands there, silent and unyielding, like a storm waiting to break.

"Vasilisa," Lila hisses under her breath, urgently tugging my arm. "Let's go."

For the first time since I heard him speak, I exhale.

Slowly, I step back.

My pulse hammers in my chest as I let Lila pull me away, her grip firm; almost desperate.

We move quickly, slipping down another hallway, and only when we're far enough does she finally release me.

Lila exhales sharply, pressing a hand to her chest.

The usual brightness in her face is gone, replaced by something serious. Something wary.

She glances over her shoulder before leaning in, voice hushed.

"Vasilisa… Santo is *not* all that he appears to be."

Her words hang between us, heavy, unshakable.

"What do you mean?"

She hesitates, chewing on her lower lip before speaking again.

"Promise me you'll be careful," she implores earnestly. "There's more to this house… and Santo… than meets the eye."

Before I can press her for more, a throat clears behind us, and Lila's eyes widen.

Slowly, I turn.

Santo stands just a few feet away.

His dark gaze is locked onto mine. The air feels heavier suddenly, charged with an intensity I don't fully understand.

"Lila," he says smoothly, his voice a low rumble that somehow fills the entire hallway. His gaze never strays from mine. "Could you give us a moment?"

Lila's spine straightens.

Her voice is steady when she replies, but there's something strained beneath it. "Certainly, Mr. Amato."

She doesn't even look at me before slipping away down the hall, her steps brisk, leaving me alone with him.

I inhale carefully. Steady.

"Santo—"

He lifts a hand, just slightly, shaking his head.

A quiet, deliberate motion.

"What were you two discussing?" His tone is light.

Almost *casual.*

But his eyes betray him.

They are sharp. Unrelenting. Pinning me in place like a wolf waiting for its prey to twitch.

My pulse skips.

I take a breath.

"Just… things about the house."

The words leave my lips before I can second-guess them.

But I *know,* he hears the hesitation.

Santo steps closer.

Not fast. Not aggressive. Just deliberate.

His presence fills the space between us, pulling the air from my lungs.

His eyes search mine, looking for cracks, for anything I might be keeping from him.

I don't break his gaze. Even as my pulse thunders in my ears.

He studies me for a moment longer, then exhales softly.

He steps past me, reaching for the library door.

"Come in."

The words are smooth. Unquestionable.

I hesitate for half a second before following him inside.

The grand library looms around me, but its beauty does little to ease the tension curling at the base of my spine.

Santo gestures for me to sit.

I don't.

He shuts the door behind us with a quiet finality.

"Did Lila mention anything else?"

His voice is measured now, slower, like he's leaving room for me to reveal something I shouldn't.

I swallow.

Take a gamble.

"She warned me." I hold his gaze. "That there's more to this house—and you.

The silence stretches.

His expression doesn't shift.

Instead, a low chuckle escapes his lips.

It's soft. Almost indulgent.

He runs a hand through his dark hair, shaking his head slightly. "She's quite imaginative, isn't she?"

His calmness unsettles me more than anger would have.

I don't know if I feel relieved or even more wary.

Letting out a slow, careful breath, I try to gather my thoughts. "Santo…"

I don't know what I'm going to say, but he doesn't let me finish.

His fingers brush against my arm, light, warm, grounding.

"Vasilisa." My name is a murmur, spoken softly, pulling me closer despite myself.

His hand moves, tilting my chin up. Not forceful, but commanding. His touch lingers. I'm forced to meet his gaze.

His dark eyes are no longer stormy, but warm. Pulling me in.

"If you have any questions or doubts, ask me directly."

His voice is softer now. Intimate.

His fingers fall away, leaving behind a phantom warmth on my skin.

For a moment, I lose myself in the quiet between us.

The library fades into the background, Santo standing before me like something carved from shadow and fire.

And then, his tone shifts, pulling me back to reality.

"Just one more thing."

I brace myself.

His next words send a chill down my spine.

"There is surveillance all over the house, including the sitting room in the master bedroom… *audio* included."

I still.

"…Santo." His name escapes me in a whisper.

My mind racing to recall every word I spoke in there. But beneath the rush of thoughts, something else blooms.

Trust.

He didn't have to tell me. He could've let me stay in ignorance. But he chose to warn me.

Santo watches me carefully, then gestures toward the easels set up by the window.

"You should paint."

The shift is effortless. Like this is nothing. Like he didn't just remind me how much power he holds.

"I'll have Winnie send up a snack since you missed lunch."

"Winnie?" I echo, still trying to catch up.

"One of the staff."

"Like Lila?"

His lips curve. Something dark. Amused.

"Just. Like. Lila."
A pause.
"Actually, Lila could use a nice, long vacation."
Before I can process what that means, he turns, heading for the double doors.

His presence leaves as swiftly as it came.

CHAPTER 20

SANTO

I leave Vasilisa in the library.

My mind begins turning over how to handle Lila.
I never expected her to be a problem.
She's young, working part-time to pay for her education.
As a favor to Mrs. Keen. I let her in.
And now I regret it.
She frightened my wife. Pressed her about me.
About the men she's been with.
That thought alone makes my jaw clench.
Now, she sits across from me in my office, wringing her hands, eyes cast downward.
A bead of sweat trickles down her temple, and she swipes at it quickly, her breath shallow.
I don't say anything.
Not yet.
Instead, I take my time. I let the silence stretch, let her squirm under the weight of it as I shoot off a quick text to Luca.
Then I check the surveillance feed.
The monitor lights up.
The library.
Vasilisa is still there, standing near the shelves, admiring the array of paints and brushes I had set up for her.
She looks... ethereal. The natural light catches in her golden hair, softening the angles of her face, making her look almost untouched by the world around her.
Untouched by me.
She was breathtaking in the garden earlier.
And now, because of Lila's careless words, she's wary of me.

My fingers tighten around the phone.

I force myself to exhale slowly before turning my gaze back to Lila. She's still refusing to meet my eyes.

Good.

She should be nervous.

But fear alone isn't enough.

She needs to *understand.*

I lean forward slightly, just enough for her to feel the shift in power. "Lila."

She jumps, her head snapping up, wide eyes locking onto mine.

"It's time you take a long vacation."

She blinks rapidly, like she's not sure she heard me right. "A vacation?"

I nod once.

Her lower lip trembles.

Her eyes shine with unshed tears. "I'm sorry, Mr. Amato, I didn't mean to—"

I lift a hand, a silent command for her to stop talking.

"What you *meant* or didn't mean is irrelevant." My voice is quiet, but the edge in it is sharp enough to slice. "What matters is the damage that's been done."

She opens her mouth, but my stare alone is enough to silence her.

"Vasilisa is my wife, Lila. And it is not your place to scare or confuse her about this household. Or *me.*"

"I-I didn't think—"

"That's right. You didn't."

That cuts through her. I can see the moment it lands.

She shifts in her seat, uncomfortable, her fingers gripping the hem of her skirt like it'll ground her.

For a second, a flicker of guilt tugs at the back of my mind.

But I dismiss it just as fast.

"When I hired you, I made it clear that this job requires *discretion.* Seducing my men for information that doesn't concern you?" I tilt my head slightly. "That tells me you've *forgotten* what discretion means."

She wilts, her entire body caving inward.

"I—I'm really sorry, Mr. Amato," she stammers, voice small.

I study her, the apology hanging heavy between us.

I can see the unspoken plea in her eyes—for mercy, for forgiveness.

I let her sit in it.

With an exasperated sigh, I finally respond.

"I don't need your apology, Lila." My voice cuts sharper than I intended. "Just make sure it doesn't happen again."

She nods so quickly it's almost frantic. "Yes, sir."

I stand, rounding the desk with slow, deliberate steps.

She stiffens when I stop beside her, her fingers twisting together so tightly they turn white.

She knows better than to move.

"And about that vacation," I murmur, looking down at her. "Consider it started."

She blanches, face losing all color, but she doesn't argue.

She just stammers out another weak "Yes, sir."

She scrambles to her feet and nearly bolts from the office.

The door clicks shut behind her.

I sink into my chair, exhaling slowly, and glance at the monitor.

Vasilisa is still in the library.

She's more at ease now, her delicate fingers uncapping tubes of paint, brushing soft strokes across a blank canvas.

Colors blend and swirl beneath her skilled touch, forming something beautiful—something soothing. The sight alone eases the tightness in my chest.

She's a goddess.

Her very soul is like crystalized sapphire held in her eyes.

Vasilisa is everything I am not—pure, kind, good, full of light.

My presence alone could tarnish that. Watching her so focused and calm twists something in my chest.

I want to protect her from the darkness of this world. From the darkness in me.

She dips her brush into a pool of cerulean blue, her fingers wrapped around the handle with quiet precision.

She moves with such ease, such grace, her brush gliding across the canvas like she was born for this.

I don't just see her.

I *feel* her.

She turns her head slightly, eyes flicking toward something off-camera, and I marvel at the sight. The elegant slope of her throat, the delicate curve of her shoulders. My gaze drifts lower, catching the whisper of lace beneath her blouse.

Too many buttons undone.

It would be too easy—too natural, to trail my tongue along the soft curve of her décolletage, to taste the warm skin at the swell of her breasts.

A sudden impulse grips me.

Not just to touch her.

To sit beside her.

To watch her create something out of nothing, to lose myself in the way she paints, she breathes, she exists.

To soak in the peace she radiates and let it settle inside me, even for a moment.

But I know myself. I'd shatter that peace the second I got too close.

A sharp knock on the door pulls me from my thoughts.

"Come in." My voice is rougher than I expect.

Luca steps inside, closing the door behind him.

"You wanted to see me, boss?"

I tear my gaze from the monitor, switching it off. I motion for him to sit.

"Yes. When you gave me your report, was it a *full* report on Vasilisa's romantic relationships?"

Luca's brows furrow as he drops into the chair. "On her relationship with Jude Olsen?"

"Besides him. And that piece of shit, Pietro."

The name leaves a bitter taste in my mouth.

Luca leans forward, quirking an eyebrow. "There was no evidence that there was ever anything between her and Pietro."

"Doubtful." I dismiss it just as fast. "What about others?"

Luca chuckles.

"She's twenty, Santo. How far could she have gone?"

"Plenty of twenty-year-old's are promiscuous."

His amusement deepens. "Since when do you care about promiscuity?"

"When it pertains to my wife."

Luca smirks, leaning back like he's enjoying this.

"We don't do the blood-on-the-sheets thing anymore, so what is this about? Was she not a virgin? Maksim said—"

"Maksim can't even keep his own sister on a leash." The words snap out before I can stop them.

Luca's expression shifts, arms crossing over his chest. For the first time, he actually looks… *displeased*.

"Is that *really* the issue here?"

"No." The irritation coils in my gut. "Go find me what I asked."

I wave a hand in dismissal, expecting him to leave.

But he doesn't move.

"I already have it."

He pulls out his phone, scrolling for a second before glancing up. "There's only one other before Jude. A Logan Doyle. Lives in London now."

I exhale, relieved. "Good. He needs to stay an ocean away."

Luca's eyes widen, his expression flickers between confusion and bemusement. He slips his phone back into his pocket, shaking his head.

"You *like* her."

His voice is quiet, careful, like he's testing the words out loud.

I frown, my fingers drumming irritably against the desk.

"This isn't about liking her, Luca." The denial is swift, firm. Even as my conscience whispers otherwise. "This is about keeping my wife safe."

Luca laughs. A low, knowing sound that grates on my nerves.

"I've seen how you are with women, Santo. This is different."

He leans forward, his smirk growing. "You don't care about their pasts. Hell, half the time you don't even ask their names."

His smirk deepens.

"But with *Vasilisa?* You want to know every man who's touched her. *You're jealous.*"

The accusation lands; sharp, unyielding. My throat tightens, heat rising up my neck before I can shut it down.

"That's—that's ridiculous."

Luca grins.

He pushes up from his chair, his gaze unwavering as he places a firm hand on my shoulder.

"Remember who you're talking to, Santo." His voice shifts, lower, knowing. "I've known you all my life."

My jaw ticks.

"And have you ever known me to be jealous?"

Luca's grin widens.

"That's just it." He slaps my shoulder lightly before heading for the door. "No one's ever known you to be this human before."

The click of the door locking is the last sound before silence swallows the room whole.

Luca's words claw at the edges of my thoughts, sinking in deeper than I want them to.

Jealous.

I clench my fists. This isn't about jealousy.

It's about control. *Security.*

Keeping what's mine untouched.

It's about making sure the ghosts of Vasilisa's past stay exactly that—*ghosts.*

But the thought of her with someone else, of another man's hands on her, another man knowing the softness of her sighs, curls inside me like a sickness I can't shake.

I need to ask her.

Or it will fester.

I push to my feet, stride out of the office, the door slamming shut behind me. The halls of the estate are quiet, dimly lit, the marble floors clicking under each measured step.

Everything is too calm. That stillness before a storm.

At the library doors, I pause.

A hesitation I don't recognize roots me in place.

She doesn't belong to anyone else. *But does she even belong to me?*

I exhale, knocking once.

"Vasilisa?" My voice softer than I mean for it to be.

A beat of silence.

Then the door cracks open, and she stands before me. Paint smudged on delicate fingers.

A messy bun barely holding up golden strands, some slipping loose to frame her face.

She smiles—small, tentative, but so fucking sweet it knocks the breath out of me.

"Santo," she peeps my name, like it's something forbidden; *something dangerous.*

I open my mouth, the question burning on my tongue, but I can't ask it.

I can't ruin this.

"I came…" I start, but the words die on my tongue. She watches me, patient, waiting, eyes full of something I can't name.

I force myself to swallow the truth, pushing past the ache that settles low in my chest.

"I—I came to see your painting."

A lie. A terrible one.

Surprise flickers across her face before she smooths it over with a soft, amused smile.

She doesn't call me on it. Instead, she steps aside, allowing me in.

She leads me to her canvas, and I don't know what I was expecting, but it sure as hell wasn't this.

The blues melt into greens, soft brushstrokes blending so effortlessly it looks almost alive.

Dabs of white scatter like distant stars, pulling the whole piece together like a dream you can't quite hold onto.

I stare, caught in it—in her.

Then, I feel it.

The warmth of her hand slipping into mine.

I look down, startled by the delicate fingers threading through my own, paint-streaked and small, like she's always meant to fit there.

"Do you like it?" Her voice is barely above a whisper.

I can't answer.

Not when my chest feels too tight. Not when my grip on her instinctively tightens, like I might never let go.

Not when I know, in a matter of days, moments, breaths, she's already more than I can afford her to be.

Not when I know I will keep her.

No man—not her past, not her future, not even fucking fate—will take her from me.

"Vasilisa..." I murmur, turning to her, and *fuck*—she's looking at me like I'm something gentle.

She blinks, waiting. Expectant. Wide-eyed.

The air thickens between us, charged with something untamed.

Finally, I force out the only answer I can manage.

"Yes."

I lift my free hand, brushing a stray strand of hair behind her ear, fingertips grazing soft skin.

"I love it."

But the truth hangs unspoken between us, thick and inescapable.

It's not the art that has me ruined.

It's the artist.

We stand in silence, caught in the moment. Something flickers in her eyes, uncertainty or something deeper.

Then, softly, she speaks.

"Is Lila in a lot of trouble?"

She hesitates. "I didn't want—"

"No." I cut her off before she can worry. "She's truly on vacation. Her job will be here when she returns."

Vasilisa searches my face, then offers a small nod before looking back at her painting.

"Can you guess what it's going to be?"

I peer at the twilight sky she's crafted, the glow of streetlights framing what looks like an overhead view of a familiar place.

And then it clicks.

"La Serenata?"

She beams.

"Yes. Our first date."

She's painting that night.

The memory rushes back, unbidden. The ambiance of La Serenata, the rich scent of wine and candle wax, the way her emerald dress clung to her frame, molding to every delicate curve.

"You're painting that night?" My voice comes out lower than I intend.

She nods, her fingers tracing the edge of the canvas. "I wanted to capture our story."

Biting her lip, a light blush stains her cheeks, her gorgeous eyes shining with something vulnerable.

I can't take it.
I reach out, hooking my thumb under her lip, freeing it from her teeth.
She stills, her breath catching, but I don't stop.
My thumb trails along her cheek, memorizing the warmth of her skin.
She's flushed. Paint everywhere.
Pure. Beautiful. Mine.
A hunger pulses inside me.
I cup the back of her neck, fingers threading into the loose tendrils of her hair, and pull her in.
Her lips part in surprise, but I don't give her time to second-guess it.
I capture her mouth, taking what I crave.
She gasps against me, gripping my shirt as I deepen the kiss, swallowing the soft, sweet moan that slips past her lips.
I freeze.
I need to stop.
Pulling back, I rest my forehead against hers, breathing her in.
"May I have it?" I murmur, my voice rough, still inches from her mouth.
Her eyes flutter open, dazed. Confused. *Wanting.*
"Have what?" she whispers, her gaze dropping to my lips.
I step back, before I take more than I should, shifting toward the painting.
"May I have the painting when you're done?"
She blinks. "You want me to gift it to you?"
"I could buy it if you'd like."
Her lips twitch, amusement flickering in her expression as she traces the edges of the canvas.
"Where would you put it?"
I don't hesitate. "In my office."
She tilts her head, considering, a shy smile playing on her lips. "Next to the *Monet?* I don't think so."
She giggles. And *fuck*—the sound grips something inside me, twisting it tight.
"Why not? You're just as talented."
I slip my hands into my pockets, fighting the urge to pull her back into me.
"I am not," she huffs, still smiling, still intoxicating. "But I'll still give you the painting."
Her tongue swipes across her bottom lip, and I know I need to leave before I kiss her again.
I nod, stepping back.
Creating *space.*

"Dinner is in twenty minutes. I'll take mine in the office."

She frowns, confused, searching my face, but doesn't push.

I make it to the door before pausing, glancing over my shoulder.

"Tomorrow morning, my men will be here." My eyes flick to the lace peeking from her blouse, the teasing dip of her neckline.

A smirk tugs at my lips. "Wear something more… appropriate."

Her cheeks flush. She chuckles, nervous, but she nods.

And before I can stop myself, before I can do something reckless, I steal one last look at her.

Then I shut the door behind me and head to my office, where I can be alone with my thoughts of her.

CHAPTER 21

VASILISA

The house is a flurry of activity in the morning, just like Santo said it would be.

Men move with quiet efficiency; nods replacing greetings, eye contact kept to a minimum.

The tension is thick, the air humming with unspoken rules.

I try to play the part of the perfect wife, but every room I step into empties just as quickly.

And to make it worse, my husband is nowhere to be found, while his brother, *Angelo,* lingers.

I avoid him just like everyone else avoids me.

It's not that I'm incapable of introducing myself, but by the time afternoon rolls around, I'm drained.

The constant movement, the sharp glances, the unspoken weight of my presence—it's too much.

I need to escape.

I slip outside and lay down on the bench beneath the shade of the magnolia trees.

The air is warm, thick with the scent of flowers, and for the first time today, I let myself breathe.

I close my eyes.

It doesn't last long.

A shadow falls over me, pulling me from my moment of peace.

My eyes snap open, and I'm met with the sight of a young man.

Sunlight catches in his light brown hair, forming a halo around his head. There's a small scar at his jaw, at odds with the easy smile that disarms me instantly.

I scramble to sit up, smoothing my dress down my thighs, forcing a polite smile.

"Is this spot taken?" he asks, nodding toward the bench.

I shake my head, shifting over.

"No, please. Sit."

"I'm Romeo Romero," he introduces himself, offering his hand.

"Vasilisa."

I take it, his grip firm but careful.

For a while, we sit in silence. It's comfortable, something I didn't realize I was craving.

Then a voice shatters the peace.

"Romero."

The warmth in Romeo's face disappears as he stiffens and rises to his feet.

His eyes meet Angelo's.

"Don Amato." His nod is respectful, but the tension in his jaw betrays him.

Angelo barely acknowledges him, his sharp gaze fixed on me.

"Vasilisa," he greets, voice cold. His eyes flick down, assessing me.

I know that look, scanning for any hint of impropriety.

I swallow hard.

"Don Amato," I say, forcing my voice steady.

He studies me for another beat before shifting his attention back to Romeo.

His lips curl into something that isn't quite a smile. "I hope Romero isn't bothering you."

A veiled threat. A *reminder*.

"He's been very kind," I answer quickly, trying to keep whatever this is from escalating.

Romeo shoots me a brief appreciative glance before straightening.

"You're needed inside, Romero," Angelo says coolly. "Santo's looking for you."

A flicker of something dark crosses Romeo's face. But he nods and heads toward the house, leaving me alone.

With him.

"Are you settling in?" Angelo asks, his voice still icy.

"Yes," I manage, my fingers curling into the fabric of my skirt, as if that will ground me.

Angelo starts pacing, hands clasped behind his back.

His movements are too measured, like a predator circling prey.

I keep my gaze trained on him, hoping, *praying*, for someone to walk outside, to interrupt whatever this is.

"Maksim speaks highly of you, Piccola." His gaze locks onto mine, unblinking. "You don't want to tarnish that reputation."

My heart pounds.

"I have no intention to," I say quickly, trying to sound confident.

Trying to sound like I belong here.

Angelo smirks, apparently not convinced by my assurance. He opens his mouth to say something else when the sound of footsteps approaching cuts through the moment.

We both turn toward the noise.

Santo.

"Angelo," he greets curtly, skipping any formalities. His gaze moves to me and softens, just slightly. "Vasilisa."

"I was just leaving," Angelo says smoothly. With one last look, something between a warning and amusement, he strides away, leaving us alone in the thick silence of the garden.

Santo watches him go before turning back to me.

"You okay?" His voice is softer now, tinged with something that almost sounds like concern.

I nod, offering a small smile. "I'm fine."

His gaze dips lower, lingering just long enough for me to feel it.

I shift slightly, and the lace tops of my stockings peek out beneath the hem of my black turtleneck dress.

Santo notices.

His jaw tightens. His expression doesn't change, but his eyes darken, just enough to betray his thoughts.

"I have a meeting to get to," he says finally, his tone quieter than usual, as if he's reluctant to go.

"When will you be back?" I ask before I can stop myself.

"Late."

His voice softens. "But I'll try to make it before midnight."

A flicker of disappointment stirs in my chest, but I push it down with a smile.

"That's okay."

He extends a hand to help me to my feet.

His fingers linger on mine. I expect him to let go once we're inside, but instead, he stops near the base of the stairs.

"You've covered up more today," he says, his gaze dragging over me again, settling on the high neckline of my dress before dropping to my legs.

"But now you've left those on display instead."

I glance down, suddenly self-conscious under his scrutiny.

"They really can't be all that distracting, my legs are very short," I say quickly, brushing off his comment, trying to lighten the tension.

His lips twitch, his gaze unwavering.

"They're also very *mine.*"

The words wrap around me, leaving me momentarily stunned.

My heart flutters.

Before I can say anything, he takes a step back. "I'll see you tonight, Vasilisa."

Then he's gone, heading for the front door.

I stand there for a beat, pulling in a slow breath, steadying myself, before finally moving toward the kitchen in search of a snack.

Julian is at the sink, washing dishes.

He looks up when I enter, flashing me an easy smile.

"Need anything, Mrs. Amato?"

"Call me Vasi, please." I wave a hand dismissively. "I just came in for a snack. I can make it myself."

I head toward the pantry, but Julian shakes his head, already drying his hands on a towel.

"Nonsense. I'll whip you up something. What are you craving?"

"Something sweet," I admit, a small grin tugging at my lips.

He chuckles, pulling open a cupboard and rummaging inside. "I think I've got just the thing."

I try to peer over his shoulder, but his broad frame blocks my view.

"Here we go." Julian straightens with a triumphant grin, holding up a small box of cupcakes, their sugary tops gleaming under the kitchen lights.

When my eyes light up, he chuckles. "Santo wouldn't be too pleased if he knew about this stash."

I wink, accepting the box.

"He doesn't need to know." I grab one and immediately take a bite, the sweetness melting on my tongue. "Does he really not allow snacks?"

"He prefers healthy snacks only."

I grimace. "He doesn't know about my sweet tooth yet."

Julian smirks. "Then we won't tell him."

Warmth spreads through me at the thought. Maybe I'm making a friend.

"What's for dinner?"

He raises an eyebrow. "Hungry already? You've got a cupcake in hand."

I laugh. "No, I just wanted to know if I could help."

"You don't have to—"

"I want to learn. Please."

He studies me for a moment, then grins. "Alright then."

He pulls open a drawer and hands me a crisp white apron.

I take it gladly, the cool fabric smooth in my hands. "What are we making?"

"Spaghetti aglio e olio."

I pause, the words familiar. "Spaghetti, garlic, and oil?"

I slip the apron over my head, tying it securely around my waist.

Julian nods approvingly. "You've been paying attention."

He turns to the counter, where a spread of fresh ingredients awaits—flat-leaf parsley, cloves of garlic, dried chili peppers, and a freshly made spaghetti. "It's a simple dish, but full of flavor."

For the next half hour, we work side by side. Julian shows me how to finely chop the garlic and parsley while he slices the chilies with effortless precision. He walks me through sautéing the ingredients in olive oil, his voice patient and encouraging at every step. The air fills with a mouthwatering aroma, making my stomach growl in anticipation.

As we wait for the water to boil, he hums an unfamiliar tune under his breath, moving around the kitchen with an easy fluidity—like he belongs here.

I watch him, admiring how naturally he handles everything, how at home he seems.

He tosses a pinch of salt into the pot with a little flair, and I giggle.

Once the pasta is cooked, he guides me through the final steps, tossing the noodles into our sizzling mix of olive oil, garlic, and chilies.

A generous sprinkle of parsley and freshly grated parmesan finishes the dish.

Julian plates it up, handing me a fork. "Try it."

I twirl a bite onto my fork and take my first taste. The pasta is perfectly al dente, the flavors bold and balanced—rich olive oil, tangy garlic, the slow burn of chilies, and the freshness of parsley tying it all together.

"This is... amazing." I swallow, unable to hide my delight.

Julian grins. "I had a feeling you'd like it."

We sit down to eat, and soon the rest of the kitchen staff trickles in, joining us for dinner. They're warm and welcoming, chatting with me about the ins and outs of the house, telling stories about Santo and how kind he is to them.

The thought makes my heart warm.

Here in this kitchen, surrounded by easy laughter and acceptance, I feel something I've been missing since arriving.

I feel at home.

CHAPTER 22

SANTO

The reflective glass windows of Beaumont Enterprises gleam against the city skyline, a symbol of wealth built on old money and even older corruption.

The Beaumont brothers—Warren, Wesley, and Wilder, have made a name for themselves off their father's empire, but power is nothing without control. And they don't have nearly as much of it as they think.

I step into the lobby, where Luca and Romeo are already waiting, the latter leaning against the reception desk, grinning shamelessly as he flirts with the woman behind it.

We head toward the elevators, but before we make it inside, the receptionist calls out for us to stop. I don't bother stopping. She can threaten to call security, doesn't matter. I own them.

The elevator ride is smooth, stopping on the seventeenth floor—Warren's favorite number.

The predictable prick.

His predictability is his weakness.

The doors slide open to reveal three security guards waiting.

Men that work for me.

I give them a brief nod, and they step aside.

We move down the hallway toward the glass conference room.

Inside, the Beaumont brothers sit in mid-conversation, laptops open, papers scattered across the sleek glass table.

The moment they see me, the air tightens.

Warren is the first to react.

"What the hell are you doing here, Amato?" he seethes, already bristling.

I smile, slow and sharp, watching his discomfort flicker beneath his anger. "Is that any way to greet an old friend?" My voice drips with mockery.

"You're far from a friend." Warren sits back, smoothing his Armani lapel. "What do you want?"

Luca and Romeo take opposite stances in the room as I address War directly.

"I want a building," I say simply. "And I hear you're not willing to budge."

Warren sneers.

Beside him, Wesley is already typing away on his laptop. "You want the Parker building," Wesley states, eyes still on the screen. "East side. Right in the middle of Maksim's territory."

"That's the one," I smirk, pointing at Wesley. "Gold star for you." My tone is sarcastic, but my eyes stay serious and alert.

Warren scoffs, crossing his arms. "Not giving it up. Especially after your little alliance with Korsakov. I'm not handing that bastard a damn thing."

There it is. *His real problem.*

I tilt my head, faux concern lacing my tone. "Still caught up in your little pissing contest with Maks?" I click my tongue. "Pathetic."

His jaw clenches. "Yet your brother's still kissing his ass, even going so far as to give you a bride," he bites out. "How is she, by the way? Vasilisa, right?"

My blood turns lethal in an instant.

The air in the room thickens. I don't react. I don't flinch. I don't let him see how much that name—*her name*—twists a knife in my ribs.

I just smile. A dangerous, warning kind of smile. "You don't ever say her name."

Warren smirks. Wilder chuckles. Wesley keeps typing.

Then Warren leans forward, eyes glinting. "Would be a shame if something happened to her. Like your—"

Click.

The sound of Luca's gun cocking cuts through the air.

Wesley's fingers freeze on the keyboard. Wilder lifts his hands in surrender, his smirk vanishing.

Even Warren, for all his bravado, flickers with hesitation.

I raise a hand.

Luca stands down.

I move. Crossing the room in two slow steps.

I lean over the glass table, grab Warren by his tie, and yank him forward until our noses nearly touch.

My voice is low.

"If you so much as utter another word about my wife, I will slit your throat—" I pull him closer, until I can feel his shaky exhale against my skin, "—and fuck her in your blood."

The room is deathly silent.

I shove him back.

Hard.

His chair nearly tips over, his hands gripping the edge of the table to keep himself steady.

Luca and Romeo move beside me as I turn toward the door.

We're done here.

But just before I step out, I glance back, watching Warren try to shake off his rattled expression.

I smirk.

"Oh, and tell Mandy I'll be seeing her soon." I add casually mentioning his sister.

Warren stiffens. His mask cracks; just a little.

And I savor every second of it.

We make our way to the elevator, the doors chime open before I even have a chance to press the button.

Surprised, I see Olivia Baker standing there, her eyes widening when she meets mine.

A moment of confusion flickers across her face before she mutters, "Did I come into the wrong building?"

Without a word, Luca, Romeo, and I step into the elevator as Olivia slips out.

Outside of the building, my phone buzzes—Angelo's name flashing across the screen.

I answer. "The meeting was a bust—"

"Meet me at the penthouse. Maksim's here." His tone sharp. The line goes dead before I can respond.

I exchange a glance with Luca and Romeo.

We move.

★★★

The elevator opens directly into Angelo's meticulously curated world.

Black and maroon décor, stark white walls; everything placed with a precision that reflects the man himself. It's sleek, controlled, calculated.

Much like my brother.

Maksim is sprawled on one of Angelo's plush sofas, a glass of whiskey balanced lazily on his knee. He looks up as we enter, his brows pulling together, his mouth set in a grim line.

With his ridiculous colorful hair, he almost looks like a sad clown.

Across the room, Nico and Vaska sit in silence, their expressions giving nothing away, their posture is stiff, their eyes sharp, assessing.

"Finally." Maksim exhales, standing to greet me. "Let's get down to business."

His gaze flicks from me to Luca and Romeo, giving each of them a respectful nod before clasping my hand in a firm shake.

Then, his grin sharpens, and with a heavy clap to my back, he adds, "Sorry for taking you away from your honeymoon, but I'm sure Kisa doesn't mind the break."

He winks.

Heat spikes in my chest. My jaw tightens before I force the anger down.

He turns, and we follow him to Angelo's dining room, where my brother sits at the head of the table.

Nico drops into the seat beside him, Vaska flanks Maksim. Scattered across the table are photographs—Gabriel Kaya and his men. A few shots of Katya and Elena.

I grab a picture of my sister, snapped as she walks past a grocery store, Riot beside her.

My grip tightens around the edges. "Where did you get this?"

"That was found in the apartment of the man who tried to take your sister," Maksim says before sliding another photo across the table. Katya. Outside Maksim's casino. "This one was with the man who tried to take *my* sister.

They're watching us.

Tracking us.

"I need to know every move they make before they even think about making it. That's where you come in."

"You want my men on surveillance. Easy enough." I study a picture of Gabriel Kaya, the Turkish bastard responsible for the attempted abductions.

He wants our attention. Now he has it.

Maksim leans forward, his expression carved from ice.

"Make sure it's easy. I want every detail—his men, his movements, his family. If he so much as fucking breathes wrong, I want to know before he does. And then, I want him delivered to me. *Alive.*"

The rage in his voice is barely leashed.

"What has you gunning this hard? We've known about Kaya for weeks."

Maksim's jaw ticks. "One of his men tried to rob my casino. Held one of my girls at gunpoint. Vaska handled the accomplice, but the bastard ran off with my money. Kaya managed to slip someone into my hired security team. That will *never* happen again."

I nod. "Consider it handled."

Beside him, Vaska runs a knife over a handkerchief, his movements slow and methodical.

"I gutted that accomplice like a fish. Sliced through him like butter. And I'll find the other one too."

His voice is low, almost bored, but the gleam in his eyes says otherwise.

"No doubt about that," Maksim mutters.

Angelo leans back in his chair, flicking a glance between Maksim and Vaska. "How many men do you need to lock down your territory?"

"Half. I want double the protection. Katya has six men on her at all times." Maksim exhales sharply.

Angelo nods. "Elena's coming home in a couple of months. Until then, I may have to put more men on her."

I pull out my phone as the conversation continues, bringing up my security feed. I rewind, backtracking to what Vasilisa was doing while I was gone.

The screen shows her in the kitchen.

Cooking.

With *Julian.*

Something sharp and ugly twists in my gut.

She's laughing, her eyes warm.

Too warm.

Warm in a way that should be reserved for me and me alone.

A simmering rage starts low. My jaw clenches as I fast-forward the footage.

The scene shifts—she's sitting with the kitchen staff, sharing a meal.

She looks happy. Comfortable. Accepted. The staff is treating her well.

But Julian shouldn't be that close to my wife.

Not if he values his life.

★★★

The master bedroom door is closed but light outlines the door frame.

She's awake.

Waiting.

I exhale past my restraint and push the door open.

The sitting area is empty. The bed, untouched.

The bathroom door is open, the space vacant.

A cold weight drops in my stomach.

She's not here

Panic sets in, sharp and immediate. I turn, striding out of the room and taking the stairs two at a time.

The library—dark. Silent.

My mind races with thoughts of where she could be.

Did she leave?

Was she taken?

While I was busy making plans on how to guard Katya and Elena; *my wife* was alone.

Alone.

Maybe she decided to visit her family, but I didn't leave her with a driver. Thoughts of her in a ride share with a stranger; unguarded, vulnerable, sends a slow, seething burn through my veins. My steps turn heavy, my jaw locking as I reach for my phone. If she's not in this house, I'll mobilize every damn man I have to find her—

Then I hear it.

Soft, steady breathing.

A faint snore.

Relief slams into me so hard my chest aches. I pocket my phone and move toward the sound, stepping into the living room.

I flip on a lamp, its warm glow casting a comforting light over the space.

There she is.

Sprawled across the couch in a silk robe that barely conceals her delicate lace nightgown. Her locks of golden hair spill around her like a halo. Her lips are parted slightly, lashes fluttering like she's caught in a dream.

I exhale, tension easing as I take in the sight. The stress, the fury from earlier—none of it belongs here.

Not with her like this.

I shouldn't have left her alone tonight.

Books are stacked neatly on the coffee table, one left open beside her.

I pause.

The tension in my body giving way to something else.

My intelligent, beautiful wife, up late, lost in literature.

A quiet smile tugs at my lips.

I adore her like this.

I carefully lift her into my arms, cradling her against me, and immediately regret it.

She's *warm,* soft, a breath of silk and lace against my skin.

The scent of her; sweet, intoxicating, seeps into my lungs, curling around something dark inside me, something feral.

Mine.

The thin fabric of her nightgown leaves little to the imagination.

Translucent lace teases over her curves, the swell of her breasts, the dip of her waist. My hands burn where they press against the smooth skin of her thighs, and my cock throbs painfully beneath my slacks.

I grit my teeth, adjusting my hold, forcing my focus elsewhere.

Not now.

Not like this.

She's too light.

The realization creeps in, tightening something in my chest.

A reminder.

A responsibility. I make a mental note; she needs to eat more.

I'll make sure of it.

As I move through the dimly lit house, I glance down at her peaceful face, the faint rise and fall of her breath. My heart aches as much as the rest of me does.

Fuck.

The second I step into her bedroom, the moonlight spills over her, silver illuminating soft skin, casting shadows along the sheets.

It's a vision that brands itself into me, searing through restraint, through the last shred of my self-control.

I lower her carefully, my fingers lingering just a second too long, my gaze trailing over the way she curls up instinctively, pulling the blanket close.

She stirs, a soft sigh slipping past her lips.

My fingers linger on the edge of the bedspread, my mind screaming at me to resist, to turn away.

But it's a losing battle, and with a soft curse I sink onto the edge of the bed.

For long minutes, I sit there, staring at her sleeping form, my heart pounding in my chest, fighting the urge to wake her and taste every inch of her skin.

She whimpers slightly, utterly unaware of the havoc she's wreaking inside me.

I exhale sharply, my fingers digging into the mattress.

She sighs again, a sound so soft, so fucking tempting, that I nearly lose the battle right then and there.

My body vibrates with restraint, my muscles locked with the effort of resisting.

With a quiet curse, I push to my feet. If I stay, I'll lose whatever restraint I have left.

I force myself out of the room, but even as I drag myself to my room, I already know—this won't last.

She's mine.

Locking my bedroom door, I strip down to my boxer briefs and slide into the cold sheets, trying to ignore the ache deep within me.

I squeeze my eyes shut, willing sleep to come, but it's fucking impossible. Because all I see is her.

Vasilisa.

Her smile, teasing and sweet. Her body flush against mine, warm and soft, the scent of her wrapping around me, pulling me under. The way she sighs as I explore her—*slow, deliberate*—like she was made for my hands, for my mouth.

The images drag me deeper, until my dreams become something else entirely.

She's beneath me, her golden hair spilling across my pillow, her body open, taking me so perfectly; tight, dripping, mine.

My cock buried deep inside her, her back arching, nails clawing at my skin as she screams my name. A silent prayer. A desperate plea.

I wake with a strangled groan, my body coiled tight, my breath ragged.

A cold sweat clings to my skin, but the heat inside me won't die down.

My cock is painfully hard, straining against the fabric of my underwear, the ache pulsing deep. I glance at the clock. Six in the morning. No chance of getting back to sleep now.

With a sigh, I push out of bed, the frustration thrumming beneath my skin, and head for the ensuite bathroom. I turn on the shower and step inside.

I let the icy spray rain down on me, hoping it will quench some of the heat building inside me. My hand instinctively travels down to my cock gripping it tightly as I stroke myself. A bead of pre-cum glistens at the tip and I capture it with my fingers, spreading it over my heated crown. The cold water does little to cool me down.

I grab the body wash from its spot on the ledge and pour some into my hand. I spread it over my length, sucking in a breath as the slick glide makes my muscles clench.

I close my eyes, and she's right there.

On her knees.

Her perfect, pouty lips parting as I feed my cock into her mouth, watching as her lips stretch around my girth. Her tongue swirls around the tip, greedy, eager.

Fuck.

My grip tightens, stroking faster as I sink deeper into the fantasy.

Her crystal-blue eyes lock onto mine, filled with adoration, surrender.

One hand fisted in her golden locks, I guide her, force her down my cock, reveling in the way her throat clenches as she takes me too deep.

She gags so fucking beautifully, tears welling at the corners of her eyes as I push her limits.

I curse under my breath, my hips flexing into my hand, chasing the high.

The pleasure builds, coiling hot and tight at the base of my spine.

My breathing is ragged, my body trembling with the force of it.

With one final thrust, I release myself entirely and ropes of thick cum spray against the shower wall.

Her name spills from my lips—a whispered mantra, a vow, a *fucking promise.*

My body shudders through the aftershocks, but the moment the pleasure fades, the ache is still there.

Because she's not here.

CHAPTER 23

VASILISA

I had woken up in my bed, so either I sleep walk or Santo brought me to my room.

Now I sit on a bar stool in the empty kitchen, enjoying a bowl of freshly cut fruit.

The quiet hum of the house surrounds me, a fragile, early-morning peace.

Santo walks in.

He stops abruptly, his sharp gaze locking onto mine.

I drink him in.

He's devastatingly handsome in a three-piece charcoal gray suit, the crisp fabric molding to his powerful frame, his hair immaculate as always.

Every movement, controlled, *effortless*, draws my attention, the flex of his muscles beneath the expensive fabric making it impossible to look away.

"You're up early," he remarks, heading to the fridge.

He grabs a bottle of water, twisting the cap off.

I force myself to look away. "It's seven. I usually wake earlier, but I guess I was tired."

He hums in acknowledgment, his eyes sweeping over me.

I had chosen a light dress for the day, as modest as possible with what Cassandra ordered.

His gaze lingers, meeting my eyes before he gives me a small knowing smile.

"*Ah, that's right.* We have that in common."

He reaches into the fridge again, this time pulling out a protein shake and setting it on the counter.

My fingers tighten around my fork.

"We have quite a few things in common, Santo," I murmur before I can stop myself.

His head tilts slightly. "What's that?"

I shake my head. "Never mind."

His gaze sharpens.

"Thank you for bringing me to bed last night," I say pushing the conversation in a safer direction. "I lost track of time while reading."

His lips curve into a grin, but his eyes remain intense, unreadable. "Not a problem."

The way he says it makes heat creep up my neck.

His gaze shifts, dropping to my bowl.

"You should eat more."

Before I can respond, he steps closer, his scent—spice, musk, something inherently him, wrapping around me.

He leans in, pressing a soft kiss to my cheek.

It's brief.

Barely there, but my skin burns where his lips touch.

Without another word, he strides out of the room, leaving me breathless, sending a spark through me, small, but impossible to ignore.

I want more.

I think back to our wedding night, to the way I had practically thrown myself at him.

Santo promised he wouldn't touch me until I wanted him.

Well, every day, I want him more than I'd like to admit.

With a frustrated sigh, I push the thought away and finish my fruit, rinsing my bowl and placing it in the dishwasher before heading to the library.

I need a distraction.

The first date painting is nearly done.

I could probably finish it tonight, but a new idea is already forming in my head.

Our first kiss.

I grab a fresh canvas, setting it up on the second of the three easels Santo had placed in here for me.

My hands move on instinct, sketching out our silhouettes.

I know the moment I want to capture.

The dresser. My legs wrapped around his waist. My dress unzipped.

Heat creeps up my neck as the memory flashes through my mind.

I trace the lines of his broad shoulders, the tilt of my head as he kissed me, the press of our bodies. Maybe he'd like it for his bedroom.

His bedroom.

The thought irritates me. We should be sharing one.

A throat clears, snapping me from my thoughts. I turn to see Luca standing at the doorway, holding a rectangular box in one hand and a massive bouquet of lilies in the other.

My heart jumps. I rush toward him, reaching for the flowers first.

The bouquet is beautiful—pure white lilies, soft and delicate, nestled among sprigs of baby's breath. The scent is clean, fresh, and unmistakably familiar.

Tucked between the blooms, a small envelope peeks out.

I slide my finger under the seal, pulling out a cream-colored card. A familiar scent clings to the paper—subtle, warm, unmistakable.

Santo's cologne.

'I didn't have time for breakfast, but wanted to make sure your day goes well.'

My fingers trace over his handwriting, my chest tightening with something I don't want to name.

This—*this*—isn't something I expected from him.

Thoughtful.

A soft smile tugs at my lips. "This is beautiful."

Luca nods, setting a rectangular box onto the nearby desk. "Santo wanted me to give you this too. It's your laptop."

I blink. "Seriously?"

The moment the words leave my mouth, excitement takes over.

I gently set the lilies down and hurry to open the box, revealing a sleek silver laptop. My fingers glide over the edges, appreciating the smooth, cold surface.

"It's fully charged, and the charger's in the box," Luca adds, as if reading my mind. "Santo also saved his card onto it, so you can shop online if you need anything."

My cheeks hurt from smiling so hard. I look up at Luca who looks unmoved, almost bored. "Thank you, Luca."

"I'm just the messenger," Luca says leaving me alone with my new gifts.

I grab my phone from where it rests beside my easel and dial Santo. The phone rings twice before his smooth, steady voice answers.

"*Mia Dea.* I take it you received my gift."

Just hearing his voice sends warmth curling through my chest. "I love the lilies—they're gorgeous. Thank you. And the laptop… it's perfect."

There's a small pause.

"The laptop was a necessity. I told you I'd get you one for your classes."

"Yes, but this is more than I expected. It's… a lot. Thank you, Santo."

My voice wavers slightly, the weight of his gesture settling deeper than I meant for it to.

"Only the best for you," he says, like it's the simplest thing in the world. "I have to go. I'll be home by seven tonight."

Before I can respond, the line clicks off.

I sit there in silence, cradling the device in my hands.

A soft sigh escapes me as emotions crash over me.

No one has ever followed through on their promises to me.

But Santo did.

He said I could paint, and now I have an entire room dedicated to it. He said I could go to school, and now it's happening.

I don't think there's anything I could ask for that he wouldn't give me. That realization settles deep in my chest, warm and overwhelming.

Happier than I've been in a long time, I throw myself back into my painting, the scent of lilies filling the air as I work. I fall into my rhythm, brush gliding effortlessly over the canvas, lost in the quiet peace of creating.

My phone buzzes with a text.

Santo

> **Remember to eat lunch Dea.**

It's a simple message, but my heart flutters all the same. I glance at the clock and sigh. He's right, of course. It's already past noon, and I haven't eaten anything since morning.

I make my way downstairs, and into the kitchen where Julian is busy chopping vegetables.

"Hey, Julian," I greet him warmly, then grab an apple from the bowl on the counter. I'm about to leave when my phone buzzes again.

Santo

> **Not just an apple.**

I pause, heat creeping up my neck as I glance around, searching for the camera. I spot it above the kitchen entryway and wave, my lips pressing into a small, amused smile.

Julian chuckles. "Thought you could get away with that?"

I sigh dramatically. "I almost made it."

Shaking his head, he plucks the apple from my hand and replaces it with a plate—a fresh sandwich, crisp vegetables on the side, and a small tub of hummus.

I take a bite, humming in satisfaction as the flavors hit my tongue. "This is really good, thank you."

"Don't thank me," Julian says with pride. "Mr. Amato told me your favorite sandwich. I made the submarine dressing myself."

I pause mid-chew, my heart doing another stupid flip.

"It's perfect," I say, taking another bite, letting the flavors linger.

The thought tugs at me—how does Santo know my favorite sandwich? But then it clicks.

The list.

The detailed file I was given about him before we got married. He must have gotten the same about me.

That realization sparks an idea.

"Julian, what's Santo's favorite meal?"

He barely hesitates. "Carbonara. Why?"

I lower my voice instinctively, hoping the camera won't pick up what I'm about to say. "Santo will be home on time tonight, and I want to make it for him."

Julian's brows lift slightly, but a slow smile spreads across his face. "Sure, we can do that. What time is he coming home?"

"Seven."

He nods, considering. "Meet me back here at four-thirty. That'll give us plenty of time to cook, then you can change and set up the dining room before he gets home."

Excitement flutters in my chest. "Wonderful! Thank you so much, Julian."

I pop my last carrot into the hummus, flash him a grateful smile, and rush off—eager to get back to my painting and to what I hope will be a perfect night.

I spend the next few hours lost in my work, the brushstrokes flowing effortlessly.

Each stroke feels like a step closer to something *real*, something that has weight, something just for me.

The afternoon melts away in a blur of color and motion, my heart light, my mind at ease.

When I finally glance at the clock, my stomach flips. Four-thirty.

I rush to the kitchen, where Julian is already waiting, a grin on his face and an apron in his hands.

"Ready to cook?"

"Yes" I reply, slipping on the apron and rolling up my sleeves, determination and excitement humming beneath my skin.

Julian walks me through each step. We start with the garlic and onions, chopping them finely before they sizzle in olive oil, filling the air with an intoxicating aroma. The pancetta crisps up next, its golden edges curling slightly in the pan. As I whisk eggs with Parmesan, freshly cracked pepper, and a pinch of salt, my hands feel steady—more confident than I expected.

Time flies.

Between playful banter and shared laughter, my nerves settle into something warm, something giddy. By the time we pour the velvety sauce over the perfectly cooked spaghetti and stir in the pancetta, a rush of pride swells in my chest.

I did it!

I made Carbonara for Santo.

I hope he loves it.

With Julian's nod of approval, I set the table carefully, choosing the blue ceramic plates Winnie mentioned were his favorite. The heavy silver cutlery is polished to perfection, the crystal glassware catching the flickering candlelight just right. I step back, taking in the setting, adjusting a candle slightly before exhaling in satisfaction. Everything is going according to plan.

★★★

Choosing my dress takes longer than I anticipated; I want it to be perfect for tonight.

Tonight could be *the* night.

He said when I was willing and I am more than willing.

Finally, I settle on a soft cream-colored silk dress that hugs me, sexy yet elegant; hopefully he will think so.

As seven o'clock inches closer, my stomach flutters.

The scent of Carbonara drifts up from the kitchen, rich and inviting, filling the house with warmth.

Tonight *will* be different everything will be perfect.

I hear the front door opening and my heart flutters in my chest. I hope he can see the want in me and make a move.

I smooth my dress one last time, stealing a glance at my reflection. My skin is flushed, my eyes bright with excitement, with hope.

This is it.

I descend the stairs, my pulse quickening with every step.

Santo steps inside, his sharp gaze sweeping over me. For a second, just a second, I catch something in his eyes.

Surprise.

He notices.

My face warms under his gaze as I reach the last step.

"Welcome home, Santo."

Chapter 24

SANTO

I'm furious.

Red-hot rage claws through my veins, burning, searing, consuming.

But she walks down the stairs.

And just like that, my fury is shackled—momentarily stunned by the sight of her.

That dress clings to her like a second skin, the color a perfect match to her flawless complexion.

My cock hardens instantly, and I shove my hands into my pockets to keep from reaching for her.

She moves toward me with effortless grace, slipping her arm through mine, guiding me to the dining room like she doesn't sense the war raging inside me.

The table is set. The aroma of creamy carbonara fills the space—a scent that should bring me comfort.

Instead, it fuels the fire licking at my insides.

She made this for me.

But she made it with *him*.

The thought sinks its teeth into me, venomous and unshakable.

"Smells good," I force out, dragging my chair back and settling into it.

She smiles, warm and inviting, as if that alone will thaw the ice running through my bloodstream.

With practiced ease, she twirls the spaghetti onto our plates, the candlelight catching in her hair, gilding her in gold. She's too fucking beautiful. Too soft. *Too perfect.*

I grip my fork too tightly as I take my first bite. It's exquisite—just as I knew it would be.

Creamy sauce, crisp pancetta, pasta cooked to absolute perfection. It's the kind of meal that should make a man weak with pleasure.

I groan despite myself.

"I see you like it." She beams, her eyes bright with something dangerous. Hope. Expectation.

I can't stand it.

"Yeah, it's good."

The words scrape out, rough and jagged, betraying the storm inside me.

Her smile falters, barely noticeable, but I see it.

I *feel* it. And I hate myself for it.

We eat in silence, the air thick with unspoken words.

She's waiting for me to say something. To give her something.

I give her nothing.

The only thing I can focus on is the memory of her with him.

The easy way she laughed, the way she touched his arm. *Julian.*

I grit my teeth so hard my jaw aches. The urge to claim her right here, right now, is a vicious, living thing inside me.

If I had my way, I'd bend her over the table, sink into her, and make damn sure there wasn't a single part of her that didn't know who she belongs to.

First time be damned. I wouldn't even care if the staff was here to watch me claim her.

An ugly thought slithers in.

Would it even be her first time?

It never mattered before.

Virginity, purity, all those ridiculous notions were beneath me.

But with her?

The idea of another man having had her—*touching what's mine,* sends a violent fury ripping through my chest.

I laugh under my breath.

It's unhinged. Hollow.

Her voice cuts through the silence, gentle but hesitant. "Did you have a good day?"

"Yeah."

The word is a slap—blunt, short, distant.

She looks down at her plate, hiding the flicker of hurt in her eyes before she speaks again.

"This is your favorite dish, right?"

I glance up at her, my grip tightening around my fork. "Of course."

But I don't taste the food anymore.

All I can taste is the jealousy curdling in my gut, the unbearable possessiveness clawing at my throat.

I'm going to lose my fucking mind.

I shove my chair back, the legs scraping against the floor with a sharp screech.

Her eyes widen as I stand abruptly, my fists clenching at my sides.

I can't do this.

Not when all I want to do is drag her upstairs and show her exactly who she belongs to.

"Excuse me," I say curtly, my voice clipped, betraying the restraint I'm barely holding onto.

She looks up, startled. "Santo?"

"I need to rest."

The lie tastes bitter on my tongue, but I force it out anyway before turning sharply on my heel and stalking toward my office.

The moment I shut the door behind me, darkness swallows me whole.

The controlled façade I wore at dinner shatters as I slam my fist onto the desk with a force that rattles the objects atop it.

A sharp sting explodes through my knuckles, grounding me in something real, something other than the jealousy clawing through my insides like a rabid beast.

I welcome the pain.

It's better than this maddening rage.

Stalking toward the bar, I grab the decanter of whiskey and pour a generous amount into a glass.

The amber liquid gleams under the dim light, swirling like molten gold—deceptively warm, just like the anger simmering beneath my skin.

I throw it back in one go, the burn rushing down my throat, but it does nothing to quench the fire.

The glass clinks heavily as I set it down, my jaw tightening as the silence presses in.

She's just outside this room. Close enough to touch, to pull into my arms.

Close enough to pin beneath me and lose myself in until every thought of any other man is erased from her mind.

Yet she feels untouchable.

Like a mirage—something beautiful and fleeting, something I can't reach without destroying myself in the process.

A soft knock sounds at the door.

"Santo?"

Her voice is quiet, laced with concern.

It spears through me, cutting through the haze of whiskey and jealousy.

I turn, but don't answer. I don't trust myself to.

If I open that door, I'll either say something I regret or fall to my knees for her, and I refuse to do either.

"Santo," she murmurs, her voice impossibly soft.

I hear a faint thud against the door—her hands, perhaps.

She's waiting for me, waiting for an answer I don't have. "What's wrong?"

I close my eyes and exhale through my nose, dragging my fingers through my hair.

My breath is uneven, ragged, but I force out the lie anyway. "I'm just tired."

Silence.

I can feel her hesitation through the damn door, but eventually, she relents. "Okay."

The soft click of her heels echoes through the hallway, fading with each step she takes away from me.

I sink onto the couch, pressing my fingers into the bridge of my nose, willing myself to calm down. To be rational.

But the image of her dances before my closed eyelids; that beautiful dress hugging her body tight, her hair cascading around her shoulders in golden waves and those bright hopeful eyes boring into mine.

How can I stay angry when every fiber of my being yearns for her?

Julian.

I can't fucking kill my chef.

The thought is so ridiculous it almost makes me laugh.

Julian has been nothing but loyal, and I know—*I know*—he did nothing wrong. This jealousy is mine alone.

This vicious, unfamiliar possessiveness is a monster of my own making.

I exhale harshly and pull out my phone, texting Julian.

Take your holiday early. Double pay.

His response is immediate, overflowing with gratitude.

The moment I see his thanks, some of the pressure inside me loosens, just enough to let me think clearly.

I text Mrs. Keen next.

Can you return tomorrow?

As soon as I hit send, my phone rings.

Reluctantly answer.

"What's going on, Santo?" Mrs. Keen's voice is warm but inquisitive.

"My wife wants cooking lessons, so I need you."

The lie slides off my tongue with ease, though it's only half a lie.

The truth is, I just need her here—to make sure Vasilisa eats, to keep her occupied, to fix the mess brewing in my head.

Mrs. Keen hums knowingly.

"Why can't Julian do it?"

There's amusement laced in her tone.

I press my fingers to my temple. "He's starting his vacation tomorrow."

"That's *odd*. He wasn't supposed to leave until I got back."

I exhale, frustrated. "I gave him an early break."

There's a beat of silence before she speaks again, and I can practically hear her disapproval.

"And Lila? Can't she fill in for me?"

"Lila's on vacation too."

I rub my jaw, the weight of my own irrationality pressing against my ribs.

Mrs. Keen laughs softly. "So this new wife of yours has already made an impression on you… and she's made friends you don't approve of?"

Heat creeps up my neck.

My grip tightens around the phone. I don't respond fast enough.

"Can you come back to work early or not?" I snap, my frustration bubbling over.

"*Santo,*" she tsks, pausing just long enough to drag out my irritation.

I grit my teeth. "Please, Amelia."

The moment her first name leaves my mouth, I know I've lost.

A soft chuckle hums through the line.

"Okay sweet boy, I'll be there," she soothes, her motherly nature shining through just like it did when I was young.

My shoulders drop slightly in relief.

"I'll send the private plane for you. First thing in the morning."

Then, in a quieter voice, I confess, "Vasilisa doesn't eat enough."

That, more than anything, earns Mrs. Keen's cooperation. "I'll take care of her, Santo."

When I hang up, the silence is louder than before. The ticking clock. My own measured breaths.

The simmering unease that never truly fades.

I push off the couch and move to my desk, flipping on the monitors. One by one, I scan the security feeds.

She's not in the bedroom.

My fingers tighten around the armrest as I cycle through the cameras.

Then, I find her.

The library.

She's still wearing that damned dress—though now, a smock is tied loosely around her waist, the fabric dusted with paint. Her golden hair is twisted atop her head in a messy knot, wisps falling loose, framing her face.

She's completely absorbed in her work, her expression contorted in deep concentration, her brush gliding effortlessly over the canvas.

Something in my chest tightens.

I watch her.

Because even from a distance, even when I should leave her alone—I can't stop watching her.

The easel is turned just enough to keep the painting hidden from view, a deliberate tease that ignites something restless inside me.

A burning curiosity.

A need.

I want to see it. *I need to see it.*

The desire propels me forward before I can think twice. I leave my office hastily, heading straight for the library.

Fuck knocking, I push open the double doors.

She gasps, startled, her brush slipping from her fingers, a streak of paint splashing against her smock.

"Santo."

My name is barely a breath, a whisper that curls in the air between us.

She doesn't get the chance to say more before I cross the room in long, urgent strides.

My gaze drops to the canvas, and the moment I take it in, my breath catches in my throat.

It's raw. It's beautiful.

It's *us.*

I reach out, my fingers ghosting over the edge of the canvas, drawn in by the emotions she's bared in each brushstroke.

The colors blend into something hauntingly intimate—passion, longing, reverence.

"Is this..." My voice is hoarse, barely above a whisper.

"Our first kiss."

I drag my gaze away from the painting, meeting her eyes.

There's something flickering in them—admiration, maybe, but laced with uncertainty, shyness.

A quiet vulnerability she's offering me in this moment.

My fingers twitch with the need to touch her, to pull her close, to feel what she's painted with my own hands.

Instead, I reach out gently, caressing her cheek.

Her skin is warm, impossibly soft beneath my touch. Her eyes flutter closed for the briefest moment before she meets my gaze again.

"Is this new?" I murmur.

She shrugs, pink blooming across her cheeks. "Yes. I just started it today."

I inhale deeply, allowing her scent to fill my lungs. There's something so familiar about it, so uniquely hers, that it aches inside me.

"I…" The words fail me for a second, my throat tightening. I clear it softly. "It's beautiful. Just like you."

Her lashes flutter, her lips parting slightly as she gazes up at me. She looks so vulnerable standing there, so delicate.

But those eyes—those brilliant, unyielding eyes—reveal a strength that has me reeling.

I swallow hard.

"Why?" The question slips out before I can stop it. "Why paint this?"

"Why do artists ever create, Santo?"

She reaches out, her fingers tracing the contours of the painting—*of us*—with such care it steals the breath from my lungs.

"To express their feelings."

The answer comes automatically, though my own chest tightens at the weight of *what* she's telling me.

A wistful smile tugs at her lips as she nods. She motions to the painting again.

"And these are mine."

Silence stretches between us, filled with something deep, something neither of us wants to break just yet.

My gaze stays on her, on the quiet sincerity in her expression, on the way she's still so open despite everything.

"I'm not tired anymore."

She blinks, caught off guard. "Really?"

I nod, reaching out, sliding my fingers between hers. She doesn't pull away. Instead, she relaxes into my touch, the warmth of her hand settling something restless inside me.

"Really." I search her face, wanting this moment, this truce, to last a little longer. "Why don't we have some dessert?"

She tilts her head, eyes brightening.

"Can we have cupcakes?"

I exhale a quiet chuckle.

She could ask for a whole damn bakery and I'd give it to her.

"We can have whatever you'd like."

I lead her out of the library, her hand still in mine.

The storm inside me quieting.

In the kitchen, she wastes no time raiding Julian's stash of cupcakes, plating one for each of us.

The way she devours hers makes me question how I ever thought she didn't eat enough.

Her delicate fingers hold the cupcake with a care that contradicts the hunger in her movements, and when she hums in satisfaction, something primal stirs in me.

She finishes the last bite, and my gaze catches on the smear of chocolate at the corner of her mouth.

I reach out, my thumb swiping it away. She stills, her breath hitching, her wide eyes locking onto mine.

I glance at the frosting on my thumb before bringing it to her lips.

Her gaze flickers down, hesitant yet intrigued, before she parts her mouth and accepts it.

A gentle suck, her tongue flicking against my skin.

Heat crashes through me like a tidal wave.

I pull my thumb from her mouth, replacing it with my lips, capturing her in a kiss as sweet and sinful as the dessert we'd just devoured.

She gasps but doesn't pull away. Instead, her arms wind around my neck, and I seize the moment, lifting her onto my lap.

The hem of her dress bunches around her thighs, baring her soft skin to my touch.

The warmth of her body against mine is more intoxicating than any liquor. Her lips move impatiently against mine, matching my intensity stroke for stroke.

A low groan escapes me as I deepen the kiss, chasing the lingering sweetness of chocolate from her mouth and replacing it with something far more potent—*us*.

I leave her lips just long enough to trail hot, open-mouthed kisses down her neck, reveling in the soft sighs spilling from her lips.

Her voice—breathy, *desperate*—rings in my ears like a siren's call.

I pull down the strap of her dress as I go, my lips following the exposed skin, lingering at her collarbone, then lower.

She shivers beneath my touch, and when I nip lightly at the soft curve of her cleavage, her fingers tangle in my hair, a gasp breaking free.

The sounds she makes are *mine*, a melody that feeds the insatiable hunger clawing at my gut.

My hands slide up her thighs, fingertips tracing slow, teasing circles over the sensitive skin.

When our eyes meet, hers are dark with unspoken longing, mirroring the storm inside me.

Satisfaction washes over me as I take in the power of desire I hold over this beautiful creature.

My lips continue their assault on her skin, drowning in her, her sounds, her *need*.

"Santo," she pleas, pulling me out of my reverie.

Her voice is strained with desire.

The way she says my name nearly undoes me.

"Yes, Dea?" I murmur, nuzzling the soft skin beneath her ear, breathing her in.

She exhales shakily. "I... I want you."

Her confession is hesitant, as if afraid to voice it aloud.

I stop, pulling back just enough to take her in—the flush painting her cheeks, the way her body sings beneath my touch, the raw anticipation in her eyes.

She bites her lower lip, waiting.

I want to give her everything she wants.

My phone rings.

The shrill sound snaps the moment in half like a blade slicing through silk.

Fuck.

I pull the phone from my pocket, my jaw clenching when I see the name flashing across the screen.

Fucking Maksim.

Vasilisa shifts, the spell broken, and slips off my lap, her gaze downcast as she smooths her dress.

I stand, turning away as I answer the call, frustration curling hot and tight in my chest.

Maksim needs surveillance pulled from one of the docks where a shipment has been intercepted.

By the time I hang up and turn back—she's gone.

★★★

I wake before the light to welcome Mrs. Keen back home.

She joins me in the kitchen, her warm smile and familiar presence instantly soothing the chaos in my mind.

"So, what really happened?" she asks, cutting straight to the chase.

I shake my head, letting out a tired chuckle. "Like I said, Julian went on vacation."

A soft voice chimes in before she can respond.

"Julian's on vacation too?"

Vasilisa enters the kitchen, looking far too radiant for this hour.

She's wearing a flowy short skirt and a soft pink button-down, the color making her look even younger, more untouched—*more mine.*

I brace myself for Mrs. Keen's reaction, but to my relief, she lights up with excitement.

She rushes toward Vasilisa.

"It's so wonderful to finally meet you!" Her enthusiasm is contagious, and Vasilisa reciprocates without hesitation.

They part but still hold onto each other's hands.

"You must be Mrs. Keen," Vasilisa says politely.

"You may call me Amelia," Mrs. Keen corrects, taking her in with approving eyes. "And look at you! Stunning!"

A blush blooms on Vasilisa's cheeks. "Thank you, Amelia."

"I've heard quite a lot about you," Mrs. Keen teases, casting a mischievous glance at me.

I barely conceal a groan.

Here we go.

Vasilisa's gaze flicks to me, curiosity dancing in her eyes. "Is that so?"

I offer a helpless shrug, an apologetic smile playing on my lips. "All good things, I promise."

Mrs. Keen chuckles knowingly and moves toward the counter, pouring coffee into three mugs.

"Would you like some?" she asks.

"Yes, please," Vasilisa answers immediately, then turns to me with a simple smile—so soft, so easy—yet it knots my stomach.

We gather around the island, sipping coffee as Mrs. Keen animatedly recounts her trip to Europe. She describes cobblestone streets and fresh pastries with such vividness that I can almost smell them.

But I'm only half-listening.

Instead, I watch Vasilisa.

The way she laughs at Mrs. Keen's stories. The way she absently traces the rim of her mug when she's deep in thought. The way the morning light catches in her golden hair.

I can't stop looking at her.

"I love her," she says suddenly when Mrs. Keen leaves the room. Her gaze lingers on her half-empty cup, a gentle softness in her voice. "My mother isn't very affectionate, so it's nice to feel wanted by someone."

A pang of something sharp and unwanted lodges in my chest.

"My mother was the opposite," I find myself admitting before I even think about it. "Amelia became a surrogate for us after we lost her."

Vasilisa looks up, her brows furrowing with quiet sympathy. She reaches across, her soft hand settling over mine. A simple touch, but it threatens to melt me.

"I would have loved to have met her."

My throat tightens.

"She would have adored you."

The words slip out on instinct, absolute in their truth.

Her lips part slightly, but before she can say anything, I lift her hand to my lips and press a tender kiss against her knuckles.

She exhales softly, a breathless sound that threatens to ruin me.

I want to stay.

To keep touching her.

To see where this moment could lead.

But I can't.

Not yet.

Reluctantly, I pull away. "I have to go to work."

She nods, a polite smile tugging at her lips.

"I'll see you later," I promise, forcing myself to leave before she captures any more pieces of my heart.

CHAPTER 25

VASILISA

A s the final brushstrokes adorn the canvas, completing the master-piece that is La Serenata, Luca walks into the library.

With a huff, he plops himself down in one of the plush lounge chairs, crossing his arms over his chest and fixing me with an intense gaze.

The colors of the painting seem to come to life in response, dancing and swirling with energy.

My heart races as I await Luca's reaction to my creation, knowing that his intense stare must mean he has an opinion—but instead, I get a furrowed brow.

"Are you alright?" I ask gently.

"Is that La Serenata?" he asks, his gaze still fixed on the painting.

I nod, a small shrug accompanying my reply.

"It's where Santo and I had our first date. Well, our *only* date. The second one was cut short by work."

Luca snorts.

"You're married now. Plenty of dates to be had."

"Is something wrong?" I ask, worried I've done something to upset or offend him.

Luca's jaw tightens.

He exhales sharply through his nose, as if weighing his words.

"There's just a lot going on, and I'm stuck—" He stops himself abruptly, his expression hardening.

I hesitate before offering lightly, "Babysitting me?"

The words leave a guilty taste in my mouth. I know he could be handling other business for Santo instead of being here with me.

Luca presses his lips into a thin line before shaking his head.

"Forget it, I'm sorry." Then, as if resetting, he straightens up in his chair and asks formally, "Do you have anywhere you want to go, Mrs. Amato?"

I chuckle.

"No, *Mr. Cattaneo*, I have nowhere I need to be," I reply in the same formal tone.

A smirk plays across his face, and the tension between us eases.

"How long have you been painting?" he asks.

"I've dabbled on and off all my life, but now, thanks to Santo, I have this."

I gesture around the room with pride.

Luca nods in understanding. "I always thought I'd be good at painting, but I'm shit at most things artistically."

"Would you like to try your hand at it?"

He exhales, tilting his head. "I don't have time for painting."

"Oh, of course not," I tease sardonically. "Too *manly* for such creative endeavors."

Luca shakes his head and chuckles.

"I never said that," he defends with a smirk. "Just... never had the opportunity."

I wipe my paint-smeared hands on a rag and turn to face him, raising a single brow in challenge. "How about now?"

He blinks. Then exhales through his nose. "I'll make a fool of myself."

"Then I'll make a fool of myself with you," I offer.

A moment passes, then he shrugs. "Fine."

I beam and hand him a clean brush, gesturing toward a blank canvas. "Paint something."

Luca hesitates, shifting the brush in his grip like it's foreign to him.

For a moment, I wonder if he'll back out, but then he dips the brush into the paint and slowly brings it to the canvas.

His strokes are rough, hesitant at first, but soon, something shifts.

The lines become more confident, the colors bolder.

We paint in silence.

I steal glances at his work, watching as a landscape takes shape beneath his careful hand—a lake, ducks included. It's simple, but there's something peaceful about it, an unspoken longing captured in the water's stillness.

I smile as I finish up my own painting—a quiet memory of my first kiss with Santo, captured in soft, blended hues.

Luca's painting is *not* what I expected.

With a final stroke of the brush, I sit back and take in his unexpected masterpiece.

The lake is calm, the ducks peaceful, and for a moment, I lose myself in the serenity it exudes.

He catches me looking, and I give him a soft smile.

"You have a talent," I say sincerely, brushing my fingertips lightly over the canvas.

Luca scoffs, shaking his head. "Well, I had a really great teacher."

I laugh wholeheartedly. "I sense sarcasm there."

"No, no sarcasm involved. Just stating facts."

He chuckles, and the camaraderie between us feels surprisingly easy. "Thanks for encouraging me to paint. I've never done anything like this before."

"Sometimes we need someone to push us to do things we wouldn't normally do." I pause before adding, "Even if it's uncomfortable or scary at first."

I glance back at my own painting, thinking about how nice it was to share this moment with someone.

An idea sparks.

"We should paint together more often," I suggest casually.

Luca exhales a short laugh.

"I won't have the time. Eventually, Santo will find someone else to—" He cuts himself off, jaw tightening.

"To babysit me?" I finish for him, my voice soft, without accusation.

Luca opens his mouth, guilt flickering across his features, but before he can say anything, my phone rings.

His eyebrows shoot up in surprise. "Damn it, if that's him, tell him I was only joking."

I glance at the screen flashing Mimi across it.

"It's not him," I smirk, "But it wouldn't matter what I say. He can hear us in here."

I gesture toward the security cameras hanging in the room.

Luca groans, running a hand down his face.

I chuckle, lifting the phone to my ear.

The moment I answer, Mimi's tearful voice crackles through the speaker.

My stomach drops.

"What's wrong?" I ask, my grip tightening around the phone as I try to steady my voice.

"Our parents are sending me to Andras Academy!" Mimi wails, her voice thick with sadness and fear.

I freeze. The name alone makes my chest tighten.

Andras Academy.

A school infamous for its rigid structure, designed to shape syndicate heirs like weapons from a forge.

My parents had once threatened to send me there—worse, they wanted me to attend *Cambion*, the university it feeds into. But I had managed to escape that fate.

Mimi, it seems, has not.

"What? Why? When?" My thoughts tumble into a chaotic swirl.

"Today," she blubbers between gasps for air. "They left for France this morning, and Pietro is taking me to the airport."

France?

My brows knit together. "Why on earth would they go to France?"

"Who's in France?" Luca's voice cuts in, sharp with curiosity.

"My parents," I reply distractedly, barely processing the question as my mind spins.

Mimi sniffles. "Who are you talking to?"

"Luca's here," I tell her, my eyes flicking toward him.

"LUCA?!" Mimi shrieks, her voice cracking through the phone like a whip. "Oh God, I'll never be able to date him now that I'm gone!"

She dissolves into another round of sobs. I pull the phone away from my ear, grimacing at the volume.

Across from me, Luca looks horrified.

His eyes widen as he mouths, *Date me?,* like the very concept has just shattered his universe.

I suppress a sigh. "Mimi, I don't think that was going to happen for you anyway."

Luca scoffs, shaking his head in silent agreement.

"Please focus," I urge. "Did Mama say anything to you?"

"No," she replies quietly, her voice muffled by her tears.

Then, softer, "Oh, Pietro's here." A sharp inhale, then another hiccupping sob. "I have to go. I'll send you letters. You have to write to me, or I'll go insane."

Her final words echo as the call cuts off.

I lower the phone slowly, staring at it as if it holds answers I'll never find. The unease festering in my chest deepens.

None of this makes sense.

"They never mentioned a trip." My voice is quiet, more to myself than anyone else. "And they *definitely* haven't talked about Andras Academy since I was in high school."

Luca watches me, his usual sharpness now tinged with something more thoughtful.

"That's strange," he admits, arms folding across his chest. "I'll talk to Santo, see if Maksim knows anything."

I nod, grateful. Luca won't let this go unanswered.

I'm left alone with my thoughts. My art. The silence.

The weight in my chest lingers, my thoughts still tangled with worry for Mimi, but I remind myself—Luca will tell Santo.

Santo will ask Maksim.

Things will be okay.

Slowly, my gaze drifts back to my painting.

La Serenata.

The memory of our first date immortalized in bold colors and soft brushstrokes. The tension in my shoulders eases, just a little.

Tonight, I'll present it to Santo. *Maybe, just maybe,* I can convince him to have dinner with me again.

And this time, I hope we'll actually get to finish it.

The way he kissed my hand this morning, the tender way he caressed my cheek, the lilies, the laptop—each gesture lingers in my mind, weaving together into something undeniable. I want to be his wife in *every sense of the word.* I want him.

I should ask Amelia to help me make another one of Santo's favorite dishes and make tonight special.

Leaving the library, I descend the stairs and make my way to the kitchen, passing a few staff members along the way.

They smile and greet me warmly, their kindness wrapping around me like a comforting embrace. I've been accepted. *I belong here.* It feels like home.

All that's left is to get my fairy-tale ending with Santo.

Amelia beams the moment I step into the kitchen, her hands dusted with flour as she kneads a ball of dough.

"Vasilisa!" she exclaims brightly. "What brings you here?"

"I want to cook dinner tonight," I explain, keeping my voice steady even as thoughts of Mimi and our parents try to creep back in.

Not now.

Tonight is for Santo.

Amelia wipes her hands on her apron, giving me a knowing look. "Are you planning on seducing Santo with good food?"

Heat rushes to my cheeks. I lower my gaze, but I nod.

"What else does he like besides Carbonara?"

She laughs heartily, shaking her head.

"There wasn't much that boy didn't eat growing up," she says, her voice laced with affection. "But another favorite of his is lasagna."

Relief washes over me.

"I can make that."

A plan begins to take shape in my mind.

"Very well, then. Let's get you the ingredients," Amelia says, moving toward the cupboards.

The afternoon is spent surrounded by warmth—flour-dusted counters, the rich aroma of simmering sauce, and Amelia's infectious laughter filling the air.

Despite the lingering tension from Mimi's call, I find myself relaxing, allowing the present moment to wrap around me like a soft cocoon.

By evening, the meal is ready—an elaborate spread, fit for a king.

I take a deep breath and adjust the thin straps of my short black dress.

Tonight, modesty be damned.

My fingers brush over my bare skin, a shiver trailing in their wake as I pick up La Serenata, holding the painting close to my chest.

Tonight will be different!

I wait for Santo.

I take in the dining room, ensuring everything is perfect—the soft flicker of candlelight, the delicate arrangement of silverware, the deep red wine shimmering in crystal glasses.

Tonight has to be perfect.

Then, I hear it—the front door opening and closing. My heart leaps, but instead of approaching, his heavy footsteps retreat.

I hesitate for only a second before grabbing my painting and rushing after him.

No. Not tonight.

Not when I've done everything to make this special.

"Santo," I call, my voice hopeful, desperate to catch his attention.

He turns his head slightly, acknowledging me, but keeps walking, his long strides carrying him swiftly down the hall.

I quicken my pace, my heels clacking against the polished floor, the canvas awkward and cumbersome in my arms.

"I made dinner," I say, breathless.

"I'll take some in my study when I can."

My heart sinks.

His words hit like a slap—distant, dismissive, uninterested.

I grip the canvas tighter, willing myself not to falter.

"I made lasagna," I add quickly, my voice wavering. "And I finished the painting for you. I thought we could spend some time together."

Still, he doesn't stop.

I push forward, determined.

I need him to see me.

But just as I nearly reach him, he stops abruptly in front of his office door.

The breath catches in my throat as he presses his thumb against the handle.

A soft beep, the quiet click of the lock disengaging.

Finally, he turns.

His piercing gaze rakes over me, slow and unreadable.

For a second, I swear I see something there—desire? frustration?

My heart jumps, desperate for any sign that he feels what I feel.

Then it shifts, it's gone.

His expression *hardens,* Like a mask slipping into place, eyes turning sharp, detached, *cold.*

A blush creeps up my neck beneath his scrutiny, but it no longer feels like warmth.

It feels like *exposure.* Like I've laid myself bare, only for him to turn away.

Without a word, he takes the painting from my arms.

He steps inside, turning toward me slightly.

"If you're looking to spend time with someone, call Luca."

The door shuts in my face.

The lock clicks.

I stand there, frozen.

Confusion and heartbreak tangle inside me, squeezing my chest so tightly it's hard to breathe.

What just happened?

For a moment, I stay rooted to the spot, hoping—foolishly—that the door will open again.

That he'll realize what he's done.

That he'll come back to me. But the silence stretches, pressing down like a weight.

He's not coming back.

My arms feel empty without the painting.

My body *feels* wrong in the dress I wore just for him.

Slowly, I turn and walk back to the dining room. The candles still flicker. The silverware is still perfectly aligned. The lasagna sits untouched. Everything is exactly as I left it.

Except for me.

Alone.

Rejected.

Once again.

Chapter 26

SANTO

V asilisa was waiting for me.

I've known this all day—saw her nod when Mrs. Keen asked if she was trying to seduce me, the anticipation building inside me like a ticking time bomb.

Every part of me wants to rush to her, to hold her, kiss her, take her, but I can't.

Not now.

I shrug off my jacket, tossing it onto the couch, before lowering myself into my chair.

My fingers drum rhythmically against the polished wood of my desk, my eyes landing on the painting she gave me—La Serenata.

The piece is breathtaking, but all I see when I look at it is her.

Vasilisa.

The way she looks at me.

Bright eyes filled with hope.

Then confusion and pain—the same look she wore when I slammed the door in her face.

Fuck.

I watched her today, as I always do.

But this time, I watched her with *Luca.*

Painting.

Since when does that fucker paint?

I've known him my whole life—there's not an artistic bone in his body, but my wife comes around and suddenly he's Van fucking Gogh.

I shake off the sharp sting of jealousy.

Luca is my most trusted man, *my cousin*—he would never cross me.

Still, the image lingers, twisting in my chest like a knife.

I lean back in my chair, rubbing my temples.

My mind wanders back to our interactions over the past few weeks; the stolen glances, soft touches, the taste of her skin on my tongue, the feel of her smooth thighs wrapped around me, her warm light frame on my lap and those lips… those damn lips have been haunting me.

I want her.

But wanting her is dangerous.

She doesn't know who I am.

What I've done.

What I am capable of.

She grew up in this life, but she hasn't seen the violence firsthand.

She hasn't seen me, not the version of me that kills without hesitation, the version that men whisper about in fear.

Not Scythe.

The thought of her looking at me with disgust, the thought of her being *afraid* of me—

It makes my stomach turn.

I run my fingers through my hair, tugging at the strands, trying to ease the pressure building in my skull.

I *need* to see her.

I flick on the monitor, scanning until I find her—alone in her bedroom, sitting on the bed we should be sharing if I wasn't such a fucking idiot.

Her face is in her hands.

For a moment, I think she's crying.

A sharp pang of something ugly and unfamiliar lodges in my chest.

She exhales, straightens, pulls herself together and heads to the bathroom.

I don't have cameras in the bathroom, so all I can do is watch the closed door.

The need to go to her, to fix this, claws at me.

My jaw tightens.

A sharp knock snaps me out of my haze.

I grab my phone to unlock the door.

Luca steps inside.

Jealousy licks at the flames of my rage.

"What do you want?" My voice comes out sharp, unforgiving.

"Report from Maksim," Luca replies sternly, unfazed. "He can't reach Miroslav or Vera. He's called Pietro in for an interrogation."

I lean forward, my jaw tightening. "He thinks Ivanov is involved?"

"Not sure yet," Luca admits. "But the Popovs' sudden departure from the country raises red flags. Maksim has men flying overseas as we speak, but there's a problem."

Luca avoids eye contact. Something very unlike him, it makes my patience snap.

"Just spit it out."

Luca exhales, his fingers flexing at his sides.

"He wants you to question Vasilisa."

I scoff, shaking my head.

"My wife has been here for weeks. I saw the feed this afternoon when her sister called—she was blindsided. That was genuine."

Luca's expression doesn't shift. "Are you sure?"

Something cold slithers through me.

"Are you questioning my ability to know where my wife is and what she's been doing since she arrived in my home?" My voice is low, sharp—a warning.

"No, I'm questioning if you really know her."

My hands curl into fists.

I narrow my eyes. "You're overstepping, Luca."

Luca holds my gaze. "I mean no disrespect. I only want what's best for the family."

I exhale through my nose, forcing myself to stay still.

"And my wife is part of the family."

My voice is measured, dangerous. "If Maksim can't keep his organization in line, that's not *my* concern. My wife is innocent—she doesn't know anything about her parents' affairs."

Luca watches me carefully before giving a slow nod. "I'll relay the message to Maksim."

He turns to leave, his hand reaching for the door when I stop him.

"Luca."

He stops, turning back toward me, his expression unreadable. A question in his eyes.

I hold his gaze. "It's time you take a couple weeks off."

Luca's face falls, but only for a fraction of a second. He schools his features so quickly I almost don't catch it.

Almost.

"And when you return," I continue, "be sure to let me know where your loyalties truly lie."

Luca hesitates. Just for a moment, then he gives a sharp nod and exits without another word.

The door clicks shut, leaving me alone with the storm in my chest. I drag in a breath, but it doesn't settle me. My eyes flick back to the monitor.

Vasilisa.

She's curled up on the bed now—still in that stunning lace dress, her delicate body folded into itself. My chest tightens. I turn up the volume, listening.

A soft sniffle.

I inhale sharply, the sound gutting me.

She's crying.

My jaw clenches, my entire body tensing with the urge to go to her. To pull her into my arms, press my lips against her hair, wipe away every tear, but something holds me back.

Shame.

Not because of what I've done, but because she doesn't know what I am.

She wants a prince.

I will *never* be that.

I drag a shaking hand through my hair, trying to steady myself. My mind flashing back to her beautiful smile, her laughter echoing through the cold walls of my heart, warming them in a way that nothing ever has before.

The thought of that smile fading into *fear*…

The thought of her looking at me like I'm a monster… It's enough to drive me insane.

I stand abruptly, my chair scraping back, my pulse pounding.

I need to tell her.

Not want.

Need.

She has to know she can trust me, she has to know she can rely on me—regardless of who I can be.

Before I can second-guess myself, I stride toward her room. I need her to see me, all of me. Just as I raise my hand to knock, I hear it.

A soft whisper filters through the door.

My stomach twists.

Is she talking to someone?

My protective instinct flares, and I push the door open gently.

I move past the sitting room threshold, my eyes scanning the dim space, then I see her and my heart cracks, she's whispering to *herself*.

Curled up on the bed, hugging a pillow tightly, her eyes shut like she's trying to keep something out.

Something claws at my chest.

This wasn't how this was supposed to go.

I was supposed to tell her.

But looking at her now—small, fragile, hurting, the words die in my throat.

I clear my throat slightly before speaking up, "Vasilisa?"

Her teary eyes snap open, wide with surprise, startled by my sudden presence.

She blinks, trying to process me being here.

Whatever words I had prepared—whatever I thought I was going to say—stick in my throat.

Because she looks so *beautiful*.

Even like this.

Even with tear-stained cheeks and red-rimmed eyes, even with her breaths uneven, she is achingly beautiful.

She wipes at her tears quickly, trying to pull herself together.

"Santo..." Her voice cracks, choking on my name.

She's trying so damn hard to compose herself, to not break, but her efforts are in vain, because another soft, wounded sob escapes her lips.

"Are you alright?" I ask gently, stepping toward her.

She lifts her eyes, blinking at me in confusion, like she doesn't understand why I'm here.

I don't even understand why I am.

She sighs, dropping her gaze.

"I'm just overtired," she lies.

The words cut through me.

I did this.

I upset her so much she's crying so hard she can't breathe properly.

I have reduced her to this.

I am indeed a monster.

I inhale sharply, the weight of my own guilt settling deep in my chest.

"I just came to tell you—" my voice is strained, "that Luca is on assignment elsewhere for a couple of weeks."

She nods quietly, accepting my words without question—without fight.

She doesn't ask why. She doesn't even seem to care.

I brush a loose strand of hair from her face, aching to tell her everything—

Who I am.

What I am.

How I can't fucking breathe without her.

But then I *truly* see it.

The redness of her nose, the slight swelling of her eyes.

The way her light is already dimmed.

Because of me.

I drop my hand.

And instead of telling her the truth, I do her a favor—

I walk away.

As I shut the door, I hear it.

A single, sharp, muffled sob. My chest tightens, my hand clenching into a fist at my side.

I should have stayed.

I should have fixed this.

I should have—

No.

I need to get out of here. I need to leave her be, let her be free. I pull out my phone and call Maksim.

He answers on the first ring.

"My wife doesn't know anything about her father's dealings," I start, my voice clipped.

"You keep her out of it."

Maksim chuckles darkly.

"Fine." He pauses. "Is Scythe interested in a kill?"

I exhale slowly, letting the anger curl around my ribs, a slow-burning fire igniting in my gut.

"Always."

"We're at the warehouse," Maksim informs, ending the call.

I text Romeo and a few of my men, sending them the address before striding outside.

The moment I step into the cool night, I let it happen.

The familiar rush of adrenaline. The slow, suffocating rise of something dark and violent and untamed. I allow the animal within me to surface.

Scythe.

The name that strikes fear into men's hearts, that makes grown men beg.

The name I earned in blood.

★★★

The warehouse looms in the distance, a skeletal ruin swallowed by the night. The scent of oil, blood, and damp concrete lingers in the air, mixing with something thicker—*fear.*

I step through the side entrance, my steps echoing against the hollow floor.

The air is alive with anticipation.

The men are waiting.

I can feel it—the shift in energy, the silent reverence as I enter. For a moment, I let myself relish the weight of it, the rush of adrenaline humming beneath my skin.

This is where Scythe thrives. Before me, two men kneel on the cold concrete, their bodies bound, their faces marred by fear and violence.

Maksim stands off to the side, his calloused hands slick with blood, a sadistic grin plastered across his face.

I don't need to ask what he's done to them.

I already know.

As Scythe, every fiber of my being thirsts for this—the power, the control, the lives hanging in my hands, waiting for me to decide their fate.

But Santo still lingers beneath the surface, restless, aching for something else.

He wants warmth.

He wants to go back home, hold Vasilisa, press her against his chest, whisper reassurances into her hair until she believes them.

He wants to dry her tears, bring back her smile, bask in the light of her presence.

But Scythe does not deal in warmth.

He deals in pain.

I lift my gaze to Maksim, who gestures toward the captives with an easy tilt of his head, his bloody fingers gesturing me closer.

I step forward.

The moment I do, she appears in my mind again; her tears glisten like stars in twilight, reflecting an ocean of emotions so deep it consumes me.

A knot twists in my stomach.

I push it down. I force her away.

These men have information. I will extract it from them.

Maksim steps closer, pressing a blade into my palm.

The metal is cool, familiar, a weight I know well.

"Have at it, Scythe," he mutters, a knowing gleam in his eye. "Make them talk."

I turn the blade over, watching as it catches the dim light, casting jagged shadows across the prisoners' petrified faces.

Maksim has already done his work—the Juggernaut never disappoints.

I stride toward the first captive, who whimpers as I draw the blade along his jaw, his chest rising and falling in frantic terror.

"You know why we're here."

The words slip from my mouth, cold, absolute.

The man's head jerks up and down, frantic, but his voice shakes. "I-I don't know anything!"

I smile.

A grim, lifeless thing.

"That," I say, pleasantly, "is what they all say."

I bring the blade down onto his shoulder. The steel bites through flesh, carving through muscle, and the room erupts with his agonized scream.

The sound bounces off the warehouse walls, swallowed into the night beyond.

A symphony of fear. A chorus of desperation. A song Scythe knows all too well.

The second man stares, terror etched onto his face, but he remains silent.

He wants to be brave.

Bravery has never been a shield against pain. In fact, it's something I enjoy breaking down. Wiping the blade clean on the captive's pants, I turn toward him.

He flinches before I even touch him.

Good.

I lower myself beside him, my voice just a whisper, soft, *menacing.*

"Your turn."

His body tenses, his breath shaky in anticipation, dread or both.

I repeat my previous actions, but this time, I take my time, dragging the blade down his face, watching as blood pools in the jagged line I create.

Pain follows, predictable and sharp, and then, he breaks.

They always do.

The grueling hours roll by as I work my way through various methods of persuasion. Slicing and cauterizing the wounds I make to prolong the necessary torture to get the information we need.

With dawn seeping in through cracks and holes of the warehouse, they finally break–spilling secrets like water from a broken dam. Miroslav's treachery unfolds before us; an unknown deal he made with our enemies, no longer a secret whispered within closed doors.

Maksim lets out a grunt of approval as I clean my blade, preparing to leave.

And then, the shift happens.

My mind returns and all I want is to go home. I want to *hold* Vasilisa, remind her that she is safe. I want to crawl into the warmth of her presence and forget what I just did here.

But Scythe won't allow me reprieve.

He reminds me that it's because of *me* that she cried herself to sleep.

CHAPTER 27

VASILISA

Santo didn't come home last night.

The morning is eerily quiet, the kind of silence that seeps into the bones, heavy and suffocating.

Amelia brought my breakfast to the library, but it sits untouched on my plate, the scent of warm eggs and herbs turning my stomach. I have no appetite.

Not after last night.

Not after the way he *looked* at me.

The memory replays in my mind, sharp and unforgiving—the cold detachment in Santo's eyes, the way he slammed the door in my face, like I had committed some unforgivable crime.

I grip the fork in my hand, my fingers tightening around the cool metal before I drop it, letting it clang against the plate, and return to my painting.

I don't understand him.

When he suggested I spend time with Luca, it felt like a slap in the face.

Like I'm something to be passed off, *discarded.*

But when he came into my room—his touch soft, reverent as he brushed a strand of hair from my face.

Gentle.

Loving.

A stark contrast to the man who had abandoned me just moments before.

Who is my husband, really?

The hot and cold nature of his affections unravel me.

One moment, he looks at me like I am something precious, something *worthy.*

Then the next, he turns away as if I'm a mistake he regrets making.

I don't know which version of him is *real*.

I swallow hard, forcing the lump down my throat, blinking against the sting in my eyes.

I was raised to be a good wife.

Stay silent.

Pay attention.

Be helpful.

Never challenge. Never overshadow.

But with Santo, I had hoped for more.

I had hoped for *kindness.*

For patience.

For something that could, one day, become *love.*

But hope is a dangerous thing, and I fear mine is wasting away.

How long can I keep waiting for a man who holds me close only to push me away again?

How long before I become just another ghost in his life?

My stomach turns again, but this time from anger.

I never signed up to be *bullied* by my own husband.

Our marriage was arranged for the sake of our families, but I'm still a person.

A woman with feelings. And I deserve respect.

I will demand it.

Tonight.

For now, I force my focus elsewhere. I turn back to my painting, dragging my brush across the canvas, finishing the image of our first kiss.

But there's no joy in it.

Not like there was before.

I step back, my arms crossing tightly over my chest. And yet, despite the ache lodged deep in my ribs, I feel pride at its completion.

At least *this* version of us is whole.

At least *this* Santo doesn't turn away from me.

The door to the library creaks open, and my heart stutters, tightening with anxiety.

For a split second, I think it's him.

I *hope* it's him.

But it's not.

Instead, a familiar face appears.

Romeo.

"Hi, Mrs. Amato, I'm assigned to you while Luca is… away," he says with a boyish grin, but his eyes flicker with something uncertain.

I still at his words.

The reminder that Santo *sent* Luca away burns through me, but I don't let it show.

Instead, I force a polite smile and turn back to my brushes.

"Call me Vasi, please. How are you, Romeo?"

"Tired, actually." He stretches, rubbing the back of his neck. "Long night with the boss."

My head snaps toward him.

"You were with Santo?" My curiosity flares before I can contain it.

Romeo hesitates.

"Family business," he answers sheepishly, clearly knowing he's said too much.

I nod, understanding but unsatisfied.

"Where *is* my husband today?" I ask, testing the waters.

He shifts slightly.

"NovaRael. Working on some file or something."

His words are vague. *He knows more.*

Romeo watches me closely as I continue cleaning my brushes. "How old are you?"

I chuckle, raising a brow. "No one ever told you not to ask a lady her age?"

His eyes widen in realization, and he stumbles over an apology.

I laugh, waving him off.

"I'm kidding. I'm twenty. How old are you?"

"Same," he smirks. "Mr. Amato is a lucky guy."

I scoff, rolling my eyes. "Be sure to tell *him* that next time you see him."

"Trouble in paradise?" Romeo probes, his smirk lingering.

I don't answer. Instead, I grab my canvas and stride toward the library doors.

Romeo follows, carefully taking the painting from my hands.

"Be careful, Mrs. Amato," he scolds gently.

That's it.

I throw my hands up, exasperated. "Vasi!"

Romeo chuckles as we make our way down the stairs to my bedroom. When we reach the door, I push it open and step inside—only to realize he hasn't followed me.

Instead, he's standing in the hallway, shifting uneasily.

"Get in here!" I huff, gesturing for him to enter.

He shakes his head. "I can't just walk into the boss's room."

I blink. "Good thing this is my room then."

Still, he doesn't move.

He just grips my canvas tighter, like he's debating running in the other direction.

"Yeah, the room you share with Mr. Amato," Romeo says carefully. "I'd rather not die today."

A sharp, bitter laugh escapes me.

"No, this is *my* room." I gesture toward myself, then motion outside the hall. "Your boss sleeps somewhere over there."

Romeo's mouth opens—then closes. His expression shifts, realization dawning.

"*Separate* rooms?" He stares at me like I've just shattered some sacred truth. "He lets you have separate rooms?"

My laugh is humorless.

"*Lets?*" I echo, arching a brow. "No. He requested it."

Romeo's gaze drags over me, slowly.

"To be away from *you?*" His voice is laced with disbelief.

I force a casual shrug, pretending it doesn't hurt.

Pretending I haven't spent too many nights questioning why.

Like I don't feel the sting of rejection every night when I lie alone, wondering if he regrets marrying me.

He hesitates for a beat longer before finally stepping inside, breaking that invisible line. It's small, but it feels like a win.

"Can you help me put that canvas up there?" I ask, pointing above my bed.

Romeo doesn't argue. "Sure, let me grab some tools."

He disappears for a few minutes before returning with a drill and nails in hand.

With ease, he pulls the bed away from the wall and begins hanging the canvas.

I watch him work, my arms crossing over my chest.

This painting—it's a moment frozen in time.

The first time Santo kissed me.

The moment I thought maybe—*just maybe*—this marriage wouldn't feel like a lifelong cage. But now, the brushstrokes feel like a mockery.

Romeo pushes the bed back and steps beside me, tilting his head as he admires my work. "It's really good," he says genuinely.

I open my mouth to thank him, but his phone rings.

He answers it smoothly.

"Go for Romero." A low rumble crackles through the speaker.

His eyes flick to me.

He says nothing, just ends the call and walks out of the room without a word.

I don't move.

Because I already know. I already know who's calling me next. Sure enough, my phone rings.

Exhaling sharply, I answer tersely. "Yes?"

Santo doesn't waste a second. His voice is a low growl through the phone.

"What was he doing in your room?"

My fingers tighten around the phone.

Not this. Not *again.*

"He was helping me hang my canvas," I reply coolly, my tone clipped, my patience already gone. "Is that a problem, husband?"

Santo doesn't respond to my challenge, but I can feel his disapproval, thick and suffocating even through the phone.

Then it hits me.

My stomach drops.

"Wait—you actually have a camera in my bedroom?"

"I told you I did."

My breath catches.

"In the bathroom, too?" I demand, my incredulity growing.

A beat of silence.

Then, his voice, low and cryptic. "I'm not sure if I want to answer that or not."

A hot, angry pulse rushes through my veins.

"It's a yes or no question, Santo!" My voice rises, frustration spilling over.

Silence.

A dangerous kind of silence.

"Is there a camera in the bathroom?" I demand.

His answer comes fast—sharp, jealousy coiled into every syllable. "If there isn't, will you bring him in *there* instead?"

Enough.

I end the call and toss my phone onto the bed, fuming.

The sheer audacity. The idiotic assumptions. The obsession, *the lack of trust,* the constant surveillance.

I can't *breathe* in this house.

Storming toward the door, I yank it open and nearly crash into Romeo.

"Everything okay?"

"No," I snap, brushing past him. "I want to go out."

Romeo hesitates. "Where to?"

I lower my voice, my eyes flicking toward the shadows in the hallway. "Not here, where all the ears are listening. I'll tell you in the car."

His hand immediately goes for his phone, but before he can even dial, I snatch it from his grasp and bolt down the stairs.

"Mrs. Amato!" Romeo chases after me, panic rising in his voice. "I need that back, seriously, you can't—"

I stop abruptly at the front door, spinning on my heel to face him.

My grip on his phone tightens.

"Are you going to *hurt* me to get it back?"

The desperation in his eyes is almost comical. "No! Never! You're the boss's wife. He would *kill* me."

I lift my chin. "Then I'm keeping it."

Romeo groans in resignation as I stride out of the house. His phone starts ringing—*again and again,* but I don't even look at it. I power it off and tuck it behind me.

Romeo exhales sharply, rubbing his temples before yanking his keys from his pocket and unlocking the door to the SUV out front.

"You know he's going to be *furious* right?"

I slide into the passenger seat, cross my arms, and glare ahead.

"Oh well. I want ice cream."

I know Santo will have a conniption about Romeo's phone being off and me leaving the house, but today is worth it.

★★★

Romeo Romero is far too kind to work for Cosa Nostra. His easy smile and carefree attitude provide a welcome break from the tense atmosphere of our household and Santo's watchful eye.

It feels good to be out and about, the warm sun on my skin and the fresh breeze in my hair.

After we got vanilla chip ice cream for me and rocky road for him, we climbed into the SUV and I make one final request—to go grocery shopping.

Romeo pauses mid-lick of his cone to study me with curious eyes.

"Julian or Mrs. Keen usually handles the grocery order, you don't have to do it yourself. Just let them know what you need."

He starts the engine while still holding his half-eaten cone.

"But doesn't Santo have final say in what gets ordered?"

"Oh, he definitely does. But do you think he would deny you anything you want?" Romeo scoffs.

I shrug, taking another bite of my cone. "Well, what I want might not be to his taste."

"What do you mean?"

"Chips, cookies, snack cakes...you know, treats."

"Ah, junk food. Yeah, Boss isn't known for keeping those around the house." Romeo chuckles.

"So can we please go?" I plead, flashing him my most persuasive puppy-dog eyes. "I'll owe you forever."

Romeo shakes his head with a small smile. "Can I have my phone back?"

"After we finish shopping," I counter playfully. "Consider it an incentive."

My trip to the grocery store takes nearly an hour, as I carefully select all my favorite treats and indulgences. Among them is a tube of cookie dough—perfect for those moments when I can't wait for Amelia to make it from scratch.

Making our way back home, Romeo asks for his phone again, and I reluctantly hand it over.

To my dismay, he connects it to the car, turns it on, and a moment later, an incoming call lights up the dashboard.

My heart sinks as I recognize the name on the screen.

Santo.

Still, I hold out hope that Romeo won't answer.

But my hopes are dashed when I hear Santo's voice filling the car.

"Romero."

Santo's voice is a low drawl, deep and commanding, his control bleeding through the speakers.

Romeo stiffens beside me.

"Yes, Boss." There's a hint of fear in his tone.

"Where are you taking my wife *now*?" Santo demands.

I open my mouth, already annoyed, ready to explain. "We're—"

But before I can finish, Santo's booming voice cuts me off. "I wasn't asking *you*."

The words hit like a slap. I sink into my seat, feeling small, powerless, like nothing more than a possession.

Romeo swallows thickly.

"We're headed back to the estate, Boss," he answers, casting me an apologetic glance.

"Be sure that you are."

My fingers clench into fists. My anger, my exhaustion, boils over.

Just when I had started to breathe, to enjoy a simple day, Santo reminds me who he *thinks* I belong to.

I don't even realize I'm speaking until the words spill out of me, sharp and poison-laced.

"We just went to get ice cream and then to the store. I thought this *arrangement* came with perks—like spending my husband's money on things I want and need. Or is that no longer the case, *Mr.* Amato?"

The car falls deathly silent.

Romeo goes rigid, his body so tense I think he might shatter under the weight of it. My heart pounds. My ears ring.

What did I just say?

Every instinct tells me to tuck and roll out of the car, but I can't move.

Through the speakers comes a slow, measured exhale.

And then Santo's voice is calm, cold, lethal. "That is correct, *Mrs. Amato.*"

The line goes dead.

Romeo doesn't say a word. Neither do I.

We drive in silence the rest of the way home.

When we get back, Romeo disappears, leaving me to unpack my stolen happiness, my contraband snacks. Amelia takes one look at my overflowing bag of treats and sweets and bursts into laughter.

"You sure have a sweet tooth, Vasilisa," she teases, shaking her head.

I grin, but my amusement is laced with defiance.

Because this isn't just about sugar cravings.

This is about choice.

This is about having something of my own, even if it's something as small as sweet treats hidden in a pantry.

Together, Amelia and I tuck the stash away, slipping the treats into a large, empty box on the bottom shelf. The box blends in seamlessly, just another forgotten item among the neatly arranged pantry goods.

I step back, arms crossed, satisfied with our handiwork.

"No one has to know." Amelia winks, dusting her hands off.

I exhale, a genuine smile pulling at my lips. For the first time in hours, I feel a sliver of relief—a reminder that I'm not *completely* alone in this house.

We settle into a comfortable silence, the kitchen filled with the soft clatter of pots and pans as we work. It's easy, effortless, and so rare to find a moment of peace here.

But I cling to it anyway.

Amelia kneads dough beside me, smirking as she tosses a glance at the pantry.

"All those treats—you could open your own store."

I let out a light laugh, twirling a spoon in my hands. "Maybe I'm trying to sweeten up Santo."

The words are half a joke, half a lie—because I know better. Santo isn't the type to be softened by something as simple as sugar or *kindness.*

Amelia chuckles.

"Don't waste your treats on him." She tosses me an apple from the fruit bowl. "He wouldn't know a good snack if it hit him in the face."

I catch it easily, the cool skin smooth against my fingertips.

"Noted." I smirk.

But the moment doesn't last. The warmth, the laughter; it all flickers out as a sound drifts in from the hallway.

A low voice.

Romeo.

My fingers tighten around the apple, my focus sharpening.

Beside me, Amelia is still rolling out dough, completely unaware of the shift in my body language.

I exhale slowly, setting the apple down.

Then, careful not to draw attention, I slip toward the hallway—toward Romeo's voice.

The closer I get, the clearer their conversation becomes.

"Scythe was ruthless," Romeo says, his voice filled with admiration.

A shadow of unease slithers through me. *Scythe?* The name is foreign, but the reverence in their voices is undeniable.

"I've heard he's an artist with his craft," the other guard responds with a dark chuckle.

My stomach turns. *An artist?*

Romeo hums in agreement. "It was an art form," he says, almost eagerly. "His methods of torture are unparalleled—like he relishes causing pain."

A sharp chill runs through me, a cold, slicing dread sinking into my bones.

Torture.

I swallow hard, my fingers curling into my palms as their words swirl like poison in my mind.

"Did he really cut out their tongues?"

Before I can stop myself, a soft, startled gasp escapes my lips.

Both men turn sharply, their conversation halting as their eyes snap to me.

Romeo's face drains of color.

"Mrs. Amato," he says quickly, stepping forward, his voice tight with panic. "Do you need something?"

I step back instinctively, my breath shaky as I try to collect myself. "No," I reply, though my voice betrays me.

The second guard hastily excuses himself, already pulling out his phone as he disappears down the hall.

Romeo remains frozen, his jaw tensing, his guilty expression only making the knot in my stomach tighten.

I know the Bratva's ways; violence, blood, ruthlessness, but this? The way Romeo spoke of Scythe…

It felt different.

Reverent.

Joyful.

A sick feeling rises in my throat.

Is that how Santo feels, too? Does he share the same dark satisfaction when taking a life? Does he enjoy it?

Can I handle it if he does…

My thoughts spiral, sharp and dangerous, as I turn on my heel, retreating back to the kitchen—to the only place I still feel grounded.

Amelia glances up as I enter, her warm smile faltering when she notices my expression, and Romeo lingering in the doorway.

"There you are," she says lightly, but her tone shifts as her gaze narrows on Romeo. "What did you do?"

Romeo stiffens beside me. "Nothing," he replies, his voice defensive but too quiet.

I don't hesitate. "Who is Scythe?"

The words leave my mouth sharper than I intended, slicing through the kitchen air.

Amelia's hands still over the dough.

For the briefest moment, I see it—the flicker of hesitation, the carefully concealed pause.

Then, she exhales softly, her expression smoothing over, practiced.

"He's an associate," she answers evenly, her familiar smile snapping into place like a well-rehearsed lie.

But I saw it.

Her eyes flick to Romeo for the briefest of moments; a silent exchange that I almost miss.

A cold weight settles in my stomach.

They're lying to me.

I glance between them, my chest tightening, a sharp sting creeping into my ribs.

I thought Amelia was on my side.

I thought she was someone I could trust.

Now, I'm not so sure.

CHAPTER 28

SANTO

My brilliant, enigmatic wife is also a *spitfire*.

She has a sweet tooth and a sharp tongue with a fiery attitude she seems to reserve only for *me*.

What Romeo knows, but my wife does not, is that each SUV I provide my men come with GPS tracking. What *neither* of them know is that each one also comes with a listening device.

And so, I *heard* her.

I heard the anger in her voice. The defiance.

I knew I upset her last night. *And again today*, but when I saw *him* standing there, in her bedroom, I saw red.

Romeo knows his place. He respects it.

But that knowledge did nothing to curb the wildfire jealousy that burned through me, fierce and relentless.

I wanted to rip him from that room. From her presence. I wanted to remind him—to remind *her,* that she is *mine*.

But then, I listened.

Hearing her *fight* for herself, demand her freedom, refuse to be controlled… it sparked something in me.

Admiration, maybe.

Or maybe it was something deeper. A *realization*.

My wife is far stronger than I ever gave her credit for.

Now that Vasilisa is home, now that she's safe, I push those thoughts aside and leave my office, making my way to the conference room where Maksim and Angelo are waiting.

After last night's interrogation, strategy must be discussed.

Because now that we *know* our enemies have made a deal with Miroslav…

We have a problem.

Maksim and Angelo stand at opposite ends of the table, voices low but sharp, their disagreement simmering just below the surface.

A heated debate.

A war of egos and tempers.

And it's only a matter of time before it boils over.

"There's no way Kaya isn't part of this! His men tried to take your sister, then turned around and came for mine," Maksim growls, his voice thick with frustration.

"Kaya wants to meet, and I think we should take it," Angelo counters smoothly, too confidently.

Maksim scoffs. "It's a trap, and you fucking know it."

"Not if it's on our turf."

"He's been after my territory for years. Now he comes for my family, and you want me to give him more access to my territory? Fuck no." Maksim's words drip with venom as his glare sharpens on Angelo.

"I'm telling you, I'm right about this."

Maksim laughs, but it's humorless, unhinged. "I've been doing this shit for almost a *decade* while you've been at the helm for—what? A fucking month?"

Angelo's jaw ticks. His eyes go dark.

"Watch yourself, Korsakov," he warns, voice low, dangerous.

"You're overstepping, Amato," Maksim fires back, stepping in close.

Tension crackles like a live wire between them.

I exhale sharply, stepping between them before this pissing contest turns into a bloodbath.

"*We,*" I say, my voice cutting, gesturing between Angelo and myself, "can set up a meeting with Kaya on our territory if necessary."

My eyes lock onto Maksim's. "You can utilize my men for intel on every enemy we have. Now cut the shit and get the fuck out of my building. I have work to do."

Maksim clenches his jaw, nostrils flaring, but after a tense beat, he gives me a stiff nod and storms out, slamming the door behind him.

Silence settles for a moment.

I arch a brow at Angelo. "I leave for one moment, and you blow him the fuck up?"

Angelo shakes his head, unbothered. "Better we meet with Kaya without him anyway. He's too hotheaded."

I laugh. "Unlike you?"

Angelo smirks, chuckling. "Fair enough, brother."

He claps me on the back. "Dinner at Serenata's tonight?"

Before I can answer, my phone rings.

One of the guards at my estate.

I answer immediately, my stomach tightening.

"Is she okay?"

Angelo watches me closely, the slightest crease forming between his brows.

The guard's voice is clipped. "She *knows*, boss."

My spine locks.

"Knows what?" My voice is sharp, a blade edged with irritation as tension coils tight in my chest.

"Mrs. Amato knows about *Scythe*," the guard responds.

The words land like a damn grenade.

How the fuck—

"How the hell did she find that out?" My pulse spikes, anger roaring to life, clawing its way up my throat.

"She overheard—"

"She shouldn't have overheard anything because no one should be fucking talking about it!" I snap, cutting him off, my rage spilling over in sharp, venomous bursts.

"Yes, boss."

I exhale, trying—and failing, to steady myself. Angelo watches me silently, his presence a quiet weight in the room.

A nuisance.

I don't want him here right now.

"Does she know everything?" My voice drops, raw with desperation.

"No, she only knows what Scythe does, not who he is," he answers carefully.

The smallest relief flickers through me before rage snuffs it out.

"I suggest you remove yourself from my property immediately—and whoever else was involved in this little slip-up. Don't even think about coming back," I seethe, fury bleeding through every word.

"But boss—"

Angelo snatches my phone and presses speaker.

"I don't give a fuck what happened or why," he interrupts, voice cutting through the tension like a whip. "All I know is that I don't need this shit right now. Anyone involved, get your asses to my penthouse and wait for me there."

Before I can respond, he ends the call and tosses my phone back at me.

I catch it, barely restraining the urge to throw it at his head.

"I was handling that," I snap.

Angelo shrugs, unbothered. "You can't just fire my men."

"They work for *me*," I remind him, my voice cold, razor-sharp.

"And *you* work for me, little brother," he counters smoothly, his tone pointed, deliberate.

The air crackles between us.

I *hate* when he pulls rank.

"Get the hell out of my building!" I snarl, my control slipping fast.

Angelo watches me for a beat, his eyes assessing, calculating—before he chuckles. A slow, amused sound, like he enjoys pushing me to the edge just to see if I'll jump.

He says nothing else. Just leaves, doors clicking shut behind him.

I storm toward the window, my fingers digging into the frame as I stare out at the city skyline.

I inhale deeply. Exhale.

Rein it in.

The last thing I need right now is a war with Angelo. We can't afford to be at each other's throats when we should be planning our meeting with Kaya.

But Vasilisa *knowing* about Scythe?

It shatters my focus. Distracts me in ways I can't afford.

She's not supposed to know.

And if she keeps digging—

Fuck.

The curse barely leaves my lips before I sense rather than hear Marcus stride into the conference room. There's weight to his presence, a thick tension hanging over him.

"Mr. Amato," he starts tentatively.

Not now.

Not fucking now.

"What?" I snap, not bothering to turn around.

"The QUEEN file—"

"What about it?" My voice lashes out, cutting him off before he can waste my time.

Marcus hesitates.

"We're in."

My interest piques, the storm in my head clearing just enough for me to turn toward him. He looks uneasy. I sigh, already irritated.

"What's the problem?"

"We got in, but..." Marcus swallows. "The documents started self-destructing as soon as we breached. We managed to salvage half, but it's in code."

I roll my jaw. *Of course, it is.*

"How long to crack it?"

"Maybe three months, give or take."

I press two fingers to the bridge of my nose, a sharp throb forming between my temples. "We don't have months. Can you do it in *weeks?*"

"With more help, maybe, but—"

"Make it happen." My patience snaps, my voice razor-sharp. "Use whoever you need." I stride past him, dismissing the conversation before he can keep wasting my time.

I need to get my head together.

These distractions aren't helping. As I storm back toward my office, I pass Evie and tell her to clear my schedule.

She stiffens. "Mr. Amato, what about your meeting with—"

"Clear it," I snap.

She falters. "But—"

"I said clear it!"

She stutters out a quick agreement as I shove open my office door and slam it behind me.

I need a minute to think.

Pouring myself a glass of whiskey, I slump into my leather chair, the city skyline stretching before me in the cold, indifferent night. The amber liquid swirls in my glass, untouched, my mind fracturing under the weight of everything.

Vasilisa knows about Scythe.

The QUEEN file will take months to crack.

We have a war on the horizon.

The problems keep stacking up.

My control is slipping through my fingers.

Rubbing my temples, I strategize.

First—Angelo.

Our disagreement has to wait. We can't afford to be divided when we need to set up a meeting with Kaya.

Next—Vasilisa.

She has to be handled delicately. Her face flickers in my mind, soft and sweet, but *afraid*.

Of *me*.

I grit my teeth.

I can't let that happen. *I won't.*

The shrill ring of my phone cuts through the quiet.

I inhale sharply, biting down the fresh irritation as I snatch it up without checking to see who it is.

"What?"

"Santo…"

The voice is hesitant. Shaky.

My stomach drops.

I recognize it instantly.

Silvio. My father's advisor.

No.

My grip on the phone tightens. "What happened?"

A beat of silence. Then—

"There's been an attack… your father."

The world narrows.

A single, razor-sharp thought slices through the noise in my mind. My father.

"How bad?" My voice is even, too controlled.

"He's alive, but… it's bad."

I don't hesitate.

I grab my coat, whiskey forgotten, problems forgotten—because in this moment, there is only one priority.

Cosa Nostra needs me.

And I need to be clear-headed—now more than ever.

★★★

My head reels. The doctor's words echo in my mind, looping endlessly.

Four gunshot wounds.

My father is alive—barely. Hours of surgery, a medically induced coma, and now he's hanging by a thread. His recovery is a gamble at best, a slow death at worst.

Angelo has locked down the hospital with our best men, stretching our resources thin. Maksim didn't hesitate to offer reinforcements, even pulling brigadiers from Nevada who will fly in overnight. I called our Capo in Chicago, who is sending soldiers as well. Even Luca was here *before* me, waiting like the true comrade he is.

All hands on deck for Marcello Amato.

My father ruled with iron and respect, and now the men of Cosa Nostra are rallying to go to war for him.

By the time I make it home, exhaustion weighs heavy in my bones. The living room is dark, the silence pressing in like a vice.

There's no light under the door to the master bedroom, and for a moment, I let myself *believe* she's asleep.

That I'll have a night of solitude, that I won't have to face her.

But then I see it.

A soft glow seeping from beneath the guest room door, shattering the illusion.

I stop in front of it and exhale.

Tonight has been a *fucking minefield*—Romeo in her bedroom, her reckless junk-food joyride, the shadow of Scythe looming like a noose tightening around my neck. I don't have the strength to deal with any of it.

Not now.

I steel myself, prepared to send her to her own room with the last sliver of patience I have left.

But the second I open the door—

She's on me.

Her arms wrap around my neck, her body colliding into mine.

I barely catch her before I stagger back a step, unprepared for the sheer force of her presence.

She's so light against me, but she *feels* like everything.

Her face buries into the curve of my neck, breath warm, delicate, soothing—a stark contrast to the war raging in my head.

"I'm so sorry about your father," she whispers, her voice muffled against my skin.

The words sink in, igniting something deep, something aching in my chest.

I freeze.

Caught completely off guard.

But then—instinct.

My arms tighten around her, pressing her closer.

She doesn't let go.

Her legs wrap around my waist, clinging to me like she's holding the weight of the world at bay.

And for a moment—*just a fucking moment*—it's like everything else disappears.

The chaos. The pain. The exhaustion dragging me under.

All that's left is *her.*

My hands glide down the silk of her robe, a grounding sensation against the storm inside me. Her scent—soft and sweet, a mixture of her cashmere perfume and something inherently her, fills my senses.

I inhale deeply, trying to memorize it, to bottle this moment of solace I didn't know I needed.

And just as I think I might drown in her, might finally surrender to the *need* for her, she lets go— leaving me gasping, reaching for a warmth that's already slipping through my fingers.

Her legs slide down, and I reluctantly release her, the loss of her hitting me like a blow.

She steps back but doesn't break away completely, her hands trailing down my arms before clasping mine.

And then she looks at me.

Really looks at me.

And damn it, those eyes—they pull at every single thread holding me together.

"I just wanted to make sure you were in one piece," she says softly, her voice steady but filled with something fragile. Something real.

I can't speak.

How do I tell her that I've never felt more undone than I do now? That the only reason I'm in one piece is because of her?

"I'm alright," I say finally, my voice low and rough. "I wasn't there when it happened."

She nods, the tension in her shoulders easing slightly. "Okay."

Her hands slip from mine.

And as she brushes past me, the absence of her touch is almost unbearable.

"Good night, Santo," she murmurs, her voice barely above a whisper—like she's afraid to say more.

I watch her leave.

Her robe sways softly behind her, and it takes *everything* in me not to reach out, not to call her back.

The door closes quietly behind her, but the ache she leaves in her wake is deafening.

The room feels emptier than before, the weight of her absence pressing down on me.

She brought me peace, however fleeting—

And now, she's taken it with her.

I let out a slow breath, the lingering warmth of her touch still burning on my skin, and one thought settles in my chest, heavy and unshakable; she's everything I need and I don't know how to deserve her.

CHAPTER 29

VASILISA

In the morning, I expected the house to be filled with Cosa Nostra soldiers given what happened to Marcello, but seeing Pietro next to Luca in the kitchen still surprises me. Relief floods through me, and before I know it, I'm rushing forward, springing into Pietro's arms.

I'm glad I wore jeans today instead of a dress with all the hugging I'll be doing. After yesterday, I've made sure to be completely modest in my sweater and jeans—I'm steering clear of upsetting Santo. He has enough on his plate.

I release Pietro and turn to hug a very startled Luca.

"I'm glad you're back," I say, beaming up at him.

"Romeo, that bad for one day?" Luca teases, raising a brow.

I laugh, but my smile fades as I notice Pietro's face. A cut mars his lip, and his black eye stands out in the morning light—details I missed in my haste to hug him.

"What happened?" I ask, reaching out to touch his face.

Pietro gently grabs my hand, lowering it before I can reach him.

A throat clears behind me, and I turn to find Santo standing at the threshold, Don Amato and Maksim flanking him.

Maksim speaks first, his voice sharp and casual all at once.

"Sinner's handling Kaya. I'm heading to Vancouver—Killian Byrne has eyes on the Turkish, and I want to see what he knows."

"In light of what happened yesterday, it's clear we're at war," Don Amato adds, his voice measured, commanding. "You've all been assigned. Santo sent out the details this morning. Check them and get where you need to be. We're an alliance; no one outranks anyone. All hands."

The men murmur their agreements before dispersing, leaving me in the kitchen with Luca, Romeo, Pietro, five other men, and Santo.

Santo's voice is firm as he addresses Pietro. "Ivanov. You, Dmitri, and Fabiano will head to California. My sister Elena is at university and currently has two guards. I need you to protect her with your life."

"I will," Pietro replies with conviction.

Santo steps forward, patting Pietro on the back. "I mean it. She's the second most important woman in my life."

A sharp pang tugs at my heart, but I shove it down, keeping my expression neutral. Our eyes meet for a fleeting second before Pietro nods and turns to me with a polite smile. My best friend leaves, off to protect a sister-in-law I've never met.

Santo shifts his attention to Luca. "You, Romeo, Enzo, Sergei, and Alexei are on Vasilisa."

I glance at him, but his stormy gray eyes remain locked on Luca.

"She doesn't leave. Anything she wants, you get it for her. No exceptions. No risks. Before she enters any room, you do a sweep."

His voice is final, his tone brooking no argument.

"Santo," I start softly, his name barely audible.

"No exceptions, Vasilisa."

"It's not that," I reply quickly. "What about Mimi?"

His eyes soften slightly as he looks at me. "Maksim has that handled. We have men at Andras."

He turns back to the men. "A moment with my wife."

The room clears. The guards leave in silence, and even Amelia, who had been serving breakfast, removes her apron and disappears without a word.

Santo steps forward, his presence swallowing the space between us, *commanding* even in exhaustion.

The dark circles under his eyes are stark against the sharp cut of his cheekbones, his gaze—usually so piercing, so unwavering, dulled by the weight of everything he carries. He's polished as always, his crisp white button-down pristine against the navy vest and slacks tailored to perfection. But even in his effortless elegance, I see it. The strain in the tight set of his jaw. The barely-there furrow of his brow. The heaviness in his shoulders that even the finest suits can't disguise.

And yet—he's still the most devastatingly handsome man I've ever seen.

My heart stutters as his hands slide into his pockets, as he watches me, his gaze *lingering,* drinking me in as if he's afraid he'll forget the details of my face before he walks out that door.

It's a look that wrecks me.

Not just because of the intensity behind it, but because it makes my insecurities coil inside me, pressing into my ribs like an iron vice.

What does he see when he looks at me like that?

In my jeans and sweater, I look plain, *unremarkable,* so small beneath his scrutiny.

And yet, he doesn't look away.

His gaze softens, deepens, burns with something I can't name.

Something *I ache* to understand.

A single finger glides under my chin, tilting my face upward in a touch so gentle it unravels me.

His lips brush mine; soft, fleeting

Not enough.

Before he can pull away, I rise onto my toes, my hands flying to his face, my fingers curling onto his jaw as I pull him down, *kissing him like I can breathe life into him.*

He exhales sharply against my mouth, and for a second, just a *second,* he *melts.*

The tension in his body falters, his hands ghosting over my waist as if he wants to hold me there, as if he wants to stay. But then the moment slips away, and when I break the kiss, we're still close, our foreheads nearly touching, my breath still tangled with his.

"Come home safe to me," I whisper, my voice breaking just slightly.

His hands twitch at his sides, and something unreadable flickers in his dark eyes. His brow creases—not in frustration, not in hesitation, but in something deep and *unspoken.* Something he can't say.

He won't promise me.

Instead, his voice drops, rough and low. "I'll *endeavor* to."

And then he straightens.

The guards return, stepping into the room like shadows, and suddenly, he shifts. The air between us feels heavy with things left unsaid, with everything we should have spoken aloud but didn't.

And then he leaves.

I don't know when he'll be home, only that I *will* be waiting up.

★★★

I loathe the shadows that follow me everywhere I go.

They are constant, lingering just at the edge of my freedom, a reminder that I am watched, that I am guarded—as if I am something delicate, something that can be taken.

I refuse to be either.

Instead of dwelling on it, I focus on my painting. Seated in the library, I let my brush move across the canvas, bringing to life the newest piece taking shape beneath my fingertips—a depiction of Santo and me, in the garden beneath the magnolia trees. A moment that is ours, captured forever in paint.

Luca doesn't join me today. He sits at a nearby table with Romeo, their conversation quiet, their presence steady. Enzo and Sergei remain outside the library door, silent sentinels. But Alexei—he is the only one who seems to pay me any mind.

He stands behind me, broad-shouldered and imposing, his dark hair cropped short, his neatly trimmed beard making him look even more severe. His entire presence is combat-ready—dressed for war, boots heavy against the floor, his piercing blue eyes constantly watching.

More often than not, his gaze lands on Luca, sharp with an unspoken fury—one that Luca returns, unbothered, unwavering.

Alexei observes my work, tilting his head slightly before commenting in Russian, a compliment slipping from his lips. "You are talented."

I nod, accepting the praise. "Spasibo."

"You married into this family solely for the alliance?" Alexei asks in Russian, his voice low, his gaze flicking toward Luca and Romeo, ensuring they don't understand.

I keep my expression neutral. Calculated. "Yes," I answer evenly. "But my husband is a good man, so the marriage is good." My tone is polite, controlled—distant, but firm.

Alexei chuckles.

I don't like it.

"None of us are *good* men," he says smoothly. His head tilts, watching me with something that makes my skin prickle with irritation. "You know... the Pakhan promised you would be one of ours before he sent you to this dump to struggle with the classless."

I pause.

Very slowly, I turn to face him.

My voice is even, my chin lifted, my pride unshaken.

"Having my own library is hardly a dump," I say in our language "And being forced to marry one of you?" I smile, but there is nothing soft about it. "That would mean I would *drop* in rank. That would truly be a struggle."

His expression shifts.

Offended.

Good.

A sharp scrape echoes as Luca and Romeo push their chairs back, rising to their feet. In an instant, they are at my side, a silent wall of protection.

Luca's voice is a low, dangerous drawl. "What did you say to her?"

Alexei scoffs, his disapproval clear, but I don't give him the satisfaction of reacting.

I exhale slowly, my composure unwavering, and switch to English as I address Luca.

"It's nothing." My voice is smooth, dismissive. I flick my gaze back to Alexei, unimpressed. "He's just a typical grunt in the Bratva with a typical attitude."

A muscle ticks in Alexei's jaw, but he doesn't argue.

Instead, he turns sharply on his heel, moving to guard the door, clearly irritated.

I watch him go, my fingers tightening briefly around my brush before I return to my painting.

I won't let men like him think they can shake me.

The rest of the day passes by uneventful. I'm worried about Santo and Luca assures me he is just at NovaRael working, but his tone suggests otherwise. As night falls, the house becomes quiet. All except the light scratching sounds of brushes against canvas and the quiet whispers of my guards conversing in secret.

The magnolia trees are coming to life under my brush, vibrant pinks and deep greens set against the blue-sky backdrop. I paint until my fingers grow numb from gripping the brush, but it's a sort of therapy that keeps me grounded amidst all the uncertainty.

"Vasilisa, you should rest," Luca suggests, his voice breaking the silence, his eyes holding a hint of concern.

"I can't sleep," I mutter back, not taking my eyes off the canvas. My heartstrings tug sharply at the thought of Santo somewhere out there in danger.

"Try," urges Romeo with a soft smile.

"Maybe you're right," I confess with a sigh.

I tidy up my materials before allowing Romeo to escort me to my room while Luca heads outside to replace Enzo and Sergei.

"Where's Alexei?" I ask.

Romeo grimaces, "Santo sent him back to Maksim."

"Santo spoke to you, you heard from him today?" I ask stopping mid stride. "Is he okay?"

Romeo nods confidently. "Yes, he's working at the office today, he's in no danger."

"I was there this morning Romeo, there's a war coming."

I cross my arms over my chest.

"And your husband is one of the most powerful men in the city, he'll be fine, and you'll be safe," Romeo chuckles, "Now relax your brow before you wrinkle."

I can't help, but crack a smile, "Okay, but next time he calls can you tell him I want to talk to him?"

"If he contacts me, I will."

I open my door, but Romeo stops me, and ushers me behind him, "I have to do a sweep."

Exasperated, I sigh, "No one has been in or out of this house."

"Alexei left, that's someone," Romeo says with finality as he enters the room leaving me in the hall.

Luca stops next to me. "Enzo and Sergei are guarding the property with the others; I'll be out here with Romeo while you sleep."

I nod but don't bother telling him I won't be sleeping, at least not in this room.

Romeo steps aside, gesturing for me to go in.

I quickly shower and throw on a robe, tying it securely. With an entourage now my shadow, modesty seems necessary.

When I open the door, both men look surprised to see me. Luca lowers his phone a little too quickly, his movements stiff.

"Who are you talking to?" I ask, narrowing my eyes.

"Angelo," Luca clips, his tone firm.

"Liar."

"I don't lie."

"To me, you do," I challenge. "I want to speak to Santo."

"He's busy," Luca says, his voice sharper now.

A deep sigh echoes from the phone in Luca's hand. Santo's unmistakable voice cuts through the tension.

"Give her the phone."

Luca's jaw tightens as he switches off the speaker and hands the phone to me. I press it to my ear, my frustration melting slightly at the sound of Santo's voice.

"Santo?"

"Why aren't you sleeping? It's late, Dea," he mutters, the weariness in his tone tugging at something inside me.

"Are you okay?" I ask quietly.

"I'm working," he replies simply, but there's a softness in his words, almost an apology.

"Okay," I whisper, defeated, before handing the phone back to Luca.

I head downstairs, Romeo trailing me silently. I can hear Luca's low voice reverberating in the background, but I don't care to listen. Santo has his responsibilities—to the Don, to my cousin, to Cosa Nostra.

My mother's voice echoes in my head: *"Your job is to help, not hinder the men in your life."*

I roll my eyes at the thought.

Subhuman, trophies, and trinkets—nothing more to men like them, to men like Santo.

Ignoring Romeo's questioning glances, I grab the blanket from the armchair, plop onto the couch, and curl up, facing the backrest. Luca's heavy steps thud behind me, stopping at the couch.

"You're going to pout in here?" he asks.

I don't answer, pulling the blanket over my head and shutting my eyes.

★★★

I wake to the sound of muted voices. The scent of him is unmistakable.

Santo is here.

My heart skips, but I don't move, feigning sleep as the men continue talking, oblivious to my consciousness.

"Why is she down here?" Santo's deep whisper is tinged with irritation.

"She chose to. Should we have moved her?" Romeo replies.

There's a pause, and I imagine Santo giving one of his silent, deadly looks before he speaks again.

"I have Nico replacing Alexei tomorrow," Santo says, his tone firm, authoritative. "What did he say to her?"

"Don't know. It was in Russian, but she looked bothered."

Santo's voice drops, a harsh edge cutting through his whisper. "If we weren't low on men, I'd kill him myself."

Guilt twists in my chest as I hear him sigh heavily, exhaustion weighing down every syllable. "You two can go. I have her."

The sound of retreating footsteps fills the room, and I feel Santo's presence beside me. His nearness radiates heat, a magnetic pull I can't ignore even though I try.

"I know you're awake." His voice cuts through the darkness.

My heart plummets, but I remain still, holding my breath.

He chuckles softly, a low, rumbling sound that sends a shiver through me.

"Fine," he mutters.

Before I can process his words, his hands, strong and sure, slip under my thighs and back. He lifts me, blanket and all, cradling me close to his chest.

I melt into his warmth, his scent surrounding me like a cocoon.

There's no point in pretending anymore, but I still don't open my eyes.

If this is the only moment I get like this, I'll savor it.

Guilt tugs at me.

He's still awake because of me.

But being in his arms, feeling the steady rhythm of his heartbeat, I regret nothing.

His steps are measured as he carries me upstairs, each stride deliberate. The soft creak of the hardwood under his feet gives away our destination—*my* bedroom.

When he reaches the bed, he sets me down gently. The plush mattress cradles me as he adjusts the blanket over me with surprising care. I crack one eye open, just enough to peek through the folds of the blanket.

He doesn't leave.

Instead, he stands there for a moment, his hand lingering on the edge of the blanket as if he's unsure whether to let go. His face is cast in shadow, but his posture tells me everything—shoulders tense, head bowed slightly, like he's carrying a weight he can't share.

My chest tightens as I watch him. I can't see his eyes, but I can feel the heaviness in the air, the storm of unspoken emotions swirling around him.

He exhales deeply, running a hand through his dark hair before stepping back. He lingers near the threshold, his hand resting on the frame as he looks back at me. For a moment, I think he knows I'm watching, but he doesn't say anything.

Finally, he steps out, then I hear the door clicking shut behind him.

I stay impossibly still, my heart racing. Even though he's gone, the warmth of his touch lingers.

I close my eyes, his scent and the memory of his arms wrapping around me still vivid. I try to resist the pull of sleep, afraid I'll lose the moment entirely, but it's impossible. Eventually, exhaustion wins, and I drift off, still wrapped in his lingering presence.

CHAPTER 30

VASILISA

Santo's gone again and as he said there is a new man in place of Alexei.

Nico.

He's Angelo's right hand, much like Luca is to Santo.

Nico is a towering figure; his broad shoulders and muscular frame showcase countless hours at the gym.

A deep scar runs down his left eye to his jaw, giving his already intimidating presence an extra edge.

He wears a stringer tank that shows off his arms covered in tattoos, paired with rugged cargo pants, he seems ready for anything.

He strides into the library switching spots with Romeo as I continue to paint.

Romeo heads towards the door to guard it. Luca eyes Nico as he walks over to me.

"This is what you do all day? Paint?" His voice is smooth and melodic, though there's a hint of skepticism in his tone.

I look up from my easel and meet his gaze evenly. "Is that how you speak to someone for the first time?"

His brows lift in surprise. But I refuse to break eye contact, even when my gaze lands on his scar, I may be intimidated by many things, but no one will *ever* see it.

"I was trying to make conversation."

"Then perhaps you lack the necessary skills."

Luca barks out laugh and Nico shoots him a dark look. "I didn't mean to offend, Mrs. Amato."

I smile and correct him, "Call me Vasi or Vasilisa."

"Vasilisa," he repeats, testing my name on his tongue. "The Don said you were shy, but he was wrong."

He smirks.

I nod and continue painting. Nico moves behind me and watches as I work.

"You have talent," he compliments sincerely.

"Thank you," I reply, surprised but pleased. "Do you paint as well?"

Luca interrupts us with a warning tone. "*Don't* let her rope you into painting!"

He points a finger at Nico dramatically.

I narrow my eyes. "Don't listen to him, Nico. He's just upset that Santo no longer *allows* him to paint."

"You paint, Cattaneo?" Nico teases.

Luca quickly flips him off and pulls out his phone, giving me a smirk before assuring me that he's not calling Santo.

Nico raises an eyebrow at me, his posture relaxed but his gaze sharp. "You don't want him to call Santo?"

"No. My husband can call *me* if he wants to, but he doesn't," I reply bitterly, setting down my brush and walking away toward the back of the library where the restroom is.

Nico falls into step behind me, his movements quiet, but his presence looms.

I glance over my shoulder, irritation bubbling to the surface.

"You don't have to follow me to the bathroom," I snap unintentionally.

"That's not what Santo said," Nico replies, a softness in his tone.

I huff, throwing my hands up.

"I'm so sick of being constantly trailed around! It would be nice to have some peace and quiet for once."

Nico's expression doesn't shift, but there's a flicker of something in his eyes—understanding?

"He just wants you to be safe."

"I'm trapped in this house. How much safer can I be?" I retort, stopping in front of the bathroom door, crossing my arms.

Luca's voice cuts in from across the room. "Just use the restroom, Vasilisa!"

Nico's head snaps toward Luca.

"Ease up," he says, an edge to his voice that makes Luca glance away.

I purse my lips, watching the silent exchange, and step aside as Nico gestures toward the bathroom door.

He opens it, stepping inside first to do his sweep. Once he's satisfied, he nods for me to go in.

When I return to my easel, Romeo is back in the library, and Luca is gone.

"Where's Luca?" I ask, sitting down and adjusting my canvas.

"Boss called him away," Romeo replies dismissively, and I know better than to press for details.

I focus on my painting, letting the tension in my chest bleed out through the strokes of my brush. By the time I finish the piece Luca returns, holding a large bouquet of lilies and roses. He sets them on the table beside me, a folded note tucked among the stems.

He clears his throat. "From Santo."

I pluck the note free, my hands trembling despite myself.

"I hope this can make up for my absence."

The words are simple, thoughtful even, but they feel hollow. My chest tightens as I look at the bouquet. The overwhelmingly sweet scent fills the air, pulling me back to our wedding day; a day I desperately want to hold on to but feel slipping further away.

I set the note and flowers down on the table, leaving them untouched, and turn back to my easel.

Nico's gaze follows me closely, his brow furrowed as if he's trying to read my thoughts.

Romeo looks confused but says nothing.

"Don't take it personally, Vasilisa," Luca says when he notices my lack of reaction.

I glance at him briefly, my expression impassive. "I don't want empty words."

Luca crosses his arms, his stance stiff. "He can't be at your beck and call every day."

"I don't *need* every day, Luca," I say sharply, picking up a new brush. "But he could call. He could *text.*"

Luca exhales through his nose, clearly frustrated. "You expect him to stop in the middle of a war to text you an apology?"

"I don't need an apology. I don't need flowers. I need *him.* I need to actually feel wanted," I say, ignoring the way Nico stiffens beside me.

"Next time, I'll tell him your request is that he drops everything and comes running," Luca quips sarcastically.

"A simple text. A good morning phone call. That's all!" I snap, setting my brush down harder than I intended.

Luca starts to reply, but Nico steps forward.

"Enough." Nico steps between us slightly, his posture tense. "She's allowed to feel how she feels."

Luca grits his teeth but says nothing, his gaze flicking between Nico and me. I don't wait for another argument to erupt.

I rise from my seat and leave the library, brushing past Nico.

"Where are you going?" Nico calls after me, his footsteps echoing down the corridor.

"Does it matter?" I shoot back, not bothering to turn around. My steps carry me toward the gardens—the only place that still feels like a sanctuary. The sunlight filters through the leafy canopy, dappling the ground and brushing my skin like a faint echo of Santo's touch.

I make my way to the stone fountain and sit on its edge, staring at the rippling water. The sound of the fountain mingles with the distant chirping of birds, filling the heavy silence between Nico and me. He keeps his distance, but his watchful eyes never leave me.

The smell of flowers drifts on the breeze, sweet and torturous. My chest tightens as the memories flood in—the laughter, the warmth, the fleeting moments of happiness I had here with Santo.

Suddenly, the stillness becomes unbearable. I stand abruptly, startling Nico.

"I'm going stir-crazy!"

"Vasilisa..." Nico starts, his tone cautious, but he falls silent when I glare at him.

"Listen," he says after a moment, his voice softening. "We're at the beginning of a war. All Santo cares about is your safety."

I scoff bitterly.

"He didn't even want me. This was an arrangement. I'm of no real value to him, and we both know that."

Nico's expression hardens, and his voice becomes firmer. "Yes, you are."

I roll my eyes. "I'm just an investment to him. Without me, he doesn't have NovaRael. If someone takes me, they take his company. That's all I am—an *asset* to protect."

Nico steps closer, his gaze piercing. "Do you want to know how many guards his mother had before she was taken off the front steps of this home?"

His words hit me like a slap, and my blood runs cold. I blink at him, stunned, the air around me suddenly too thick to breathe.

At the look on my face, Nico nods grimly.

"Lucia meant *everything* to Marcello. He thought he could protect her by keeping her in a separate home. But our enemies found her. They took her... and sent her back to Marcello and his sons in pieces."

The weight of his words sinks in, pressing down on my chest like a boulder. My legs feel weak, and I sink back onto the fountain, my thoughts reeling.

My stomach churns, and tears blur my vision. I raise a hand to stop Nico from continuing, my voice barely a whisper.

"Enough... I don't want to hear more."

Nico nods, his sharp edges softening as he watches me. "You should rest," he says gently.

I nod, feeling too overwhelmed to argue. Nico walks beside me as we head back into the house.

The evening ends the same as the last. I fall asleep on the couch; my husband takes me to my bed and in the morning he's gone.

★★★

I start on my new painting, this time of Santo at his desk in NovaRael. He had been busy scribbling notes when I entered the room that day, his brow furrowed in deep concentration. The memory feels distant now, hazy at the edges, as I struggle to capture him on canvas. Without a refresher—*without him,* I'm grasping at fleeting details.

It's been weeks since I last saw him, and all I have in his absence are the countless lilies Luca delivers almost daily.

Romeo and Enzo sit in the library with me when Nico and Luca enter, Sergei trailing behind them. I glance up as they set up at the table, a large tin can in Sergei's hands. He nods at me.

"This is from Gilded Ace," he says, and my heart stops at the name of Maksim's casino.

"What are you doing with that?" I ask, rising from my seat.

Luca smirks, taking the tin from Sergei as they settle in. "We're going to teach you a little poker."

Luca gestures to an empty seat beside him, and I sit beside him. A slow smile tugs at my lips. *They assume I don't already know how to play.*

I let them get comfortable, their expressions already painted with self-assured superiority. I keep my own poker face intact, barely resisting the urge to roll my eyes when Nico tries to explain the basics.

"Alright, guys, let's not overwhelm her." He glances at me through thick lashes, concern visible in his hazel eyes. "Poker is a game of chance and strategy, Vasilisa. The goal is to have the best set of cards by the end."

I nod, feigning a demure look of gratitude, as if his explanation is news to me. They don't know that poker had once been my favorite pastime with Maksim, who had taught me himself.

The game begins in earnest, their joviality quickly dissolving into intense concentration as they try to decipher each other's strategies. I play my part well—gasping at losses, giggling at wins, letting them believe I am exactly the naïve girl they expect me to be.

The first round comes and goes; I lose by a hair's breadth to Luca. My defeat seems to bolster their confidence.

As we shuffle for the next round, my fingers move deftly with years of experience hidden behind faux hesitation.

Silently, I compose myself for the strike. The room falls into quiet anticipation as everyone checks their hands.

"What do you think? Is it your lucky round?" Enzo teases, his grin faltering the moment I reveal my cards.

It takes them a second to register what just happened—Nico blinks rapidly at my full house, while Luca raises an impressed brow, but by then, it's too late.

The third game ends with me victorious again, the pot significantly larger this time. Their egos take a hit, but I see something else dancing in their eyes—respect.

"Let me guess," Nico breaks the silence, chuckling. "You've played before?"

I smile, collecting my winnings, leaving them to their wounded pride. My point is clear: *I am not just Santo's wife. I'm my own person.*

Another month passes, still no word from Santo—only more lilies in his absence. The guys eventually switch from poker to baccarat, assuming once again that I don't know how to play. With each passing day, my camaraderie with them deepens, their respect for me growing.

They even go out to buy more easels, joining me in painting.

Every night, I fall asleep on the couch, and every night, my husband carries me upstairs. That is the extent of our interactions.

One night I choose to sleep in my own room and that becomes my new habit.

Over time, I grow used to his absence and come to cherish the presence of my new friends.

Even cooking together with Amelia at the helm becomes part of our routine.

Then one day, something shifts. Sergei reveals his hidden talent for the violin, and soon, music becomes part of our evenings. One by one, the others join in; Nico surprises us all with his skill on the guitar, while Enzo and Romeo turn everything into a dramatic performance.

One night, over warm cups of coffee and half-finished canvases, Luca confides in me about his siblings back home in Italy, whom he hasn't seen in over a year. There's a strain in his voice, longing laced with worry, but a glimmer of hope remains.

Slowly, these men—Sergei with his sharp gaze, Romeo with his thoughtful demeanor, Enzo quick with a witty remark, Nico with his unwavering kindness, and Luca with his infectious laughter—become more than guards. *They become my brothers.*

Despite the warmth of their friendship, I still miss Santo.

Every night, I slip into his room. His presence lingers in the careless way his clothes are strewn about, in the scent of him woven into the sheets. He's everywhere. A ghost inhabiting every corner of my life, keeping me captive in his irresistible aura.

Then one morning, I wake to find a note on my bedside table. My heart pounds as I unfold it. His handwriting sends a jolt through me, my hands trembling.

I miss you.

That's all it says, but it's enough. Enough to undo me completely. My tears fall freely, staining the paper.

From that night on, I sleep hugging the note, holding onto it as if it can bring him closer.

I yearn for him—to share this newfound warmth of companionship, to let him see what I've built in his absence. But he is buried in his work, swallowed by this war.

I sigh, shifting my focus back to the canvas in front of me.

This time, it is not a painting of Santo.

"Vasilisa," Enzo calls from across the room. "Could you pass the red?"

I hand him the requested paint. As he thanks me, I glance back at my nearly finished painting—a portrait of me and my brothers gathered around a poker table, frozen in a moment of laughter and competition. A testament to this strange yet beautiful chapter of my life.

A sudden cacophony of beeps and buzzes erupts from the five men's cell phones, causing them to abruptly drop their brushes and exchange concerned glances.

"We have to go," Sergei's voice carries a bitter edge.

"All of us except Luca," Nico interjects with a somber tone.

Confused, I turn to look at Luca who subtly shakes his head, seeming to warn me not to protest their sudden departure. My brothers quickly bid me goodbye with hugs and forehead kisses before exiting, leaving me alone with Luca in a tense silence.

"Is everything okay?"

"Nothing bad has happened," Luca assures me with a confident tone, but it does little to ease my concern.

The day continues as normal, except for the absence of four of my closest friends.

As evening approaches, I slide in to bed clutching Santo's note in my hand.

I miss him. The memories I have of him are hazy and distant, but it doesn't stop my hand from trailing down my body and touching myself to the thought of him as I have for the past month now, eager and hungry for release, hoping he watches me come with his name on my lips.

CHAPTER 31

SANTO

The past months have been grueling—days trying to figure out Miroslav's deal, nights breaking men for a name that

It's consumed everything—my time, my energy, and, worst of all, time I could have with *her*.

Kaya has finally decided to meet with Angelo and me tonight, another night away from my wife.

The thought of Vasilisa, alone in that house surrounded by guards, tightens something in my chest.

I used to keep her close in other ways—watching her on surveillance when I couldn't physically be with her, but even that has fallen by the wayside.

It wasn't just about seeing her. It was about *memorizing* her; the way she moves when she thinks no one is watching, the way she tilts her head when she reads, the way her fingers linger at her lips when she's lost in thought. Not being able to do that anymore feels like starving. Now, I only hear about her through Luca's texts, brief updates that don't do her justice.

Every night, I carry her sleeping form upstairs, her body warm and pliant against mine, but it's not enough. For the past month, she hasn't even been on the couch. Instead, she's already asleep in her room, the door closed, the space between us stretching further. I haven't held her in weeks, and the ache of it is constant, gnawing at me in the quiet moments I can't ignore.

I send her flowers. I left her a note; a pathetic attempt to bridge the distance, but she hasn't called or texted. I don't blame her. The phone works both ways, and I've failed her as much as she's silent now. Luca says she's fine. I know she isn't.

And that silence terrifies me more than any enemy we're about to face.

I sigh, sinking back into the passenger seat of Angelo's SUV as we head into enemy territory. The weight of everything presses down on me, Miroslav, Kaya, the war—and underneath it all, her.

Always her.

The thought of Vasilisa waiting for me, feeling abandoned, is a wound I can't seem to heal.

She's a light, *the* light in this dark, ruthless world, and yet I'm the one extinguishing it.

Angelo glances at me briefly, his brow furrowing. "You good?"

I nod, brushing off his concern. But the truth is, I haven't been good in months. *Not without her.*

As far as Kaya knows, we're alone. We're not. Maksim has snipers on the perimeter, and Irish intel Maksim got are suggesting the Turks aren't the ones pulling Miroslav's strings.

The road leading to Kaya's estate is as dark as the fog surrounding it. The cobblestone pathway grows more uneven the closer we get; the perfect metaphor for our shaky meeting with him.

Entering the compound, the guards at the gate are tense, their stiff postures revealing more than their stony expressions.

Inside, Gabriel Kaya is everything you'd expect from a ruthless mob boss: tall, imposing, and every inch a predator, just like us. His cold eyes trace over Angelo.

"Amato's," he greets coolly, his voice edged like a blade. His focus stays on Angelo. He drapes himself across the couch in a casual display of dominance, his posture relaxed, but not careless. He gestures to the couch opposite him.

We don't sit.

No pleasantries. No wasted breath. Angelo's voice is a sharp command. "We don't appreciate your men encroaching on Korsakov's territory, let alone attempting to take our women."

Gabriel exhales a humorless chuckle, slow and calculated. "And I don't appreciate pieces of my men arriving at my doorstep in gift boxes. Yet here we are."

Angelo's expression doesn't shift. "You're ordering an unprovoked attack."

Gabriel leans forward, his mouth curving into something resembling amusement. "If I wanted to strike a blow, I'd go for the jugular. Your sister? That's small time, a warning shot." His gaze flicks to me, calculated, deliberate. "*Your* wife would be the kill."

A cold, quiet rage settles in my chest. My muscles coil with the instinct to move—to strike before another word can leave his mouth. But Angelo is faster. His arm slams across my chest, a silent warning. I don't push against it, but I don't relax either. My fingers twitch at my side, itching to rip Gabriel apart.

Angelo's voice remains steady, but the steel beneath it is unyielding. "Are you saying you can't control your men and they're going rogue?"

"I'm saying my men are being targeted, taken, their families threatened to do bidding for others," Gabriel counters, his jaw clenching.

"Bullshit." The word leaves my lips before I can stop it.

Gabriel's laugh is cold, slicing through the room like ice. "Believe what you want, but Korsakov is a liability. He's made enemies beyond just me."

"Give me a name," Angelo demands.

Gabriel tilts his head slightly, feigning thought. "And what do I get in return?"

"A ceasefire between our families," I offer, my voice flat. "Until we resolve this war with whoever is *actually* behind the attacks."

Angelo glances at me, his jaw ticking with unspoken tension, but he nods. "Deal."

Gabriel's expression sharpens, satisfaction flickering in his eyes. "Sarkisian. Arsen Sarkisian."

"The Armenians?" Angelo's confidence falters, just for a moment. "No fucking way."

Gabriel nods, his face devoid of humor. "Ask Korsakov what he did to Sarkisian years back to make him an enemy."

I want to ask more questions, *to dig*, but Angelo ends the meeting abruptly, his voice firm. "We'll be in touch."

As we leave, something catches my eye—a delicate face peeking out from behind a curtain. She's a ghost of a woman, barely there, her features pale and fragile against the shadows of the room. Big brown eyes widen in fear as they meet mine, shimmering with a silent plea. Her trembling finger presses to her lips, begging for my silence.

I nod imperceptibly, leaving her and Kaya behind as we step into the night.

The drive back to my office is interrupted by Angelo's phone buzzing. *Our father is awake.*

Angelo doesn't say a word as he speeds toward the hospital, his grip white-knuckled on the wheel.

We screech into the hospital parking lot, leaving the car running and sprint inside.

The sight of our father connected to so many machines is jarring, but his eyes are clear and alert. He looks at us with intensity before Angelo can speak.

"The Armenians," he rasps, his voice barely audible over the steady beep of the heart monitor. "It was them."

His confirmation validates Kaya's information.

I step out of the hospital room, to call Korsakov, the beep of machines and Angelo's murmured reassurances fading as I bring the phone to my ear. Maksim picks up after the first ring.

"Scythe," Maksim says, his tone as steady and sharp as always.

"It's confirmed. It was the Armenians."

There's a pause, and then Maksim swears under his breath. "Shit."

"Kaya said you did something years back," I press.

Maksim exhales. "Kaya embellishes. His intel is shit."

"Korsakov, what the fuck did you get us into?"

"Nothing," Maksim replies smoothly, but the slight pause in his voice betrays him. "Kaya's intel is shit."

"Angelo knows something. If I ask him, what will *he* say?"

"The same thing I just told you," Maksim snaps, deflecting. "Did you find more on Miroslav?"

I grit my teeth at his evasiveness but answer anyway. "It's not the Turks he made a deal with, that much is clear. Everything points to the Armenians."

Maksim sighs deeply. "I just landed. Now that we know who we're after, we can end this shit."

"We can start by dissolving this fucking alliance," I snap.

Maksim's voice turns cold. "The *Sovereigns* remains standing, Scythe. Whether you like it or not."

"Fuck the Sovereigns, this alliance has already put my sister in danger and almost *killed* my father. After I speak with Angelo, we're getting out of this shit," I spit.

Maksim's laugh is low and dark, sending a chill through me. "What about NovaRael? Are you willing to let that go, too?"

"I have ZEUS. I'll build on it," I reply confidently, though the weight of his words lingers.

"And what about Vasilisa?" Maksim adds.

The sound of her name stills me.

"You didn't think I would *let* you keep her, did you?" Maksim continues, his tone cruel and calculated, designed to cut deep.

A growl escapes my throat, anger and fear intertwining in a way that makes my skin prickle. "Fuck you, Korsakov." I end the call with a swipe, my hand trembling in rage, my grip tight on the phone.

The only thing that can calm me is her.

I pull up the feed and watch from the beginning—painting, laughing, too open with the guards. I scrub backward through days of footage.

Games. Cooking. Shared meals. Hands on her shoulders. Smiles she gives *too freely.*

I want to crush the phone in my hand.

I switch to live footage of her now, in the library that *I* gave her, painting with the guards. A surge of anger courses through me. I text every guard except Luca, ordering them to the hospital.

Fury blurs my vision as I watch them leave her side, their lips touching her forehead in goodbye. Instead of relieved, she looks sad.

Always a ray of sunshine, my wife. Too friendly.

Overly friendly.

Luca's disapproving stare burns through the surveillance screen, his silent judgment sharper than any words he could say. I refuse to acknowledge it. She belongs to me. That is the only truth that matters.

I shut off the screen, but the image of her lingers—her sad, distant expression etched into my mind like a wound that won't close.

I push it away. I have to.

I need to find Angelo. Focus on Maksim's evasions, on the war slipping through my grasp—not the ache my wife stirs in me.

By the time my men arrive, my anger has cooled to a simmer. Controlled. Contained. I give them their orders, stationing them outside my father's hospital room before leaving without another word.

Home. *To her.*

★★★

The house feels *wrong* when I return. Midnight is early for me, but the silence still unsettles. For the first time in months, the thought crosses my mind—*she might still be awake.* A flicker of something I refuse to name stirs in my chest.

Hope.

I glance toward the living room. Empty.

Upstairs, Luca is stationed outside her door, his presence both a reassurance and an irritation. A permanent shadow between my wife and me.

He doesn't move when I approach, but his eyes flick over me, assessing. "Your father well?" His voice is neutral, but there's a quiet edge to it.

"As well as can be expected," I reply curtly, my gaze shifting to the closed door behind him. "Is she asleep?"

"She went to bed early." His tone stays even, but something in it makes me bristle.

Anger.

"You have something to say, Luca?" I demand.

His jaw tightens, but he doesn't hesitate. "She's happy. She feels *good.* Free instead of alone. Instead of *trapped.*" His gaze sharpens. "You didn't need to take them from her."

The words slap harder than they should. My muscles coil, my voice lowering to something dangerous.

"I take what I want—from *her*, from *anyone*." I step closer. "Her happiness doesn't concern you, Luca. Tell me, is there something I should know?"

Luca doesn't flinch. "Vasilisa is a loyal woman. And I'm loyal to *you.* Remember that before you throw your jealousy in the wrong direction."

He brushes past me, shoulder clocking me hard, leaving me alone in the hallway with nothing but the weight of his words.

My hands curl into fists at my sides.

I stare at the closed door, anger simmering, jealousy burning through my veins like a sickness. She doesn't deserve this. And yet…

The image of her, surrounded by them. *Laughing.* At ease. Free in a way she should only be with *me*. It gnaws at me like a wound that refuses to close.

I force myself to move, retreating to my own room. Stripping, I collapse onto my unmade bed, exhaling sharply.

My fingers twitch toward my phone.

I shouldn't.

But the thought of seeing her, just for a moment—peaceful, warm, untouched by the burden of my name, *tempts me.*

It's been too long since I felt her skin.

Too long since I held what's *mine.*

Giving in, I pull up the surveillance feed to her room.

I tell myself it's just to check on her.

It's a lie.

But the moment the screen lights up, every thought evaporates.

Vasilisa isn't asleep.

She's writhing on the bed, her body arching, her thighs parting, soft moans spilling from her lips, moaning *my name* into the dark like it's a secret.

Heat scorches through me, my grip tightening around the phone as my pulse pounds, cock aching.

My wife is touching herself.

Touching what's *mine.*

A sharp possessiveness grips my chest like a vice. The sight of her fingers gliding between her thighs, disappearing beneath the thin scrap of lace she wears, is a sin I'd die to commit.

I should be the one touching her. It should be my hand. My mouth. My name breaking her apart..

She's mine. *Every inch of her belongs to me.*

I can't stop myself. I don't even try.

I drag my free hand down, wrapping my fingers around the hard length of my cock. A shudder rips through me as I stroke myself to the rhythm she sets for herself, my breath sharp, my restraint unraveling with every soft gasp she gives.

The little nightgown she wears has bunched around her waist, giving me a perfect view of her fingers slipping deeper into her panties, her body twisting with every slow, torturous stroke. Her other hand fists the sheets, knuckles white as she fights for control, but *I know* she's close.

Her breath hitches. Her thighs tense.

A broken moan, a sharp cry as her back bows off the mattress. Her legs snap shut, her body quaking as she comes apart—*on her own, without me,* but it's the way she says my name that ruins me.

My jaw clenches, my grip tightening as I chase the high she's already lost to. The possessiveness in my chest turns feral, burning through my veins like fire as my body tightens, need consuming every last thread of control.

She wants me. *She's reaching for me.*

Pleasure explodes behind my eyes, my body tensing as I spill into my hand, heat smearing across my stomach and the sheets beneath me. My breath is ragged, my pulse hammering as the last waves of release shudder through me.

Not enough.

I turn off the surveillance, tossing my phone onto the nightstand before yanking the soiled blanket off the bed. A heavy sigh rips from my chest as I head to the bathroom, frustration and satisfaction tangled inside me.

She's right down the hall. Soft, spent, still flushed from the pleasure she gave herself.

And I should be the one in that bed, wrecking her until she has no choice but to *crawl* into my arms.

The freezing shower does nothing to extinguish the heat simmering beneath my skin.

I wrap a towel low around my hips, scrub a hand through my hair.

Stepping out of the bathroom, my heart stutters.

She's here.

Perched on my bed in a white silk robe clinging to her like a second skin. She looks impossibly innocent. Dangerously forbidden. And I'm unraveling.

She shouldn't be here.

Her gaze drags over my chest, slow and deliberate, then meets mine—an unspoken question in her eyes.

"You're home early," she murmurs; soft, tentative.

"I thought you'd be asleep." The smirk is instinctive, especially when her cheeks flush pink.

Her eyes flick to the guest bed and its rumpled sheets, then back to me, brow furrowing.

"Were you asleep?" she asks, curious.

I don't answer.

I keep my eyes on her face; not on the parted robe, the flash of skin, or the way her fingers fidget like she doesn't know why she's here.

But then her eyes drop, to the towel slung low on my hips.

She doesn't look away fast enough.

She knows.

The way she watches me, the way she lingers on the sharp ridges of my body, on the tension in my stance—it's a dare. A challenge.

For a moment, I let myself feel it. The ache.

For *her*.

For the taste of what I've craved since the moment she stepped into my world and made it hers.

But I won't take it. *Not like this.*

"Why don't you go back to bed?" My voice is even, though my muscles coil. I turn to the closet, grab sweats.

Behind me, she exhales—too soft. Too much like the sound from moments ago, when she thought she was alone, writhing.

My grip tightens around the waistband of my pants.

Her voice slices through the tension. "Did that hurt?"

"What?" I ask from the closet.

"Your tattoo," she clarifies.

I inhale slowly, discarding the towel, dragging the sweats on.

"I knew what she meant. I just hoped she wouldn't ask.

The scythes carved into my back—sharp, unmistakable. A mark of who I became. *Of Scythe.*

I keep my voice steady, careful. "It didn't hurt. I'm used to pain." A pause. "It just took a while."

"I can only imagine it took days to finish," she says softly.

"Actually, it took weeks," I correct, stepping out of the closet, tying the drawstring on my sweats.

When I glance at her, her eyes meet mine, and for a second, I see something I haven't seen before.

A look I can't place.

Curiosity. Realization. Maybe even suspicion. It tightens something deep in my chest.

"Is it supposed to symbolize death?" she asks, her voice soft but probing.

I hesitate.

The scythes don't just symbolize death—they *are* death.

But I can't tell her that.

"Sort of," I say carefully, lowering myself onto the edge of the bed beside her.

She gives a slow nod, but her gaze lingers, searching. *Piecing me together.* Her fingers brush against my arm, the touch featherlight—a reassurance, or maybe a question she's not ready to ask.

"Santo?"

"Yes?"

I take in the delicate lines of her face, the warmth of her flushed cheeks, the small crease in her brow.

"I missed you," she whispers, her eyes dropping—hovering over my lips.

The words slam into my chest, hitting harder than they should.

A jolt of desire burns through my veins, sharp and searing, and before I can stop myself, I lean in, the space between us dwindling to nothing.

"I missed you too, Mia Dea."

Her breath catches. Her chest rises and falls faster, matching the unsteady rhythm of my own.

But she doesn't flinch. Doesn't retreat.

Instead, she holds my stare, her pulse thrumming in the delicate line of her throat.

"Santo," she whispers, her voice carrying the same breathless plea I heard earlier in her room—except now, *I'm right here.*

I swallow hard as her fingers trail up my arm, slow and deliberate, before coming to rest against my chest.

A single touch.

A fucking brand.

"Yes?" I whisper, matching the quiet intensity in her voice.

Her lips part, her breath shaky, but her gaze never wavers.

"I *want* you."

Not a plea. Not a request.

An assertion.

My body locks up, every muscle coiled with restraint.

For a split second, I hesitate—the weight of everything I've held back pressing against my ribs like a vice. *This is a line I can't uncross.*

But then she looks at me, *really looks at me,* with a need that burns through every last thread of control I've clung to.

Fuck it.

She's mine.

I cup her face, fingers threading through silk-soft hair. Her lips part—but I don't give her time to think.

I *take* her.

Pulling her flush to me; nothing between us but heat, hunger, and everything we've denied.

My mouth claims hers—soft at first, teasing. But the second she melts, it turns raw, desperate—a tangle of breathless moans and biting need.

Her hands slide up my chest, fingertips pressing into my skin, as if she's been waiting for this moment as long as I have.

Her silk robe shifts, slipping against her body, revealing flashes of bare, heated skin. It's torture. It's heaven. It's her—all of her.

And I want to taste every inch.

I break the kiss, forehead pressed to hers, trying to breathe through the unraveling. "Do you have any idea what you do to me?" I rasp.

Her lips curve into the faintest, teasing smile, her fingers skimming along my jaw.

"Maybe," she whispers, lips brushing mine. "But you could show me."

Fuck.

That's all I need.

I haul her into my lap, her thighs straddling mine, her heat grinding down on my cock—and I devour her.

My hands roam; memorizing, claiming. She grinds in slow, torturous circles. I fall back onto the bed, letting her lead, letting her wreck me.

Her tongue dances with mine, tasting of honey and sin, leaving me lightheaded with the need to taste more, *take* more. She nips my lip, defiant, wicked, and I snap.

With a growl, I flip her, pressing her into the bed. Mine again.

Her robe falls open. She's bare. Flushed. *Perfect.*

Her hair fans out like molten gold, wild, against the delicate beauty of her body. It shimmers in the dim light, strands catching silver where the moon touches them, making her look ethereal, untouchable—except she *is* mine to touch.

Her nipples are already taut, flushed a deep rose against her flawless skin, rising and falling with each shallow breath. My gaze traces the subtle dip of her waist, the gentle curve of her hips, the smoothness of her thighs—each inch of her pristine, *untouched* except by me.

She flinches, moving to cover herself. I stop her.

I brush her arms aside, covering her with my body. My mouth claims hers again; fierce, unrelenting.

She moans into my mouth, her hands exploring the hard planes of my back, nails dragging just enough to make me shudder. My lips travel down the delicate column of her throat, leaving goosebumps in their wake as I trace patterns with my tongue, savoring the taste of her skin. Each gasp, each soft plea that spills from her lips urges me on, consuming me with the need to devour her completely.

Between kisses, I murmur against her flushed skin, "How many fingers did you use?"

She gasps, a sharp inhale that makes me smirk against her throat. "What?" she breathes.

I answer by dragging my lips lower, my tongue flicking over the swell of her breast before I take one pert, pink peak into my mouth. She arches instantly, a breathless moan slipping free as her fingers tangle in my hair, holding me to her.

I release her with a graze of my teeth, my lips brushing over her heated skin as I murmur, "How many fingers did you use when you touched yourself tonight?"

A shudder courses through her.

"I *knew* you were watching," she whispers, her voice trembling as I swirl my tongue around her other nipple, watching her eyes go hazy with pleasure.

I bite down gently, just enough to have her gasping and pulling at my hair.

"Answer me," I demand.

Her lips part, a whimper slipping past them. "Two," she moans.

Her honesty making something dark and possessive coil in my gut.

"That's my girl." The praise rolls off my tongue like a reward, and the way she shivers makes me crave more.

Trailing kisses lower, I let my fingers ghost down her stomach, teasing the lace at her hips.

"Did you clean up after you came?" I murmur, dragging my mouth lower. "Or are you still dripping for me?"

Her breath stutters.

"I'm still…" She hesitates, her voice barely audible.

I lift my head, arching a brow. "Still what, Vasilisa?"

"For you."

A dark chuckle rumbles low. "Such a good girl." I hook my fingers into her panties and drag them down, slow. Torturous.

She shivers, anticipation flickering in her lust-blown eyes.

I trail my fingers along the inside of her thigh, light as a whisper, teasing her. Watching as she squirms, her breath hitching, her body already desperate for more.

She gasps when I reach the apex of her thighs, parting her with my fingers.

Dripping. Slick. Perfect.

"You weren't lying," I rasp. Hot. Wet. Mine. "You really are soaked for me."

She watches me, chest heaving, pupils blown. Her body is ready, but I won't rush.

Aching slow, I slide one finger inside.

She gasps, hips lifting, hands fisting the sheets as my thumb circles her clit; lazy, slow, teasing.

"Did you imagine it was me?" My voice is husky, dark, my need dripping from every syllable.

She whimpers, her thighs trembling.

I push deeper.

Her breath catches, her nails digging into my shoulders, she clings to me like she was made for this.

"Yes."

My restraint shatters.

I slide in another finger, curling just right; until she chokes on a moan, walls clamping tight.

My mouth finds her breast again, tongue flicking, sucking, teasing, as I work her over, as I push her closer and closer to the edge.

"Good," I murmur. "I want you thinking of me. *Only me.*"

A cry escapes her as I plunge deeper, her walls clenching, her body begging for more.

I capture her lips once more, our tongues tangling in a heated kiss as I drive her higher, my fingers working her into a desperate frenzy.

"Tell me you need me." I growl it into her mouth, pace punishing now.

She stiffens—then shatters, orgasm slamming through her. She tries to speak, but another wave steals her words.

My fingers work her through it, cock straining against my pants—desperate to be inside her.

As the last shudders ripple through her, she lies beneath me; wrecked, glistening, chest heaving. A vision drenched in moonlight.

Finally, she breathes the words.

"I do... I need you."

Her words set me ablaze. I can barely breathe.

I pull my fingers from her dripping pussy, her soft whimper only spurring me on as I bring them to my lips—sucking them clean, savoring her perfect taste, my eyes locked onto hers.

She shudders. She gasps as I push my pants down, my cock springing free, thick and aching for her. I position myself between her legs, the head of my cock dragging against her soaked entrance, teasing.

Her legs wrap around my hips, dragging me in. I groan against her lips, ready to take what's mine—

Then a fucking phone ring

Sharp. Jarring. Like a blade.

I ignore it. Claim her lips. Her body. Let her feel how close she is to being mine.

But the ringing persists.

Insistent. Grating. A fucking curse.

Someone is going to fucking die.

"Fuck, my phone," I growl, dropping my forehead to hers.

The sound is a reminder of the world beyond her—one I want nothing to do with right now

Sensing my withdrawal, she clings tighter, nuzzling into my neck with a soft moan.

"Ignore it," she whispers, voice warm against my skin.

I almost give in.

Then comes the knock.

My grip tightens. My jaw locks.

"What?" I snap, dragging myself off the bed, already missing her warmth.

"It's *Maksim*," Luca says from the other side of the door.

She sits up, flushed and breathless, tugging her robe tight. Modest—after what we were about to do. *It drives me insane.*

"You have to go," she whispers, trying to mask her disappointment.

I smirk at her shyness. I tug at the robe's knot, exposing the skin she's trying to hide. "He knows you're in my bed, you don't have to whisper."

She blushes. I cradle her face, brush my thumbs over her cheeks, and kiss her slow—deep. Lingering. Savoring.

"We're married," I murmur against her lips. "Don't be embarrassed."

She nods, still red-faced, and I brush my fingers over her jaw before pulling away to grab my phone.

The second I answer, Maksim's voice pulls me back into the world I despise.

"Two of my men were sent back to me maimed at my doorstep. I need Scythe."

The name snaps me out of the heat and silk and her. Scythe. Not Santo. Not her husband. The killer.

I glance at my wife—*my wife*—her soft, gorgeous face watching me with quiet concern, a worry she won't voice. She deserves better.

Better than me.

"On the way," I say gruffly, ending the call.

Vasilisa straightens, searching my face, holding in whatever she wants to say. Her fingers twitch in her lap.

She wants to stop me. I can feel it in her silence. But she won't.

"I'll send Romeo and Nico back to join Luca to guard you, okay?"

I know it won't be enough.

She inhales deeply. "Okay."

She nods. Brave. But that flicker in her eyes? *Knife to the ribs.*

I force myself to move, to change quickly, but her gaze is on me, watching every movement, every muscle. I catch the way she bites her bottom lip, eyes dark, needy, and it takes everything in me not to say fuck it all and climb back into bed with her.

Instead, I lean down, palm the side of her face, and kiss her hard, deep—enough to bruise. Enough to remind her.

And I leave her.

Again.

CHAPTER 32

VASILISA

I don't remember when I drifted off, but the sharp bang of the front door slamming downstairs yanks me from sleep like a bucket of ice water.

My heart slams against my ribs, foggy but alert. The weight of last night presses against my skin, the ghost of Santo's touch lingering in places that still throb with warmth.

Santo.

He's home.

I barely take a breath before I'm up, tightening my robe around me as I hurry down the stairs, my pulse a frenzied beat in my ears. The anticipation of him drives me too fast. I miscalculate the last step, my footing slipping out from under me. A startled gasp escapes me just as strong arms catch me, steadying me before I can fall.

Spicy tobacco and mint flood my senses, a scent so achingly familiar that my stomach knots with unease.

Not Santo.

My gaze snaps up, locking onto the wrong pair of eyes—light, sharp, filled with amusement. My stomach twists as a slow, knowing smile spreads across Angelo's face.

"Well, Piccola," he muses, his voice laced with humor. "What a lovely way to greet me."

I wrench myself out of his grasp, my robe slipping dangerously off my shoulder in my haste. His eyes trail the movement before flicking back to mine. There's something in his gaze I don't like.

I clutch the fabric tighter around me. "What are you doing here?" My voice betrays me, shaky with confusion and something else—something colder.

Angelo smirks, tilting his head like he's amused by my reaction. "Santo sent me to check in. He's still working."

"Santo can delegate *the Don* to watch his wife?" I ask, the disbelief thick in my voice.

His smirk falters just enough to show the flicker of annoyance beneath his easy arrogance. "No one *delegates me*," he says smoothly, but there's an edge now, a quiet warning. "This is more of a brotherly favor."

His arm drapes over my shoulders before I can react, the weight of it heavy, possessive. I don't like it.

"Come on," he says, guiding me toward the kitchen like I don't have a choice. "Why don't we get some breakfast? Have a little chat. Get to know each other."

There's something unsettling in how casual he makes it sound. I swallow hard and nod, forcing my body to move, even as my jaw clenches against the unwanted proximity.

"Tell me, tiny," he drawls, the amusement creeping back into his tone, "have you ever fired a gun?"

I step out from under his arm, shrugging him off like his touch is something I can scrub away. "Can I get dressed first?"

His chuckle is low, dark. "If you have to."

I don't wait for a second dismissal. I turn on my heel and bolt up the stairs, my skin prickling with unease.

Getting dressed is harder than expected. My hands hover over my options—one part of me reaching for the dresses I've been trained to wear, another considering Santo's insistence on modesty. Jeans or decorum? I hesitate, the war inside me unfamiliar, frustrating.

In the end, my training wins. I pull on a corduroy dress over a crisp white shirt, black tights hugging my legs, and finish with platform heels. Something about it feels like armor. I brush my hair into a ponytail, smoothing stray strands before inhaling deeply.

I step into the hall—only to collide with Luca.

His expression is tense, cautious.

"Angelo's here," he murmurs.

"I saw him already… unfortunately, not as dressed as I am now."

Luca's brows draw together, his concern evident. "He wants us to leave."

The weight of his words settles in my chest, pressing tight. "He wants me to leave *my home?*" My voice rises with indignation, sharp and unwavering.

"Not you," Luca clarifies, shaking his head. "Just us. Romeo and me."

A chill creeps down my spine. Grabbing Luca's arm, I plead, "Please don't go."

His expression softens, but his stance remains firm. He pats my arm gently, his touch reassuring, but it does nothing to ease the unease twisting in my stomach. He carefully pries my fingers off him. "Angelo won't hurt you, Vasilisa. I don't know what he wants, but I do know that much."

That's not enough. Not for me.

Romeo appears at the end of the hall, his sharp eyes assessing the tension between us. "Did you tell her?"

"I was getting there," Luca mutters.

"Tell me what?" I demand, looking between them, my pulse hammering against my ribs. A tight, suffocating sensation creeps into my chest. "Is Santo okay?"

Luca holds up a hand, stopping my thoughts before they spiral. "He's fine."

I exhale sharply, the relief short-lived as Luca continues, "It's your parents. They still haven't been found."

The air shifts, turns thick and oppressive. My breath catches in my throat.

"Do you think they're—" The words lodge themselves there, too monstrous to voice.

"No," Luca interjects, his tone firm, unwavering. "The intel we've gathered suggests your father made a deal with some of our enemies. It may involve the Armenians."

The floor tilts beneath me. My body is still, but inside, everything is shattering. My father?

A deal with the Armenians.

A betrayal of the Bratva.

A betrayal of us.

I force myself to breathe, to pull my mind out of the chaos threatening to drown me. He left. My mother left. My sister and I...discarded.

I swallow hard, locking my emotions behind a wall of ice. "So, Angelo doesn't want to hurt me, but *interrogate* me?"

Luca and Romeo exchange glances, their hesitation feeding my unease.

"We don't know," Romeo admits, his words careful.

"I'm not leaving," Luca states with finality.

I press a hand to his shoulder, grounding myself in the moment.

"No," I murmur, forcing steadiness into my voice. "You have to follow his command. I'll be okay."

The words taste like a lie, but Luca's hesitation cracks just enough for him to nod.

Together, they escort me downstairs to the kitchen.

Angelo sits at the breakfast bar with Nico beside him. Julian is serving them, and I can't contain my joy when I see him.

"You're back!" The relief surges through me, and before I can stop myself, I rush forward, throwing my arms around Julian.

His strong arms wrap around me, lifting me slightly off the ground in a bear hug. The warmth of his embrace is a momentary reprieve from the tension coiled in my chest, a familiar comfort in a sea of uncertainty.

"How was your trip?" I ask as we pull apart, though I keep hold of his hands, unwilling to sever the connection just yet.

Julian's face lights up. "It was amazing. I spent time with my brothers, we went camping, fishing—it was—"

A sharp throat-clearing cuts him off.

Angelo's sharp gaze zeroes in on him, then flicks to our hands.

"You touch my brother's wife like that all the time?" he drawls.

Julian pales, his hands slipping from mine as if burned. "No, sir, of course not. I've been on—"

"Enough." Angelo waves a dismissive hand, cutting Julian off as if he's no longer worth his attention.

My fingers twitch at my sides, the sudden chill of Julian's absence leaving me more unsettled than I'd like to admit.

Angelo turns his attention fully to me now, his darkened eyes assessing, calculating.

"Come here, Piccola," he commands smoothly, motioning for me to step closer.

I hesitate.

Every instinct screams at me not to move, but defiance is a luxury I'm not sure I can afford. Gritting my teeth, I force my feet forward, stopping beside him as he swivels in his stool to face Luca and Romeo, who hover uneasily in the doorway.

Without warning, Angelo loops an arm around my waist. His grip is heavy, branding the fabric of my dress. My muscles lock up at the contact, a prickle of discomfort traveling up my spine.

"You two can leave for the day," he says, flashing a smile that doesn't reach his eyes. "You too, Nico."

Nico pauses, his fork halfway to his mouth. His brow furrows, and for the first time since I entered the room, real tension crackles in the air.

"I thought you wanted me to stay while you and Vasi—"

"No, you're not needed," Angelo interrupts smoothly, that smile widening. "I have Vasilisa."

His hand slides gently down my side, slow, deliberate. I suppress a shudder, my stomach twisting.

"I don't think that would be appropriate, boss," Nico says, his voice hard, controlled. He sets his fork down with a quiet *clink* and stands, his shoulders squared, his scar more pronounced under the shadow of his growing anger.

"Challenging me, Nico?"

"Just suggesting," Nico replies, steel beneath his words.

The two men lock eyes.

The room goes still, the unspoken power struggle thickening the air. My pulse pounds against my ribs.

Then, Angelo laughs, a slow, dark sound that makes my skin crawl. "Fine," he says, waving a dismissive hand as if he's humoring a child. "You three stay. Tiny and I have business to attend to *downstairs*."

Confusion flickers through me. My gaze shifts to Angelo's profile, his smirk unwavering. "Downstairs?"

He finally turns to look at me, his expression unreadable, but the glint in his eyes unsettles me. "Yes, Tiny."

Before I can protest, he stands and presses a guiding hand against the small of my back. Firm. Insistent. Not forceful—yet.

I glance back at Luca, Romeo, and Nico, their faces set with silent concern. But no one stops him.

I force my spine straight as Angelo leads me toward the kitchen pantry.

At first, confusion clouds my thoughts. But as we pass my large stash of junk food, something catches my eye. A glint of metal peeks from the shadows—a small silver button embedded in the back wall.

Angelo presses his finger to it.

A low vibration hums through the air, deep and resonant.

Then, with a soft whoosh, the wall splits apart, sliding open in smooth, mechanical precision.

An elevator.

A *hidden* elevator.

My breath catches, my pulse kicking into high gear. I've lived in this house for months. *Months.* And I had no idea this existed.

Angelo chuckles, the sound vibrating low in his chest as he nudges me forward. "Surprised, Piccola?"

I step inside hesitantly, my eyes flicking over the sleek interior. The control panel has five buttons, each labeled with a single letter.

Angelo presses the last one labeled 'B.'

The doors slide shut.

We begin to descend.

The ride is smooth. The silence, unbearable. I keep my arms tight around myself, my mind racing through every possible reason why this hidden place exists.

The doors open with a quiet ding, revealing something I never expected.

A sprawling underground space, brightly lit and expansive.

To the left, a fully equipped gym, glass walls encasing an arsenal of weight racks, punching bags, and machines.

To the right, a gun range, targets lined up at varying distances, bullet casings scattered like discarded confessions.

Further back, the entrance to a luxurious pool and sauna.

Angelo gestures toward a locked door. "That one's for guy's night." His smirk deepens at my unimpressed expression.

Beyond that, a hall stretches into the unknown, leading toward what I assume is the underground garage.

Angelo watches me, his amusement evident. "You really didn't know about this?"

I shake my head, unable to find words.

He laughs. "You really are Santo's caged bird."

The words sting, but I lift my chin. "What exactly are we doing down here?"

Angelo's smirk lingers, but his gaze sharpens.

"You," he murmurs, stepping closer, "are going to learn how to survive."

***

Spending time with my brother-in-law isn't as bad as I thought it would be. With expert care, he teaches me how to dismantle and clean a gun, emphasizing safety—keep my finger off the trigger, treat all guns as if they're loaded. I practice with his Glock 17, and to my surprise, Angelo calls me a natural when I hit the bullseye.

Despite his intimidating exterior, I've come to see that Angelo is *not* what I expected. I try to remember his instructions, planting my feet shoulder-width apart, slightly bending my knees, and taking aim.

"Don't tense up, Tiny," Angelo says, pulling me from my thoughts. His body presses against mine from behind, his hands covering mine on the gun. The scent of his cologne fills the space between us, and I swallow hard, trying not to focus on the heat radiating from him.

"Relax," he murmurs, his voice low and steady, guiding. "You'll shoot better if you're loose."

My heart pounds. Santo wouldn't like this—Angelo standing this close, touching me this way. Even though it's innocent, I know exactly how it would look to him. A flicker of unease tightens my stomach, and guilt

257

settles in my chest like a weight. I grip the gun tighter, more out of necessity than anything else.

"You got it?" Angelo's finger curls around mine on the trigger, the question hanging heavy between us.

I nod quickly, forcing myself to focus. "Yes."

"Good." His breath brushes the top of my head. Together, we pull the trigger, and the sharp crack of the shot echoes in the air, striking the bullseye once again.

Angelo steps back, taking the gun from my hands as I exhale a shaky breath. "You're a quick learner, Piccola," he says, his tone softer than before, almost… approving.

I watch as he safely disassembles the weapon, his movements confident, precise. For the first time since we started, I allow myself to relax. He's not Santo. Not even close. But if he's here, it's because Santo trusts him—and that has to mean something. Besides, he's my brother-in-law, and I could use family.

I take a breath and glance at him. "Do you want to have lunch together?"

He smirks, lips curling up mischievously. "What are we having?"

"I have leftovers from dinner last night that I made," I say with pride.

"Sure, I can stay for a bit, Tiny." He winks. "But then I got to head out."

He gestures for me to go ahead of him, and together, we step into the elevator, its metal walls gleaming under the soft lighting.

The ride is quiet. I watch him from the corner of my eye. His usual smirk is gone, replaced by something distant, lost. His jaw clenches as he stares at the closed doors, lost in thought.

I wonder what he's thinking, but I don't dare ask questions I don't want answers to.

The doors slide open with a soft chime. I shake off my curiosity and step into the kitchen. Julian glances up as we enter, his gaze flicking between me and Angelo.

"Are you two in need of a snack?" he asks with a smile.

"No, thank you," I reply, heading straight for the fridge and pulling out containers of leftovers from last night's dinner. "Just heating up some lunch."

Angelo sits at the breakfast bar, his eyes following me as I pull the leftovers from the fridge, the faint aroma of garlic and herbs already making my mouth water. Julian steps in to help, carefully taking the containers from me.

"Will you be joining us for dinner, Don Amato?" Julian asks.

Angelo keeps his eyes on me and shakes his head. "No, I can't tonight."

When the microwave beeps, Julian grabs the containers.

"This is too hot for you to handle, Mrs. Amato," he teases, offering a friendly grin. "Why don't you sit down? I'll plate it for you."

I hesitate but follow his suggestion, slipping onto the stool beside Angelo. His gaze is still steady on me, and I can feel the weight of it even as I focus on the sound of Julian arranging our plates.

"So, tell me about Santo when he was younger," I ask, breaking the silence with a small smile.

Angelo's brows lift in amusement.

"Younger Santo? He was a pain in my ass," he says, chuckling. "Smart as hell, though. Always outthinking everyone, including me."

I laugh softly. "I can't relate. I'm the eldest, and clearly the smartest."

His chuckle deepens, a low, rich sound that catches me off guard. "I'll take your word for it, Piccola."

Julian sets our plates down, nodding politely before excusing himself. Angelo watches him go, his gaze lingering, before returning to me. "I hear you're a talented artist," he says, his tone shifting to something softer.

"Yes," I reply, surprised by the question. "Painting is… an escape for me."

His eyes sharpen slightly, the teasing glimmer replaced by something more thoughtful.

"Do you often need an escape?" he asks, his voice low before taking a bite of his spinach and feta ravioli.

I shrug. "Sometimes."

"This is delicious," Angelo hums. "You did a great job, Tiny."

"Thank you," I say with a smile. "Amelia helped me."

Angelo nods and we continue to eat our meals in comfortable silence. Surprisingly, I am thoroughly enjoying my time with him.

The simple act of sharing a meal and having an easy conversation makes me miss Santo even more.

I watch as Angelo roughly wipes his mouth with a crisp napkin, his light eyes sparkling with amusement. "What's your favorite dish?" I inquire, genuinely curious.

"Pasta with vodka sauce, or any kind of rich red sauce," he replies with a hint of pride in his voice. "I like the color."

"Simple tastes," I remark, surprised at his answer.

"I'm a simple man," he retorts with a smirk, but there is a glimmer in his eyes that hints at a deeper complexity.

I scoff and playfully roll my eyes, "You are far from simple, Mr. Amato."

"You call me Angelo, Piccola," he teases, pointing a finger at me as if scolding a child.

Angelo's phone begins to ring, and Luca enters the kitchen.

Excusing himself, Angelo steps away to take the call, leaving me alone with Luca.

"Where have you been?" I ask curiously.

He leans against the counter, watching me.

"After he took you away, I went to Santo," Luca replies, his eyes scanning me intently, as though searching for cracks in my armor. "Are you okay?"

I nod, forcing a smile. "Yes, I'm fine. I actually had a great day. Is Santo okay?"

Luca's posture softens slightly. "Yeah, he's just working."

Angelo returns, his expression noticeably harder than before. The shift in his demeanor sets me on edge.

"Piccola," he starts, his voice lower, "Some business came up. I have to go."

Unease prickles at my skin. "Is everything alright?"

His gaze softens briefly, the hard edges of his face relaxing for just a moment.

"Don't worry yourself over it," he says, stepping closer. His fingers brush against my temple as he tucks a loose strand of hair behind my ear.

The gesture feels too intimate, too *careful*. Luca clears his throat loudly, his discomfort impossible to miss.

Angelo doesn't even glance at him. "Maybe get some water for that throat, Cattaneo."

"Is *Santo* alright?" I ask Angelo with more urgency. My heart pounds at the weight of his gaze.

"He's fine," Angelo replies, his voice steady, but his eyes linger on mine too long, their scrutiny heavy and invasive. His thumb grazes my cheek briefly, a touch that makes my chest tighten with unease. Before I can respond, he drops his hand and strides toward the kitchen door. "I'll be back tomorrow."

"Wait," I call after him, a sinking feeling settling low in my stomach. "Is Santo coming home?"

For the briefest moment, something flickers across Angelo's face—guilt, hesitation, or both. His eyes drop for a fraction of a second before he schools his features into a stern mask.

"Not tonight."

Then he's gone.

The weight in my chest grows unbearable, and tears threaten to spill. I quickly brush them away, refusing to let myself fall apart here. But I can't shake the pressure in my chest, the lump in my throat.

Santo.

Chapter 33

SANTO

Silence suffocates Angelo's penthouse as I step inside, the weight of my rage pressing against my chest like a loaded gun.

I barely made it through the drive from NovaRael without turning back to confront them.

The surveillance footage still burns behind my eyes—*him with her*—the easy way he touched her, the fucking way she *let* him.

My hands clench, itching for violence.

The image of her beneath me; writhing, gasping my name, should drown everything else out.

It doesn't. The sight of Angelo's arm around her waist, his hand brushing her cheek. It festers like poison, fueling the inferno inside me.

The penthouse is pristine, every surface polished to a cold, soulless gleam. It's fitting. It reflects him—my brother and his snake's grin. I stride to the bar, pouring myself a drink with steady hands that betray the storm inside. The whiskey burns as I take a slow sip, but it does nothing to extinguish the fire in my gut.

The elevator doors slide open.

Angelo saunters in, that lazy, knowing smirk on his lips. Like he's already won. The fire inside me roars to life.

"Hello, little brother," he drawls, arrogance dripping from every syllable.

I turn just enough to look at him, my grip tightening around the glass in my hand. "Why were you with her?"

Angelo strolls to the bar, unfazed, and pours himself a drink. "Why wouldn't I visit my cognata?" He smirks, swirling his glass. "She was all *alone.*"

My teeth grind together. "She had three guards. She was *fine.*"

"I sent them away," he says smoothly, taking a sip. "Spent the day with her instead."

The words crack something inside me. The thought of Vasilisa—*my wife*—alone with him shoves a knife into my gut. My fingers flex around the glass.

"She's a needy little thing," he muses, taking another slow sip.

The whiskey in my hand nearly sloshes over the rim as my grip tightens.

I down the rest of my drink, slam the glass down, and shove him back—hard. His own whiskey sloshes, spilling over his fingers as he stumbles back a step, his smirk deepening.

"Don't talk about her like that."

Angelo raises a hand in mock surrender. He eyes the whiskey dripping down his fingers and clicks his tongue before setting the glass down on the bar with exaggerated care.

"Relax, Scythe," he taunts. "I meant no disrespect."

He wipes his hand off on his shirt, then grins. "We had a great time—*went for a swim.*"

My vision tunnels.

"You didn't swim with her." The words scrape from my throat like jagged glass.

"Oh, but I did." He grins, that same fucking grin that used to drive me insane as a kid—only now, it's worse, because I know he's doing this on purpose.

I think of the pool. I think of how they disappeared into the kitchen pantry and never came back for hours. Then, it hits me.

"You didn't." I sneer, "She didn't have a bathing suit with her. Her clothes and hair were dry when she came back."

Angelo shrugs, lazy as ever, settling onto the couch across from me. "Who's to say we didn't swim nude?"

The world snaps.

Before I even register moving, my hands are on him, fisting his shirt, dragging him forward until our faces are inches apart. My breath is ragged, my pulse a war drum.

"No. You. Didn't." The words are a growl, low and deadly.

Angelo doesn't flinch. Doesn't resist. His hand grips my wrist, squeezing just enough to remind me that he's not afraid.

"We didn't," he finally says, prying my hands off him. He straightens his shirt like it's just another night, then leans back.

Then he smirks. "But I am seeing her again tomorrow. And the next day. And the day after that. Until you pull your head out of your ass and go home to your *wife.*"

The rage inside me is molten, unbearable. I shove a hand through my hair, but there's no relief, no comfort. Just the sickening truth that he knows—he sees the cracks in my armor.

"Why do you even care?" I grit out.

Angelo's smirk fades. His eyes—sharp, unforgiving—pin me in place. "Because she's a kind, smart, beautiful woman who doesn't deserve to be abandoned in *that* house."

"I'm keeping her safe," I snap.

"By leaving her alone?"

"She's safe in that damn house!" The words explode from me, raw and desperate.

Angelo's stare doesn't waver. And then he delivers the killing blow. "Like our mother was?"

The room drops into silence.

My chest tightens.

"Don't you *dare* bring her into this," I snarl, but it's too late. The damage is done.

"Why not?" Angelo's voice is ice. "You're doing the same thing Dad did."

I shake my head. No. No.

"I'm not," I spit. "She has round-the-clock surveillance, guards, an entire staff. Our mom was truly alone."

"And look what happened to her." His voice is razor-sharp. "She was taken, tortured, sent back to us in pieces. Surveillance or not, she wouldn't have stood a chance." He leans forward, eyes burning into mine. "So I'll ask again—why are you hiding from your wife?"

"I'm not," I snap, but my voice cracks at the end.

Angelo's smirk creeps back, but this time, it's cruel. Knowing. "You are," he murmurs. "And I know *why*."

I shake my head. My pulse pounds against my skull.

"You're hiding Scythe."

The name slams into me like a blade. My gut twists.

"No," I deny, but it sounds weak even to my own ears.

Angelo scoffs. "You don't think she can handle that?"

I open my mouth. Close it.

"She's innocent," I finally say, the words rasping from my throat. "She's good. And I'm—"

"What she's used to," Angelo cuts in. "She grew up with Maks. He's worse than you." He chuckles darkly. "Hell, the son of a bitch is worse than me half the time."

My hands tremble. I flex my fingers, forcing control back into them.

"I'll go home to her," I mutter. "Just... not right now. Not in the middle of all this." I gesture vaguely, my chest tightening as I try to grasp something—anything—to make sense of this.

Angelo watches me for a long moment. Then he sighs, shaking his head in disbelief. "If you don't want to protect your wife, then I will." His voice is final. "Maksim entrusted you with her safety, and you just passed her off to your fucking guards."

"She's fine," I repeat, but it sounds hollow.

"Whatever helps you sleep at night, little brother." Angelo stands. "Get some sleep, you look like shit. I'll take the meeting with Maks tonight and fill you in in the morning."

And just like that, he's gone.

★★★

I spent the night watching surveillance footage of Vasilisa sleeping peacefully.

Now I sit in my office, eyes locked on the live feed, exhaustion drowned out by anger. She's at breakfast with Luca and Romeo, laughing—radiant.

It's the kind of laughter that makes a man forget the world is cruel. The kind of happiness I should be giving her.

But I'm not there.

A sudden urge grips me—to call them away, to remind them they're soldiers, not her damn entertainment. They should be watching the perimeter, not her face.

But I stay silent, transfixed, caught in the sheer light of her.

And then he walks in.

Angelo.

He moves straight to her, his confidence so casual it's infuriating. He leans down, places a kiss on her cheek—*my* wife's cheek—and his hand settles possessively at her waist. My blood turns molten as he helps her off the stool, leading her toward the pantry.

Before he disappears with my girl, he turns his head—eyes locking onto mine through the surveillance camera.

And the asshole grins.

A sharp, taunting grin that sends a white-hot surge of fury through me.

My fist slams against the desk. The impact echoes through the room, but it does nothing to quell the rage boiling beneath my skin. I curse myself for not installing cameras on the ground floor. It never seemed necessary—only Angelo and I had access.

A mistake. One I'll correct the second I return home.

But I can't go home.

Not yet.

With my responsibilities. *Scythe doesn't get breaks.*

I push the anger down—lock it in a corner of my mind where it will simmer until I have the time to deal with it.

The intercom beeps. Evie's voice fills the room.

"Marcus is ready for you."

I exhale sharply, standing, rolling the tension from my shoulders before making my way to the cyber security floor.

As the elevator doors slide open, I expect good news. Maybe another breadcrumb leading to whatever deal Miroslav made with the Armenians.

What I don't expect is to see *him.*

Wesley fucking Beaumont.

I loathe the rich bastard. The entitled smirk. The effortless wealth. The arrogance. He's the kind of man who thinks power is bought, not taken.

A bullet between the eyes would be an immediate solution to my irritation.

Problem is, it would also be impulsive and stupid. Not to mention, hiding the death of a billionaire would be a logistical nightmare.

Still, my fingers twitch at my side.

"What the fuck, Marcus?" I demand, my voice sharp enough to cut glass.

To my surprise, Marcus looks genuinely taken aback. "You said to use all resources and anyone available."

"Anyone who works for *us.*"

The smug bastard raises his hands in mock surrender. "I come in peace."

"The Beaumont's weren't enemies of Mr. Popov," Marcus continues, his eyes flickering between Wesley and me. "But... are they enemies of *your* organization?"

"You have got to be fucking kidding me," I mutter under my breath before locking eyes with Wesley. The fucker smirks like this is a business deal and not an insult to my very existence.

"It's common knowledge that you're mafia, Santo," Wesley says, extending a hand.

I don't take it. Instead, I glare at him in silent warning.

He drops his hand with a shrug. "I couldn't care less about that. It's War's issue, not mine." His smirk widens. "If anything, I want an alliance. A truce. To work together."

"You shouldn't be touching my shit, let alone *be* in my business."

"But I found something." He turns back to the computer, fingers flying over the keyboard. "See?"

He pulls up images. Myself. Luca. Nico. Angelo. Maksim. Vaska.

I move before I can think, shoving him aside to take control of the computer. I scroll through document after document, confirming what I don't want to believe.

Miroslav has been embezzling from his own company. From NovaRael.

Using *my* NovaRael as his own personal piggy bank.

The transactions are right there, money funneled into offshore accounts under his name. Years of betrayal buried beneath careful accounting.

But that's not the worst of it.

My fingers tighten on the mouse as I click through more files. And then I see it.

A date. A time. A location.

"A drop-off." The words leave me in a whisper.

Wesley leans in. "Looks like Miroslav is supposed to make a delivery at the docks."

I barely hear him, my mind already moving miles ahead. What the hell is he delivering? What's valuable enough to risk making a deal against the Bratva? Against Maksim?

He has a death wish. And soon enough, it'll be fucking granted.

I force myself to step back, inhaling deeply before turning to Wesley.

His stupid, square-jawed face is set in satisfaction

"What do you want?" I ask.

His grin widens. "A collaboration."

"Of what?"

"I don't know yet," he says, too casual for my liking. "But I'd like to schedule a meeting in the near future to discuss it further."

I don't trust him. Not even a little.

But I can't deny that he's just handed me exactly what I needed.

Reluctantly, I nod. "Fine."

We shake on it, and I resist the urge to break every damn bone in his hand.

As Wesley leaves, I shift my focus to Marcus. He's tense, watching me carefully, as if bracing for my wrath.

"We gained a lot more with his help than we ever could have alone," Marcus says, voice cautious.

I watch him for a long moment, then exhale sharply, clapping a firm hand on his shoulder. "You're forgiven this time. But *never* again."

Marcus nods, understanding the weight behind my words.

I leave without another glance at the computer. As soon as I'm behind the door, I pull out my phone, typing a quick message to Maksim.

'Found something. Miroslav's been using NovaRael to funnel money. Deal at the docks. Date, time attached. Also, fucking Beaumont's involved. Will explain later.'

His response comes instantly. *'Got it.'*

I exhale, sinking into my chair, running a hand down my face.

The truth settles over me like a storm cloud.

Miroslav played us.

But that isn't what weighs on me the most.

It's the upcoming drop-off.

What the hell is he moving?

And more importantly—who else is involved?

The remaining days of the month blur into a cycle of intel gathering by day, bloodshed by night. The weight of each kill presses against my soul, but I push it aside.

Instead, I drown myself in my work.

I spend sleepless nights at Angelo's penthouse, his taunts about his time spent with my wife pushing me further into the darkest recesses of my mind.

Vasilisa is a beacon.

And I?

I am nothing but a shadow.

CHAPTER 34

VASILISA

The month flies by, and my brother-in-law—or *cognato*, as he's taught me, is surprisingly fun to be around.

He visits every day, sending Luca and Romeo away. I miss them. And Nico; I never see him at all. The bond I had with my pseudo brothers wears thin, but time spent with Angelo is an adventure of its own.

He gifted me my very own Glock, and together, we work on my shooting skills. He makes me spar, teaching me to use my speed and size to my advantage.

'If you ever find yourself in danger, Tiny,' he says, wiping blood from my lip after a particularly rough takedown, 'make the fucker regret breathing. Go for the nose.'

We even use Santo's gym, where we work out together—him lifting weights while I run on the treadmill.

Training becomes my escape.

Because Santo never calls me back.

Never answers my goodnight texts.

And with Luca gone, I don't know if he's safe. Or if he thinks of me at all.

Angelo tells me that Santo gets to the penthouse late and leaves early, much like he did when he was here.

I Despise it.

But Angelo—though he doesn't soothe me with pretty words or empty reassurances—distracts me. He has breakfast and lunch with me, pulling my thoughts away from the dangers my husband might be facing. He lets me in, tells me things I don't think he tells anyone. About his mother's death. About why they call him Sinner.

The story is brutal.

It makes my heart bleed for younger Santo.

When Angelo leaves in the afternoons, I paint. I paint memories of my husband, afraid I'll lose them. As short and fleeting as they were, they are my *most* favorite.

As I slow down on the treadmill, Angelo drops his dumbbells with a heavy clank, wiping sweat from his face with a towel before walking over. He hands me my water bottle that Lila had brought down for me earlier, I take it, but it gnaws at my feelings that she refuses to look me in the eye.

I didn't have any gym clothes. Angelo calls Cassandra. Suddenly I have gym clothes. Now I have seven brand-new running shorts with matching tanks, while Angelo sticks to his usual—sweatpants and no shirt. His torso is a canvas of ink. And his back…

His back is captivating.

A pair of large, black-and-red angel wings spread across his muscular frame.

Santo has a tattoo.

Santo has a *better body.*

I like that he only has one large tattoo instead of multiple ones. It lets me see his body better. The way his muscles shift. The way his skin looks when it's damp. Like the night before he left…

The memory of his fingers between my legs hits me hard.

I can still *feel* him.

Santo makes me feel *feral.* I've never been so uninhibited in my life, never *wanted* like that before. But his body is a masterpiece—his smooth chest, his defined abs… those abs…

They're to die for.

Before Santo, I'd never even been close to having sex.

Sex.

With Santo.

With his cock…

I don't know how I'll ever be ready to take it. It's… *big.*

I figured, like Luna once said, men with great bodies were compensating. The bigger the man, the smaller the…

But I was *so* wrong.

So incredibly wrong.

Lost in my fantasies about my husband's body, I don't realize I've been staring at Angelo until he speaks.

"You like what you see, Tiny?" he smirks, the cockiness dripping from his voice.

Heat rushes to my cheeks. I recover fast. I point to the red ruby tattooed on his chest.

"Actually, I like that one."

He glances down at it, smiling faintly. "One of my favorites. What do you want to do now?"

"Can we go for a swim?" I ask eagerly.

Angelo chuckles and shakes his head. "Not unless you want a Santo shaped hole through the garage door."

"If it'll bring him home, I say yes!"

"We can't," he says with finality. "Let's go."

We make our way to the elevator and Angelo lets us in, once inside, I watch him quietly.

"Go ahead with your question, Tiny. I know you have one."

"Did Santo say I *can't* swim?"

"No," Angelo replies simply.

"Then why did *you* say we can't?"

Without warning, Angelo stops the elevator and locks eyes with me. His shirtless form is intimidating as he traps me against the wall and his frame. His breath brushes my face.

"Let me ask you something, Piccola. Do you think I'm a good man?"

I blink at him. "I— being a good man is relative," I answer carefully.

His head tilts slightly, considering my words. "Do you think *Santo's* a good man?"

I hesitate for a second, but the answer feels easier. "I'd like to think so."

Silence stretches. I can tell he's about to say something else, but the words catch in his throat. So, I speak first.

"It depends on who you ask and what you're asking them." I shift my weight and meet Angelo's eyes. "For instance, Maksim. If you ask me about him, I'd say he's a good man. I've only known him to be good to me; piggyback rides when I was younger, patching up a scraped knee. Maksim's always been *Mishka* to me. But…" I trail off, biting the inside of my cheek. "It wasn't until I got older that he started using me to date prominent people, to build alliances… or to marry me off to men like Santo."

Angelo's gaze lowers as he pulls away from me, but I catch the flicker of something else there, hesitation. It passes quickly, tucked behind the usual ease he wears so well.

"In order to swim with you, it would make Santo think I'm *not* such a good man." His tone is light, but the words sit heavier than before. "And when it comes to my brother… I'd like to be a good man."

I nod slowly, unsure why the sudden shift in his mood makes me uneasy.

But just as I think the conversation is over, Angelo's eyes linger, watching me a little too intently. His next question catches me completely off guard.

"Has he hurt you?"

I freeze, my heart skipping. "In what way?"

Angelo holds my gaze for a long moment, but there's something behind his eyes, as if he's trying to fit together pieces of a puzzle I can't see.

His silence stretches a little too long.

"Never mind," he says eventually, but the dismissiveness feels forced.

I almost let it drop, but something about the way he asked lingers. Before I can think too much, Angelo speaks again, softer this time.

"If he ever does… let me know. I'll remind him how lucky he is."

I manage a faint smile, but I can't shake the feeling that he wasn't joking.

The elevator resumes its ascent as Angelo releases the stop button, resuming our ascent. I watch him out of the corner of my eye, catching the faint trace of a smile tugging at his lips as if he's already shaking off the moment.

"Pack your things for tonight and a dress for the charity event tomorrow at Exile."

"Where are we going tonight?" I ask nervously.

"To my penthouse," Angelo replies, a hint of amusement in his voice.

The thought of seeing Santo tonight makes my heart soar with anticipation. Ignoring Angelo's amused chuckle, I rush past him as soon as the doors open and head upstairs to pack.

"I have to shower first, Piccola," Angelo calls after me. "You should do the same."

I shower as quickly as possible, toss a robe around me, and rush to pack my things. I tear through the closet, searching for my overnight bag. Frustration builds as I tug at the handle, knocking a shelf with my elbow so forcefully that it rattles.

A small white card flutters to the ground.

I stifle a cry, rubbing my elbow as I glance down.

Then my heart stops.

The name *Rachel* is scrawled in casual script above a red kiss mark, a phone number scribbled underneath.

I stare at it, my chest tightening as my mind races.

Rachel.

A past conquest, no doubt. This has been my room since our wedding. This…this *thing* shouldn't even exist in our space.

A hollow laugh escapes me before I can stop it.

Of course.

It had to be from *before* me. Right?

Because the alternative—the thought that this was from *after,* from *now,* makes something curdle in my stomach. My fingers crumple the card before I even register the motion, crushing it into my palm before tossing it into the bathroom trash.

Refocus, Vasi.

Not tonight.

Tonight, I have one thing on my mind. *Santo.*

With renewed purpose, I hastily pack my bag—nightie, toiletries, makeup. For the charity event, I select one of my sexiest yet elegant dresses, slipping it into a garment bag to keep it pristine.

A reminder.

He's spent too long away. Let's see how long he can keep resisting me.

Picking an outfit for tonight is easy, it feels almost liberating to shed the soft, simple dresses and the jeans-and-oversized-shirts I'd worn in his absence. The modesty was for him.

But tonight, I want to be seen.

Tonight, I *want* him looking.

I descend the stairs slowly, my heart pounding in anticipation at the thought of seeing Santo soon. At the bottom step, Angelo waits, dressed in his usual all-black attire, his posture relaxed but his sharp gaze immediately locks onto my outfit. His dark brows lift in surprise.

"What are you wearing?"

Confused, I glance down at my ensemble. "Clothes."

Angelo raises a hand as if to stop me. "I know what clothes are, and that's not it. You're basically in a bra."

"It's a bustier," I clarify, still unsure of the issue. "And nothing is showing," I add confidently, handing him my overnight bag.

"Those pants are too tight."

"And yet they fit me just fine," I say, gesturing toward the leather that clings to me perfectly.

"Do you always dress like this around the house? Around my brother?" His tone shifts, amusement curling at the edges of his words, his light smoky eyes glinting with mischief.

I stiffen slightly.

"Sometimes," I answer nonchalantly. "Why does it matter?"

Angelo lets out a low chuckle, shaking his head. "He's stronger than I thought."

My brows knit together. "Excuse me?"

But before I can press for an explanation, he shifts gears, nodding toward my feet. "What's with the heels?"

I glance down at my three-inch stilettos. "What do you mean?"

"They're too high for you. You're going to snap an ankle," he teases, though I catch the slight edge of concern.

I roll my eyes playfully. "Thank you for your input on my fashion choices. But don't worry, these heels are quite comfortable."

Angelo smirks, his teasing unwavering. "Alright, Tiny, do you need anything else before we leave?"

I shake my head. "Nope, I'm all set!"

The SUV moves smoothly through the bustling city streets, headlights reflecting off the wet pavement. Inside, the conversation flows naturally, Angelo's voice warm as he shares little pieces of Santo's past.

"He used to take apart household appliances just to see how they worked," Angelo says with a chuckle. "Our mother would always hide the blender."

I smile, picturing a young Santo with an insatiable curiosity.

"He was always buried in a book too," Angelo adds, his tone shifting slightly. "I used to tease him about it, but honestly? I admired it. Still do."

My chest tightens at the rare glimpse of affection he lets slip.

I tell him about Mimi—how much I miss her, how she's always been my anchor. We talk, we share, and soon the conversation lulls into a comfortable silence.

Then Angelo breaks it.

"I have to know—were you really trained to be a made man's wife?" His voice is even, but there's a layer of something beneath it.

I shift uncomfortably. "Not trained... just never really had a choice. I was always told I'd marry a powerful man. It wasn't necessarily limited to the syndicate, but it was a high probability."

"Did you have to learn anything?"

I exhale, mentally sifting through the years of conditioning Maksim forced upon me. "CPR. First aid. Accounting. Etiquette. Interrogation training." I give Angelo a pointed look. "Guess that one came in handy."

He laughs. "Who made you take these classes?"

"Maksim."

Something unreadable flickers across Angelo's face. "He was grooming you to be the wife of someone like him."

His expression darkens slightly. "Although, not teaching you how to use a gun, let alone defend yourself was an idiot move."

"I don't think he ever thought I'd be alone or need to use a gun," I admit quietly.

Angelo's lips press into a firm line. "I understand. We never taught our sister either."

I blink, caught off guard. "How *is* Elena?"

"Stubborn as ever," he says with a smirk. "She won't leave until she finishes finals."

"I get it," I nod. "I had to defer my studies for this... arrangement."

Angelo glances at me. "You go to school?"

I lift my chin slightly. "I do."

"And Santo is okay with you being on campus where other men can see you in that bra you call a shirt?"

Heat rises in my cheeks. "Not exactly," I admit. "But he agreed to online classes. Hopefully, that'll be enough for the school. I really don't want to drop out."

Angelo's voice is smooth, certain. "You won't have to. They'll accept your terms."

I narrow my eyes. "You seem pretty sure."

He smirks. "Let's just say I'm owed a favor almost everywhere. I'll cash them in if needed."

Something about the way he says it makes me believe him.

We pull into a dimly lit parking garage, the soft glow of LED lights reflecting off sleek cars. Angelo maneuvers the SUV into a reserved space near a reflective elevator. The moment we stop, my eyes catch on a figure standing by the doors.

Nico.

Excitement rushes through me, and before I can think, I'm out of the car, crossing the space between us in a heartbeat.

"Nico!"

I throw my arms around him, holding tight, feeling a sudden wave of relief at being in his presence again.

He pats my back, stiff at first, before finally allowing the hug. When I step back, his eyes flick past me toward Angelo, his expression sharpening.

"You brought *Santo's* wife here?"

Angelo's jaw tightens as he steps forward. His voice is smooth, but there's an unmistakable edge to it. "Yes, Nico. She's spending the night."

Nico's gaze flickers between us before he exhales sharply, pressing the elevator button.

The doors slide open, and I step inside with Angelo. He pulls a black card from his wallet, taps it to a sleek panel, and we ascend.

To the penthouse.

When the doors glide open, my breath catches.

The living room is stunning—two plush black couches, elegant glass end tables, and a state-of-the-art television descending from the ceiling. Maroon curtains frame massive windows, the city skyline stretching endlessly beyond them, glittering like scattered diamonds against the night sky.

A slow exhale leaves my lips.

Angelo's penthouse is immaculate. From the sleek, modern stainless-steel appliances in the large kitchen I can just make out to my left. A hallway leads off to my right, and I can see a room at the end of it. Angelo turns to me with a warm smile.

"Your home is beautiful," I say, my voice soft as I take it all in.

"Thank you, Piccola," he replies, a ghost of pride in his tone. "I'm going to put your things in the guest room. Make yourself at home."

I sink into the plush couch, my fingers running over the smooth fabric as I glance out the massive windows. The city sparkles below, stretching endlessly into the night. My gaze drifts to the bar against the wall—two glasses sitting on the counter, a quiet remnant of Santo's presence.

I wonder when he will return. Nervous energy flits about my body at the thought of seeing him again after so long without any contact.

I hope he isn't upset with me for showing up unannounced.

Angelo's company has been a welcome distraction, but I can't shake the ache of not knowing what Santo is thinking and feeling like an afterthought in my own marriage.

Angelo returns, phone pressed to his ear. His voice is calm, laced with that ever-present authority. "Yeah, be here around six in the morning... Yeah, the charity's at eight. See you then." He pockets his phone before turning his attention back to me.

"So, Tiny, I made a few calls. Isabella will be here in the morning to do your hair and makeup."

I blink. "I can do my own hair and makeup, that's not an issue."

"I'm sure you can. But this is my treat. Consider it a gift from your cognato."

The generosity catches me off guard. I offer him a small smile. "Thank you."

I pause for a moment, trying to keep my voice steady. "When will Santo get here?"

Angelo hesitates, just long enough for the dread to creep in as he takes a seat beside me. "He won't be coming back here tonight."

The words hit harder than I expect. My heart drops.

"Where is he?" I ask, my voice thinner now. "Is he going back home? Maybe I should go back there—"

I move to stand, but Angelo's hand closes around my wrist—firm, grounding. "I don't think he'll be there either."

A knot tightens in my stomach.

"Let's order a pizza, watch a movie," he suggests, pulling me back onto the couch. "You'll see Santo tomorrow at the charity."

I should nod, should smile, should accept the casual reassurance. But my mind is already spiraling.

Why isn't he coming?

Is he… angry?

Or is it worse?

A thought claws its way to the surface, sharp and poisonous. *Is he with someone else?*

My throat tightens. I hate that I even let the thought cross my mind. I don't want to be that woman—the insecure, jealous wife. But the doubt is there, growing like a vine wrapping around my ribs, squeezing tighter.

"Where's the restroom?" I manage, my voice quieter now.

Angelo gestures toward the hall. "First door on the left. Guest room is right across from it."

I nod, forcing my limbs to move, to escape before the emotion overwhelms me.

The cool marble countertop grounds me as I brace against it, staring at my reflection. My face is pale, my lips pressed into a thin line. Get it together.

I splash water on my face, letting the icy bite drag me back to reality. But it doesn't erase the image in my head—the idea of Santo with someone else. The betrayal I shouldn't even assume, but can't help but feel.

Would Angelo tell me if he was?

Or is this whole night meant to distract me?

I hate this.

I step back, inhaling deeply, and head into the guest room. The moment I open my bag, I realize my mistake—I only packed a nightie. No robe. No cover-up.

I stare at the delicate blue silk in my hands, frustration bubbling beneath my skin.

I'd picked this outfit for Santo. What a waste.

Maybe I can just spend the night in this room and avoid any further interaction with Angelo.

I undress and slip into the blue nightie before crawling into the bed. I press my face into the pillow inhaling deeply. It smells like Santo. Like the remnants of something I miss so badly it aches. A single tear escapes, then another.

A sharp knock breaks the moment.

"Are you alright in there, Tiny?"

Angelo.

I swallow the lump in my throat. "I'm okay."

"Are you coming out or not?"

With a quiet groan, I push myself out of bed, rubbing away any trace of tears before opening the door. I pass by Angelo quickly entering the living room, keeping my gaze averted to hide my redden face, but the moment I face him his expression shifts.

"Do you own anything that covers more than half your body?" His tone is incredulous, laced with amusement.

Heat floods my face, and I wrap my arms around myself. "I forgot my robe at home."

Without another word, Angelo disappears down the hall and returns moments later, tossing me sweatpants and an oversized shirt. "Wear these."

Grateful, I hurriedly pull the pants on, cinching the drawstring tight and rolling up the legs to fit. I pause, glancing up at Angelo, who has, thankfully, turned away to give me some privacy. I discard my nightie and put on the burgundy shirt with *Stanford* written across the chest.

"You went to Stanford?" I ask, surprised.

Angelo shakes his head. "No. Just Santo. Those are his clothes."

A strange feeling washes over me—bittersweet. I'm wrapped in his scent, his belongings, but not him.

The elevator chimes.

"Pizza's here," Angelo announces turning around as the doors slide open to reveal Nico, two boxes in hand.

The moment he sees me, his face hardens. His gaze flicks to Angelo as he hands over the pizza.

"I didn't know what you wanted on yours, so one has pepperoni, and the other is just cheese," Angelo explains as he sets the boxes down on the coffee table in front of the couch.

Nico remains at the elevator door, his intense gaze fixed on me with an angry glint in his eye that makes my blood run cold.

"You're really going to keep her here?" He directs at Angelo.

Angelo's jaw tenses. "Say what you got to say Nico."

The weight of whatever's unsaid hangs heavy between them. Their exchange shifts into rapid Italian, their voices sharp, controlled. My name is mentioned more than once, but I can't piece together what's being said. Then Angelo's voice lowers, the final words clear.

"Se vuoi vivere, te ne andrai."

Nico exhales sharply before turning on his heel and leaving.

I let out a slow breath. "He's angry at me."

"He thinks I'm going to fuck you."

Shock slams into me. "He—what?!"

I barely recover before another wave of panic hits. "He wouldn't tell Santo that, would he?"

Angelo shrugs, utterly nonchalant. "No. I'd kill him if he did."

His words should be a joke. But they're not.

Angelo sets down the pizza, grabbing two plates. "One or two slices?"

★★★

The night winds on. We eat too much pizza and watch a cop show Angelo claims taught him everything he knows about the law.

At some point, I'm sprawled across the couch, my feet resting on Angelo's lap. When he grabs my foot, I shriek.

I try to pull away, but he keeps a firm grip on me.

"Do you love Santo?" His voice is quiet.

He begins to expertly massage my foot with his skilled hands. Each touch sends waves of relaxation through my body.

His thumbs knead slowly, deliberately.

"I don't know... I think I could, I want to, but he," I take a deep breath and will myself not to cry. "He just left me."

Angelo studies me. "I was in love once."

I sit up at this confession, pulling my foot away and crossing my legs in front of me.

"What happened?"

His eyes darken. "She left."

The air shifts.

"I'm sorry. Do you know where she is now?"

"Florida," he answers immediately.

"Why did you bring her up now?" I lean forward as if the closer I get to him the more I can read.

He looks away, his eyes shadowed.

"We spent a week together once. Ended up on a couch like this. Her feet in my lap." He looks at me again, the intensity of his stare penetrating me. "This moment just reminded me of her."

A chill runs up my spine.

"Don't worry Tiny, I don't want you. "You look nothing like her," he shrugs nonchalantly his familiar grin plastered on his face.

I let out a breathless laugh. "Good. Santo would maim you."

"He could try." Angelo smirks. "Now, time for bed."

CHAPTER 35

SANTO

A month away from Vasilisa is torture.

Thirty fucking days, and I'm unraveling.

If I hear one more word from Angelo about what an idiot I am for leaving her, I will commit fratricide. I don't need my brother cataloging every damn thing I've missed—her habits, her moods, the way she's been waiting for me. I *know*.

Instead of going home, I steer toward Luca's, telling myself I'll take a nap, shower, and then go to that stupid charity event. It's not avoidance. It's not cowardice.

It's fear.

Fear of what I might find when I walk through that door.

But as I drive through the city, my grip tightens on the wheel, my pulse hammering louder than the engine. I think about *her*. About Vasilisa in our bed, curled up, her hair spread across the pillow. About crawling in beside my gorgeous wife, burying my face in her neck, whispering apologies against her skin; begging for forgiveness for abandoning her while worshiping her body for days on end.

To hell with the event. To hell with everything.

I jerk the wheel, making a sharp, reckless turn. My foot slams on the accelerator, sending the car flying down the street. I need to see her. I need to be home.

By the time I hit the winding drive leading up to my estate, my pulse is a thunderstorm in my veins. The tires screech as I slam on the brakes, barely putting the car in park before I throw the door open.

I take the steps two at a time. I don't care if I wake her. *Dio, let me wake her.* Let her be in bed, warm and waiting. Let me see those sleepy, confused eyes as I pull her into me. Let me hold her.

The house is silent.

The kind of silence that feels *wrong.*

My stomach clenches as I reach her bedroom door and shove it open, flicking on the lights.

Empty.

My breath catches.

I step inside, searching for anything—some sign that she's still here. The bed is perfectly made, the sheets undisturbed. Her things are scattered across the room, her clothes tossed aside—but the closet— I yank it open.

Her overnight bag is gone.

A sharp, jagged breath rips from my lungs.

No. No. No.

She wouldn't *leave me.* She *couldn't.*

Without thinking, I bolt from the room, ripping open the door to the guest bedroom.

Empty.

My pulse roars in my ears, drowning out the stillness.

My phone is in my hand before I even realize it, my fingers dialing on instinct.

Luca.

He picks up on the second ring.

I don't let him speak. "Where is she?"

There's a beat of hesitation. "Angelo said he told you."

My breath turns sharp. "Told me what?"

Impatience coils like barbed wire in my chest.

"He took her to the penthouse. I thought she was with you when you didn't show up here."

I don't bother responding. I hang up and immediately dial Angelo.

It rings.

And rings.

And rings.

Voicemail.

I try again.

Same fucking thing.

A growl rips from my throat as I shove my phone away and bolt down the stairs, my body a live wire, my head pounding with a single, blinding thought—

I need to see her. I need to get to her. *Now.*

I don't remember the drive, only that I press my foot to the floor, weaving recklessly through traffic. The city blurs past, nothing existing outside of my singular goal.

By the time I tear into the parking garage of the penthouse, it's eight in the morning and Nico is not at his post.

Something in my gut twists.

I shove the feeling aside, storming toward the elevator. Tapping my access card on the panel, the doors sliding open as I step inside, my pulse hammering in my ears.

The moment the doors open, it hits me.

Her scent.

Warm. Sweet. The unmistakable perfume that clings to her skin.

She's here.

My breath leaves me as I move, following the faintest trace of her. I need to see her. To touch her. I rush toward the guest room, her scent strongest here. My heart slams against my ribs as I grab the handle and turn—

Empty.

The room is void of her presence.

My relief evaporates.

"Vasilisa!"

Her name tears from my throat as I turn toward the master bedroom. My mind spins, my blood hot with rage, my vision already darkening at the edges.

If she's in his bed—

I will rip her from his arms and kill my own brother with my bare fucking hands.

I shove the door open—

Empty.

My stomach churns.

She isn't here.

I stagger back into the living room, frustration, jealousy, and an all-consuming rage rolling through me in violent waves.

Then I see it.

Two mugs of coffee.

Empty plates.

My hands curl into fists as I reach for one of the mugs, my fingers brushing over the ceramic.

Warm.

Still fucking warm.

My heart stumbles in my chest as my eyes flick to the delicate lipstick print on the rim.

She was *just* here.

The realization slams into me like a freight train. I sink onto the couch, my lungs dragging in uneven breaths.

Then something else catches my eye.

Blue.

On the floor, crumpled by the couch, is a silk nightgown.

Hers.

Vasilisa's.

The delicate lace trim, the fabric that frames her body skin tight, softness I've traced as I carried her up the stairs…

And now it's discarded.

Here.

In *his* living room.

A roar builds in my chest, my vision blurring as red creeps into the edges of my mind.

He *took* her.

Brought her *here.*

Without my knowledge.

Without my *permission.*

The betrayal cuts through me, jagged and merciless, and before I can stop myself, my fingers are dialing again.

This time, he answers.

He doesn't speak.

Neither do I—not at first.

"Where. Is. My. Wife?"

There's no hesitation. No guilt. Only that cool, fucking infuriating calm.

"We're at Exile. Charity event." A pause. Then, smoothly, "Get your shit together and get here."

The call disconnects before I can respond.

I stare at the phone in my hand, my pulse hammering, my blood still boiling—

But one thing is certain.

I'm not taking orders from *Angelo.*

I'm *not* going to Exile.

I'm going home.

And when she walks through that door, she'll face her husband.

VASILISA

Exile in the daylight is almost unrecognizable. Sunlight pours through large windows, revealing polished floors and curated décor where shadows and strobe lights usually reign. Tables are arranged for the charity auction—bidding on trips, artwork, and rare collectibles, all to support public schools. Maksim hosts this event once a year, though with everything happening, I half-expected him to postpone it.

Angelo returns to my side, tucking his phone away. His face is neutral, but something in his eyes is off—troubled.

"Everything okay?"

He flashes an easy smile.

"Yeah, Tiny, all good. Why don't you go say hi to your cousin? Bid on whatever you want, I got it if you win." He nods toward a table where Katya is inspecting a painting, her lips pursed in thought.

I smooth out my dress and prepare myself. I love my cousin, but she carries herself like she's worlds ahead of me. She's effortlessly put together, her rose-pink dress shimmering under the lights, her posture impeccable.

As I approach, she turns, and to my surprise, a wide smile spreads across her face. She glides toward me with effortless grace, looping her arm through mine as we move through the room.

"Mrs. Amato," she drawls, her tone teasing, "how's married life treating you?" Her dark blue eyes sparkle as her brows rise and fall.

"It's treating me well," I lie with a small smile.

"Where's that husband of yours?" She scans the room until her gaze lands on Angelo, deep in conversation with Maksim. "I thought you married the other one."

"I did. Santo had to work, so Angelo brought me."

Katya rolls her eyes. "That's all these men do."

I huff a quiet laugh. "How have you been? Are you alright?" My voice softens at the memory of her near-abduction.

She waves a dismissive hand. "Please. If I locked myself away every time my life was threatened, I'd be a hermit." She chuckles, utterly unfazed. I envy her—her fearlessness, the way she stands unshaken. Meanwhile, all I seem to do is worry. About Santo, about my pseudo-brothers, about Mishka. The weight of it is constant.

Before I can respond, we collide with someone, the woman's drink spilling across Katya's dress.

"What the hell?" Katya shrieks, stepping back and letting go of my arm, staring down at the spreading stain.

"I am so sorry," the redhead gasps, grabbing a napkin and dabbing at the fabric.

Katya snatches the napkin from her and storms off toward the restroom, leaving me alone with the stranger.

She's beautiful. Her auburn hair cascades over bare shoulders, her black dress a little too tight, a little too casual for an event like this. Her cat-like eyes crinkle as she offers a sheepish smile.

"I'm so clumsy. Sorry about your friend."

"She's my cousin. And accidents happen," I reply, keeping my voice light.

Her expression shifts, recognition lighting up her face. "Oh, you must be Vasilisa."

Something in her tone makes my stomach turn.

She extends a hand, her voice syrupy sweet. "I'm Rachel. Santo has told me so much about you."

My pulse stutters.

Santo told her about me.

I take her hand out of habit, my mind spinning. *Rachel.* The name clicks into place. The kiss mark on the card Rachel. The woman I brushed off as a past fling. But he spoke to her—about me.

"When?" The question comes out sharper than I intend.

She tilts her head. "When what?"

"When did he tell you about me?" My voice is even, but my heart pounds against my ribs.

Rachel's lips twitch, as if she enjoys this. "Oh. This is awkward." She bites her lip in mock sympathy. "Don't be upset—that's just how *these* men are."

"When?" My patience snaps, my tone turning cold.

Her eyes flash. "The day before—and *after*—your wedding."

The words slam into me, but she doesn't even look apologetic.

"I don't believe you," I say stepping past her, intent on leaving, but she grabs my wrist.

"Was he *home* on your wedding night?" she murmurs, her grip tightening. "No? Because he was at Opulent. With *me*."

A sharp pain blossoms in my chest.

"Everything okay?" Luca's voice cuts in, his attention locked on Rachel's hand around my wrist. She releases me instantly, all saccharine smiles.

My mind shuts down.

"We're good," she says breezily before turning and walking away.

Luca touches my shoulder, snapping me out of my daze. "Vasilisa. What did she say?"

My throat tightens. "I want to go home. Can you take me home?"

His brows furrow. "What happened?"

I swallow hard. "What's Opulent?"

Luca stiffens, eyes flicking away for half a second. A second too long.

He exhales. "It's a strip club. Angelo and Santo own it."

The air is sucked from my lungs.

My tears are pushing forward, but I refuse to let them fall. Not here. Not now.

"Take me home."

I move toward the exit, but Luca steps in front of me, his voice low. "Vasilisa, *what* did she say?"

My hands curl into fists. "If you don't take me home, I'll ask Angelo to do it."

Luca studies me, his jaw tight. Finally, he steps aside and follows me out.

The car ride is long, suffocating. The silence is only broken by the occasional sound of Luca typing on his phone at red lights. My own phone sits useless in my lap—I have no one to call. No one to turn to.

By the time we arrive, I barely register the guards ignoring me, Amelia's wary gaze as I pass her, the quiet stillness of the house that has felt more like a prison than a home.

I should pack. I should leave.

But I have nowhere to go.

My parents are fugitives. My sister is far away. My phone, stripped of all contacts, is a cruel reminder of my isolation. Every friend I've made here? Loyal to Santo. And more than likely, every single one of them *knew*.

I am utterly and completely alone.

I push open the door to my bedroom—and stop cold. Santo sits at the edge of my bed, waiting.

"Santo, what are you doing here?" My voice is sharper than I intend, but I don't bother hiding it.

His jaw tightens. "What? *Home?*"

"In my room is what I meant. But yes, also home," I fire back. "I'm surprised you aren't working. Or at *Opulent.*"

His brow furrows. "Opulent?"

I cross my arms. "Yes. Weren't you there on our wedding night?"

He doesn't move. His gaze stays locked onto mine, unreadable.

But I *see* him—disheveled, tired, a far cry from the put-together man I met months ago. His shirt hangs open, his knuckles are scabbed, dark circles shadow his eyes, and the stubble on his jaw is more than a couple of days old. He looks wrecked.

Good.

I refuse to let that sway me.

"You don't have to answer," I say breezily, striding past him toward the closet. "Rachel already let me know you went to see her."

I yank out a suitcase and toss it onto the bed beside him. Still, he doesn't react.

"Not going to deny it?"

"No."

That's all he says. *No.*

I see red.

My fingers curl into fists at my sides, but I don't let them shake. Instead, I turn, standing in front of him, meeting his storm-dark gaze with fire.

"I didn't realize this arrangement was an open one."

His jaw flexes. His eyes narrow. "Didn't you?"

"No, Santo, I didn't," I bite out.

His gaze sharpens, and then he reaches behind him, pulling out a delicate blue nightie, dangling it between his fingers. "Then explain this."

I frown, thrown off. "What?"

"This was on the living room floor at my *brother's* penthouse."

A laugh bursts from me—harsh, bitter. "That's not even what you think it is."

"Isn't it?" He tosses the nightie onto the bed as he stands stalking toward me.

I instinctively step back, fury burning through me, licking up my throat.

"You think that *low* of me? That I would sleep with your brother?"

"I think if he commanded it, your duty to the family would force you to."

The sheer audacity of it sends my control snapping. I shove at his chest, but he doesn't move, doesn't budge. Instead, I force my way around him, nearly shaking with rage.

"I have a mind of my own, Santo!"

His head tilts. "Do you?"

My breath stutters. "What the hell is wrong with you?"

Santo crosses his arms over his chest, his jaw locked tight, eyes dark as a storm. "Are you just polite to *every* man you meet, or are you being the dutiful, proper wife of the underboss?"

I stare at him, my pulse roaring in my ears. "I'm not going to apologize for being kind and wanting to make friends."

His eyes flash. "You're always making friends. You're *too* friendly."

I shake my head with a scoff and head to the bathroom, grabbing the stupid card I found and toss it at him, he ignores the paper ball as it falls to the floor. "You act like I'm out here parading myself around!"

"You think I'm wrong?" He grabs the paper off the floor, "Explain Ivanov."

"Pietro is my *friend*," I say, my voice firm.

Santo opens the paper, rolls his eyes and tosses it back on the ground before continuing his interrogation, "What about the way you went to touch his face?"

It takes me a second to even remember what he's talking about. Then it clicks—the morning the war was announced, Pietro's bruised face in the kitchen. "He was *injured*."

"And the way he looks at you?"

I throw my hands in the air. "I can't control how others look at me, and neither can you!"

His voice drops, lethal. "Yes. I *can*."

Santo tilts his head, a dark chuckle leaving his lips. "You think my brother won't die for fucking you?"

My breath catches.

"Then I'd be in charge." He steps closer, voice a quiet threat. "And what would happen to you then?"

I lift my chin, refusing to back down. "What *would* happen to me, Santo?"

He shrugs, "Depends on how many more *friends* you decide to make."

A sharp, bitter laugh rips from me. "I can't make friends, Santo. As soon as I do, they all magically disappear on *'vacations.'*"

I storm forward, and for the first time, he steps back. But I don't let up.

I stab a finger into his chest. "You deleted Luna from my life." Stab. "Lila came back and won't even speak to me." Stab. "You send guards away like they're disposable pawns." Stab. "You force the staff to ignore me like I don't even exist." Stab.

The last words rip from me, raw and aching. "And then you *leave* me for months at a time."

Santo's expression flickers—his shoulders tense, his mouth parts like he's about to say something, but I don't let him.

"I feel so alone, Santo." My voice cracks, the tears breaking free. "This doesn't feel like a marriage. It doesn't even feel like a real relationship."

His storm-dark eyes soften, guilt creeping into the lines of his face. "I don't know how to be in a relationship," he mutters, voice low.

I let out a hollow laugh. "Oh, please. Yes, you do."

His brow furrows. "Casual sex doesn't equal a relationship."

Casual sex. The words are a slap to the face.

"Yet you have the nerve to complain about me being *friendly*?"

His jaw ticks. "I haven't been friendly with anyone since we were arranged."

I meet his gaze, unflinching. "And I've had two relationships and *no* sex."

His nostrils flare. "I'm supposed to believe that?"

I shake my head, done. "I don't care what you believe anymore."

Santo exhales sharply, his frustration mounting. "I just find it hard to believe, given the way you've *thrown* yourself at me." He steps closer, his voice dropping. "Or is that part of your duty as a wife?"

"Enough, Santo!"

But he doesn't stop, his accusations cutting deep. "You're jealous of women who meant nothing to me, yet you have active relationships with every man you meet."

"I do *not!*" My throat tightens. "You're jealous because I smile or laugh or banter with anyone."

Santo's gaze darkens. "Because all those things should be reserved for *me.*"

I let out a sharp, exhausted chuckle. "My God, Santo, you have to reel that in. I've *tried* for you."

I lift my chin, meeting his gaze head-on. "I stayed up late waiting for you. I made dinners you never ate. I had doors slammed in my face. I tried to make something out of nothing—because I'm *your* wife."

Santo's jaw tightens. "And what a dutiful wife you are."

The words are a blade.

His tone is bitter, dismissive, and it lights a new fire in my veins.

He turns, heading toward the sitting room, but I chase after him.

"Why do you keep using that as an insult?" My voice quivers with anger, frustration—pain.

Santo stops, turning slowly. "Because you were born into this." His voice is sharp, controlled, but beneath it, something breaks. "You were *bred* to be the perfect, obedient wife."

His eyes flicker, his fists clenching. "You don't feel anything for me. You don't love me."

I take a step back, stunned. "Oh, and you do?" My voice wavers, the words daring, bitter. "Santo, you tolerate me at best."

Santo steps closer, fists clenched at his sides, but his expression softens, raw and unguarded.

"You think I tolerate you?" His voice is low, rough, weighted with frustration and something far deeper. "You think I can just tolerate the woman who consumes my every thought? My every breath?"

I freeze. His words are thick, vibrating with an intensity that makes my pulse stutter.

"You don't understand, Vasilisa." His jaw flexes, his dark eyes burning into mine. "I don't need *air* when you're near because you *are* the air. You fill every space, every moment, with light. Without you, there's *nothing*. No life. No meaning."

His chest rises and falls sharply, his control slipping.

"From the moment I saw you at Exile, everything changed. I couldn't breathe—not because you suffocated me, but because I needed you *more than anything*. Every time you're in a room, it's like nothing else exists but *you*."

He swallows hard.

"When I said '*I do,*' it wasn't because I *had* to. It was because, in that moment, I *knew*—I couldn't spend another day without you tied to me. Without you being *mine*."

His voice cracks, exposing the depth of what he's held back, what he's fought against.

"I tolerate you?"

He exhales sharply, shaking his head. "No, Vasilisa. I've loved you in ways I never thought possible, and it *terrifies* me. If love means losing control—if it means *needing* someone so much it burns a hole through my heart—then yes, I love you more than I can handle."

He steps closer, the air between us charged, suffocating. "But it's you—" his voice lowers to something dangerous, something aching, "*you* are the one who tolerates."

The silence that follows is thick, stretching between us like something tangible. My pulse hammers so loudly I can barely hear.

He loves me.

The words linger, refusing to settle, refusing to make sense. My body feels weightless, my mind at war with itself. I want to believe him.

I *want* to desperately.

But I can't move. I can't speak.

Santo doesn't push. Instead, he exhales, forcing something down before he murmurs, "I want to show you something. Get dressed—something suitable for outdoors."

And just like that, he turns to leave.

"Wait," I breathe.

He stops.

I turn my back to him indicating the zipper of my dress. "Can you?"

For a second, he doesn't move. Then, slowly, he steps behind me.

His fingers graze my spine as he pushes my hair aside, knuckles trailing heat down my skin. My breath hitches, goosebumps rising in the wake of his touch. When he finally tugs the zipper down, the brush of his fingers feels different, not just intimate, but deliberate.

Meaningful.

My heart stumbles, my throat tight.

He loves *me*.

His breath lingers near my neck, the space between us humming with the weight of everything unsaid.

This is what I wanted.

But I can't afford to believe in fairytales. Not yet.

Still… my heart is already slipping. Hoping. *Yearning.*

His voice is low, smooth, a quiet vibration against my skin. "Meet me in the kitchen. Bring a jacket."

And then he's gone, leaving me standing there, undone, my mind a tangled mess.

CHAPTER 37

SANTO

I've made a mess of everything.

Her face when she said I only tolerated her, it gutted me. The shock in her eyes when I told her I loved her, it will haunt me.

I can do this. I can push Scythe away, keep that part of my life separate from this side of my life. I can bask in her light and keep her far from the shadows of my darkness.

I can do this.

In the guest room I change into my dark jeans and pull on a light gray t-shirt, the soft fabric feels cool against my skin. I reach for my brown leather jacket in the closet, the familiar weight of it settling comfortably on my shoulders. I lace up my sturdy boots, ready to take Vasilisa for a ride.

I wait for her in the kitchen where Mrs. Keen gives me a weary glance.

"Is everything alright?" she asks concerned.

"Yes, I was wrong, just as you suggested," I admit. "I'm going to take her for a ride."

Mrs. Keen's eyes crinkle with a soft smile. "That is an excellent idea."

"I need a favor."

"Anything."

"Have the staff move my belongings back into the master bedroom and then everyone has to leave."

Her head rears back, her eyes blink many times before she utters, "Leave?"

"Yes, I need time with my wife. *Alone.*"

Mrs. Keen bursts into a wide smile, "We'll be gone before you return."

Before I can say anything more Vasilisa walks in wearing fitted jeans that hugs her form just right, paired with ankle boots that add a hint of height just how she likes it. Her lightweight knit top drapes elegantly over her, with a soft texture that catches the light. Over her arm, she carries a leather jacket and once again I'm breathless at her beauty.

Her eyes soften when they meet mine. "You look handsome," she mutters unsurely.

"Thank you, you look breathtaking as always," I compliment taking her hand and pressing a kiss to her knuckles enjoying the blush that creeps on to her cheeks.

She tugs at her hand, but I hold it instead, lacing her fingers with mine, she narrows her eyes playfully, "So, what's the plan for today that required pants?"

"We're going for a ride," I grin and escort her in to the pantry—to the elevator. I pull out my phone and set up access.

"Give me your finger," I say, lifting our intertwined hands.

I guide her hand to the biometric scanner disguised as a simple silver call button, placing her finger on it. It beeps twice and I reluctantly release her hand.

"Now you can use the elevator whenever you like. Just press your finger on the button and choose a floor," I explain stepping inside with her.

Her eyes widen in surprise. "How far does it go?"

"To the roof," I reply with a smirk, pushing the basement button to start our descend.

"So..."

"Basement, kitchen, bedroom, library and roof," I explain with a chuckle.

"I walk up and down stairs every day for nothing," she playfully bumps me with her shoulder.

The door slides open, we pass by my home gym and make our way to the garage. I grab an extra helmet and lead her to one of my prized possessions - a sleek, powerful motorcycle. But as soon as she sees it, she stops dead in her tracks.

"Absolutely not!" She takes a step back like the bike itself is a threat.

"Why not?"

"It's a motorcycle," she states matter-of-factly, looking at me as if I've just suggested something absurd.

I chuckle and place the helmet on her head, carefully strapping it on.

"It is, and here's a helmet for you," I take her jacket from her arm and put it on her.

She shakes her head, "No way, these are dangerous!"

"I assure you, I'm a skilled driver and it's perfectly safe," I put on my own helmet and take a seat on the bike, steadying it for her to get on. "Come, hop on behind me."

She hesitates for a moment before cautiously getting on.

"Wrap your arms around my waist and hold on tight," I instruct her.

Her arms encircle me tightly and secure. With a flick of the ignition switch, the engine roars to life and we speed out of the garage onto the open road, soon we are speeding down a scenic route.

As we zoom past trees and fields of wildflowers, she squeals with both excitement and fear but holds onto me tightly.

A thrill of satisfaction courses through me at her trust and I can't help the wide grin that splits my face.

The wind whips around us, tugging at our clothes. It's an unusual sensation, feeling her body pressed against mine. Between the roaring engine beneath us and the feel of her body against mine, I am hyper-aware of everything around and within me.

Her fear seems to ebb away with each mile we cover. The death grip she has around my waist stays secure but less intense.

Her head leans against my back. Her fingers begin tracing patterns against my stomach through my shirt - absent-minded doodling or a silent communication - either way it seizes my attention instantly.

It feels *right*.

As if every wrong turn in life has finally led me to this spot on earth where everything feels balanced.

We arrive at a small lake surrounded by towering trees, I cut off the engine and steady the bike helping her off first. Her legs are a bit wobbly from the long ride, and she stumbles slightly before steadying herself against me.

We remove our helmets, and she breathes out in awe taking in her surroundings.

Her eyes drink in the serenity of the lake under the golden sunlight. Her awe stirs something inside me.

"I used to come here a lot," I start to explain, "to think...to just get away."

She looks at me and there's an understanding in her eyes that makes my throat tighten. She doesn't say anything but gives me a small nod of appreciation and understanding.

We walk along the edge of the water in comfortable silence, watching as ducks float idly by. She seems lost in thought, gazing at our reflection on the shimmering surface of the water.

"It's beautiful," she says softly, not tearing her eyes away from the scene before us.

I glance at her, watching the way the sunlight dances on her golden hair and adds a soft glow to her features.

She is beautiful. There's a pang in my chest.

"Yes," I breathe, "it is."

I love this place, but the woman standing next to me... the woman who makes my cold heart feel a warmth it hasn't felt in a long time; *she's* what's beautiful.

"These are so pretty," Vasilisa says crouching down to admire the bluebells growing by the lake bank, careful not to touch them.

"My mother loved them too, always said they were beautiful but knew better than to handle them."

Vasilisa stands and regards me, her eyes on my profile as I look at the steady water. "She came here with you?"

"She introduced me to this lake," I reply, "When we were younger, she would bring my siblings and I to have picnics, and she would read to me. Angelo would get bored, and he'd always end up jumping in the lake."

She giggles and takes my hand in hers. Her fingers are warm against mine, and her touch is light and delicate. Her fingers intertwine effortlessly, she leans her head on my arm, and she takes a soft breath. "That sounds wonderful. She sounds wonderful."

"She was," my voice tight with emotion, "I spread her ashes here so she's always here when I am."

Vasilisa squeezes my hand, "It's nice to meet you Mrs. Amato," she whispers, causing the lump in my throat to triple.

"She would have loved you." I whisper shifting toward Vasilisa and meeting her gaze. "I need you to know some things."

Sensing the seriousness in my voice, her eyes grow wide as she takes a step back, releasing my hand. The sudden lack of her touch sends a pang through me.

I reach out and pull her back to me, the warmth from her body seeping into mine as she looks up at me, concern clouding her eyes.

"Is it about Rachel?" she quietly asks.

I shake my head, "Nothing has ever happened with her."

She worries her bottom lip and nods slightly. "Then what is it that I have to know?"

"I've done things... things I'm not proud of," I start, swallowing down the lump of guilt in my throat. "There's blood on my hands, Vasilisa. More than I can ever wash away."

"I've hurt people. I've destroyed lives," I admit, my voice raw.

"I know," she says quietly, her gaze steady on mine. "I grew up in the same lifestyle, remember?"

"But it's more than that," I continue, anxiety knotting in my chest. "After my mother passed, I became someone I *never* wanted to be."

"What do you mean?"

"I can't tell you," I reply, hating myself for the secrets I'm keeping from her.

She deserves so much better than this.

"Why?" Her voice is pleading and filled with confusion, "Why can't you tell me?" She takes a step back wrapping her arms around herself.

"I want to protect you."

The words hang heavily between us, echoing my fears.

"From what?"

Her eyes flicker with uncertainty.

"Me."

The weight of my confession settles over me like lead.

We stand there on the lakeshore for what feels like an eternity, neither of us moving or speaking.

Finally, she breaks the silence.

"Santo," she says softly, reaching out to take my hand in hers. "You could never scare me."

Her words feel like a balm on my wounded soul, her acceptance washing over me. She squeezes my hand.

"Thank you, Vasilisa," I say, the tension roll off of me. "Let's go home."

Our ride back home is silent but peaceful. Her hands reach under my shirt for warmth as she traces patterns on my skin.

She melts into me, her beating heart thrumming against my back syncing with my own.

The estate looms into view, the only people around are the guards at the gate and the front door. I pull into the garage and take the elevator to the kitchen, as I help her remove her jacket she looks around.

She frowns.

"Where is everyone?"

"I sent them away."

She spins around to face me, "Why? Are you leaving too?" her eyes spark with panic.

I cup that gorgeous face between my hands.

"No," I say firmly. "Never again, Vasilisa. Never again will you be alone. Never again will you wonder where I am. Never again will I let you feel unwanted."

"Never again?" her brow furrows.

"If I have to leave, I will always come home, you will always have friends and I will never leave without telling you why."

I will spend the rest of my days making up for the months she was left lonely. I will be the man she deserves and keep Scythe far from her.

She gives me a brilliant smile, "We have the rest of the day?"

"We have the rest of the *month.*"

Her eyes glitter, her hands coming up to drape around my neck as he pulls me closer. "That's a lot of time," her voice is quiet, warm.

"It is, and I want to spend all of it with you." I say, pulling her in tighter as she rises onto her tiptoes for a kiss.

Our lips meet and my heart pounds in my chest as if it's trying to catch up with something that's been missing for too long.

I hook my hands beneath her thighs and lift her. She gasps, her legs locking around me as I take her mouth, stealing every breath, every sound, every piece of her she'll give me.

We pull away from each other after what feels like forever, her lips bruised and kiss-swollen, her face flushed and glowing.

She pushes back gently, breathless, eyes shining. "I think we should make dinner together," she says, grinning in that way that dismantles me completely. That infectious, hopeful smile—one I could never resist.

★★★

Cooking together feels like a dream. We move effortlessly around each other, our bodies naturally in sync. It's effortless, instinctual, like we've done this for years.

After we finish eating, the weight of the last few days settle heavily over me.

"I'm going to shower, Dea," I murmur after we load the dishwasher.

She smiles, but surprises me by following me upstairs.

She doesn't say anything.

Just watches.

As I strip down and turn on the water, I glance back to find her standing in the doorway, a vision wrapped in soft curiosity and something deeper—something uncertain but willing.

She is so goddamn beautiful.

The soft glow of the bathroom light catches the angles of her face, the delicate line of her throat, the subtle rise and fall of her chest. Her hair spills over her shoulders in a way that makes my breath hitch.

I step into the shower, letting the warm water cascade over me, loosening my muscles, washing away the weight of my sins.

I forget she's still here—until the lights dim.

Until I feel her.

Her arms slide around my waist, soft, cautious fingers brushing over my stomach.

I inhale sharply, a violent shiver tearing through me.

I don't deserve this.

I bring her hand to my lips, kissing each fingertip, reverent, worshiping as I turn to face her.

She presses herself against me, her bare skin meeting mine. Warm. Wet. Perfect.

A low chuckle rumbles from my chest.

How bold to come into the shower with me—yet too shy to let me see her completely.

Fuck, I want her.

I take her hand from my mouth and press it to my chest, right over my heart. Let her feel it. Let her know I'm not some untouchable monster. I'm hers—whether she realizes it yet or not.

"Look at me," I murmur, tipping her chin up.

Her eyes meet mine—nervous, wide, beautiful—and then I'm kissing her. Deep and slow. No space left between us as I drink her in.

She melts into me, body softening, surrendering, and it hits me so hard I have to grip her tighter. She trusts me. Even here, even now.

My hands trace the wet, silken planes of her body, my fingers spreading over the curve of her ass, gripping, lifting her effortlessly into my arms.

She clings to me, the water falling between us, bathing me from my sins as I'm blessed by the sanctity of her lips and her body against mine.

She writhes and it makes my cock throb. The need to plunge deep inside her up against the shower wall is immediate.

She gasps when I pin her back against the marble. Fuck, she sounds like a dream. A breathy, desperate dream I never want to wake from.

Her pupils are blown wide, her blue irises nearly swallowed by the darkness of her desire.

She's fucking divine. All that light, all that need—wrapped in this soft, trembling body that's about to come undone just for me.

Her lips are red and kiss-drunk, her pupils blown wide. She's wrecked already—and I haven't even touched her where she needs it most.

I kiss along her jaw, then her neck, her pulse fluttering like a trapped bird under my mouth.

"Please," she whispers against my lips, her voice so needy it makes my cock twitch hard enough to hurt.

She rolls her hips against me, shameless. Begging without words.

I slide my hand between us meeting her warm, wet pussy.

She gasps into my mouth, a sound that makes me ache.

She's soaked; ready for me.

"Fuck," I breathe against her skin. "You're this wet for me?"

She whimpers.

I press my thumb to her clit and rub slow, dirty circles until her body jolts in my arms.

I want to bury myself inside her, feel the tight clutch of her body wrapped around me.

But not yet.

Her mouth parts in a cry that gets swallowed by another kiss, her nails dragging down my back. Every moan she makes sounds like a prayer I don't deserve to hear.

I sink one finger inside her.

Christo.

She clenches around me like she was made for this—for me.

She throws her head back, mouth open, eyes fluttering. I still, needing her to say it.

"Words, Dea. Tell me."

Her breath hitches. "Please," she whines. "Please, Santo."

That's all I need.

I curl my finger inside her and press deeper, adding another, fucking her slow with my hand while the water pounds around us.

She's panting now, high and frantic, grinding against me like she's lost every ounce of control.

I mouth at her neck, her shoulder, her breasts—everything I can reach. She's trembling in my arms, shaking so hard I know she's close.

"So pretty like this," I murmur against her skin. "So good for me."

She's gone. Her head drops forward, face buried in my shoulder, and then—

She breaks.

Her whole body spasms, legs tightening around me as she moans out my name like it's the only thing anchoring her to the world.

I hold her through it. My fingers still moving, slow and deep, coaxing every last wave of that orgasm out of her.

"Fuck. That's it," I whisper. "Give it all to me."

She sobs a little—soft, breathless, overwhelmed.

And I'm ruined.

I ease my fingers from her and cradle her tighter. She collapses against my chest like she's weightless, like she knows I'll never let her fall.

Her arms wrap around my neck, and I swear I feel her heart beating with mine. She's quiet, calm, breath soft against my skin.

We stay like that while the water cools, until her body stops trembling. Then I carry her out.

I dry her off slowly, kissing every inch I expose, before wrapping her in a warm robe and tying it tight.

She looks up at me, cheeks flushed, lips swollen, and glances down.

My cock is still rock hard.

Her eyes widen a little. "Santo…"

I shake my head, stepping back just enough.

"Not tonight," I say, my voice rough. "I told you. I'm not taking you until you're ready to beg for it."

I smirk as her breath catches again.

"We've got time, Dea. And I'm going to ruin you right."

She watches me with those gorgeous eyes as I towel dry her hair, as I tuck her into bed, as I pull on sweats and slip in beside her.

And when I wrap my arms around her, when I breathe her in, I know—

I will *never* deserve this… to bask in her light.

But I will spend my life worshipping her anyway.

CHAPTER 38

VASILISA

I wake up to an empty bed, the sheets cool where Santo was.

My fingers tangle in the fabric, his scent still clinging to it.

A smile tugs at my lips as I roll onto my side, letting the remnants of his scent sink into me. The room is bathed in a soft, golden hue, the early morning light slipping through the cracks in the curtains.

With a content sigh, I push myself up, stretching as the memories of last night flutter through my mind. A blush warms my cheeks.

The tenderness in his touch, the way he held me afterward, like I was something fragile and precious. Like he *wanted* to keep me.

His emotion was palpable; it filled me up in ways I never thought possible.

A distant clatter pulls me from my thoughts, grounding me back in reality. I wrap my robe tightly around me and pad barefoot across the cool floor, following the sound into the kitchen.

And there he is.

Santo stands at the stove, his broad, bare back facing me, muscles shifting with each precise movement. The soft morning glow glances off his skin, tracing the tattoo etched along his skin, highlighting the ridges of his shoulders. My mouth goes dry.

"Good morning," he says without turning, his voice low and husky. It's the kind of voice that lingers, that curls around my spine like silk.

"Morning," I manage. I lower my gaze, cheeks warm, before stealing another glance at him. I take a seat at the breakfast bar, watching as he plates up scrambled eggs and bacon with the same careful precision he applies to everything in his life.

"If you don't like it, I can make you something else," he says, setting the plates down before moving to pour fresh juice.

I take a bite, humming in delight at the perfectly cooked eggs. "It's delicious."

His full smile breaks across his face then—rare, breathtaking. It stutters my heart, knocks the breath right out of me. His eyes soften when they meet mine, and there's something unspoken there, something warm and steady. A promise. A quiet offering of moments like this, of mornings spent together, of tenderness and care in the spaces between the chaos.

Breakfast passes in easy silence, the kind that speaks of familiarity, of something deeper settling between us. After we finish, Santo collects our plates and sets them in the sink, but instead of stepping away, he turns back to me, bracing his forearms against the counter.

"Vasilisa," he begins, his voice measured, his gaze serious. "Last night—"

Panic flutters in my chest. I don't want to have *that* conversation. I don't want to hear him say it was a mistake, that it was obligation, rather than desire.

So I do the only thing I can think of, I beam at him. "I want to show you something!"

His gaze sharpens. "Show me what?"

"It's in the library," I announce brightly, already hopping off my stool and making my escape toward the stairs. But Santo moves faster.

His arm sweeps around me, lifting me off the ground. A surprised squeak leaves my lips as I find myself cradled against his chest.

"We can take the elevator," he utters, turning toward the pantry.

A giggle esca "I can walk, you know."

He smirks. "Yeah. But you don't have to."

His hold tightens just a fraction and I wrap my arms around his neck. Before I can say another word, he presses a lingering kiss to my forehead, his lips warm against my skin as we ascend.

The elevator doors open to a dark wooden wall. Santo reaches out, pressing against it revealing the bright lights of the library and I gasp at the realization that the elevator is hidden behind a bookshelf.

"I don't know anything about this house," I whisper in awe, running my fingers along the nearest row of books.

Santo's jaw tightens, his expression guilty. "I suppose that's my fault."

I laugh softly, reaching up to cup his cheek, tracing my thumb over the sharp line of his jaw. "It was a joke, Santo. Now, can you put me down so I can show you?"

His gaze lingers on mine for a moment, something flickering there before he exhales and lowers me gently to the ground.

I grab his hand and pull him toward the front of the library, where my easels stand in a quiet, reverent display. The look on his face as he takes in every canvas is worth the wait.

Every painting is of him.

Santo in his office the day we met. Him across from me at La Serenata on our first date. Standing at the end of the aisle. Us in the garden. Sitting at the dining table before walking away from me. His face before he slammed the door on mine. His back tattoo, wrapped only in a towel. Leaning in the doorway in that navy suit.

Each brushstroke is a memory—some tender, some painful. But all of them are him.

I watch the way his fists clench and unclench as he moves from one canvas to another, his expression shifting. He is silent as stone, absorbing every detail with something close to reverence, but there's an undercurrent of sadness in his gaze, something raw and unspoken.

He lingers in front of the painting of him across from me at La Serenata. Our first real night together. The moment we tried to connect despite the circumstances pressing in on us. In the morning light streaming through the tall windows, I see his shoulders ease, his stormy eyes softening.

"Vasilisa," he finally speaks, his voice raw. "Why...?"

I swallow hard. "Because each moment mattered to me... good or bad, because it's *you.*"

His gaze locks onto mine, heavy with something I can't name. He steps closer, cupping my face in his hands, his thumbs brushing along my cheeks with aching gentleness.

"I didn't realize... you didn't say it after I did," he mutters, studying me as though the answer is written on my skin. "But you don't say it, do you? You show it."

"I'm an artist," I whisper. "We express, not tell."

We stand there, suspended in time, faces close, breath mingling, surrounded by painted fragments of our story. The air between us hums with something electric—understanding, longing, something deeper than words.

"You're not just..." I hesitate, then press on. "You're not just a duty. I'm not just being a dutiful wife."

His eyes darken with emotion as he presses his forehead to mine. "And last night... it wasn't just about lust."

A shiver runs through me at his admission, my heart pounding, my throat tightening. Before I can find words, his arms tightens around my waist, pulling me flush against him. My arms wind around his neck, and he lifts me, my legs wrapping around him, his lips finding mine.

I murmur against his lips, "Does this mean I can have more orgasms without the serious conversations?"

His laughter rumbles, deep and warm.

"Only if you stop trying to hide this body from me," he whispers, slipping a finger beneath the shoulder of my robe and easing it down, exposing my bare skin to his hungry gaze.

I freeze.

He knew.

He knew I hadn't wanted him to see my body last night.

Santo nuzzles against my neck, his lips pressing soft, open mouth kisses along my skin, sending shivers down my spine.

"Did you think I wouldn't notice?" His voice is quiet, not accusing, just knowing.

My breath hitches, but the words won't come. His hands skim down my sides, grounding me in his touch.

Before I can gather myself, he's carrying me out of the library. I stammer, "I... I'm not hiding."

He says nothing, just holds me tighter.

When we reach our bedroom, he sets me down gently, but instead of stepping back, he studies me, his stormy eyes filled with quiet determination.

"Then let me see you, Vasilisa. All of you."

His words aren't a demand. They're a plea. A request for trust. And it shakes me to my core.

My throat tightens as he takes my hand, leading me into the bathroom. He turns me toward the mirror, standing behind me, his presence solid and unwavering.

"I'd never force you to do anything you're uncomfortable with," he says solemnly, his gaze locked on mine in the reflection. "But, Dea, I want to love you completely... and that includes loving every part of your body."

My heart pounds so hard I swear he can hear it. His words unsettle something deep inside me, something I don't know how to face.

I meet his gaze in the mirror and immediately shift under the weight of it. The heat in his eyes, the way he looks at me like I'm something worth cherishing—it's too much.

I drop my head. "You don't have to say that."

His hands tighten on my waist. "Why wouldn't I?"

"Because I know I'm not your type." The words tumble out before I can stop them. The second they hit the air, I regret them.

Santo's eyebrows raise, his expression equal parts amused and exasperated. He grips my shoulders and turns me to face him fully.

"Says who?" His voice is low, edged with something I can't quite place.

I blink at him, caught off guard. "Cassandra said she wasn't surprised we were arranged because I'm not your type."

A flicker of irritation passes over his face.

"Cassandra's known me a long time," he says, his voice darkening. "She knows who I've been seen with. That doesn't mean it's the only thing I want."

I huff softly, not ready to let him dismiss this so easily. "Rachel?"

"Never been with her, never will be with her. We established that."

"You wanted me to eat more," I point out, regretting the words as soon as they leave my lips.

Santo furrows his brows, his confusion clear. "Because you were going to eat an apple after skipping breakfast. That's not enough for anyone, Vasilisa."

I roll my eyes, frustration bubbling over. "It's not just that. You've said it more than once."

"When?"

I glare at him, crossing my arms. "Right before you left, when I was eating fruit for breakfast. And on our first date—we shared a charcuterie board, and you told me I should eat more."

Santo blinks at me, exasperation flickering in his expression. "A charcuterie board doesn't feed anyone. That's snacks, not a meal."

"There were *three* other appetizers on that table, Santo."

"That's still not dinner. It's not enough," he counters, rubbing the back of his neck like he's trying to keep his patience.

"Enough for *you* or enough for me?" I ask, tightening my arms around myself.

His gaze darkens—not with anger, but something else entirely. "Enough for a human being," he says simply.

"Oh my gosh," I groan, throwing up my hands. "If you're just going to have an excuse for all of my feelings, why should I even try?"

Before I can step away, his hand cups my cheek, tilting my face until I'm forced to meet his gaze. His thumb brushes lightly over my skin, and I hate that it calms me, that it makes my frustration waver.

"What is it," he asks softly, "that you think my type is?"

The words knot in my throat, but I resign myself to the truth. "Curvier women. Women with more... body to offer."

Silence.

It stretches between us, thick and suffocating, broken only by the unsteady rhythm of my heartbeat echoing in the quiet room.

Then, Santo laughs.

A deep, rich sound that rumbles through his chest, lighting up his face in a way I've never seen before. Before I can protest, he turns me toward the mirror, positioning himself behind me, his legs pressing against the ottoman as he towers over me.

His touch is featherlight as he caresses the side of my face, his eyes meeting mine in the mirror's reflection. His breath is warm against my ear when he whispers, "Vasilisa, there's no one like you. You're beautiful in ways they couldn't begin to understand."

His words strike something raw inside me, and tears prick at my eyes. Slowly, he peels the robe from my shoulders, pressing a kiss to my bare skin. His hands are warm as he unties the fabric and lets it fall open and his gaze remains locked on mine in the mirror.

"Look at yourself, Vasilisa," he whispers, his hands trailing reverently down my sides, over my breasts and stomach, as if he's memorizing every inch of me. "You're beautiful. And you're *mine.*"

The words settle deep in my chest, curling around something fragile. I lean back against him, needing the solidity of his presence to keep me grounded.

"Don't ever think your body needs to be more or less than what it already is," he breathes against my skin, his lips brushing just below my ear.

Then, the warmth of his hands disappears as he steps back, taking a seat on the ottoman.

I glance toward him, confused, but his voice halts me.

"Sit," he commands gently.

My breath catches. "What?"

"Hook your legs over mine," he says, his tone calm yet insistent.

Heat floods my face.

If I do, I'll be completely exposed—to him, to the mirror. The thought paralyzes me for a moment, but Santo's gaze is patient, filled with something deeper than desire. "Trust me," he urges, holding out his hand.

With a shaky exhale, I take it. Slowly, I straddle his lap, my legs hooked over his, my thighs spread open. My gaze flickers to the mirror, but the moment I see myself, I instinctively look away.

Santo's fingers tighten on my waist, grounding me. He pulls me back against his chest, his warmth seeping into my skin.

"Look at us," he murmurs, his lips trailing just behind my ear.

"I'd rather not," I say softly, forcing a laugh, but the nervous edge in my voice betrays me.

His hand moves slowly, tracing the length of my arm, deliberate and reverent. "Why not?"

"You know why," I whisper.

I finally force myself to look at him in the mirror. His reflection is steady, unwavering, while I can't stop searching for flaws I know are there.

His head shakes slightly before he even speaks. "No. We just talked about this." His eyes lock onto mine in the glass, his voice firm but tender.

I hesitate, my chest tightening under his gaze. "I'm just… not enough. I don't look like—"

"Stop." His voice is gentle but leaves no room for argument.

I swallow the rest of my words.

His palm settles over my ribs, fingers spreading as if to hold me together. "Do you know what I see when I look at you?" he asks quietly.

I shake my head, unable to find my voice.

"I see the woman who makes me forget how to breathe," he says, his tone soft but unshakable. "The one who holds more power over me than anyone ever has. Do you realize that?"

I try to look away, but his fingers catch my chin, forcing me to meet our reflection's gaze.

"Santo—"

"I'm not asking you to believe it yet," he cuts in gently. "Just… let me show you."

His hands skim down my sides, deliberate and slow, like he's tracing devotion into my skin; like he's painting over every part I've ever criticized.

"Every inch of you is mine to *admire*, to *touch*, to *fuck*. And I plan to do all three"

A shudder rolls through me. I exhale shakily, my heart a relentless rhythm against my ribs.

His forehead presses lightly to the side of my head, his breath warm and steady. "You're perfect exactly as you are. And if you ever doubt that…" His fingers intertwine with mine, guiding our joined hands across my stomach, my hips, the places I've always avoided, the parts of myself I'd never let anyone claim. "I'll remind you."

I close my eyes, letting the words settle in the deepest parts of me, in the spaces that once held doubt. When I open them again, the mirror feels different. *I feel different.*

Santo's gaze never wavers, burning through the reflection.

"There you are," he murmurs in approval, his hands leaving mine to mold themselves around my waist.

He is silent for a moment, allowing both of us to take in our reflections. I watch us in the mirror; his stormy eyes are intent on my face while mine are drawn towards our intertwined form.

My chest rises and falls, my body trembling—not from fear, but from the sheer force of his presence. His hands start to move again, fingertips whispering over my skin, exposing me inch by inch to the cool clarity of the glass. His touch is electric, tracing over the lines of my body as if he's savoring me.

I watch as his eyes drink me in, dark and consuming, as if he is starving for me. My skin hums under the weight of his attention, every touch a silent promise.

Each touch is a testament to his words - I can feel reverence in his fingertips as they explore the contours of my form, each caress lingering with a tenderness that reduces me to breathless silence. My heart pounds so loudly I'm sure he can hear it echoing in the silence of the room.

His fingers pause at the swell of my breasts, tracing their outline before capturing one in his hand, his thumb grazing over a sensitive peak. My breath hitches and he smirks, his hands leave my breasts that are mere handfuls compared to what I thought he wanted, they go past my stomach which I feared was too flat for a man who needs robust, and they glide past my hipbones, that I expected him to be repulsed by for being slightly visible.

He slides his hand lower, his fingers dipping between my legs where I ache for him most. I'm bare before him, open, wanton.

I gasp when his fingers brush over my clit, pleasure sparking through me. My eyes flutter closed, but his grip tightens on my hip.

"Look at yourself, Mia Dea."

His voice is a command wrapped in velvet. It ripples through me, stealing the air from my lungs, forcing my eyes open.

And what I see leaves me in awe.

The girl in the mirror is powerful. She is raw and uninhibited, her skin flushed, her lips parted, her body trembling under his worship. Santo's eyes blaze with unfiltered possession, with love. He isn't just touching me—he's claiming me.

He *loves* what he sees. The proof evident, not only in his eyes, but the hardness of his thick cock pressed against me.

His hand leaves my pussy only to glide down the inside of my thigh, leaving slick trails on my skin, marking me with my own arousal. His smirk deepens, the kind that makes my knees weak, the kind that tells me he's far from done.

"Vasilisa," he whispers my name like a prayer, like a sacred vow. His hand cups my breast again, his fingers rolling my nipple between them, and I let out a soft moan, my back arching. "You're a fucking goddess, and I'd worship at your altar every night if you'd let me."

Heat blooms across my cheeks, down my neck, all the way to my chest. It isn't embarrassment. It's something deeper. *Pleasure.* It's the pleasure of being seen, of being desired by *him* in a way I never thought possible.

I've been craving this feeling since I met him.

His hand moves back from tracing circles around my thighs, his finger teasing, before sliding inside me. My breath hitches. My body clenches greedily around the intrusion, seeking, needing.

"Watch it happen, Vasilisa," he orders, his voice thick with arousal.

My eyes obey, locked onto the image of his finger disappearing inside me, of my body yielding to him so beautifully. He adds a second, stretching me, filling me, and I let out a trembling whimper, pressing my nails into his thighs. He hums near my neck, his warm lips vibrating against my skin.

"Perfect," he murmurs appreciatively as he begins to pump his fingers in and out slowly. A wave of heat rushes through me at his words combined with his actions.

His fingers still and he slides them out. I whimper at the loss, my hips instinctively tilting toward him, searching, pleading. But Santo has other plans.

He brings those fingers to his lips.

And sucks.

My mouth falls open as I watch him taste me. His eyes close, a low, pleased hum escaping his throat, as if savoring the very essence of me. The sight alone shatters my last thread of restraint.

He groans, his tongue flicking out to chase the taste before his fingers return, slick and relentless against my clit.

Every movement sends electric jolts of ecstasy coursing through my body, rendering me speechless and lost in the throes of euphoria.

My grip tightens on his thighs as he rubs circles around my clit with one hand while caressing my breast with the other. The dual sensation is enough to have me arching off his chest, my moans echoing off the bathroom walls.

"Santo," I gasp, clenching around nothing, desperate.

He chuckles, dark and wicked, as his fingers keep their rhythm.

"Show me how you fall apart."

His words unravel me. Sending pleasure crashing through me in relentless waves.

I shatter.

I come with his name on my lips, my body bowing against his, my reflection a vision of sheer, unrestrained bliss.

His hands are gentle now, coaxing me down, smoothing over my shivering skin. His mouth presses a kiss to my shoulder, his arms a fortress around me as I sink into him, spent.

"Ti amo," he whispers against my temple.

The words are more beautiful than any painting could ever be. To know that he loves me, adores me just as I am... *It's everything.* His love for me feels like gravity, constant, steady and impossible to escape.

He holds me tightly to him, his hands soothingly caressing my body. As I meet his eyes in the mirror once more, something new blooms inside me—a delicious thought. A need to give back the same reverence, the same devotion.

I want to try something too.

CHAPTER 39

SANTO

I should stop her.

The thought fires off like a warning shot the second she slides from my lap, her hands trailing down my chest hesitant, but determined.

This was supposed to be for her.

I brought her here to remind her how beautiful she is- to make her believe it.

Not to take from her.

Yet as she kneels between my legs, gazing up at me with those trusting eyes, something inside me fractures.

Something primal coils low in my stomach, heavy and aching, my cock already tightening despite every warning screaming in my head.

I don't deserve this.

Not her.

Not the way she's looking at me, like I'm something more than what I am.

Her hands tremble, barely brushing the edge of my belt.

She doesn't know what she's doing.

She's too soft for this world. Too innocent for someone like me.

But fuck, I am not strong enough to stop her.

My fists clench at my sides, jaw locking tight as I fight against the instinct screaming at me to pull her back up, to lift her onto my lap, to keep her safe there. *Unscathed.*

But I don't.

Because I want this.

I want her.

And that realization rips through me like a storm.

Mine.

Her lips part, hesitation flickering across her face. She's waiting for me to stop her.

Waiting for me to say no.

I should.

Instead, my hand moves on its own, cupping her cheek, tilting her head up until our eyes lock.

The sight of her kneeling there so seemingly eager to please me, so willing, so devoted—knots something sharp and dangerous in my chest.

"You don't have to Dea," my voice is low, but rougher than I intend.

She blinks, searching my face for something—permission, reassurance, restraint. Something I'm not sure I can give.

"I know." She whispers it like a confession.

She knows.

She's *choosing* this.

I've never wanted anyone more, but I cant.

I shouldn't.

I drag my thumb along her lower lip, feeling the way she shivers beneath my touch.

There's no hesitation in her eyes now.

She's made up her mind.

Maybe she isn't as fragile as I think.

Still, I lean down, pressing my forehead to hers, letting the warmth of her skin sink into me, trying to steady myself.

"This isn't about me Dea."

Her fingers tighten against my thighs.

I exhale, feeling the cracks in my restraint widen.

I'll give her anything she asks for.

I shake my head, barely.

Then, her voice.

Soft. Barely more than a breath. "Please."

Fuck.

For someone with no experience my wife knows how to take me apart.

I inhale, long and slow, trying to settle the fire burning low in my stomach. She has no idea what that single word does to me.

I pull away just enough to look into her eyes, to see the quiet plea there.

The need.

I give her a small, approving nod.

"You set the pace," I manage, my voice hoarse. Unsteady.

Her breath catches.

"You can start by stroking me." The words feel like sacrilege.

My hands move to unbuckle my belt, the sharp click of metal the only sound between us. I ease my zipper down, releasing my hardened cock, watching her expression closely.

Her lips part.

Her fingers tremble slightly as she wraps them around my length.

A sharp hiss rips through my teeth.

Her touch is tentative, unsure. But intoxicating nonetheless.

Her hand moves slowly at first, fingers adjusting, finding the right pressure. I fight to keep my breathing steady, but when her thumb swipes over the tip, spreading the pre-cum gathered there, my restraint fractures.

A sharp exhale leaves me, jaw tightening as I fight the urge to thrust into her palm.

I watch her.

The way her brows furrow slightly in concentration.

The way her lips part just enough for me to catch the softest peek of her tongue.

She's mesmerizing.

And I am utterly wrecked by her.

Her hand moves slowly, finding a rhythm that has me gritting my teeth, trying to keep myself from unraveling too soon.

She's learning me.

I can't help but place my hand over hers, guiding her gently, showing her where it feels best. She follows. She doesn't resist, doesn't hesitate—she allows herself to learn from me.

Her thumb brushes over the tip, grazing a particularly sensitive spot, and I can't hold back the groan that escapes me.

Her eyes flicker up, something new gleaming there—*satisfaction*. She knows she's making me come undone.

And fuck—it makes me smile.

"Like that?" she whispers.

I nod, jaw tightening. Words aren't possible right now.

My hand drops away, leaving her to explore on her own, and when her grip tightens, I suck in a breath, my muscles going rigid as a low, pleased hum leaves her lips. She likes this. She likes seeing what she does to me, the control she has over my body.

Her confidence grows, each stroke more sure than the last.

I let my fingers tangle in her hair, twisting lightly, just enough to feel her.

The sight before me is ruinous.

The head of my cock, disappearing and reappearing from her grip, her fingers slick with my arousal, the way she stares, fixated, absorbing every reaction.

A growl rumbles low in my chest as her thumb circles the tip again, spreading my slickness with a deliberate touch.

"Use your mouth, Vasilisa," I encourage her, my voice trembling with need.

She licks her lips, hesitating for a brief second before she leans in, her breath warm, teasing as it washes over me.

I shudder.

Then, finally—her lips part, and she takes the head into her mouth.

Fuck.

A sharp inhale rushes through me as she sucks softly, her tongue darting out to taste me.

Her inexperience only fuels the fire, making every hesitant lick, every slow pull, feel even more erotic.

I grind my teeth to keep from groaning too loudly, but the sheer possessiveness rolling through me makes it impossible to stay silent. My grip in her hair tightens slightly.

She flinches; but doesn't pull away.

I force myself to loosen my hold, but then my gaze catches her reflection in the mirror.

Vasilisa.

Naked. Kneeling. Lips stretched around my cock, eyes glossy as she looks up at me like this is exactly where she belongs.

The image is beautifully fucking devastating.

A raw, primal surge of need tears through me.

Scythe wants to claim her. *Mark her.*

I watch as she grows bolder, taking me deeper, her movements more certain.

"Dea," I whisper, my voice hoarse, wrecked.

She hums in response, the vibrations sending a jolt of electricity down my spine causing my body to jerk and tense beneath her.

She's so goddamn perfect.

And she's *mine.*

The obscene, wet sounds fill the space between us as she pushes herself deeper, testing her limits.

Then, she gags slightly, her throat tightening around me.

My fingers twitch in her hair.

I want—*fuck*, I want to take over.

"Breathe through your nose, relax your throat," I instruct, my voice strained, desperate to hold onto control.

She nods, her eyes locked on mine, determination gleaming in those stunning, clear depths.

She takes a deep breath and relaxes, sinking further down, taking me deeper than before.

I shudder violently.

Her name slips from my lips, a hushed, broken whisper.

And she smiles around me.

Fuck.

"Beautiful, Vasilisa..." I murmur, running my thumb along her stretched lips. "You're doing so well."

She glances up at me again, and the sight of her— Flushed cheeks. Shining eyes. Lips swollen around my cock.

It nearly destroys me.

She's too much.

"Deeper," I gasp, my voice rough, raw, breaking.

She doesn't hesitate.

Her lashes flutter as she pushes herself further, pushing past the snug resistance of her throat, the sensation sending a violent shudder through me

My fingers tighten in her hair, her tongue moving in slow, deliberate strokes, her lips forming a perfect, wet seal.

Every instinct in me screams to take over, to fuck her throat, to make her understand exactly who she belongs to.

But she's learning.

And fuck—watching her learn is going to ruin me.

I press my thumb to the slight bulge in her cheek, feeling the way my length stretches her mouth, the way she struggles to take all of me.

"That's my girl," I rasp, my voice trembling with the force of my restraint.

She hums softly, the vibrations sending another shockwave of pleasure through me.

"Faster," I find myself begging, my own control snapping apart at the seams.

She obeys.

Her hands grip my thighs, her nails biting into my skin as she works me, swallowing into each thrust.

My stomach tightens, heat coiling, pooling, an undeniable pressure threatening to spill over.

"I'm close," I admit, voice breaking.

Her cheeks flush darker, her movements more fervent.

She knows.

She *wants* this.

Never has anyone held such power over me.

I lose myself.

I gasp out her name as white-hot pleasure rips through me, my cock pulsing in her mouth as my release coats the back of her throat.

"Fuck," I groan, my fingers digging into her shoulder, shaking as the sensation wrecks me completely.

Wave after wave crashes over me, my breath ragged, uneven, my entire body trembling.

Out of breath and completely sated I open my eyes and see her. Vasilisa, kneeling before me, her eyes wide, cheeks flushed, lips wet and swollen from taking me so beautifully.

I shudder at the small drop of my release on her chin.

I swipe it away with my thumb, bringing it to her lips.

She licks it off, never breaking eye contact.

My cock twitches in response.

Scythe wants to keep her there. On her knees. Wants the world to see what she gives so freely.

I crush the thought immediately— tuck myself away and lift her into my arms instead.

"Perfect."

Her legs tremble—whether from kneeling for so long or from the intensity of the moment, I'm not sure.

"Did you like it?" she asks, hesitant.

I meet her gaze, the answer absolute.

"You were perfect. Every sound. Every look. Every second."

She bites her lip, as if holding back, but then—softly, hesitantly asks, "Can we do it again?"

I chuckle, shaking my head. This woman will be the end of me.

"Not right now, Dea," I murmur, lifting her fully into my arms and pressing a kiss to those swollen lips. "Now, it's your turn."

She rears her head back, breathless. "My turn?"

"Yes," I growl, lifting her into my arms. "I need to taste you."

Her eyes widen—anticipation warring with uncertainty.

"Calm down, Vasilisa," I whisper, my fingers trailing down the curve of her throat, over her collarbone, until they graze the soft rise of her chest.

She shivers beneath my touch.

A smirk tugs at my lips. She's so responsive. So beautifully mine.

I lay her down, the mattress shifting beneath her weight.

"I—" she stammers, trying to push herself up, but I gently press her back down, covering her with my body before she can protest.

I silence her with a kiss.

Soft at first, coaxing, but deepening when she melts beneath me, surrendering.

"Just lie back," I whisper against her lips, tasting the quickened rhythm of her breath. "Trust me."

Her throat bobs as she swallows hard, trying to relax.

And fuck—

The sight of her beneath me, flushed, eager, despite the nervous tension in her body, sends a sharp pulse straight to my cock.

I kiss my way down her neck, lingering to suck lightly at her pulse point. A sharp gasp escapes her, her fingers curling into the sheets beneath her.

"Easy," I soothe against her skin before moving lower.

Her nipples are already pebbled, hard and aching as I circle one with my tongue.

Her gasp turns into a moan, then a whimper, as I tease her, suck her, drag my teeth lightly across the sensitive bud before soothing it with a broad stroke of my tongue.

My other hand trails light, lazy circles around her other breast, pressing just enough to make her squirm, to make her writhing, breathless, needy.

"Santo…" she whispers, and fuck.

The way she says my name, reverent, pleading, surrendering, nearly sends me over the edge.

But this isn't about me getting *my* taste.

This is about her.

Worshipping my wife in the way she deserves.

My hand trails lower, past the soft dip of her stomach, until I reach the apex of her thighs. She jerks up at the first brush of my fingers against her clit.

"Still sensitive?" I ask, lifting my head to meet her gaze.

Her chest rises and falls erratically, her cheeks burning. "Yes," she breathes. "But don't stop."

The corner of my mouth lifts into a wolfish grin.

That's my girl.

I circle my finger around her clit again, slow, deliberate; watching as her thighs tremble, her lips part, her brows pull together in sweet agony.

She's soaked.

So fucking wet for me.

A deep, satisfied groan rumbles from my chest.

"Such a beautiful mess you've made," I praise removing my hand to a distressed whimper. My mouth follows the path my hands took, trailing kisses down her stomach.

Her breath hitches.

I graze my lips along the sharp dip of her hip bone, my tongue darting out to taste the skin there.

A violent shudder rips through her.

"Patience, love," I whisper against her skin, smirking when a weak laugh escapes her—cut off by a sharp gasp when I move lower.

My fingers skim up her inner thighs, and she parts them wider for me.

A perfect invitation.

A perfect offering.

Legs parted, slick and glistening, trembling with need; she's open for me. Laid out like a fucking feast.

I take a moment to appreciate the sight before me before kissing the inside of her thigh.

She shakes.

"Santo..." she whispers, her hands tangling in my hair.

I press a kiss to her pussy, feeling her body jolt from the contact.

"Just let me," I soothe. My voice thick with need, with reverence, with possession.

Her sharp inhale is the only sound I hear before my tongue finally touches her.

And fuck me—

Her taste is heaven.

Warm, salty, sweet; like need and sin and something made just for me.

I groan against her, the vibration drawing a broken cry from her lips.

Her hands tighten in my hair, her hips rolling instinctively, searching for more.

I lap at her, flicking my tongue over her swollen clit, drawing slow, precise circles before sucking it between my lips.

She arches off the bed, crying out, her fingers yanking at my hair, legs shaking around my head.

I hold her down, spreading her wider, drinking her in, completely addicted.

Every sound, every gasp, every plea she gives fuels something dark and primal inside me.

She is my finest addiction.

I will *never* get enough of her.

"Santo..." she breathes, barely able to form words.

I pull away for a fraction of a second, my lips glistening with her slickness.

"Please what?" I rasp, pressing an open-mouthed kiss to her inner thigh.

She whimpers, her body trembling beneath me. "I need... I..." She bites her lip, unable to say it.

"You need to come?"

Her cheeks flush even more, if that's possible. She nods desperately.

I flick my tongue over her aching clit before demanding, "Say it."

"I—I need to come. *Please.*"

A dark thrill rolls through me.

She's so undone, so wrecked, and it's all because of me.

"Good girl."

I dip my head back down, licking and sucking, my fingers sliding inside her, curling, finding that spot.

She gasps, writhing, moaning my name, high and desperate now.

"Santo... I'm—"

I feel it.

The way her pussy clenches, tightens, hovering at the edge.

I circle my tongue over her clit, whispering the command into her skin, "Come for me, Dea."

And she shatters.

Her body shudders, a keening cry tears from her throat as she convulses through waves of pleasure crashing over her.

I don't stop.

I drink her down, savoring every last tremor, every last moan, until she is completely spent.

Only when her body finally relaxes, trembling in the aftermath, do I pull away.

She reaches for me, breathless, pulling me up, crushing her lips to mine.

She tastes herself on my tongue—and *fuck,* the way her eyes darken, the way her hips lift to pull me closer—I know she loves it.

"More," she whispers against my lips, her legs wrapping around my waist.

My cock throbs painfully, desperate for her.

But I pull away, smirking against her skin as I trail kisses down her neck.

She's still twitching beneath me, chest heaving, eyes half-lidded.

I want to mark every inch of her with my mouth.

She deserves to know what it feels like to be worshipped.

"Not yet, Dea," I whisper against her skin. "We have the whole month."

CHAPTER 40

VASILISA

"There. Perfect," Santo boasts, stepping back to admire his work as he hangs the final canvas in the living room.

After what had been the best experience of my life, Santo had gotten the idea to display the rest of my paintings, inspired by the one he'd been admiring above our bed. An hour later, every piece of my art is proudly on display throughout the house. My heart soars—I've never had the chance to showcase my work anywhere before, let alone in a home of my own.

I giggle at the thought of the guards walking past all these portraits. "I didn't think you'd want so many paintings of yourself around the house."

"How could I not when you make me look this good?" he teases, pressing a quick kiss to my lips.

The warmth of his gesture settles deep inside me, and emotion wells in my chest. "It means a lot that you did this for me." My voice trembles, the weight of the moment pressing on me.

Santo cups my face, his thumb stroking away the tears before they can fall. "Mia Dea," he murmurs, reverence in his tone. "Your art is a part of *you*. I want you in every corner of this house."

His words mean more than I can express. A confession rests on the tip of my tongue—I feel so much for him, *too much,* and I want to say it. But before I can, his phone rings, slicing through the quiet of our day. My stomach twists, dread pooling in my chest. *Not yet.* We're supposed to have a month.

He presses a gentle kiss to my lips, as if reading my mind, soothing me before he pulls out his phone.

I hear a muffled masculine voice on the other end.

Santo's expression hardens. "Alright, what do you plan on doing?" His voice shifts, cold and sharp, edged with authority. "I can resend them, but there weren't any extra details—just a date, time, and location."

Tension tightens the air between us as he listens in silence. Then, his jaw clenches. "Yeah, I'll do it now."

My heart shatters. *Now.* That means he has to go.

He ends the call and pockets his phone, turning to me with an apologetic look. But it's too late—the dam breaks. Tears blur my vision and spill freely down my cheeks.

Santo's face twists in horror, almost comical if I weren't so devastated. He brushes a strand of hair behind my ear, crouching to eye level, his lips pressing warm, featherlight kisses along my tear-streaked cheeks.

"Dea," he whispers, soothing. "Why are you crying?"

Through shaky breaths, I try to explain—how my heart aches at the thought of him leaving me so soon. But instead of a sympathetic response, he lets out a low chuckle.

I blink at him, caught off guard.

Straightening, he takes my hand and leads me toward his office.

"I'm not leaving, Dea," he says, amusement laced in his voice. "I'm just sending an email."

Relief floods through me, but I can't stop the sniffles as I wipe my tears. I follow him down the hall, only to pause at the threshold of his office.

He unlocks the sensor with his thumb pushing the door open. But I don't move. I drop his hand, hesitating.

Santo turns, his brows furrowing. "What are you doing?"

"I'm waiting," I say softly.

His gaze softens in an instant.

"Telling you you couldn't come in here was a mistake." His voice is firm, resolute. "You're my wife. There's nothing in this house you don't have a right to."

Pulling out his phone, he opens an app and takes my hand, pressing my thumb to the door handle. It beeps. Just like the elevator, I now have access.

To him. To everything.

Santo's home office mirrors the one at NovaRael, but instead of a sleek glass desk, this one is solid wood—warm, familiar. I trail my fingers across the grain, the texture grounding me.

"Is this...?" I start to ask, feeling him move in behind me, his presence a steady heat.

"It is," he confirms, his hands covering mine on the desk, his body pressing flush against my back.

I turn to face him, searching his unreadable gaze. "When did you do this? I thought you got rid of it."

"After you left the office, I called my men. Had them track it down and bring it here."

My breath hitches. "Santo…"

Moving around the desk, I crouch beneath it, my heart stuttering when I see what's carved into the wood. Right where I used to hide as a child—my initials. And beside them, *his.*

I peek up at him from across the desk. "You put your initials here too?"

He smirks, shrugging like it's nothing, but there's a knowing warmth in his eyes. "You did say the wood was magical when two lovers carved their initials in it." His gaze locks onto mine, steady. "Guess that means you're stuck with me forever."

A smile breaks across my face as I run into his arms, letting him lift me into a soft kiss. Santo sinks into his chair, settling me onto his lap. "I still have that email to send. Give me a second, Dea."

His monitor flickers on as he navigates through files. I rest my head on his shoulder, arms draped around his neck, content just being here, feeling him.

I watch as he sends a file over to Maksim—the QUEEN file.

"You opened it?"

He nods, typing out a quick message before hitting send. "We did, but it's incomplete. Still, it helps."

"That's what Maksim called about?"

Santo's fingers brush my cheek, his expression shifting. "Partly." He studies me for a moment, hesitating. "He also told me something else. And I need to share it with you… but I don't want to see those beautiful eyes fill with tears again."

A chill runs through me. My arms fall from around his neck. "Tell me."

His face darkens, his voice careful, measured. "Maksim found your mother."

The world stills. My heartbeat pounds in my ears, deafening. Santo watches me, his dark gaze unreadable, waiting.

"Is he going to kill her?" The words leave me before I can stop them. I don't want to know the answer. But I *do.* Her betrayal to the Bratva won't go unanswered.

Santo exhales. "I don't have all the details yet. He's going to question her first." His grip on me tightens slightly. "Maksim said he'd explain everything later."

I try to form words, but nothing comes out. My mind is a storm—anger, fear, confusion, all crashing into each other.

Santo's gaze sharpens, his brow furrowing. Then his touch is on me again, knuckles grazing my cheek. "You're shaking."

I barely register it until he pulls me closer, wrapping his arms around me like a shield against the world. I breathe him in, trying to anchor myself in his warmth, but the fear is there, coiling tight in my chest.

"I don't know what to do," I whisper, voice barely audible. "What if I'm next?" I can't fathom Maksim hurting me, but I know what betrayal means. Even by proxy, the Bratva doesn't forgive.

Santo stills. Then, his voice drops—low, lethal. "That will never happen." His grip tightens, his hold turning possessive. "You're innocent. And you're *mine*."

There's a promise in his words, one that comes with unrelenting violence. The kind of vow that means nothing in this world will touch me—not while he's breathing.

I rest my head against his chest, listening to the steady thrum of his heartbeat, but the knot in my stomach refuses to unravel.

His fingers stroke through my hair as he murmurs, "No one is going to come after you, Dea. Not while I breathe." His voice is unwavering, absolute. "Your parents' sins won't fall on you. I swear it."

The words hang between us, heavy with meaning. And though the fear lingers, one thing remains undeniable his promise holds a truth that resonates deeply within me — he will keep me safe.

★★★

Santo takes me back to the lake, an easel and canvas in tow so I can paint the bluebells as I watch them sway in the breeze. He sets up a picnic, just like the ones he had when he was younger with his mother, a quiet homage to memories that shaped him. The day is spent wrapped in each other's company, lost in stories of our childhoods—his days at Stanford, my classes and my monthly café visits with Luna. Between kisses and bites of food, we weave our pasts together, savoring this fragile sliver of peace amid the storm brewing on the horizon.

His stories make me laugh; his kisses make me forget and for a moment, we are not bound to duty or bloodshed; we are simply us, languishing in the sun, in the sanctity of each other.

When he picks up a paintbrush, he smirks. "I am no artist, Vasilisa, but I'm willing to try for you." His fingers move clumsily over the canvas, creating abstract forms that lack precision but hold warmth—real and raw, just like him. There is a beauty in his attempt, in the way he exists with such quiet, unshakable strength despite all he has endured. When he catches me watching him, the curve of his lips, the one he saves only for me, melts something deep in my chest.

322

As the sun begins to set, we pack up and drive home. Santo holds my hand, his thumb occasionally brushing over my skin, a silent promise that whatever waits for us beyond this moment, we will face it together.

The house is still and quiet when we arrive. He leads me upstairs, his touch gentle as he helps me get ready for bed. An unspoken agreement lingers between us—tonight, we will not speak of our worries.

Wrapped in his oversized shirt, I slip into bed beside him. His arms encircle me, pulling me close, anchoring me.

"I love you," he murmurs, his breath warm against my ear. "I will keep you safe."

His words settle over me like a lullaby, soothing away the unease that lingers beneath my skin. In his arms, I believe him. Sleep claims me to the rhythm of his heartbeat.

★★★

When I wake, the bed is cooler beside me. Santo sits at the edge, his back rigid, the glow of his phone illuminating the sharp lines of his face. I shift, and he ends the call, turning toward me.

"Good morning," I murmur, my voice still thick with sleep. But when our eyes meet, the weight in his gaze tells me everything.

Bad news is coming.

"What happened?"

He exhales, rubbing a hand over his jaw. "Maksim's flight landed last night." He hesitates, then delivers the blow. "He brought your mother with him."

The air leaves my lungs. A cold dread spreads through me, curling around my ribs like ice. My mother, in the hands of Maksim—angry, scornful Maksim—is a nightmare I have feared more than any other.

I push the covers away, my voice urgent despite the tremor beneath it. "You have to go."

Santo cups my face, shaking his head. "No, I don't have to go. He didn't ask for me."

"But I *need* you to," I whisper, my throat tightening. "You need to make sure Mishka doesn't lose control. Please."

Something flickers in his expression; understanding, resignation. Then, his features soften. "Of course I'll go. I'll check on her."

A shaky breath escapes me as I lean into him. His arms fold around me, his lips pressing to my forehead, his hand rubbing soothing circles along my back as if he can quiet the storm inside me.

By the time I step out of the shower, dressed and still trying to steady my nerves, Santo returns to the room.

"You look far too beautiful for me to be leaving," he says, his gaze trailing over me, dark and devouring.

I glance down at the simple white dress I had hurried into, nothing remarkable about it, but in his eyes, I might as well be adorned in diamonds.

A half-smile tugs at my lips. "I should be saying the same to you."

He stands tall, striking in a crisp black button-down that fits snugly over the broad lines of his chest. The sheer presence of him—commanding, effortlessly powerful—steals my breath.

He steps closer, taking my hands in his. "I promise it won't take long," he assures me, voice steady, unwavering.

I bite my lip to keep it from trembling. "Please be careful."

His thumb traces over my knuckles; he lifts our joined hands to press a lingering kiss to them.

"Always," he murmurs, then flashes me a knowing look. "I have a surprise for you downstairs."

A mix of excitement and apprehension swirls in my stomach as I follow Santo downstairs. The moment I catch a glimpse of Luna in the living room, all anxiety vanishes. I sprint toward her, and we collide in a squealing embrace, jumping up and down like schoolgirls, utterly unbothered by the stares from Nico, Romeo, and Luca. When I finally pull back, my face aches from smiling so hard.

Luna grabs my hand and gasps as her eyes land on the glimmering ring adorning my finger.

"This is huge!" she exclaims, wide-eyed. "This whole place is huge! Girl, you lucked out."

Santo clears his throat behind me, and Luna chuckles knowingly. He walks over, his touch possessive yet gentle as he pulls me snugly to his side, his arm wrapping around my waist.

Luna's gaze flicks between us, sharp with realization. She hums, lips curling into a smirk.

"Damn." She tilts her head, eyes glinting with mischief. "Does he have a brother?"

Santo's smile deepens, amusement flickering in his stormy eyes. I can feel heat creeping up my neck under Luna's perceptive gaze—she's always been able to read me like an open book.

Before I can respond, Nico steps forward, his expression serious as he looks at Luna but speaks to Santo.

"You ready to go?"

"I don't need you to take me, Nico," Santo responds coolly. "I'm heading there alone. Maksim doesn't know I'm coming and I need you here with my wife... unless Angelo needs you?"

Nico's answer is immediate, his gaze flickering to Luna. "No, I'll stay."

Santo nods before turning to me. Without warning, his lips crash onto mine in a kiss that steals my breath, sending a shiver down my spine. His hands tighten briefly at my waist before he pulls back, leaving me dazed as he makes his way to the front door.

Luna whistles low under her breath, her eyes sparkling with amusement. "Girl, he is delicious."

I exhale shakily, fingers brushing over my tingling lips. "I know."

Luna plants her hands on her hips, her expression shifting into something far more pointed. "Okay, I've got a bone to pick with you."

Uh-oh.

"Why didn't you tell me you got married off?" Her voice is firm, but there's a hint of hurt beneath it.

Guilt pools in my stomach. "I'm sorry, Luna. Everything happened so fast, and then Santo changed my phone and erased all my contacts except for family, himself, and Luca," I grumble, rolling my eyes.

Luna's eyes widen. "I had to call Pietro!"

A low murmur ripples through the guys standing behind her.

My brows shoot up. "You called Pietro?"

Luna smirks. "Girl, you know I've had his number."

A sharp grunt of annoyance comes from Nico, and Luna immediately shoots him a warning glare. "Pipe down, Beastly."

I blink, intrigued. "Beastly?"

Luna jerks her chin toward Nico. "Yeah, him. Pretty boy over there," she nods at Romeo, "and the Italian Stallion," she winks at Luca, "basically abducted me today."

Luca lets out an exasperated sigh. "You weren't abducted."

"It didn't happen to you, Rico Suave," Luna deadpans, shooting him a glare. Luca just shakes his head and walks away, clearly not taking the bait.

Luna turns back to me with an exaggerated eye roll. "Beastly had the nerve to just walk into my apartment and tell me I *had* to go with them," she huffs. "If it wasn't for Pretty Boy over there telling me I was coming to see you, I would've kicked their asses."

Nico chuckles under his breath, and Luna immediately narrows her eyes at him. They lock into a silent battle—a staring contest so charged it makes me wonder if there's something deeper brewing between them.

CHAPTER 41

SANTO

T he drive to Maksim's takes a couple of hours, but for Vasilisa, I'd endure longer. Even though I know I shouldn't be here, Vera is important to Vasilisa, and that makes this important to me. Maksim is either going to force me to leave—which will end badly for us both—or he'll have to let me stay as he interrogates his aunt.

I expect resistance when I call up to Maksim's penthouse, but to my surprise, I'm waved through. Either he's feeling generous—or he's planning something. As the elevator doors slide open, Vaska greets me at the entrance.

"Scythe," he drawls, lazy but alert, his blade spinning between his fingers like an afterthought. His eyes are sharp, but his grin is sharper.

"Vaska," I acknowledge with a curt nod.

"Maksim didn't call for you," he says darkly.

"No, but I have a right to be here," I reply, brushing past him.

I hear the quiet scuff of his boots as he follows me down the hall toward the room Maksim reserves for his "special guests." Before I can grab the handle, Vaska steps in front of me, a smirk tugging at the corner of his mouth.

"Did little Vasi send you?" he mocks. "You can run along and tell your wife her mama will be just fine.

A dark chuckle escapes me as I lean in closer. We're the same build, but I'm faster, and Vaska knows it. He's lost to me in every spar we've had.

My voice drops low, deadly. "Step aside, Vaska, before I decide that blade of yours belongs in your throat instead of your hand."

"Scythe," Maksim's voice carries down the hall, easygoing but edged. "Didn't think you'd make a house call. Here to check on your mother-in-law, or just miss me?

Vaska glares at me before stepping aside, but I don't miss the warning in his eyes. I turn to face Maksim, who stands a few feet away, his hair now a ridiculous shade of pink. The snakebites under his lips catch the light, glinting as wickedly as the smirk stretching across his face

"Vasilisa would like to request you don't kill her mother."

Maksim clutches his chest in mock horror. "Kill my aunt? How could you think so little of me?" His smirk returns. "Besides, my mother would have my head if I laid a finger on her sister." He takes a key out of his pocket, "I'm just holding her, so she won't have any way of warning Miroslav."

"She's given you information then?"

"Of course, she squealed as soon as we found her."

"What has she said?"

"Nothing of use, except she had no choice, her duty as a wife, it was all his idea," Maksim waves his hands around. "In either case, Miroslav has to return if he's to make his drop off with the Armenians."

"So, she has no idea where he is now?"

"She claims he's in Russia. I've got men at every port and border—if he so much as breathes wrong, I'll know."

He hands me the key, "Still need proof of life? Be my guest but lock the door when you're done."

I take the key from Maksim and unlock the door, shutting it firmly behind me. The room is nothing like I remember. What was once barren—a mattress on the floor, a bucket in the corner—is now furnished extravagantly. An ensuite bathroom, a television mounted on pristine white walls adorned with art, and a plush mattress replace the cold emptiness.

Vera Popov sits at the edge of the bed, poised and regal, a statuesque vision in couture. She is Vasilisa's mirror, but where Vasilisa is soft warmth, Vera is sharp edges and cold steel. A magazine rests in her manicured hands, but as she looks up at me, surprise flickers across her features.

"Mr. Amato."

Her voice is composed, but the way she stiffens betrays her unease.

"Vera." I regard her evenly.

She sets the magazine aside, her gaze wary, shoulders taut.

"I'm not here to hurt you. I'm here for Vasilisa."

Her breath hitches. "Is she okay?"

It's telling that her first thought is fear. "Why wouldn't she be?"

She wrings her hands. "I thought when word got to you, that you would..." She trails off, and anger coils in my chest.

"I would *never* hurt her."

Her head snaps up, shock flashing across her face. "You wouldn't?"

"No." My brows furrow. "Did Miroslav hurt you?"

Sadness flickers in her eyes before she schools her expression, lifting her chin with practiced grace.

"I am a dutiful wife," she says evenly. "Loyal to my husband. Loyal to the Bratva. He would have no reason to hurt me."

That word—dutiful. It grates against me like a dull blade.

"So, you fled willingly?"

"I followed my husband and did what he asked of me, as any wife *should*."

It's like talking to a robot. "Vasilisa can do what she wants so long as she's safe."

Vera's brows furrow, but she fixes her face and scoffs. "So long as she's safe and under your control. That is how it is for a woman in this world. Under our husband's thumb, under his *watchful* eye."

I stare at her and her eyes don't waver from mine. "Miroslav never misses a thing. Not with his *obsession*." Her voice drops, almost conspiratorial, before she lifts her chin, feigning indifference. "I suppose Vasilisa's used to that by now."

Her words offend me until I catch the rise in her brow and her emphasis on obsessed. She's giving me a clue, that I immediately put together. I incline my head—just a fraction—in acknowledgment. Her face remains impassive, but her fingers twitch, a small betrayal of tension. I leave the room, locking the door behind me, the key cool in my grip.

Maksim and Vaska are talking by the elevator when I approach.

"Leaving so soon?" Maksim smirks.

"Not yet. Did you check the surveillance at the Popov estate?"

Maksim tilts his head, considering. Vaska answers first. "We grabbed his computer. Footage was wiped."

"The cameras at his residence might have stored data on their memory cards. He could've deleted files from the system but not from the source."

Maksim exhales sharply. "He's as sharp as you, Scythe. He'd know to take those too."

"Maybe. But he left in a hurry—either he was threatened, or he saw the storm coming. When you rush, you make mistakes."

Vaska nods, already moving. "I'll get a team on it."

"I'll call Marcus, let him know to expect you at NovaRael," I add. "He and his team can help comb through the footage."

Maksim claps a hand on my shoulder, grinning. "Knew choosing you for Kisa would pay off."

My jaw tightens, but I let it slide.

"Vera told you this?" Maksim asks, more serious now.

"Not outright. But yes."

He mulls it over, expression unreadable. I don't wait for his next thought—I step into the elevator, already focused on where I need to be.

Home. With my wife.

The city blurs past as I drive, my thoughts fixed on one thing—getting home to Vasilisa. My phone vibrates against the console, Angelo's name flashing across the screen. I grit my teeth. Whatever this is, it's about to cost me time with her.

"What." I answer flatly, already irritated.

"You hear Maksim has Vera?"

"I went to see her, Vaska's pulling memory cards out of the cameras at the Popov estate as we speak."

"Good, I need a favor."

"My last favor to the family is sitting at home waiting for me."

"And what a pretty little favor she is."

My grip tightens on the wheel. "Watch yourself. What do you want?"

"I need you to take over for a bit," Angelo says reluctantly.

"Fuck no, why?"

"I can't say right now, but it will be for a week at most."

"Not happening. I'm not cutting my time with Vasilisa short."

"You can just bring her around with you, she never leaves that house."

That lands harder than it should. Vera's words echo back at me, the weight of them settling deep in my chest. "It isn't safe."

"It's not safe if she's alone, but she has a small army including Nico, that you've somehow roped into your orbit." Angelo spits. "Take her out, show her your life, show her who you really are."

"She knows who I am."

"What the fuck ever. I need you to step up and take over for a week."

"Get your consigliere to do it."

"*You're* my brother."

"Then tell me where you're going."

He hesitates before responding. "Florida."

I let out a sharp laugh, full of disbelief. Angelo curses under his breath. "Are you serious?"

"Yes, now will you do the fucking favor or not?"

"Fine, tell her I said hello."

The call cuts off before I can get another word in. Fine. I slam my foot down on the gas. Every second wasted is a second too long away from her.

***

The sun has set when I make it back home. Luca and Romeo are in the foyer when I enter.

"Where's my wife?"

"She's upstairs," Luca responds. "Nico took Luna home."

I nod, briefing them on the memory cards now secured at NovaRael. "Head over there in the morning," I instruct. "Meet with Marcus, assess the situation, and if necessary, reel Vaska in."

I take the stairs two at a time, driven by an ache that gnaws at me. Even a few hours without Vasilisa feels like deprivation, like something vital has been carved from my soul. My heart pounds in anticipation, and when I push the door open, the sight of her steals my breath. She's sitting cross-legged on the bed, her laptop balanced on her lap, fingers dancing across the keys. The glow of the screen illuminates her delicate features, and for a fleeting moment, jealousy nips at me—what could she be doing that captures her attention so completely?

But then she looks up, and the moment her gaze locks onto mine the world rights itself. Her smile is a beacon, warm and full of love, her eyes shimmering like constellations, and just like that, every insecurity vanishes.

"You're home," she breathes, her voice a mix of relief and happiness. She shuts the laptop, placing it on the nightstand, and bounds off the bed. In a heartbeat, she's in my arms, her warmth colliding with mine, her lips crashing into me with the urgency of someone starved.

I hold her close, the scent of her warm cashmere perfume wrapping around me like a memory I never want to forget. I scoop her up effortlessly, laying her onto the mattress as my lips map the soft curve of her jaw, trailing down her neck. Her giggles spill into the air; light, unguarded, a sound so perfect, I'd bottle it if I could.

When I finally stop, I gaze down at her. She bites her bottom lip nervously, her big, expressive eyes searching mine. "I missed you," she whispers, her words carrying the weight of her heart.

"Did you not have fun with your friend?" I ask gently, brushing a strand of hair from her face.

"Luna wasn't happy she couldn't come to our wedding," she admits, her tone tinged with guilt.

A pang of remorse shoots through me, and I cup her cheek, my thumb stroking her soft skin. "Now that she's been here, she can come by whenever she wants. I'll make sure of it," I say, my voice low but firm.

She smiles, but it's small, hesitant, her eyes betraying a flicker of sadness. "What is it?" I ask, my chest tightening.

"She and I used to meet up once a month at this little café after class," she says, her lips twisting as if trying to keep her emotions in check. Her nose crinkles, and I know she's holding back tears. "I miss that. I want to do that again."

"You want to go to cafes with Luna?" I ask, though I already know the answer.

She nods but adds softly, "And I want to go back to school."

Her words hit me like a cold wind. "I thought you were going to take online courses."

"I am, but…" She pauses, her gaze dropping. "It's not the same," she murmurs.

I exhale, the weight of her words pressing against my chest like a vice. "I see," I say, barely above a whisper, as I push off the bed, needing space before my guilt consumes me. She sits up quickly, her worry unmistakable.

"Are you upset?" she asks, her voice trembling.

I shake my head, forcing a tight-lipped smile that barely holds. "No, I just want to get out of these clothes," I lie, my voice hollow. I kick off my shoes and socks, unbuttoning my shirt and tossing it into the closet. My hands shake slightly as I undo my belt, the weight of her unspoken sacrifices pressing down on me.

When I glance back, I catch her watching me, her eyes darkened with longing. For a moment, the tension between us eases, her lips curving into a playful smile.

"Why don't you come cuddle?" she purrs, her voice laced with something between a plea and a dare.

I chuckle, shaking my head slightly. "Cuddle, huh?"

She nods, her teeth sinking into her lower lip in a way that makes my pulse race. She's effortlessly the sexiest woman I've ever seen, and she has no idea just how much she affects me.

"If you want something, you have to ask… explicitly," I tease, my voice dipping lower, watching as she squirms under my gaze.

Her lips curve into a sweet, innocent smile, but her eyes gleam with mischief.

"I really just want you to lay down with me. If you do, I'll give you *anything* you want."

Her words are a slow-burning fuse, igniting something deep inside me. I slide the belt free, letting it slip from my fingers and hit the floor with a quiet, deliberate thud. I close the distance between us slowly, savoring the way her breath hitches with every step. "That's a dangerous thing to offer a man like me."

"Maybe I like danger," she whispers, her voice soft yet laced with challenge.

I smirk, leaning in. "No, you think you do," I murmur, my lips ghosting over hers before I finally claim them in a slow, consuming kiss. Her arms loop around my neck, pulling me closer.

She's intoxicating, her every touch, every sigh, sending my resolve teetering on the edge. When I deepen the kiss, she lets out a soft moan—needy, perfect, and wholly mine.

But then, I stop.

I pull away, even as her lips chase mine, lingering in the space where I was. A pang of hesitation grips me, and I shift, settling beside her instead. The confusion in her eyes is a knife to my gut, but I can't go on; not with this weight pressing against my ribs.

"What's wrong? Did something happen with my mom?" she asks, her voice tender but tinged with worry. She props herself up on her elbow, her brows drawn together in concern.

"No, no she's fine, safe," I assure her, but then I hesitate, the words lodging in my throat. With a steadying breath, I ask, "Do you feel trapped here?"

"Trapped?" she repeats, her voice rising with uncertainty.

"Yes," I say carefully. "Like… under watch. Under my thumb."

Her gaze flicks upward, to the camera positioned in the corner of the room. "You mean because of the cameras?" she asks, her voice thoughtful.

"Yes."

She smirks, shrugging a little. "I mean, they're weird and invasive, sure. And I don't like when you take people away from me because of what you *think* you see. But I understand why you have them."

Her words sting, even if they're delivered with a soft smile.

"I don't take people away," I say defensively, trying to keep my tone light as I give her a mock angry glare. "And I've already fixed that."

Her giggle breaks through the tension, a sound so pure it makes my chest tighten. I can't help but smile as I reach out to caress her cheek.

"So… you don't want to leave?" I ask, the words slipping out before I can stop them.

She chuckles softly, her eyes twinkling with amusement. "If I *did* leave, would you try to find me?"

My expression grows serious, my voice low and unwavering. "I would tear through heaven and hell to find you. Until the world ceases to exist."

Her breath catches, surprise flickering across her features. A blush blooms on her cheeks, making her look even more beautiful than she already is. "That's… sexy, Santo. Maybe you should change your threat if you're trying to be scary."

"No," I say firmly. "I don't want you to ever be scared of me."

Her playful smile fades, and the room falls quiet. She looks at me then, her eyes full of something that pierces straight through me—hope, light, beauty. Slowly, she places her small, soft hand on my cheek, her thumb brushing over my skin in a touch so tender it almost undoes me.

"I don't feel trapped," she says, her voice soft but steady. "You've given me more than I ever had before. I have a *home*, a place to express my art, a library full of books, a space to decorate with my creations, a laptop for school, a whole new wardrobe, a staff that feels like friends… brothers I never knew I needed… I'm happy. I don't want to leave."

Her gaze locks onto mine, unwavering as she says the words that stop my heart. "I love you."

She says it so sincerely, so easily, that for a moment, I can't breathe. My chest tightens, her words sinking deep into a place I didn't know existed. I never expected to hear those words—not from her.

My mind races with a thousand things I want to say, but all that comes out is a stunned, "What?"

"What?" she echoes, confused, her brows knitting together.

I cup her hand on my cheek, holding it there for a second, feeling the warmth of her touch like a brand on my skin before I lower it slowly. She watches, her confusion deepening, uncertainty flickering across her face. "What did you say?" I ask, my voice hoarse.

"I love you?" she repeats, her tone unsure now, her eyes narrowing slightly as if trying to gauge my reaction.

A slow smile spreads across my face, breaking through the haze in my mind. "Yes. Say it again."

She laughs, rolling her eyes in exasperation. "Santo!"

"Again," I demand, my voice rougher now, more desperate than I'd like to admit..

She smirks, her confidence returning as she leans closer. "I love you."

Her words barely leave her lips before I roll us over, pinning her beneath me. A squeal of surprise escapes her as I press my mouth to hers, pouring everything I can't put into words into the kiss—my gratitude, my devotion, my unrelenting love for this woman whose changed everything.

She turns her head away breathless, her cheeks flushed and eyes shining. "Well, at least now I know how to get you to kiss me like that," she teases, wrapping her arms around me.

I cup her cheek and press my forehead against hers. "It's not just about the words Vasilisa," I tell her, my voice more at peace than it's ever been.

"It's about the feeling behind them. The sincerity in your eyes when you say them."

I pull back slightly to look at her. Her hair is spread out on the pillow around her, the lamplight turning it into a golden halo around her face. She's looking at me with those beautiful eyes of hers, filled with warmth and trust. I kiss her once more, never getting enough of those lips and then I roll off her, pulling her into my side as we lay there in silence. The steady rhythm of our breathing fills the room. It's peaceful. Contentment washes over me as I run my fingers gently through her hair. This was what happiness feels like.

Breaking the silence, Vasilisa speaks up suddenly, "Did you mean it?"

"Mean what?" I ask.

She lifts her head from my chest and looks at me seriously. "When you said you would tear through heaven and hell for me."

I stare back into her eyes just as seriously and nod. "Every word."

A small smile forms on her lips, and she nestles her face into my neck, I wrap an arm securely around her, hugging her close. Her lips skim my neck, slow and soft, like she knows exactly what she's doing. My cock twitches at the tease. Her breath, soft and steady, fans over my skin, each exhale igniting a slow-burning fire that spreads through me, curling at the edges of my restraint.

She moves her lips slowly, as if savoring the moment.

Her fingers trail over my chest, soft and slow, making my abs tighten under her touch. I fight the urge to flip her and fuck her right then. Her touch is soothing and electrifying at the same time, sending shivers down my spine and making every hair on my body stand on end. I close my eyes and let out a content sigh, savoring the sensation of her hands roaming over me. Her hand slides lower toward the waistband of my pants and I catch her wrist gently, my heart pounding in a sweet rhythm. She looks up, eyes dark and searching, uncertainty flickering beneath undeniable need.

"Santo," she whispers, her voice a breath of want against my skin. "I need you."

My heart races at her words, and my grip tightens slightly on her wrist. She swallows visibly, her gaze searching my face for any signs of rejection. But I couldn't possibly say no to her. To Vasilisa. *Mia* Dea. My Goddess.

I've wanted this, craved this from the second our eyes met.

"Are you sure?" I ask with a ragged breath, needing to make certain she's aware of what she's asking for. That the moment she's completely mine, there will be no turning back. Her eyes darken, and she nods, a small smile gracing her lips.

"Yes," she whispers, reaching up with her free hand to stroke my jawline gently. "I *need* you."

Those words are enough to push me past any lingering reservations. I shift flipping her beneath me, my lips crash down on hers with an overwhelming intensity. She responds instantly, her thighs parting in silent invitation as my hand trails up the silken skin of her leg, pushing her dress higher with agonizing patience. I know she's wet for me; I can feel the heat radiating from her. My tongue plunges into her mouth, claiming, devouring, as my fingers slip between her legs, pressing against the damp lace covering her perfect, soaked pussy.

A choked moan spills from her lips. Desperate. Needy. *Mine.*

I break the kiss to drag my mouth along her throat, tasting her pulse, feeling the erratic rhythm against my tongue. Beneath me, she trembles, her fingers digging into my back as I continue to ravish her body.

"This needs to come off," I growl huskily, pulling at the fabric of her dress as she sits up until it reveals that she's braless underneath. The lamplight casts a golden glow over her bare skin, accentuating every delicate curve.

My fucking temptation. Spread out, nipples tight, eyes dark with need. She's offering herself to me and she doesn't even know what it's doing to me.

"Dea," I drawl, pressing a lingering kiss to her collarbone before gently pushing her back onto the bed.

Her body melts beneath me. Open. Yielding. *Ready.*

I devour her with my mouth, trailing wet, open-mouthed kisses over the elegant line of her neck, down the delicate swell of her breasts. My tongue circles a hardened peak before I suck it into my mouth, teasing, licking, grazing it with my teeth until she gasps and writhes beneath me, her fingers tugging at my hair, desperate for more.

Slowly, I make my way down her stomach, relishing in the sound of her ragged breaths and pleasurable gasps. When I reach the edge of her panties, I feel her tense in anticipation.

"Faster," she begs breathlessly.

A wicked smirk tugs at my lips.

Not yet.

I tease her first, pressing my mouth right against the damp lace, inhaling the scent of her soaking wet pussy. My tongue flicks out, tracing a slow, deliberate stroke over the fabric, barely giving her what she needs. She whimpers, her thighs trembling.

"Patience, Dea," I murmur, my voice dark and indulgent. "You know I love to take my time."

Her breath hitches and I slide off her panties, revealing every inch of her to me. My cock jerks at the sight. For a moment, I am captivated by the sheer beauty of her naked body beneath mine as if I'm seeing her again for the first time, spread out, slick and glistening for me.

She is a fucking dream.

And all mine.

"Look at you," I rasp, my fingers gripping her thighs to admire what's mine. "So pretty and wet for me."

A blush stains her cheeks, but there's no shyness in her gaze—only raw, liquid desire.

She wants this. *She wants me.*

"Perfect," "I whisper it like a vow. Like if I say it enough times, the gods will keep her mine.

I press another slow, lingering kiss to her abdomen, savoring the soft shudder that runs through her before continuing my devotion and worship of every inch of this goddess before me.

A shiver rolls through her, a delicious tremor that courses through her lithe body. A growl rumbles low in my throat as I lower my head, determined to commit every inch of her perfection to memory. From her entrance to her aching clit, savoring every drop of her arousal. With each slow, deliberate lick, her moans grow louder, breathless little whimpers that have pride swelling in my chest. I'll never get over her taste—pure fucking heaven, the perfect blend of sweetness and the intoxicating musk of desire. And it's all mine.

She is mine.

Her hands tangle in my hair, tugging hard as I suck her clit between my lips, teasing and flicking the sensitive bud with my tongue. I groan against her, the vibrations pulling a sharp gasp from her lips. I could stay here forever, lost in the way she writhes beneath me, her hips rolling to chase the pleasure only I can give her.

I slide a finger into her tight, hot pussy, feeling her walls clench down around me, greedy and desperate. Fuck, she's so tight. My cock aches with the need to take her.

"If this weren't your first time," I growl, voice raw and fraying, "I'd already be buried inside you—fucking you until you cry."

But I force myself to go slow, despite the desperation tearing through me. She deserves more than need. She deserves to be ruined with reverence.

As she moans out my name, I curl my finger inside her, pressing against that sweet, sensitive spot, and she gasps. Adding another finger, I start to thrust, stretching her open, preparing her for me, and *relishing* in the way she whines and pants beneath me.

"There you go," I rasp, my voice thick with need. "Come for me, Dea."

My fingers continue their relentless pumping as I watch with rapture as she moans, writhes, and bucks her hips. Her hazy eyes lock onto mine, full of raw, desperation. I seal my mouth over her clit once more, sucking hard as my fingers fuck her without mercy. She cries out, her body seizing up before shattering, her walls pulsing around my fingers as she comes, soaking my hand in her release.

Tears spill down her cheeks as she whimpers my name, her body still trembling from the force of her orgasm.

She is fucking divine; truly a goddess in this moment, wrecked and perfect beneath me, her pleasure laid bare for me to witness.

As her breath steadies, I remove the rest of my clothes before positioning myself between her thighs. I kiss her, slow and deep, and she moans against my lips, licking at them, tasting herself with a soft, needy sigh.

And fuck, if that isn't the most perfect fucking thing I've ever seen.

Chapter 42

VASILISA

Santo claims my mouth with a searing kiss—his tongue ruthless, deliberate, tasting, taking. It's not just a kiss, it's a warning. A promise. His flavor is addictive, laced with the remnants of my own arousal, and it sends a molten rush straight between my thighs. There's no gentleness in the way he kisses me; only hunger and ownership.

His eyes lock onto mine, blackened with possession and reverence so deep it feels like worship. My arms wind around him, fingers dragging down the ridges of his back, clinging to the only anchor I have. He gazes at me like I'm sacred. His to ruin. His to revere.

His cock grinds against my swollen clit, dragging a gasp from my lips as he glides against me with slow, controlled force. The thick press of him against my most sensitive spot is a torment, one I crave. A promise.

"Eyes on me." His voice is a velvet command, soft yet unyielding.

The first thrust steals my breath. He pushes inside slowly, thick and unrelenting, stretching me around him inch by inch. Pain and pleasure war in a blinding flash, but his mouth captures mine, silencing any sound with a kiss that demands surrender. His fingers curl into my hair, anchoring me, guiding me through the ache like I'm breakable. But he knows I'm not.

I want this. *I want him.*

He stills inside me, his forehead dropping to mine as my body trembles around him. Every nerve is screaming, stretched tight, full in a way I've never known.

"Breathe," he orders quietly.

"Look at me."

I force my eyes open.

His gaze is locked on mine, dark and intent, like he's watching something sacred unfold. Like he's memorizing every second.

"That's it," he murmurs, voice rough, threaded with restraint. "You're taking me perfectly."

My breath stutters.

"You feel that stretch?" he asks, his tone low, intimate. "That's me. That's your body opening for mine."

A shiver tears through me.

The discomfort fades as quickly as it came, replaced by the overwhelming sense of him—of *us*—and how right this feels.

"Stay still," he commands when my hips instinctively try to move. His hand clamps on my thigh, firm, grounding. "Let me feel you."

He rolls his hips once—slow, deliberate, dragging himself almost all the way out before sinking back in with agonizing control.

I gasp.

"Fuck," he breathes. "Listen to that sound you make for me."

Another slow thrust. Deeper.

"You're mine like this," he continues, voice dropping into something darker. "Wrapped around me. Looking at me like I'm the only thing you see."

My hands clutch at his shoulders.

"That's it," he praises softly. "Hold on. Let me take care of you."

He moves again, still slow, still measured—but heavier now. Every thrust feels intentional, claiming space inside me, teaching my body his rhythm.

"Good girl," he murmurs when my breath finally evens out. "You're adjusting. I can feel it."

Heat coils low in my belly.

His thumb brushes my jaw, tipping my face up.

"Tell me how it feels," he says quietly. "I want to hear it."

My voice shakes. "I—I like it."

Something fierce flashes in his eyes.

"Good," he growls.

His breath changes.

It's subtle—but I feel it before I understand it. The way his chest expands deeper. The way his jaw tightens like he's biting back something sharp and dangerous.

Then I see it.

That flash in his eyes.

Dark. Ravenous. Starved.

Need.

His gaze drops to where we're joined, watching himself slide inside me like the sight alone is undoing him.

"Fuck," he mutters, barely restrained. "Do you know how long I've wanted this?"

My breath stutters as he fills me.

"How many nights I've imagined what you'd feel like wrapped around me?" His voice is low, rough, scraped raw by honesty. "How tight. How warm."

His hands grip my hips, fingers digging in just enough to remind me he's holding back. He rolls his hips again—slow, punishing—and my cry breaks free.

"There," he growls. "*That's* what I've been starving for."

His thumb finds my clit, circling slow.

A bolt of lightning shoots through me, my body seizing at the exquisite pleasure

His control starts to fray—not in speed, but in depth. Each thrust presses deeper, heavier, claiming space inside me like he's determined to carve himself into my body.

My fingers clutch his arms, my body already responding, opening, aching for more.

He notices.

Always.

"Look at you," he murmurs, reverent and feral all at once. "Already taking me better. Already pulling me in."

His thumb leaves my clit and brushes my lower lip, pressing there.

"Open."

I obey without thinking.

He watches me—*watches*—as he slips his thumb into my mouth, eyes darkening when my lips close around it and I suck.

"Good," he rasps. "You learn fast."

The praise hits harder than any thrust

I can't think.

I can only *feel.*

My cheeks burn.

His thumb leaves my mouth and slides down between us, finding my clit again.

His thrusts deepen—slower, heavier, every movement deliberate torture.

My body is unraveling.

His thumb circles my clit with maddening precision, his cock filling me so perfectly I can't tell where he ends and I begin. Every thrust is deeper, harder, but still controlled, like he knows exactly how much more I can take before I break.

And he's aiming for it. My body shudders.

"There it is," he growls as I gasp, my thighs trembling. "That little flutter—your body's about to give me everything."

I cry out, gripping his shoulders, nails digging in.

He doesn't stop.

"Let it go," he commands, his voice rough, desperate now. "Come on my cock, Dea. I need to feel you come apart for me."

My vision blurs.

The pressure builds, tightens, coils—until it snaps.

I shatter.

A scream tears from my throat, raw and broken, as my climax slams into me like a wave, pulling everything under. My walls pulse around him, and I feel him groan—feel it in his chest, in his cock, in the way his hips stutter.

His control breaks.

"Santo—"

"I'm here," he growls, losing himself in the heat of me, the way I grip him like I never want to let go. "I've got you. *I've got you.*"

He thrusts deeper, harder, chasing his own edge now. His breath is ragged, voice wrecked.

"Fuck, you're perfect," he pants through each thrust. "So fucking perfect—*mine, mine, mine.*"

And then he's gone.

His whole body seizes as he comes inside me, burying himself to the hilt. He buries his face into the crook of my neck, a primal sound tears from his throat, like the release is pain and pleasure in one. His teeth graze against my skin, applying just enough pressure to leave a mark but not enough to break the skin—a reminder of this moment forever sealed into my flesh.

I gasp at the pressure of his teeth and I feel it, the pulse of him filling me, claiming me completely.

He doesn't pull out right away.

He stays buried inside me, panting, his forehead pressed to mine, our bodies slick with sweat, trembling from the aftershocks.

Silence as the pleasure comes down.

Just our breathing. Our hearts.

Then slowly, he shifts.

Pulls out with a quiet groan, then gathers me to his chest, cradling me like I'm something sacred. His lips press to my temple, my hair, the curve of my cheek.

I tuck myself into his side, still dazed, still shaking.

And he just holds me.

Breathes me in like I'm the first calm he's had in years.

"You were perfect," he says simply, placing a kiss on my forehead. His arms wrap protectively around me, my heart fluttering at the intimacy of the moment.

"Finché il mondo non cesserà di esistere," he whispers against my hair before pressing a soft kiss to the crown of my head. "Until the world ceases to exist."

I glance up at Santo to find him already looking at me with soft eyes, a content smile playing on his lips.

I've exposed myself to him completely tonight, given him a part of me that no one else will ever touch, and in return he's given me a piece of himself - his devotion, his protection, his love.

★★★

When I wake, it's still dark outside, Santo's softly breathing asleep beside me. I am deliciously sore, and I immediately think of taking a nice warm bath. Slowly, I ease myself from his grasp, careful not to wake him. He stirs slightly, his lips twitching into a slight frown as he tightens his grip on the pillow I was just laying on. I smile softly, running my fingers through his sleep-mussed hair before slipping away. I shut the door carefully, then flick on the light. I catch myself in the mirror, my reflection is practically glowing. My hair is a wild mess, faint love bites scattered along my neck and shoulders. A blush rises in my cheeks as the memories flood back—the way Santo had worshipped me. Owned me. *Loved* me.

I shake off the memories—for now—and run the bath, adjusting the heat until the steam curls in the air, promising relief. As steam begins to fill the room, I add some of the jasmine scented bubble bath that sits on the edge of the tub.

A dull ache lingers in my muscles, and my stomach protests with a quiet growl. I think of my stash of snacks waiting in the kitchen, but first—*a book*. A quick trip to the library will make the bath even better. A book, a bath, and something sweet. The perfect way to ease both my mind and body.

I flick off the light and slip through the door, silent as a whisper, careful not to wake him. I slip on Santo's discarded button-down, his scent wrapping around me like a second skin, and tiptoe toward the library. The sound of my footsteps echoes through the empty mansion, shattering the silence.

In the library, I quickly locate the S. J Nandez book I had been wanting to read and rush towards the back of the room where a hidden elevator awaits. With a firm pull on the bookshelf, the elevator appears, and I press my finger onto the call button. It beeps softly before sliding open its doors and welcoming me inside.

With my book tucked under my arm, I descend to the pantry where my snacks await. My thoughts flutter back Santo and my body thrums as my face heats, I have never been happier.

The doors slide open, and I flick on the pantry light, spotting my box of snacks. I place my book safely on the shelf and dig through my treats, my stomach grumbles again in anticipation, maybe I'll have a quick snack cake now before I return to my bath.

SANTO

344

CHAPTER 43

SANTO

My wife thinks she slipped away unnoticed, but the second she left my arms, *I felt it.* For a moment, I thought about following her, slipping into the tub behind her, pressing kisses down her back until she melted into me again. But then the lights went out, so I closed my eyes and listened to her scramble around the room and leave.

At first, I'm furious; ready to chase her down. But then I check the time. I've watched my wife long enough to know her habits. Right about now, she's raiding her stash of snacks, one she foolishly thinks I don't know about.

I hear the hum of the elevator descending, either she called in down to her or she went upstairs to the library. I leave the warmth of our bed and head to use the bathroom.

I'm immediately hit with the scent of jasmine and a faint smile plays on my lips. The room is still warm from the steam that had filled it earlier, making me long for her even more. Begrudgingly I take care of business and then wash my hands. I glance at myself in the mirror and smirk at the sight of a slight hickey on my neck.

My eyes focus on the counter before me, our toothbrushes side by side, her makeup scattered on the counter next to my razor and shaving cream, and not far away, a stray lock of her hair wound around my comb. She's mine. In every way, in every moment.

And fuck, I love it.

Tidied and freshened up, I decide to surprise her. I pull on some sweatpants and call up the elevator.

I had her in my arms minutes ago, but somehow, I miss her.

The doors slide open and the sight that greets me as I step into the pantry is delightful beyond words: she's sitting cross-legged on the pantry floor, a box full of snacks spread out before her and an open book resting on her knees.

Her hair, which was a wild mess when we went to sleep, is now pulled back into a loose bun revealing the hickeys that litter her neck and shoulders and all I want to do is add more, *mark her* for everyone to see.

She hears the elevator and looks up, eyes wide, caught mid-chew like a guilty little thief.

My little thief.

The look in her eyes is worth every moment of holding back my laughter. It's pure panic but also adorably endearing.

Crossing my arms over my bare chest, I lean back against the elevator doors taking, in every detail of this sight because this—this right here—is a memory worth cherishing.

She swallows hard, then gasps, "Santo!" like I just caught her committing a crime. Her face is flushed as she stammers, "I thought you were asleep."

I push myself off the door and stalk towards her, a smirk playing at my lips.

"And I thought my wife was relaxing in the bath, not hiding in the pantry like a little gremlin," I retort before crouching before her.

Picking up a piece of chocolate, I hold it out to her.

"How about we share this stash?" I suggest, tracing her lower lip with the chocolate.

"*My* stash," she corrects with a pout but doesn't resist when I slip the chocolate between her lips.

As she takes a bite of the decadent treat, I lean closer to capture her lips with mine.

My goddess indulges in chocolate like a fiend, and it shows on her fingers, nose, and lips, all coated in melted sweetness.

"How did you know about my secret stash?" she asks, closing her book and giving me a playful glare.

"Usually, you eat them in the kitchen in front of the camera," I tease, "I've seen you slam back six snack cakes in a row. I don't know where you put it all."

"Hey now, I used to have to climb a million stairs before I had this elevator. I might just get fat now," she playfully sticks her tongue out at me, "But you probably would enjoy that, wouldn't you?"

"Enough teasing," I say as I scoop her up from the floor, causing her to squeal and giggle in protest as she wraps her legs around me.

"Look at you," I murmur, swiping my thumb over her bottom lip, stealing the chocolate she missed. "A complete, delicious mess. And now, I have to clean you up."

"No, my book!" she whines, reaching out for it as I carry her towards the elevator.

"I'll bring it with us," I promise, picking up the book, but before I can take another step she squeals again.

"My snacks!"

"They're all over your face," I chuckle, gently wiping away some of the chocolate smudges with my thumb.

"But I still need them," she huffs, clinging onto me.

"Alright, alright," I give in and grab a few more snack cakes for her before finally making it to the elevator doors.

As we ascend, she buries her face into the nape of my neck, and I've never felt more powerful or vulnerable than I do right now. I am holding my entire reason for existence in my arms and the thought of ever losing this feeling I have right now, is earth shattering.

I had reserved myself to a life of bachelorhood, building my business and helping Angelo lead Cosa Nostra. I never believed there was more for me, but here she is in my arms.

The elevator doors open into our closet, but I don't let her down until we make it into the bathroom. I set her snacks and book on the edge of the tub and wipe her face with a washcloth.

She hides her face against my chest, her cheeks flaming. I chuckle, my fingers nimble as they deftly unbutton my shirt off her body and let it pool around her feet. "Look at me," I coax her gently, my fingers tugging lightly on her chin. She shakes her head in to my chest. "Please," I whisper.

Slowly, she lifts her gaze to mine, a hint of uncertainty swirling in the depths of her eyes. "I love every fucking inch of you, and you know it. You're perfect," I reassure her, swooping down to capture her lips in a soft kiss. Her body relaxes against mine, any resistance fading away as I hoist her up once more

"Ready for your bath now?" I question, carrying her towards the large marble tub still filled with warm water and bubbles. Despite protests about *'not needing help,'* she doesn't resist when I lower her into the tub, a sigh escaping her as the warm water envelopes her body.

I stay on the edge of the tub, tracing idle patterns on her knee peeking out of the water while she feeds herself snack cakes. The sight is endearing enough that I can't help but to tease, "You're like a mermaid feasting on land food."

"That makes you my pirate then?" she retorts with a giggle.

Leaning down, I captured her lips in a searing kiss. When we pull apart, her face is flushed, and her eyes are hazy with desire. "Oh, Dea, you have no idea what I'd do to you as your pirate," I warn her before standing up.

Her breath hitches and I remove my sweats, her face blooms a soft pink as she lowers her gaze.

I surprise her when the water splashes onto the floor as I gather her up into my arms again and she squeals. I step into the tub, lowering us both into the warm water. Her grip around my neck loosens as she lets out a hum of satisfaction, situating herself to lean back against my chest.

"See, isn't this better?" I murmur into her ear, pressing a gentle kiss to the side of her neck causing her to giggle and snuggle further into me. She grabs her book and hands it to me, "Lets read."

I look at the cover. "S. J Nandez? You like her work?"

She nods. "I love it."

"Hmm, I actually know her."

Vasilisa eyebrows raise, suspicious.

I laugh. "Not like that."

"Good, I would have to burn that book if that were true, and I hate harming books," Vasilisa murmurs.

In this moment, as I hold her in my arms and read to her, her laughter echoing off the bathroom walls and filling my heart with a warmth I've never known before. I am *certain* that I am undeniably in love with this woman. My darkness fades when I'm around her, her scent grounds me in peace.

I've *found* my light. And I'm never letting go.

★★★

Morning light filters through the curtains, carrying the scent of warm amber and jasmine…*her*. I stretch, basking in the warmth of Vasilisa's body pressed against me, soft and claiming even in sleep. Her face is nestled against my chest, her arm draped across my torso, and her leg draped over my hips. I can feel the heat radiating from her body, and if she shifts even slightly, she may brush against my hardened cock beneath the sheets.

Last night, after our bath, I couldn't resist taking her again and again. As we dried off, my hands couldn't help but wander over her silky skin. One touch led to another until I was carrying her to bed, unable to resist plunging inside her once more. I had wanted to bend her over the bathroom counter, but I restrained myself. Vasilisa needs time before she can handle that kind of intensity. I don't want to scare her. She may act boldly at times, but deep down I know she is sensitive and sweet.

I watch as she stirs in her sleep, her leg shifting over my cock causing me to stiffen even more. I look down at her sleeping face and see that those gorgeous eyes are wide awake now, a faint blush spreading across her cheeks.

She starts to pull away from me, but I pull her naked body back into mine. I pepper kisses all over her face and neck until she giggles that infectious melodic sound that I adore so much. She lets out an idle sigh and begins to lower her hand down my chest, past my abs and toward the base of my cock. Before she can get too close, I grab her hand gently.

"You're sore, Vasilisa."

"So what?" She replies with a mischievous glint in her eye.

I chuckle.

"You need a couple of days to recover."

Her lips purse, frustration flashing in her gaze.

"I don't want to wait that long. And besides…" Her eyes drop, bold, unashamed. "You're already hard."

Now, she doesn't shy away from staring at my cock. It's as if all her inhibitions have disappeared.

"That's because I have a beautiful naked woman in my bed," I tease, tightening my hold on her.

Vasilisa's eyes remain fixed on my cock.

"Then fuck the beautiful naked woman," she says, her voice unapologetic.

I almost choke at the word *'fuck'* passing her lips.

"My, what have you turned into?" I playfully scold, holding her tighter.

"Do I have to *beg*, Santo?"

"No, my goddess, you're too sore, but I can take care of you," I reply with a smirk.

Her lips curve into a bright, confident smile as she pulls me closer and presses her mouth against mine. The way she kisses me now is different—hungry, claiming, unafraid.

She grasps my hardened cock and strokes it firmly, causing me to let out a deep groan of pleasure.

I roll on top of her, tracing my lips over the marks I left on her skin last night. I've marked her countless times - her neck, shoulders, and breasts - and it gives me a possessive thrill to see her bearing my marks.

She is *mine*.

I kiss down the valley between her breasts and lick my way along her smooth stomach until I reach her wet, hot pussy. She has to be sore from last night; the proof is there, her pretty pussy slightly red where she stretched around my cock. I bring my lips to her sensitive clit, I kiss and lick gently, worshiping what belongs to me and only me.

Possession rolls through my body in waves.

She starts to buck under me, moaning with pleasure. My tongue swirls around her clit, focusing all my attention there so I don't cause any discomfort. I want to give her relief but also give her body time to recover. Her moans grow louder as my tongue keeps a steady rhythm on her sensitive clit.

"No, I need more," she gasps as I suck on her clit.

"Stop," she breathes out, her hands gripping my hair. "I want you inside me."

"No Dea," I mummer into her skin.

Her breath stutters

"What?"

I shake my head, firm in my decision.

She pulls away from me and scrambles off the bed.

"You're not going to hurt me," she says arms folded over her chest, "Just lay on the bed."

"What?" I chuckle, taken aback by her sudden demand.

"Lay on the bed," she repeats.

"No," I refuse just as sternly. "Not until you tell me why."

"Well, if you won't fuck me, I'll fuck *you*, get on bed and teach me how to ride."

I let out a low, dangerous laugh.

"You'll regret those words, Dea."

Her eyes flash with defiance. "No, I won't."

That's all it takes.

I lunge, grabbing her with both hands and hauling her onto the bed. Her wrists slam against the mattress, pinned tight in one of my fists. My knee forces her legs apart, exposing her soaked, swollen pussy like an offering I didn't ask for—but I'll fucking take.

She gasps, but I don't let her speak.

With a brutal thrust, I slam into her, burying myself to the hilt.

She cries out—part surprise, part need, and her back arches beneath me, her pussy clenching around my cock like she's already coming undone.

"You wanted this?" I snarl into her neck, biting down just hard enough to mark. "You want to be fucked, Dea?"

"Yes," she moans, her voice high and wrecked. "*Please,* harder—"

My hand tightens around her wrists. "Look at you. Spread open and dripping for me." I drive into her again, watching the way her eyes roll back, the way her body trembles. "You were made for this cock."

She whimpers, her thighs shaking, I release her hands and her nails dig into my back.

"You like it when I use you like this, don't you?" I growl, gripping her hip and slamming in deeper. "You *want* me to fuck you until your voice is gone."

She nods frantically, too far gone to speak.

I sit back on my knees, dragging her hips with me, making her arch. My gaze drops to where I'm disappearing inside her, her pussy soaked and swollen, stretched wide around me.

"Look at this perfect little pussy," I sneer, grabbing her ass with both hands. "You think you can talk back and ride me? Try walking after this, Dea."

She cries out as I thrust harder, faster, slapping against her so loud it drowns out her gasps.

"It's too much," she sobs, twisting under me.

I slap her thigh. Not hard. Just enough to shock.

"You don't get to decide that." I grab her face, forcing her to look at me. "I do. *I own this body.* Understand?"

Her mouth falls open. She nods, dazed, and whispers, "Yes."

I slam into her again. *"Try again."*

"Yes, Santo! Fuck—"

She's a fucking gift.

I want to devour her, wreck her, claim her in every way possible. I grip her throat gently, keeping Scythe at bay, just holding, grounding her. "You'll answer with my name while I'm inside you."

Her body shudders. She clenches around me like a vice.

"You're gonna come, aren't you?" I taunt, smirking down at her flushed face. "Soaked, shaking, ready to break… and I haven't even touched your clit."

She's moaning incoherently now, her hands clawing at my chest. I lean down, biting her earlobe.

"Beg."

"Santo, please—let me—let me come, *please!*"

"Such a fucking good girl when you beg." I finally let my fingers find her clit, rubbing in tight circles.

That's all it takes.

Her scream rips through the room as she comes—hard, violent, shaking beneath me. Her pussy milks my cock, dragging me to the edge with her.

"Fuck, that's it! Take it—take every fucking inch—"

Her body spasms, locking down around me, and I lose it.

I groan, raw and guttural, and slam into her once more before I explode inside her, emptying everything I am, everything I've been holding back.

My orgasm hits like a wave of fire, my hands clutching her hips hard enough to bruise. I stay buried deep, grinding against her as I pulse inside, claiming her in every way that matters.

And then I feel it.

That urge.

That low, twisted pulse at the base of my spine, in the back of my mind, in the place I lock him away.

Bite her.

Break her.

Sink your teeth in and make sure she never forgets.

My jaw tightens.

My mouth is already brushing her shoulder, lips parted, teeth grazing the flushed skin where her neck meets the curve of her shoulder.

One bite.

Just one.

Hard.

A mark, a scar, she'll carry forever, carved into her by the part of me I swore she'd never meet.

No.

I rip myself away. I pull out too fast.

She winces.

A flicker—so quick I almost miss it. But it's there.

And suddenly, nothing else exists.

She *winced.*

Scythe *hurt* her.

I hurt her.

The thought slams into me, a fist to the ribs, stealing my breath.

My hands tremble, unsteady, unsure as I brush a stray lock of hair from her face. She's watching me with dazed, but still trusting eyes. There's no accusation in them, no blame, but I can't help but feel as if I've crossed a line. I swallow hard, my throat suddenly dry.

"Are you okay?" The question escapes even though it sounds absurd. It's a little too late for that.

She offers me a weak smile. "More than okay," she whispers, her voice barely audible. Her fingers find mine and she interlaces our hands together, squeezing gently.

"No, I mean..." I trail off, unable to vocalize my concern. My gaze falls on the red trails left by her nails on my chest, then to her hips reddened from where I had gripped too hard.

Her eyes widen, and before I can retreat into my own mind, she's reaching for me, cupping my face in her hands—soft, grounding, real.

"I wanted this. *Every second of it.*"

Her words seep into me, slow and warm, a lifeline against the guilt threatening to pull me under. She pulls me in, and I let her pull me down beside her as I wrap my arms around her and pull her close. She sighs and cuddles up to my chest.

Scythe doesn't belong here. Not with *her*. Not in this bed, not in the softness of our world. He doesn't fit. And yet, I can still feel him, lurking, *waiting*, a shadow that refuses to fade.

"Vasilisa," I begin, my voice barely above a whisper. "Do you remember the lake? When I told you that after my mother died, I became someone I never wanted to be? That I *hurt* people?"

Vasilisa meets my gaze and nods, her fingers tracing the faint red lines she left on my chest

"That's Scythe," I confess, the words tasting like ash. "He's ruthless. Violent. He has no place near you."

Her hand roaming my chest feels like a lifeline, her touch grounding me in reality as I grapple with my darker self within.

"Santo," she says softly, her fingers stilling over my chest. "I've known about Scythe."

I blink. "You have?" Surprise flickers through me, tightening my chest.

"Yes." She shrugs, casual, unbothered. "You kill your enemies. So does Maksim."

"But Scythe *enjoys* in it!"

"*You* enjoy it." Vasilisa replies plainly. "You talk about Scythe as if you aren't him, but you are."

I freeze. Her words land like a punch to the ribs, knocking the air from my lungs. Simple. True. Unforgiving. For a moment, silence hangs heavily between us as our eyes lock in unspoken understanding; she sees me for what I truly am and accepts it unabashedly and I don't deserve it.

I stare at the ceiling, exhaling slowly. "I became him because I had to. To do what needed to be done. To avenge my mother."

Her fingers move again, slow, grounding, as if pulling me back from that place.

She presses tighter against my side, her warmth seeping into me. "We all do things we never imagined to survive. This life *demands* it. And I support you, Santo."

"You do?"

"Yes," she admits quietly. "Because I know that underneath all that ruthlessness and violence is a man who loves deeply and ardently. A man who's afraid of hurting the one he loves."

Her hand slides up to my cheek and she turns my head to look at her. "I love that man; Santo and I understand the darkness he carries within him. It doesn't scare me."

Her confession steals the breath from my lungs. I'd always feared my darkness would be too much, too heavy, *too cruel*. But seeing her compassion and understanding now makes me realize how wrong I was to think she couldn't handle it.

"I don't ever want to hurt you, Vasilisa," I sigh, lifting her hand to my lips, pressing a kiss to her palm like a vow.

"You won't and you didn't," she replies with certainty in her eyes.

Relief washes over me as I pull her close, planting soft kisses on her forehead.

CHAPTER 44

SANTO

She is resting now, curled up on the couch, the afternoon sunlight spilling over her like a golden halo. I stand by the doorway, barely breathing as I watch her.

How did she do this to me?

One look, one smile, and my chest tightens with something I can't quite describe—but I know it is hers.

I'm hers.

She is my reason, my anchor, my everything, and yet, I can't shake the fear that I might ruin her.

Vasilisa doesn't just accept me—she said she accepts all of me. Even Scythe.

"I've known about Scythe."

Her voice echoes through my thoughts, her eyes were filled with something I don't deserve. How could she not be afraid? Scythe is nothing but darkness and destruction, and she is light.

My light.

She is warmth. She is… perfect.

Too perfect for a man like me, with a life made on blood and violence, I don't deserve her.

But damn it, I want to. She isn't afraid, and that both terrifies me and breaks something loose in my chest. For the first time in my life, I feel *seen*—completely seen.

But I should keep Scythe away from her.

I *will* keep Scythe away from her.

One wrong move could tarnish her, stain this thing we were building together. The thought alone makes me want to lock her away, keep her safe.

From me.

I sigh, running a hand through my hair as I lean against the wall. This month, I promised myself, was ours. No guards, no outside threats, no distractions.

Just us.

And if I have to spend every second reminding her that she is the best damn thing to ever happen to me, I will.

I cross the room, crouching down beside the couch, my hand reaching out to brush a strand of hair from her face. Her lashes flutter, and I smile despite myself. "Vasilisa," I murmur, my voice low. "Wake up, Dea. What do you want to do for the rest of the day?"

She stirs, her lips parting in a soft sigh before her eyes open to meet mine. A small, sleepy smile curls at the corners of her mouth. "Swimming," she whispers, her voice light but certain.

"Swimming," I echo, brushing my thumb across her cheek.

"Yes," she smiles, "I never got to try the indoor pool, can we?"

"Of course," I respond, pressing a gentle kiss to her forehead before rising. "I'll get everything ready."

★★★

This pool used to mean nothing to me. Just water. Just silence.

Now?

It's where I watch my wife peel off her robe and ruin me in a pale pink bikini that leaves far too little to the imagination—and yet, not nearly enough. She is breathtaking. *Ethereal.* A masterpiece sculpted by gods, and somehow, impossibly, she is *my* wife.

My breath catches, my pulse stuttering in my chest. She's delicate in ways that make me want to shield her from the world, but there's confidence in her now. A grace, an awareness of just how stunning she is. Because she *knows.* She knows she's *mine.*

She catches me staring, her lips curling into that soft smile that's both shy and teasing at the same time.

"You're staring," she says, turning her back to me as she dips her toes into the water.

"How could I not?" My voice is rougher than I intend, and I clear my throat, trying to get a grip.

She glances over her shoulder, her eyes sparkling. "You picked this bikini on purpose," she accuses, stepping into the water. "You could've just gotten me naked upstairs."

I smirk, leaning against the wall, crossing my arms. She's right. I had all her clothes picked out, *that* included.

"You've been wanting to swim since you got here. I'm just giving you what you want."

"What *I* want?" she asks, stepping deeper into the pool until the water laps at her waist. She tilts her head, her hair catching the light. "What I *want*, Santo, is for you to stop hovering at the edge like some bodyguard and get in here."

She turns her back, floating. My eyes eat her alive. She's mine, and she knows it. She fucking knows what she does to me.

I strip off my shirt and dive in.

She shrieks, instinctively trying to escape, but she doesn't stand a chance. Not against me. I surface behind her, looping my arms around her waist and pulling her back against me. She squirms in my hold, laughing breathlessly as she tries to break free.

"I've got you now," I tease into her ear while nuzzling the side of her neck, eliciting a soft gasp from her lips.

She slows down her struggles and relaxes against me, playfulness giving way to something more intimate. Her back molds perfectly against my chest, every curve fitting me like a puzzle piece. I close my eyes and breathe in deeply; cashmere, warm amber...Vasilisa.

"You're dangerous Santo," she gasps, her body shivering with goosebumps as my lips graze her neck and my tongue leaves a trail of fire in its wake.

"I am," I say, my voice low as I leave my mark on her skin. "But you'll always be safe in my arms."

Her breath hitches as my lips linger on her skin, and her heartbeat quickens against me. The warm water ripples softly around us, but the air between us crackles with something far more potent. Her hands come up to grip my forearms, her fingers tracing the veins there as if grounding herself.

"Always safe?" she whispers, her voice barely audible over the gentle lapping of the water.

"Always," I murmur, pressing my lips to the shell of her ear. My arms tighten around her, holding her flush against me. "Do you trust me, Dea?"

Her head tilts back slightly, resting against my shoulder as she looks up at me with those luminous eyes. "With my life," she breathes.

Her words ignite something primal in me, a fire that I can't contain. I turn her in my arms, her body gliding effortlessly through the water until she's facing me. My hands find her waist, fingers splayed against her warm, slick skin as her legs brush against mine.

"You shouldn't say things like that, Dea," I murmur, my voice dark. My thumb strokes slow, torturous circles over her hipbone, watching the way her breath hitches. The way she feels me.

"Why not?" she challenges, her gaze steady, unflinching. She's bold right now and it's maddening.

"Because I'll *never* let you go," I confess, my forehead resting against hers.

"Good." Her voice is steady but tinged with a softness that breaks me. Her hands slide up my chest before wrapping around my neck.

I can't hold back anymore. My mouth claims hers, urgent, starved, pouring every unspoken promise, every ounce of devotion, every wicked thing I want to do to her into this single kiss. Her lips part for me, and the kiss deepens, the taste of her driving me wild.

The water swirls around us as I lift her, her legs instinctively wrapping around my waist. I carry her to the edge of the pool, her back pressing against the cool tiles. The contrast of the cold against her warm skin makes her shiver, and I take advantage, trailing my lips down her jawline, her throat, and lower.

"Santo," she breathes, her voice trembling with anticipation. My name on her lips is a prayer, a plea, and I'll worship her the only way I know how.

"You're mine, Vasilisa," I murmur against her collarbone, my hands exploring her body that have been driving me insane. "Every inch of you."

She arches against me, her nails digging into my shoulders as a soft moan escapes her lips. The sound is intoxicating, and I know there's no going back now.

"Say it," I growl, my tone razor-sharp, my control snapping as Scythe claws his way to the surface. "Tell me who you belong to."

Her luscious, wet lips part in a shaky sigh, her voice coming out as a sweet whisper of surrender. "I'm yours, Santo."

Those three words are my damnation and salvation all at once. They strip me bare, leaving me raw and exposed to this woman who has managed to weave herself into the very fabric of my being.

I kiss her again with a ferocity that leaves us both breathless. Her hold on me tightens as she loses herself in the kiss, matching my urgency with her own. My fingers trailing down her body between us, gently tugging at the hem of her bikini, her gasp swallowed by my lips.

My skin is on fire where it touches hers. I want her, but not in here.

In one swift motion, I lift from the water, cradling her in my arms, her legs still wrapped around my hips, the cold air hitting our skin making her shiver. I move quickly, carrying her out of the pool, but Vasilisa has other ideas as her nails rake across my back and her lips kiss down my jaw.

"I don't want to wait," she whimpers.

My eyes lock onto the nearest wall, my instincts taking over. The smooth surface will anchor us, but it's *her* I need to ground me. I stride toward it, her body melting against mine, her lips trailing fire down my neck.

"I *can't* wait," I growl against her skin, my voice raw and unsteady. I pin her against the wall, my grip firm on her hips, her warmth searing through me like a brand. My mouth crashes into hers, claiming, consuming, leaving no space for anything but me.

★★★

Vasilisa sits across from me at the kitchen table, legs tucked beneath her, wearing my shirt—the one she grabbed from the basement floor. Too focused on food, she didn't bother putting on anything else. She pops another piece of ravioli into her mouth and tilts her head, her eyes curious.

"So, ZEUS… you named your company after the king of the gods?"

I smirk, leaning back in my chair. "Not quite. It actually stands for Zonal Electronic Universal Surveillance."

Her brows lift. "That's… actually pretty smart."

I shrug, watching the way her eyes brighten. "It fit. Zeus commanded power and control. When I built the company, I wanted it to reflect that same authority in tech—complete oversight, complete dominance. Everything under my command."

She rests her chin on her hand, a playful smile tugging at her lips. "How fitting considering," she says gesturing toward the cameras in the kitchen. "So, first Athena, now Artemis. What's next? The goddess of even *more* surveillance cameras?"

I laughed, low and deep. "Artemis is more specialized, alarm systems and security integrations. It's still in development, though. My co-operator, Salvatore, has been handling things while I've been focused on NovaRael, but his wife's about to have their first kid. I might have to juggle both soon."

"That's a lot to handle," she says, her voice soft with genuine admiration. "I think it's fascinating, though, how into mythology you are."

"As a kid, I was obsessed," I admit, running a fingertip along the table's edge. "The gods, the myths… and the stars. The stars held everything, the constellations, the stories. I read about them all the time."

Her eyes light up as she leans closer. "I love the stars too. I used to stare at the night sky for hours when I was little, counting them. Then I started learning about constellations, and it became my favorite thing. I always wanted one, as if I could pluck it from the sky." She shrugs, her voice soft, almost wistful.

I grin, my chest tightening at the thought of her as a child, wide-eyed and full of wonder. But now, as her gaze drifts back to me, I see something else entirely. Her eyes linger a beat too long on my face, then flick lower, her teeth catching her bottom lip. It's not the stars she's thinking about anymore.

"The gods are in the stars," I murmur, leaning in just slightly, my voice dipping. "And you're staring at me like I might be one."

Her breath catches, color blooming high on her cheeks as her gaze flicks back to mine. "I wasn't—" she starts, but the way her voice catches betrays her. She quickly averts her gaze, confidence wavering into something softer…shyness. "I mean, you're just… you're hard not to look at."

Her honesty catches me off guard, and I smirk, reaching across the table to tip her chin back toward me. "You don't need to be shy, Dea. You're mine, remember?"

Her lips part, and for a moment, she looks like she wants to argue, but then she sighs softly, her shoulders relaxing.

"I—" she tries, but the hitch in her voice betrays her. she hesitates, her fingers brushing her flushed cheeks. "Sometimes you look at me like I'm the only person in the world, and it makes me forget how to think."

Her words punch through me, soft and sure, and for a moment, I can only stare. "That's because you *are*," I say, my voice steady, my thumb brushing along her jaw.

"It's just different with you," she says softly, her fingers fidgeting with the hem of my shirt. Her words stir something in me, and I lean back slightly, studying her.

"Different how?" My voice is careful, curious, as if her answer could shift the ground beneath us.

She hesitates, gaze dropping to the table, silence stretching between us before she finally speaks. "When I used to take art classes, I had to paint nude models. Men would come and go, and it was just…" She shrugs, her voice casual, as if the idea of her staring at other men naked wasn't something I'd latch onto.

My jaw clenches, jealousy sparking hot and fast in my chest. "Nude models?" I repeat, my voice a little sharper than I intend.

Her eyes dart up to meet mine, and she must have caught the edge in my tone because she gives me a tiny, nervous smile. "It wasn't like that, Santo. It was just for art."

"For art," I echo, my fingers drumming once against the table before I fold my arms across my chest. My mind betrays me, conjuring an unwelcome image of her, brush in hand, studying some faceless man with a focus that should belong only to me. "So you spent hours staring at other men?"

Her lips part in surprise, and then she laughs, the sound soft and disarming. "It wasn't like that," she say again, shaking her head. "You really are ridiculous sometimes."

"Ridiculous?" I raise a brow, but before I could press further, she cuts me off.

"It's different because…" She trails off, biting her lip, her cheeks blooming with color.

"Because what?" I press, my voice low, still doused in a possessive edge I can't quite suppress.

Her fingers still, and she glances up at me through her lashes, her voice barely above a whisper. "Because you're *mine*, Santo."

I freeze, her words hitting me harder than I expect. The vulnerability in her steady gaze, her cheeks flushing deep causes something inside me to shift. The jealousy, the frustration—all of it melts away, leaving behind only the undeniable truth.

She's right.

I am hers, as much as she is mine.

A slow smirk tugs at my lips, and I reach across the table to take her hand in mine. "Yeah, Dea. I am."

Her blush deepens, and she ducks her head. I can't help but chuckle as I stand, pulling her gently to her feet. "Come on. Let's get you that sweet treat I know you want."

I lift her tossing her over my shoulder as her squeals fills the room. Her laughter is infectious, and I feel it surge through me like a live current. My heart pounds in rhythm with her giggles, and a warm satisfaction curls within me. I've made her happy.

Her happiness now belongs to *me.*

Just like she does.

CHAPTER 45

VASILISA

I steal a glance at Santo his eyes already on me as I paint my newest work of art. His lips tug into a smirk as he lounges on the plush chaise, book in hand. He's always handsome, but there's something about seeing him like this—casual, relaxed. His grey shirt clings to his torso, the hem slightly lifted, revealing just a hint of firm muscle beneath. A distraction I do not need right now

"Stop staring at me like that," I huff, my brush faltering slightly. I try to ignore the heat creeping up my cheeks, but his smirk tells me I'm failing miserably.

"We've been over this, Dea. You're mine. If I want to look at what's mine, I will." He smirks, eyes dark with amusement.

"It's distracting," I huff, pretending to be annoyed when in reality, I relish his attention.

"I can't help it if my wife is so beautiful I have to stare," he responds smoothly, closing his book and rising from the chaise. He moves with purpose, crossing the room and sliding his arms around my waist. His lips find the nape of my neck, warm and deliberate, his breath fanning over my skin.

My heart skips a beat and I melt in to him, but as I do his phone begins to beep.

Santo groans in mild irritation, and sighs before he pulls his phone from his pocket. "It's my alarm to get ready for the meeting I have at NovaRael," he says annoyed.

"A business meeting?" I ask turning to face him.

"No, it's—" he cuts himself off and gives me an apologetic look, "It's about the footage we took from your parents estate and with Angelo in Florida I have to go."

"He's in Florida?" I ask remembering the conversations I had with Angelo about the woman he loved.

The corner of Santo's lip rises, "Yes."

I hesitate before blurting out, "Is it because she's there?"

Santo's eyebrows raise, "You know about Adriana?"

"That's her name?"

Santo chuckles with a nod, "I think he went there to see her too, but he didn't tell me the specifics."

"I wonder if they'll fall in love again."

"In love?" Santo scoffs, "As if Angelo could ever fall in love."

"You have," I respond quietly, "Haven't you?"

"Of course, I have," he says, his voice quieter now, more certain. His eyes hold mine, unwavering. "I think I've made that abundantly clear."

I give him a coy shrug, "Well, you can't blame a girl for wanting to hear it every now and then."

A slow, sly smile spreads on his face. His fingers trace the curve of my jaw before he leans in close, whispering against my ear. "I love you, Dea. That's why you're coming with me. I'm not wasting a single second of this time we have together."

"I am?"

"Of course, like I said, I'm not wasting a second I get with you."

My heart melts at his words, "Alright, but do I have time to finish this painting?"

Santo looks at the canvas then back at me, his expression unreadable as he shrugs, "You can, but we'll be late and… Luca, Romeo, Nico… they were all looking forward to seeing you," he muses as he walks toward the library door.

"They were?" I ask cautiously reading his face for any signs of jealousy.

He nods seriously. "Enzo and Sergei too."

"They'll be at the meeting?" I ask excited at the possibility to see my pseudo brothers.

"Yeah," he says and I narrow my eyes at him. "What's that face for?"

"Wait a second—are you using them to manipulate me into getting ready on time?" I say, crossing my arms.

"They *will* be there, I have to address Maksim's men as well," he smirks, "But yes maybe a little."

I playfully slap his chest and he grabs my hand placing a kiss on my paint stained knuckles. "I thought you didn't like me being friends with them," I question.

"That was before," he mummers on to my knuckles. He releases my hand and cups my cheek, "Now you're completely mine," he notes, his tone deep, certain. "And you know it. Just like I know there will *never* be anyone else."

His eyes burn into mine, molten, possessive; branding the words into my soul.

"All yours Santo."

★★★

I love NovaRael. Walking these halls, I feel like I'm seven years old again—wide-eyed, full of wonder. But now? Now, I am the most powerful woman here, not because of my name, but because of the man at my side.

Santo Amato, owner of NovaRael. Underboss of Cosa Nostra. *My husband.*

I never thought I'd crave power, but there's something intoxicating about it—the way people move aside for us, the way they glance at him with equal parts fear and respect. And all of it, every ounce of that power, is wrapped around the man beside me. The conference room is up ahead, but Santo's grip on my hand turns us elsewhere.

"Where are we going?" I ask, surprised by the sudden change in direction.

"You'll see," he replies, leading me down a long hallway towards a door at the very end.

"But the meeting..."

"We'll be okay if we're two minutes late," he interrupts, stopping in front of the door and turning to face me. "I wanted to show you something first."

Without another word, he opens the door and ushers me inside. My breath catches as I take in the sight before me. It's an empty office, with large windows, but there are huge canvases leaning against one wall and an easel standing in the center of the room.

"I know you wanted to finish your painting before we left, and it got me thinking..." He trails off, exhaling softly, running a hand through his hair. I don't see Santo hesitate often. When he does, it's usually about something that matters.

"Got you to thinking what?" I ask, eager to hear his response.

"Well... I thought that maybe you would like to come here after your classes since you want to go in person when you return and while I'm working, you could paint. I would have Luca or Romeo pick you up and drop you off here, we could be together and go home together."

My heart swells, too full of love for this man. He's giving me more than space to paint; he's giving me *freedom*, trust. He's silencing his jealousy, offering me something I never even asked for, simply because he knows what it means to me. More than anyone ever has.

"Thank you," I whisper, pulling him into a tight hug that he leans down for. "I love it."

He laughs softly into my ear. "I thought you might." His hand slips through my hair and cups the back of my neck gently. "You *never* have to hide your talent anymore, Dea. I want it everywhere in my world."

I lean into him, but there's a flicker in his expression—one I catch even as his arms stay wrapped around me.

"What is it?" I ask, pulling back just enough to search his face.

He studies me for a moment, thumb brushing over my jaw like he's deciding whether to speak. Finally, he lets out a slow breath.

"NovaRael… it was supposed to be yours."

I blink. "Mine?"

He nods. "Your father had it in your name. It goes to you, but a proxy can handle it and I was the proxy." There's a beat of hesitation. "But I signed the papers taking full ownership before we got married so you wouldn't know."

I stare at him, the weight of those words hanging between us. "You–"

"I wanted it," he admits, his voice low, certain, utterly unapologetic. "NovaRael is power. And I was never going to let anyone else have it." His thumb pauses at my chin, tilting it just slightly. "But if you told me right now you wanted it, it's yours."

My chest tightens. He's looking at me the way he always does—like he'd tear down empires if I asked.

I smile softly, brushing my fingers against his cheek. "Santo… I don't want NovaRael. I *love* it, but I never wanted to own it."

His brow furrows, not in confusion but in that focused way he gets when he's trying to understand me better. "But you're in school for business."

I nod, feeling the warmth of his hand still resting against the small of my back. "I am, but… I thought maybe I'd open a boutique. Or now that I get to paint, maybe a gallery instead."

His gaze sharpens, and I can see the shift instantly, the weight of his full attention landing on me like a silent promise.

"Where?"

I blink at him. "It's just a thought, Santo."

"Where?" he repeats, cutting me off gently but firmly. His eyes burn with that same possessive focus I've come to know too well. "Where would you like it located?"

I laugh under my breath, leaning up to kiss him softly. "I don't need a gallery right this second."

His gaze doesn't waver. "That wasn't the question."

I shake my head, tucking my face into his chest for a moment, letting the warmth of him ground me. "I love that you're like this," I murmur.

His lips press against the top of my head, and his voice drops to that quiet tone that's only ever for me. "Good. Because I don't plan on stopping."

And I know he means it. If I told him I wanted a gallery tomorrow, there would be a team breaking ground by sunrise.

But I don't need a gallery. I don't need power. I just need him.

CHAPTER 46

SANTO

I debated bringing Vasilisa here today. The meeting will be about her father and the surveillance found from his estate, but I don't want her away from me.

Not even for a moment.

She looks up at me, that sweet smile lighting her face as we reach the conference room doors. I hold the door open, reeling in the jealousy that claws at my throat when she rushes excitedly to her *'brothers.'*

I know it was necessary to have them guard her, but the bond she's formed with them still twists something dark inside me. I shove it down, reminding myself she's mine—over and over—because every time she smiles at them, it feels like a brand against my skin.

I guide her to a seat at the head of the table, but as I sit, I pull her onto my lap. It's not just a statement—it's a *warning*. She is mine, and that will never change. She stiffens for a moment, a blush appearing faintly across her nose before she lets out a soft, almost inaudible giggle.

My gaze sweeps the room, sharp and unyielding. "Keep your eyes off my wife," I order, my voice slicing through the quiet like a blade. "Unless you want to lose them."

The subtle shift of gazes around the room is immediate, except for Vaska, who barely lifts a brow in response.

"Santo," Vasilisa murmurs, a gentle admonishment in her voice as she places a hand softly against my chest. Her touch is light but grounding, a tether pulling me from the edge. I breathe her in, pressing my forehead into the crook of her neck.

The fire inside me cools into something quieter, softer. Her warm, familiar scent wraps around me, calming the beast clawing at my chest. As if sensing it, she adjusts against me, relaxing into my hold.

"Alright, let's get this started," I mutter against her skin, my voice softer. But as I shift my attention to the room, my tone sharpens once more. "I'm sure you're all aware why we are here," I begin, my voice echoing off the conference room walls. "It's about Miroslav Popov and what we found from his estate."

I glance at Vasilisa, wide-eyed with curiosity and worry. Without thinking, I grab a snack cake out of the inside of my breast pocket, open it, and hand it to her. Her once-worried eyes shift to excitement as she grabs it from my hand. The noise of the wrapper crinkling between her fingers fills the room, and it's a welcome distraction from the heavy subject we're about to discuss. She takes a small bite, carefully chewing as she waits for me to continue. I rub my thumb along her thigh absently, grounding myself in her presence.

"Vaska. Report."

Beside me, Vaska spins his knife between his fingers, the blade flashing under the lights. Controlled. Precise. His calm, calculating gaze meets mine before he finally nods, rising to his feet.

"We pulled surveillance from the Popov's estate, as ordered," he begins, his tone sharp and to the point, the knife still moving as he speaks. "Luca and I found several instances of Arsen Sarkisian being on the property. Multiple visits. Multiple conversations."

The second Sarkisian's name leaves his mouth, the room shifts—a crack of tension snapping through the air. Vasilisa tenses against me, her fingers tightening around my arm, gripping like she needs an anchor. She knows what that means, even if the full details aren't clear yet.

Vaska flips the knife once more, catching it cleanly by the handle—casual, practiced, like he already knows the answer before he even speaks. "The problem is, we don't have audio of the meetings yet. The surveillance was cut, but there's an underlay of audio we're trying to extract now. It'll take some time to pull the files, but once we do, we'll know exactly what they were discussing."

I nod, satisfied with the explanation but not entirely relieved. Sarkisian has been a ghost for years. Seeing him at Miroslav's estate isn't just business—it's leverage. It's secrets. It's a ticking fucking time bomb.

"Work the audio. Find out exactly what was said. Fast." My voice is ice. "Sarkisian isn't someone we can afford to lose track of."

Vaska nods, pocketing the knife as he sits back down, the tension in the room still thick, hanging over us like smoke.

Vasilisa crinkles the empty wrapper in her hand and shifts slightly on my lap, her eyes filled with concern. I can see the worry creeping in, her mind no doubt running through every possible scenario.

"Anything else we need to know?" My tone is brisk, I want this meeting to end and get Vasilisa back home.

"There's one more thing," Luca cuts in, his voice tight. His usual easy smirk is nowhere to be seen—just a grim set to his jaw, the weight of whatever he's about to say pressing into his shoulders.

"The transfers of money," Luca begins sliding over a document my way. "He transfers quarterly to an offshore account that is his *and* monthly to Sarkisian's account, but one deposit twelve years ago was much larger than any other deposit."

Twelve years ago. The same year my mother was murdered. The same year Sarkisian vanished. This isn't a coincidence—it's a link. One that chills me to the fucking bone. "Elaborate."

"The deposit, it's sizable," Luca starts, wringing his hands together. "It's not like an average business transaction. This amount is enough for a bribe… small war… ransom," Luca shrugs and Vasilisa stiffens. I glance at her. She's staring at the wall, unseeing, body trembling like she's fighting against something rising inside her. I barely get the chance to speak before Nico cuts in.

Nico exhales sharply. "It's almost as if he was buying something." He pauses. Then, quieter, graver. "Or someone."

Vasilisa's breath hitches. Her eyes go wide. This is too much for her.

"Find out exactly what that money was for. No delays. No excuses."

Luca nods as he gathers the documents. Vaska remains silent, his dark gaze on my wife.

"You're all dismissed." My voice is final, but my eyes stay locked on Vaska as his linger on Vasilisa.

The men begin to file out, but Vaska remains. Once the door closes, I speak, my voice sharp. "What do you know?"

Vaska finally drags his gaze from my wife. Then, with quiet certainty, he speaks; "She hasn't told you?"

The words hang in the air, sharp as a blade against my throat. A tear slips from Vasilisa's eye, carving a silent path down her cheek.

"Please, Vaska," she whispers, voice shaking.

Her broken plea shreds through me, and the silence stretches until I can't stand it.

His eyes soften. "Vasi, you still can't speak of it?" he asks gently, his tone filled with something I can only describe as brotherly affection.

My eyes narrow, locking onto Vaska.

"Speak of what?" I snap, my irritation rising like wildfire.

She turns to me, her eyes spilling over with tears. "Of the ransom, Santo," she whispers, her voice barely audible.

The word slams into me like a hammer to my ribs, stealing the breath from my lungs. I go still, my muscles locking, my pulse pounding like war drums in my ears. The room blurs, fades—but that word stays.

Loud. Sharp. Inescapable

Vaska's voice cuts through the fog. "Twelve years ago… Vasilisa was kidnapped."

The room tilts, the walls pressing in. The silence is suffocating, the air thick with something heavy—something wrong. Vasilisa's grip on my arm tightens, her fingers digging in hard enough to bruise. I don't move. I can't.

"We assumed it was the Turkish," Vaska continues. "Miroslav chose to pay the ransom even though Korsakov had a plan to get her back…" he trails off and shakes his head. "I guess now we know why he paid. If he let us go for her we would have discovered it wasn't Kaya who took Vasilisa and that he was working with Sarkisian."

My mind reels, the shock too fresh to process. The pieces were falling into place, forming a picture that was far from comforting. I look at Vasilisa and she drops her gaze, her eyes red and lips trembling.

"Where did they take you?" I ask, my voice barely over a whisper as I address Vasilisa.

She shakes her head slightly, the memory obviously still too painful for her. "I… don't remember, I was eight," she whispers. I pull her close.

"That's all for now, Vaska. Get me the audio as soon as it's ready."

Vaska nods giving Vasilisa an apologetic look as he leaves. As soon as the door clicks close. Vasilisa crumbles. A sob breaks free from her throat as she clings to me, her body trembling violently. Something inside me fractures; I can't stand seeing her like this. I can only hold her tighter in an attempt to soothe her with the sound of my heart echoing within my chest, but it does little to assuage the horror that clearly haunts her.

"I'm sorry…I should've told you sooner," she mutters through choked sobs. But I shake my head, my fingers threading through her soft hair.

"It's not your fault. You were just a child, Dea," I reassure her, despite the knot of anger and despair tightening in my stomach. The thought of her being taken, hurt, and frightened is unbearable. The pieces are finally falling into place, forming a grotesque puzzle.

I see it—them touching her, their filthy hands on my angel, and something dark and uncontrollable unfurls inside me. My fists clench, nails biting deep into my palms, but it's nothing compared to the fire raging in my veins. The air is too thick, the weight of what almost happened suffocating.

I want to kill them. *Slowly.*

"I'll make them pay for what they did to you." The words snarl from my throat, not just a promise—a death sentence.

It's too late, but I'll hunt them anyway. I'll rip them apart piece by piece, until there's nothing left but dust, screams, and regret

She pulls back from me slightly just enough to look into my eyes. Her own clear pools shimmer from the tears spilling over. "They didn't… they didn't hurt me like that, Santo." Her voice shakes, but there's strength in it, unwavering.

"I was lucky." Her breath catches. "But there were others. Women. Girls. They weren't as lucky."

These words do nothing to extinguish the fire burning in me - the desire for revenge on those who dared lay their hands on what is mine. I tighten my hold on Vasilisa as if it would erase the past horrors she had to face alone. "That will never happen to you again."

"I love you, Santo," she whispers into my chest, her fingers tracing patterns over my heart. "I'm sorry I didn't—"

"Shh…," I cut her off, pressing a kiss on her head, breathing her in. I don't care what it cost—blood, fire, or ruin. She's mine. As long as she's safe, the rest of this city can burn. I'd do anything for her.

Her.

All I need is her.

"Let's get out of here, get you some real food." I suggest easing her out of her tears.

She giggles, the sound like the first crack of light after a storm. A small smile lifts her lips, and just like that, my world steadies again.

"Do you have another snack cake in there?" she asks pointing to my chest.

I chuckle, "No, Dea. I said real food, let's go."

★★★

I step into the bathroom, loosening my cuffs as I roll my sleeves up. The moment I cross the threshold, my eyes find her.

Vasilisa sits on the ottoman in front of the mirror, brushing her hair, the soft strokes hypnotic. The golden strands shimmer under the light, falling over her shoulder like silk. She looks peaceful, lost in her own world, and for a second, I just watch.

She's beautiful—my goddess. But like this, in the quiet intimacy of our space, she's untouchable.

Mine.

I move toward the sink, reaching for my toothbrush, but something near the mirror catches my attention.

A small, blistered packet.

I freeze.

Slowly, I pick it up, turning it over in my palm. The tiny pills gleam under the bathroom light, unassuming, insignificant. But their purpose is anything but.

"What's this?" My voice is calm, steady, but there's an edge beneath it.

Vasilisa doesn't stop brushing her hair, she barely even glances over as she answers. "The pill."

I exhale slowly through my nose. I know *what* it is. That's not the question. My grip tightens around the packet. "Why are *you* on it?"

"To prevent children," she answers so casually I almost crush the packet.

Prevent. Not delay...

"I see."

She finally glances at me through the mirror, her expression unreadable. "The arrangement contract never mentioned an heir."

I hold her gaze, my reflection staring back at me in the glass.

"No, it didn't," I say carefully. "And I understand that. But..." I trail off, stepping closer, my voice lowering. "Has nothing changed for you?"

A small crease forms between her brows. I see the exact moment the question unsettles her.

"What are you saying?" she asks.

I swallow, choosing my words carefully. Vulnerability doesn't come easily to me, but for her—I will always try.

"I want them with you, Dea." The words come out quieter than I expect.

She stills, her brush pausing mid-stroke. Her lips part slightly, but no sound comes out, her mind clearly working through what I just said.

"Them?" she repeats, like the idea has never even occurred to her.

"Or one," I amend. "I don't care how many. I just... didn't realize you were actively preventing it."

She puts the brush down exhaling slowly, then meets my gaze fully. "Well... you weren't."

I blink. "What?"

"*You* weren't preventing it," she says, nodding toward the pill pack in my hand.

The realization unfurls inside me like a slow burn.

I place the packet down on the counter, stepping closer, my body towering over her as I tilt my head, watching her carefully.

"Of course not." My voice is low, certain. "Why would I wear protection with my wife?"

Her breath hitches, just slightly.

"You're *mine,* Dea."

I've *always* used protection before her. Never even considered going without.

But with Vasilisa? It never even crossed my mind.

She looks down, fingers twisting slightly in the fabric of her robe.

Silence stretches between us, thick with unspoken things.

"Do you want kids, Dea?"

She hesitates.

I catch it immediately.

"Why did you hesitate?"

She lets out a slow breath, shifting slightly on the ottoman. "Because I didn't know *you* wanted one."

I frown, stepping in front of her, tilting her chin up so she has to meet my gaze.

"That shouldn't be why you hesitate," I mutter. "This isn't about what I want. It should be something we *both* want. If you don't... then we won't."

She watches me, searching my face for something.

Then, softly, "I just don't want one *right now.*"

I nod, understanding but... slightly disappointed.

Not because I expect her to be ready, but because for a moment, the thought of her carrying my child—*ours*—felt right.

Still, I push it down.

"That's smart," I say finally. "Not with the war going on."

She nods quickly, as if relieved to have a tangible reason. But then—her expression shifts.

Lips parting. Hesitating again.

"Actually... it's not just that."

I frown, something shifting inside me, tilting my world just slightly off balance.

This is about Scythe. It has to be. That I'm dangerous. That she's afraid.

"Then what is it?"

She exhales, rubbing her temples, as if debating whether to say it aloud.

"I'm just... *really* scared the babies will be too big."

I blink. "What?"

She gestures vaguely at me. "Have you seen yourself? What if we make a giant baby? I can't push that out!"

I stare at her, processing.

Then—a laugh bursts from my chest, unexpected and unrestrained.

"Dea." I shake my head, still smirking as I cup her chin, tilting her face up to me. "*Nothing* bad will happen to you. Even if we do happen to make giant babies."

She still doesn't look convinced.

"Santo, I'm serious."

"So am I." My thumb strokes her jawline, my voice dropping. "You think I'd ever let anything happen to you?"

She swallows, still searching my eyes. And whatever she finds there… it seems to settle her.

For now.

CHAPTER 47

VASILISA

The rest of the month slips through my fingers like sand—fast, warm, impossible to hold onto. One moment, it's the start of the week, and the next, I'm tangled in Santo's world, wrapped in him. We paint side by side, mixing colors until our hands are stained and our laughter echoes off the walls. We challenge each other in the kitchen, arguing over spice measurements, stealing tastes off each other's fingers. We push each other harder in workouts, sweat-slick and breathless, fighting for dominance in a game neither of us wants to win.

Santo promises an orgasm for every set of lunges I complete, and let's just say, my legs are stronger than ever.

"Dea, shoes off, it's time to stretch," Santo murmurs, snapping me out of my thoughts.

I glance up just in time to see him set the heavy weights down like they weigh nothing. His arms flex, his defined abs glisten, and a bead of sweat trickles down his temple. His storm-gray eyes flick to mine, warmth softening their usual storm. His lips curve into that small, rare smile—the one that makes my pulse trip over itself.

I discard my shoes as he reaches for me. His hands finding their place like they belong there, like they always will. With effortless strength, he guides me onto the mat, easing me onto my back before stretching out my legs.

"Remember to breathe," he instructs, his fingers kneading into the muscles of my calves as he bends my knee, pressing it toward my chest. His touch is warm, firm, commanding, and a shiver of pleasure races down my spine.

His eyes lock onto mine, and my breath catches. He smirks—dark, *knowing*—before lifting my other leg, guiding it over his shoulder as he leans forward, pressing me deeper into the mat. The stretch sends a slow, sweet ache through my limbs, but all I can focus on is the way the distance between us is disappearing.

I meet his gaze, caught in the storm of his hunger—raw, unrelenting. Tiny specks in his irises flicker like lightning in a dark sky, and when a low growl rumbles from his chest, I smirk at the needy, possessive sound.

"Are we still only stretching, Santo?" I tease, my voice low, breathless.

His smirk widens into something wicked. "Just part of the exercise regimen," he murmurs against my lips, pressing forward and capturing them in a deep, demanding kiss. His tongue teases the seam of my lips, a silent command—one I obey without hesitation.

Our tongues tangle, the kiss turning hungry, consuming. He lets my leg slide down, his hands trailing up my thighs, fingers tangling in the hem of my shorts. He pulls back slightly, amusement twinkling in his gaze as his lips ghost over my jaw.

His kisses descend—slow, deliberate, tracing heat down my throat, along my collarbone. His hands flex against my thighs, his touch possessive, claiming. The thin fabric of my sports bra does nothing to dull the sensation of his mouth as he pays special attention to each sensitive peak, drawing a gasp from my lips.

One of his hands slides lower, cupping me through my shorts. He pauses, his smirk brushing against my skin. "Are you bare under these, Dea?"

I bite my lip, relishing the way his voice wraps around me—dark, sinful, filled with promise. "I might be," I reply coyly, my voice trembling just slightly under the weight of his gaze.

His fingers stroke along the hem of my shorts, teasing. "Well… let's find out." His voice is pure gravel, pure Santo.

My heartbeat stutters as his fingers dip beneath the fabric, tracing slow, torturous lines against the sensitive skin beneath. A gasp escapes me, and he chuckles, the sound rich with satisfaction.

"Naughty Dea," he whispers into my ear, amusement laced with dark hunger.

His fingers toy with the waistband, then hook into it. A beat of stillness—just long enough to make me ache. And then, agonizingly slow, he peels my shorts off, his knuckles grazing my thighs as he slides them down my legs.

He tosses them aside, his gaze dragging over every inch of my exposed skin.

"Legs up, Dea. Let me see what's mine." His voice is pure possession.

I obey, bending my knees and parting my legs, my pulse pounding with anticipation.

His gaze darkens to something primal, reverent, his lips parting just slightly.

A growl escapes him, low and raw, full of everything he doesn't say out loud. His hand runs up my thighs to my hips and lift them slightly.

His thumb grazes over my clit lightly, causing me to gasp and squirm beneath him.

"I can never get enough of you, Dea," he breathes out, admiration seeping through every syllable.

A soft moan escapes my lips as he dips two fingers inside me, slowly curling them.

"Santo," I whimper out his name, the sound echoing in the spacious room.

His eyes stay on mine, dark and dilated, tracking every flicker of pleasure that crosses my face. His thumb continues to make lazy circles around my clit, and I can feel myself winding tighter and tighter. He pulls back, just enough to make me whimper.

"Patience, Dea," Santo says, his voice filled with wicked delight. He withdraws completely, causing me to groan in protest. Then his mouth replaces his fingers.

The sensation of his tongue against me is overwhelming. I hook my arms around my legs and pull them tighter against my chest, giving him complete access. His lips close around me and he sucks, drawing a sharp gasp from me. Then his tongue is flicking back and forth, pressing into me, swirling around my clit. I can barely hold back my cries of pleasure.

"Let it out Dea," he murmurs against my skin. His fingers replace his mouth briefly, thrusting in a dizzying rhythm that has me clenching around him.

I'm teetering on the brink, my eyes squeezing shut as his tongue stays on my clit as his fingers continuing their relentless pace. I tremble beneath him, every nerve alight. I'm right there, teetering on the edge.

"Santo, *please*," I manage to gasp out his name once again, begging without words for that final push.

There's a low chuckle against my skin that sends vibrations through me. His tongue presses hard against my clit while his fingers curl inside me one more time, hitting that spot that makes me see stars.

The wave of pleasure slams into me—sharp, blinding, all-consuming. I gasp, his name breaking from my lips in a desperate, wrecked cry. Santo doesn't stop, *won't stop,* until I'm trembling.

Santo looms over me, his dark eyes burning with satisfaction and something deeper, something barely leashed. His arousal is insistent, his thick length pressed against my skin, but he doesn't move. he waits, watching, letting me feel just how much he's holding back.

"You're fucking perfect when you fall apart for me," he whispers in my ear.

I can only look at him in post orgasmic bliss before slowly dropping my legs and pulling him down towards me to capture his lips in a sweet kiss. His taste is intoxicating and combining it with the lingering essence of myself on him sends another shudder through me.

"That's enough stretching. Any more and I'm taking you right here on the mat," Santo murmurs against my lips.

★★★

Santo had work to do after a quick shower, disappearing into his home office. I told myself I wouldn't bother him—I'd be patient, *understanding*. But patience isn't my strength, especially when I know exactly how he looks behind that desk, sleeves rolled up, head slightly bowed, all sharp focus and control.

I try to distract myself, painting yet another memory of us together, but I'm restless. Two hours pass. My brush slows, my thoughts drifting. He's in there, buried in responsibilities, and I know I should leave him be. But I don't want to.

Finally, I give in.

I press my finger to the lock and enter his office. Santo looks up instantly, his expression shifting—realization, regret.

"I didn't forget about you, Mia Dea," he murmurs, his voice filled with the weight of the apology. He runs a hand through his hair, a small sigh escaping him. "I just... lost track of time."

I stride toward him, his legs parting automatically to make space for me between them. The warmth of his body pulls me in, an unspoken promise that no matter what's weighing on him, he's still mine. My hands find his chest, fingers tracing the fabric of his shirt, feeling the steady rhythm of his heart beneath my touch.

"Did you get the audio?" I ask softly.

"Not yet." Santo's voice is low, controlled—but the tightness in his jaw tells me he's barely holding back frustration. His hands find my waist, grounding himself in me. "They intercepted more of our shipments. *Again.*"

I barely react to the words themselves—I know the war he's fighting, the endless strategy. But I see the weight it's putting on him, the pressure building behind his eyes.

"Do you have to go?" I whisper, hoping against hope. "Are you needed?"

"No, Dea. Nothing is more important than you."

His voice is firm, leaving no room for doubt, but there's a sadness in his eyes that makes me feel like he's carrying the weight of the world for us both. "But..." He hesitates, running his hand gently along my cheek. "I've been reviewing the surveillance footage from Sarkisian's visits with your father."

I stiffen slightly at the mention of my father, guilt already creeping in. "Did you find anything worse than... than him being a traitor?"

Santo sighs, his hand still on my cheek, thumb brushing against my skin. "Unfortunately, yes."

I blink, my mind scrambling to keep up. "What do you mean?"

He doesn't answer immediately. His grip tightens on my waist, almost bracing me. "We caught Sarkisian leaving your father's office an hour before you arrived with—" Santo stops, his expression flickering with something darker. He doesn't want to say the name. But I already know.

"Jude."

Santo nods once.

A strange coldness creeps up my spine. "Okay...?" My voice is hesitant, waiting for the part I don't know. "What aren't you saying?"

His jaw clenches, and then finally—he says it.

"Jude was also on the surveillance. In your father's office. The same day."

The room spins.

My pulse quickens. "No," I say, shaking my head, stepping back. "That's not possible. Jude never came to my home. Not once. He always... he would pick me up at the gate and drop me off there."

Santo gives me a look, one filled with apology and pain, as if he doesn't want to break my heart but has no choice. "I don't have audio yet," he says softly, "but once I do, we'll know what was discussed."

I can't help but ask, my voice trembling, "And then... what? You're going to kill my father?"

His answer is immediate. "I won't," he says, his voice calm but firm. "But Maksim..."

I nod, knowing what that means. "Maksim will."

The reality hits me harder than I expected. The betrayal, the lies... they seem to be closing in on me from all sides. I know what has to happen. I take a breath, trying to keep my voice steady. "With Maksim, betrayal is punishable by death."

I let the weight of those words settle between us.

Santo pulls me closer, his arms wrapping around me tightly as if he can protect me from all the darkness swirling around us. He lifts me onto his lap, and I let myself sink into him, my body trembling from the truth that's unraveling around me. He kisses my forehead, his lips lingering as he breathes me in.

"No matter what happens, Dea," he whispers against my skin, "you will be safe."

I close my eyes, letting his words soothe me, even though I know the storm hasn't passed. "I know," I whisper back. "I'm safe with you."

For a moment, we just hold each other, finding comfort in the silence. My thoughts begin to drift—away from my father, away from Jude—and for just a second, it's only us. Santo's voice pulls me back to reality.

"Oh," he murmurs, "you got a letter from Mimi." He reaches into his desk and hands me the envelope.

I perk up instantly, taking it eagerly, my fingers tracing the letters of my sister's name. "About time," I tease, though the ache of missing her is still there.

Santo's phone vibrates, breaking the moment completely. He retrieves it, his expression hardening at the name on the screen. A video call.

Angelo.

I move to get up, ready to slip out of the room. But before I can, Santo grips my wrist.

"No, I don't want to be on camera," I whine. He ignores me.

He presses accept.

I groan and drop to the floor, crawling under the desk for cover.

"Little brother," Angelo's voice crackles through the speaker.

Santo chuckles low, glancing down with a look that makes my breath catch—amused. Dangerous. In control.

"Have you landed yet?" he asks.

I ignore them both. Instead, my fingers trail along the bottom of his desk, stopping at the familiar carving of our initials.

I love that he kept this desk, that he carved his name next to mine. People see Santo as intimidating, ruthless, untouchable—but I know better. Deep down, he's still the little boy who believes in happily ever after.

Santo's voice sharpens. "We don't need a new one. We just got that model last year."

Frustration.

I smile. I know *just* how to relieve it.

My hands glide up his thighs, teasing open the button of his pants.

His grip snaps to my wrist, stopping me cold.

I shoot him a look—half challenge, half promise.

He says nothing, but a slow smirk curls across his lips.

And then, deliberate as sin, he unzips his pants, dragging it down just enough.

My mouth waters. The moment his cock is free, I wrap my fingers around him, savoring the heat, the heft, the twitch of restrained need.

"I'll need you to meet me tomorrow," Angelo says as I take Santo into my mouth.

"Sure," Santo chokes out.

"You good?"

"Yeah."

I slide deeper.

"Tell Tiny I said hi. Unless… she's busy."

I freeze mid-suck, cheeks flushed, but Santo doesn't flinch. His only response is a grunt that toes the line between frustration and pleasure.

"Will do."

I resume with slow, sinful strokes. The thrill of being hidden, of him keeping his cool while I devour him, turns me on even more. He shifts his hips, just slightly—enough to let me know he's losing control.

The call continues for a minute more. I don't stop.

I know he loves it.

Finally, the call ends.

His phone drops somewhere on the desk, forgotten. A heavy breath escapes his chest as he threads his fingers into my hair.

"You're going to kill me, Dea," he growls. His voice is wrecked, rough with need.

"Then die happy," I whisper, and take him deeper again.

His hips jerk, a strangled sound escaping him.

"Fuck," he hisses.

He's so close. I feel it in the way his thighs tighten, in the way his cock throbs on my tongue.

A knock shatters the moment.

Santo goes rigid. We both freeze.

"Boss?" a familiar voice calls from outside the office – it's Luca.

Santo takes a shaky breath before responding though gritted teeth "Yes?"

"I have news."

"Just a moment Luca," Santo grits out, his patience razor-thin. Santo's jaw tightens. His eyes drop to me. He tilts his chin, and I know exactly what that means.

He places his hands on either side of my face. "Open for me," he rasps.

I obey.

He doesn't ease himself in.

He grips my hair and pushes, hips rolling forward in a slow, ruthless thrust that steals the air from my lungs.

Deeper.

Harder.

The weight of him fills my mouth completely—thick, hot, pulsing, his cock sliding past my lips until my throat burns and my eyes sting. The taste of him floods my tongue, sharp and salty, unmistakably Santo. Possessive. Overwhelming.

"Look at me."

I lift my gaze.

He's wrecked.

Jaw tight. Breathing uneven. Eyes dark and blown wide as he watches himself disappear between my lips. Watches me take every inch he gives.

Something snaps.

A low, animal sound rips from his chest as he thrusts again, using my mouth, taking what he needs without restraint. My nails dig into his thighs, grounding myself as he fucks my mouth in slow, punishing strokes—measured, deliberate, brutal in their control.

"So fucking perfect," he growls, voice torn. "Taking me like this."

He's shaking now. Thighs tense. Grip in my hair tightening as his hips lose their rhythm.

Too close.

Dangerously close.

I relax my throat, letting him slide deeper, swallowing him down until he swears—loud, broken, desperate.

"Fuck—"

His control finally shatters.

I do my best to swallow it all down, feeling a sense of satisfaction in pleasing him. As he slowly pulls out, a warm trail escapes, sliding down my chin. I catch it with a finger, licking it up deliberately, meeting his gaze as I do. Santo's jaw flexes, his nostrils flaring—his hunger barely sated.

"You're perfect," he rasps, eyes molten. "As soon as Luca's gone, I'm fucking you on this desk."

He tucks himself back in, adjusting his tie with shaky fingers. "He has the worst fucking timing," he mutters, unlocking the door.

"Come in," he calls, voice cool and commanding again.

I stay beneath the desk, the door opens, my heart pounding with adrenaline. Our little secret.

"We have the audio, Beaumont forwarded it to you, and Sarkisian is in the city," Luca announces. I hear something light hit the desk.

"The city?" Santo's head snaps up, his brows furrowing sharply. He flips through papers, his movements quick, impatient.

"Yes. He's not even trying to hide." Luca's tone is grim, certain. "We need to send Katya and Vasilisa to a safe house. Immediately."

"Excuse me?!" I blurt, shoving against the desk to stand—only to slam my head on the way up. Santo pulls his chair back as I scramble to get out from under the desk rubbing the top of my head.

Luca stares, his expression flickering between horrified and deeply, deeply regretful.

"What the hell were you—" His face scrunches. "You know what? Forget I asked."

Santo chuckles and my anger rises.

"I'm not going anywhere."

"This isn't up for debate," Luca says, his voice hard as steel, his frown deepening. "You have to leave. End of story."

"The hell I do!" I snap back, my fists clenched at my sides.

Santo's hands firmly catch my waist, lifting me onto his lap before I can lash out again. His grip is steady. "I won't decide anything without your say, Dea. But you need to breathe."

I inhale sharply, my arms crossing tightly over my chest, my nails digging into my sleeves. My eyes burn into Luca, my whole body rigid with frustration—but the slow circles Santo traces on my reddened knees start to unravel me, little by little.

CHAPTER 48

SANTO

There's a way Vasilisa's eyes burn when she's angry—a wildfire licking at the edges of an unforgiving winter. It's beautiful. *Maddening.* Magnetic. A force meant to consume or command, and I don't know which I want more.

She's wound tight in my lap, every muscle humming with restraint, thrumming against my control. When she finally turns those smoldering eyes onto me, I see a twinge of irritation but also defiance. It makes my heart swell with something akin to *pride.*

Luca shifts his weight, exhaling through his nose like he'd rather be anywhere else. Vasilisa pins him in place with a look, and for once, he doesn't have a smart remark.

"I don't want to hide," she finally breaks the silence, her voice low and surly. "I want to stay here."

"You don't know Sarkisian like we do, Vasi," Luca interjects and immediately regrets it as she shoots him an icy glare.

She turns her focus on me, sharp and unyielding. "I'm not made of glass, Santo. I don't shatter."

Her conviction strikes like a knife, sharp and undeniable. I know Vasilisa is strong, but hearing it from her lips makes it absolute.

"I know," I say just to her, my thumb pressing into her knee, not tracing anymore, just holding her there. "I've *always* known."

The silence stretches between us, heavy with unspoken things. Luca watches me, waiting for my call. Vasilisa watches me, waiting for my *trust.*

"Alright, but I can't make any decision about your safety until we hear the audio… maybe you should," I say to her arching an eyebrow as her frown turns into a deep scowl.

"No," she says with conviction. "I'm not leaving this room, I want to hear it."

I exhale, dragging a hand down my jaw before looking at Luca. "When did Beaumont send the file?'"

"Right before I got here, to your secure email."

I ignore Luca's stare and open the file. The first crackles bleed through the speakers—garbled, broken—but then, a voice slices through the static.

Miroslav Popov.

Vasilisa goes completely still, her breath hitching.

"Please one more chance."

"You've run out of chances Popov, you over promised and didn't deliver."

"This was out of my hands. Korsakov—"

A sharp metallic click cuts Miroslav off, the unmistakable sound of a gun cocking. The silence that follows is suffocating.

"I can give you what you want plus more money."

"I don't need your fucking money, I want what was promised."

"Both my daughters are upstairs, please, my youngest is fifteen."

"Fifteen?"

"Yes."

A chair scrapes, footsteps shuffle—then another voice cuts in, low, urgent. *"Miroslav, I— holy fuck."*

Vasilisa jerks upright at the sound of Jude Olsen's voice, her breath catching as shock flares in her eyes.

"Jude, now is not the fucking time!"

"The boyfriend?"

"I— yes."

"Come with me."

The sound of the door shutting and Miroslav cursing under his breath ends the audio.

Vasilisa is frozen, her breath shallow, her wide eyes locked on the screen as if she can will the audio to change. The fire that usually burns in her is dimmed, clouded with worry.

A pang of helplessness settles in my chest, sharp and unwelcome. All I can do is hold her tighter.

"He wants Mimi," she breathes, her voice laced with worry.

"We won't let that happen," I murmur, pressing a firm kiss to her temple. My gaze flicks to Luca. "Is that what we think the drop-off is for?"

"It's a strong possibility."

"Do we have eyes on Olsen?"

"Not yet. Last report had him back in Seattle."

"I can call him," Vasilisa says suddenly.

"The *hell* you will," I snap, jealousy flaring hot in my throat.

She meets my gaze, calm but insistent. "He *can't* be in Seattle," she says quietly, glancing between Luca and me. "He *has* to be here for his father's banquet."

"We can send men to crash it, but you're not being used as bait."

"Why not?" she challenges, her chin tilting defiantly. My breath hitches at the fire in her eyes—strong, unrelenting. Inspiring. Infuriating. Irresistible.

"Because it's dangerous," I grit out, forcing my voice to stay even. "You're too valuable to risk."

Her brows pull together. "But Mimi—"

"Mimi is safe," Luca interjects. "Andras has twenty-four-hour surveillance, and Santo has men there."

She regards Luca for a moment, then turns to me, her eyes searching mine. *Pleading.*

"She'll be safe?"

"Of course," I soothe, wrapping my arms around her as she presses into me, laying her head on my shoulder. I glance at Luca, giving him a grateful nod.

"If any more audio is deciphered, send it over immediately," I order, dismissing him.

Once we are alone, I press a soft kiss on Vasilisa's forehead, then her nose before brushing her lips with mine. Her body melts into mine; a testament of trust that fills me with an inexplicable sense of contentment.

Her body's warmth against mine reminds me of our unfinished business. My voice is a low command: "Hop on the desk."

She pulls back slightly, brows knitting together—then they lift, excitement flickering in her gaze. "Always so demanding."

"You enjoy it," I drawl.

She grins and obeys, sliding onto the desk with a confidence that makes my cock twitch. Her skirt rides up as she settles, thighs parting just enough to make me lose every ounce of restraint.

I roll the chair in, grab her legs, and throw them over my shoulders. She lays back as I push her skirt up and hiss through my teeth.

"Bare *again*, Dea?"

She blushes and nods.

"Messy too," I rasp, dragging two fingers through her slick heat, spreading her open. "So wet already, Dea. You were waiting for this."

She shudders beneath my touch, her breath catching.

I stand and shove my pants down just enough to free myself, the need too sharp to waste time. I rub the head of my cock against her entrance, groaning at how her wetness coats me.

"Say it," I command. "Say what I need to hear."

She looks up at me, flushed, panting. "I need you."

"Yeah?" I grip her thighs tighter, pulling her to the edge. "You're going to come for me then?"

She nods, breathless.

I thrust into her in one sharp movement, burying myself to the hilt. Her gasp echoes off the walls, and my name breaks from her lips in a gasp.

"Fuck, yes," I groan, grinding deeper. "This pussy was made for me."

I brace one arm above her, gripping the edge of the desk and pull back just enough to slam into her again. The desk shudders beneath us with each thrust, papers scattering, her moans getting louder, wilder.

"Look at you," I pant. "Spread out on my desk, dripping for me. Taking every inch like you were made for it."

She throws her head back, the motion pulling a guttural sound from my chest.

"You're so close" I groan, pounding into her harder now, chasing that tight, fluttering grip I know means she's right on the edge.

"Yes, Santo! Don't stop—"

I don't. I can't. I reach between us, rub her clit with the pad of my thumb, and her body convulses, walls clenching around me as her orgasm tears through her. The way she comes—mouth open, back arched, fingers digging into my arms—wrecks me.

I follow, hips stuttering as I spill inside her with a ragged curse, buried so deep she'll feel me for hours.

I shudder, looking down at her.

Dio, I love this woman.

I press soft kisses all over her face - on the corners of her eyes, on the tip of her nose, on those swollen lips that have driven me crazy since I met her. Her eyes flutter open, soft and unguarded. And there it is—the raw, unspoken trust that's mine alone.

"I love you," I whisper against her lips.

★★★

I take Vasilisa to La Serenata for dinner. This time, I don't clear out the restaurant, but Vincenzo still serves us personally. We take a booth tucked into the corner, and instead of sitting across from me, Vasilisa slides in beside me. The ambient lighting casts a soft, ethereal glow over her skin. She rests her head on my shoulder as we wait for our orders, a sweet gesture that sends a wave of contentment through me. Her fingers trace lazy circles over the back of my hand. My girl is happy.

Content.

Safe.

I never thought I'd have this—let alone deserve it.

We sit there, lost in our own bubble, and I can't help but marvel at her softness. Vasilisa. *My Vasilisa.* The woman who took a man steeped in darkness and turned him inside out with her light.

She shifts against me, parting her lips in a soft sigh. Her eyes take on that faraway look that tells me she's lost in thought. She doesn't speak, and I don't push. I've learned that with Vasilisa, silence is never empty—she'll share when she's ready.

Our dinner arrives, and we eat in comfortable silence. Dea picks at her food slowly, savoring each bite. Her eyes light up when she finds a flavor she likes, and the soft hum of pleasure she makes after a sip of wine sends warmth curling through me. It's the little things that enchant me most—the ones she doesn't even realize she does.

After we finish our meal, Vincenzo comes by and asks us if we'd like dessert. I can see Vasilisa hesitating; she's got an insatiable sweet tooth, but I can tell she's thinking about her stash at home.

"Order whatever you want, Dea," I murmur, lips brushing her ear. "You can raid your snack stash later."

She smiles at me sweetly before ordering tiramisu for us. We continue to chat about everything and nothing. Tomorrow, the staff returns, and I'll have to leave her with guards while I meet with Angelo. The thought of it gnaws at me. I'm consumed by her—an hour apart already feels unbearable.

On the drive home, Vasilisa links our fingers and hums happily. I look over at her as she stares out the window, the soft glow of the streetlights illuminates her face. "What's going on in that head?"

She peeks over at me, her smile tinged with sadness. "I'm going to miss you."

I lift our conjoined hands and kiss her fingers. "I will come home to you in *our* bed, every night."

She worries her bottom lip before giving me a nod. I park the car out front, and I follow her inside, she begins removing clothes as she heads to the kitchen.

With effortless grace, she kicks off her heels and lets her dress slip to the floor, leaving her in nothing but lace. My brow lifts in amusement, and she meets it with a playful smile, hand outstretched. "Shirt, please."

I shake my head playfully, but comply by unbuttoning my shirt and handing it to her. She puts it on hastily, barely bothering to button it up properly. I lean against the countertop, taking in the view of my petite goddess bustling around the kitchen. She returns with snack cakes in hand, tossing one to me with a mischievous grin as she takes a seat. I catch it easily and take a moment to appreciate her adorable beauty. *I am completely and utterly in love with this woman.*

Placing the snack cake on the counter, I grab a glass from the cupboard and make my way to the fridge. I pour her a glass of milk and slide it towards her, watching as she dips the already half-eaten cake into the creamy liquid with a self-satisfied hum. Unable to resist any longer, I press my lips against hers in a sweet kiss. "You're beautiful," I murmur against her chocolate-coated lips.

Her tongue darts out to lick my lips and I deepen the kiss, savoring the taste of chocolate on her tongue. Her arms wrap around my shoulders and she moans softly into my mouth.

The moment is perfect. Blissful. Until a voice ruins everything.

"Ugh, that's disgusting," comes my sister's unmistakable voice.

We both freeze, turning to see Elena standing in the threshold of the kitchen with her hand up to shield her eyes like she's been personally offended by the sight of us. Behind her, Riot stands with a smirk plastered on his stupid fucking face.

A rush of possessiveness surges through me, instinctive and immediate. I step in front of Vasilisa, blocking Riot's line of sight to her. He shouldn't be looking at her. No one should.

"Get the fuck out of here, Riot," I snap, my voice low, dangerous.

He chuckles like the asshole he is but lifts his hands in surrender and saunters out, all too amused with himself. I watch him go, jaw clenched, before turning my attention to Elena, still lingering with an attitude like she owns the place.

"Why are you here?" My voice is clipped, my irritation bubbling just below the surface.

I should be happy she's back. I should be relieved. But her timing is fucking terrible, and I'm still wound tight from the interruption.

Elena raises a brow, unimpressed. "I came home since no one thought to tell me our father almost died."

Her tone is pure Elena—sharp, challenging, and laced with attitude. Hands on her hips, she glares at me like I'm the one who's wrong for not rolling out the red carpet for her grand return.

I scoff. "Oh, so *now* you care to come home? We didn't think you gave a fuck about Dad, considering you didn't even bother after you almost got taken."

Elena grimaces, clearly unbothered by my fury. "Ew, if you're going to yell at me, at least put on a shirt."

I take a threatening step forward, my patience already razor-thin. "This is my fucking house. I want my key back."

She folds her arms, not backing down. "No. You gave it to me."

"In case of *emergency*."

"Dad in the hospital constitutes an emergency."

"Why didn't you go to Angelo's?"

"I did," she says, flipping her hair over her shoulder. "But I wanted to meet your wife."

Vasilisa shifts behind me, peeking out from where she's been pressed against my back.

Elena's gaze flicks to her, lips curling slightly before she lifts a hand in a small wave.

Vasilisa waves back.

I groan, already seeing where this is going. "Don't encourage her, Vasilisa."

VASILISA

I peer over Santo's shoulder. The pretty brunette still stands there, watching me.

She's a striking combination of her two brothers—dark-haired and sharp-featured. But her eyes, a warm light brown, soften her overall appearance, giving her an air of quiet observation rather than cold intensity.

Her clothes are effortlessly expensive, her hair sleek and styled, and even though Santo is practically growling at her, she seems entirely unbothered. She exudes an air of sophistication that tells me she's used to commanding a room without needing to raise her voice.

She meets my eyes, and I instinctively sink back behind Santo, half-hidden by his broad frame.

At the mention of my name, her lips twitch. "Vasilisa?" she repeats, her tone laced with curiosity.

Santo grunts, muttering something under his breath, before turning toward me. Before I can process what's happening, he scoops me up, arms firm around me, and strides toward the pantry.

I blink, startled. "Santo—"

He doesn't respond, just steps into the elevator inside the pantry, jaw tight. The doors close behind us, sealing us in silence, leaving Elena behind.

The elevator doors slide open into our closet. Santo puts me down without a word, his grip lingering for just a second before he steps back.

"Get dressed," he grunts out.

I grab a pair of leggings and a t-shirt, pulling them on as Santo puts on a shirt. I wrap my arms around his waist, "Talk to me, what's wrong?"

He presses a lingering kiss to the top of my head. "It's our last night alone before everything gets too busy again."

I look up at him, his face hardened and angry. "I'm sorry," I whisper, pressing my cheek against his chest. "We can tell her she can come back tomorrow and I can get to know her then."

He exhales, the tension in his shoulders easing just a fraction. Leaning down, he kisses me—slow and grounding. "Alright."

He laces our fingers together, leading me out of the bedroom and down the stairs

Elena is in the living room with Riot, the model looking guard she came in with, "Listen, I screwed up, alright?" Elena sighs, crossing her arms. "Angelo just got back from a trip, he wasn't exactly in a welcoming mood. It's too late to see Dad, and—I should have come home sooner. I get it."

Santo sighs, "Next time we ask you to come home, *come home.*"

She nods, and Riot's hand skims over her back in a gesture that feels too familiar.

"Hands off my sister," Santo snaps, his voice sharp enough to cut. Whatever restraint he had before is gone in an instant. Riot withdraws his hand quickly, raising it and backing up with a smirk.

"Understood, boss," Riot responds, his voice smooth as silk even though the tension in the room is cutting edge sharp.

Elena rolls her eyes, clearly unfazed. Then, just like that, she pivots her attention to me. "Vasilisa, right?"

"Yes," I smile removing my hand from Santo's to extend towards Elena.

Instead of shaking my hand, she bats it aside and pulls me into a hug. I barely have time to react before I'm wrapped in her warmth, her perfume filling my senses. "It's so nice to finally have a sister," she says kindly.

We part, but hold hands. "I have a younger sister, but she's away at school, it will be nice to get to know you… tomorrow?" I ask.

She nods understandingly, "Yes, tomorrow." She gives Santo a sideways glance. "Is that alright with you, *Boss?*" she asks sarcastically.

"Don't push it," Santo grumbles. Elena holds her hands up in mock surrender, a smirk playing on the edges of her lips, before she pivots and heads to the front door.

"I will see you tomorrow then," she calls over her shoulder, Riot trailing behind her like a loyal guard dog.

Their departure leaves a silence that rings heavy in the air. I turn to Santo. His eyes are still glued to the now-closed front door, jaw held tight.

I pull him out of his thoughts by slipping my hand into his. His fingers tighten reflexively around mine, his gaze shifting down to me. The anger has faded from his features, replaced by a softness that makes my heart flutter.

"We, okay?" I ask softly, looking up at him through my lashes.

"Always, you're never the problem, you're perfect," he murmurs, his thumb tracing circles on the back of my hand. "We can deal with Elena tomorrow," he replies gruffly.

I chuckle, but before I can say anything, Santo pulls me flush against him, lifting me effortlessly into his arms. His lips find mine in a kiss that's deep and claiming.

He pulls back just enough to murmur against my lips, "Upstairs. *Now.* I need to be inside you."

VASILISA

My eyes flutter open to Santo's soft kisses, gentle and lingering, turning into us making love; he's reverent with me as if he were saying goodbye.

Even though it's only for the day, I hate him leaving.

He showers while I soak in the bath, letting the warm water engulf me, easing the ache of his absence before he's even gone. My gaze never strays from my husband. I watch as he shaves, as he effortlessly styles his hair, each movement practiced and confident.

In the mirror, his smirk finds me—lust-filled, knowing. He strides to me, leans in pressing a slow, teasing kiss to my lips before stepping away. I watch, admiring the ripple of muscle beneath his tattooed back, the way the towel hangs low on his hips, a *perfect* temptation.

Reluctantly, I leave the comfort of the bath, wrapping myself in a towel as I pad toward the closet to get ready for my day with Elena, she's effortlessly chic—I need to look like I belong at her side.

I slip into a navy blue button-down, the crisp fabric soft against my skin, tucking it loosely into my fitted black jeans. A pair of sleek, black-heeled loafers complete the look—simple, sophisticated, polished.

For makeup, I keep it subtle, adding just a swipe of gloss over my lip stain for a touch of shine. My hair, I sweep into a loose updo, making sure my delicate pearl earrings are visible, a soft contrast to the sharp lines of my outfit.

After last night, with Santo so tense, I want to make a good impression. I want Elena to see me as more than just his wife—I want her to *like* me.

I grab my purse and stride toward the door, ready to leave, but I barely make it two steps before stopping short. Santo stands in our sitting room, brows furrowed, a gun in his hand.

My gun.

"What is this?" he asks, his voice edged with both surprise and concern.

I blink, still trying to process. "A gun?"

"Yes, but why do *you* have it?"

"What?" I stammer, my brain scrambling.

He exhales, jaw tightening. "I found this in a box. In your window nook." He lifts the box where I had tucked the gun Angelo had given me, his fingers resting against the lid. "Why do you have it?"

I hesitate, eyes flicking between the gun and his face. *Think, Vasilisa.*

"Oh. Why were *you* in my window nook?" I counter, trying to shift the focus away from me.

His gaze sharpens. "Vasilisa."

I sigh, knowing I've lost this battle. "Angelo gave it to me," I admit, stepping toward him as he slides the gun back into the box.

"Why would he give you a gun?" Santo asks, his expression stern, his grip tightening slightly around the box.

I shift under his gaze, feeling small but refusing to shrink. "He taught me how to use one," I admit sheepishly. "Said it would be good for me to protect myself."

Santo exhales sharply, shaking his head. He's clearly not thrilled. "I'd feel safer if you *didn't* have one… but it's not a bad idea." He reaches for my hands, his thumbs rubbing slow, soothing circles over my skin.

"You always have a gun around me, Santo," I chuckle, nodding toward his waist where I know he keeps one concealed.

"True," he concedes, his smirk soft but laced with something deeper. "But seeing one in your hands just feels *wrong.*" He lifts my hand to his lips, pressing a lingering kiss to my knuckles.

Then, suddenly, something clicks in his expression. His eyes narrow.

"Is that what you and Angelo have been doing this whole time?" His voice drops slightly, tinged with realization. "Learning how to use a gun?"

"Yes… that and sparring." I hesitate, feeling heat creep up my cheeks. "Are you angry?"

His brows lift in mild surprise before he exhales, rubbing the back of his neck.

"I'm not angry, Vasilisa," he sighs, shaking his head. "Just… surprised."

"But why?" I press on refusing to let this drop. "Isn't it better that I can protect myself? Especially given… well, your line of work."

"That's exactly what I don't want you involved in," Santo replies sharply, his eyes flaring with anger. "This is *my* world, Vasilisa, not yours. You should be far away from danger."

"But I'm part of this world too, I was born into it," I argue. "Whether we like it or not."

We stand in silence for a moment, both too stubborn to back down from our respective stances. But then Santo sighs again, his shoulders dropping in defeat.

"Okay," he eventually concedes. "You're right. It's good that you know how to use one."

"Thank you," I breathe out in relief.

"But I promise you one thing," Santo adds seriously, his grip tightening around my hands. "As long as I'm around, you will never have to use it."

I nod, giving his hands a reassuring squeeze. "I know."

He pulls me into his arms and buries his face in my hair. "I love you, Dea," he mumbles.

"I love you too, Santo," I reply softly.

Santo pulls back and presses a soft kiss to my lips, "Romeo is on his way," he reminds. "Elena is already waiting for you downstairs."

"Got it," I acknowledge taking one last look at him before I rush out of the room to join Elena.

I find Elena in the living room lounging in an armchair, her presence effortless and cool. Behind her stands Riot, posture perfect, his frame filling out the tailored designer shirt like he was born to wear it. With sharp, chiseled features and tanned skin, he looks more like a runway model than a bodyguard. Even his perfectly styled hair adds to the illusion. If I didn't know better, I'd think he was here to sweep Elena onto a red carpet instead of protecting her.

"Good morning," I greet, "You look chic," I gesture toward her outfit; ripped jeans, ankle boots and a simple white tank that somehow looks expensive on her. With a bold red lip and her wavy ponytail she looks perfectly put together.

"You look lovely," she responds standing to embrace me.

I hug her back, catching Riot's gaze over her shoulder. He gives a brief nod in acknowledgement.

As I release Elena, I turn to see Santo entering the room flanked by Luca and Romeo.

Santo slides an arm around my waist, his presence grounding me as he addresses his sister. "Behave today, Elena."

Elena rolls her eyes. "I always behave."

Santo ignores her sarcasm. "Have you gone to see dad?"

"Yes, I saw him early this morning," she says casually. "He's glad I'm home, *unlike* you."

Santo exhales, clearly used to her jabs. "I'm glad you're back little sister, I just—"

"Yeah, yeah," she waves him off, "Don't get your wife into any trouble. Got it."

Santo sighs deeply, pressing a lingering kiss to the top of my head. "I'll see you tonight. Luca has my card, buy whatever you want."

With that, he turns and strides out. The sound of the front door closing barely fades before Elena lets out a dramatic sigh.

"He's so annoying."

I frown at her, and she quickly gives me a sheepish smile. "Sorry he's my older brother, so he's annoying to *me*. I'm sure he's great to *you*." She waves her hand dismissively before shifting her attention to Luca "How have you been Cousin?"

Luca, arms crossed, replies "Fine."

Elena smirks. "Still angry at me for that little prank?"

I glance between them, sensing the tension immediately. "What prank?" I interject.

Luca shakes his head once, jaw tight, and I drop it. The tension is palpable, and I don't know what it is about Elena, but her homecoming definitely doesn't seem welcome.

"Still stirring shit up Elena?" Romeo's sharp smile cuts through the moment.

Elena glares at him, but ignores the jab. Instead she lets out an exaggerated sigh. "Anyway," she drags the word out, linking her arm through mine. "Let's go girly."

Without waiting for a response, she tugs me along, leading us toward the door. The guys follow silent, but ever-present.

The sleek black SUV purrs to life as Luca slides into the driver's seat, his stern face reflected in the mirror. Riot takes the front passenger seat, while Elena and I settle comfortably in the middle, with Romeo in the back.

The tension is thick enough to choke on, but if Elena notices, she doesn't show it.

"Could you turn the radio on, Riot?" she asks, flashing him a sweet smile.

Riot gives a silent nod, reaching for the dial. A cheerful pop song filters through the speakers, breaking the heavy silence. Elena bobs her head beside me, her wavy ponytail swishing in rhythm with the music.

I glance at her before hesitantly asking, "So… where are we going?"

Elena doesn't turn to look at me. Her gaze stays fixed on the passing scenery. "A day of shopping, followed by a quick lunch, and maybe a movie if we have time."

Her voice is light, almost careless, but something about it doesn't sit right with me. Beneath the easygoing tone, something is off.

"Isn't it dangerous for us to be out?" I ask, my voice trailing off before I can finish the thought—but Elena understands.

She waves a hand dismissively. "We have enough security around us." Finally, she turns to look at me, flashing a grin that doesn't quite reach her eyes. "You worry too much."

I nod silently, the unease still there, but I push it down. I want to bond with her. "Where do you go to school?"

"California," she answers smoothly, her smile practiced, avoiding the actual name of the university.

"Do you go to school?" she asks in return.

I shift slightly. "I'm currently deferring, but yes."

Elena hums. "Oh, yeah. I guess an arranged marriage would hinder you, wouldn't it?" It's not really a question—more of a statement.

I shrug, feeling a flicker of embarrassment.

"Vasilisa isn't hindered from anything," Romeo interjects, his voice firm. "She'll be going back to school, but right now she's fulfilling the obligation she has to her family—and ours."

Elena raises her hands in mock surrender. "No need to be a hero, Romeo. I didn't mean any harm."

"Well, it sounds like you lost all your couth in California," he retorts.

Elena huffs, turning back toward the window, and the tension in the car thickens once more. My stomach knots, and I find myself wishing I had just stayed home.

Despite the tension in the car, the day passes surprisingly quickly. While trying on clothes, Elena lights up, effortlessly discussing fashion. This is where she thrives—where she excels. She helps me pick out a few outfits, explaining how they'll elongate my short stature, her enthusiasm undeniable.

It feels good to be out, to step away from the weight of war, if only for a little while. This small slice of normalcy is a welcome relief.

As the late afternoon sun filters through the windows, we return to the estate. Lunch is quiet, the conversation minimal, mostly just filling the silence with idle chatter.

Shortly after, we retreat to the library. The guys leave us alone, giving us space to spend time together. I sit before an easel, focused on yet another portrait of my husband, my brush moving instinctively across the canvas.

But I can feel her eyes on me.

Across the room, Elena lounges in the plush chair Riot carried up from the living room, her legs draped over the sides. She doesn't speak, just watches, her gaze impassive as it bores into me.

"What?" I finally break the silence, shifting under her intense stare. It feels like she's trying to see through me, unraveling my thoughts, scrutinizing every detail.

"Do you have social media?" she asks. "I was thinking it'd be fun to tag you in something—maybe a picture from trying on outfits."

The question catches me off guard.

My cheeks heat. I don't face her, keeping my eyes on the canvas as I answer.

"No, I don't have social media anymore."

Her brows knit together. "Why not? I've seen plenty of girls in our world with social media accounts—designer gowns, luxury vacations. You'd be perfect for that. Plus, you could post your art."

I let out a nervous laugh, avoiding her gaze. "Well… it's not exactly by choice." My fingers tighten around the paintbrush. "Santo got me a new phone before we got married, but it doesn't have access to social media. I think it's his way of protecting me."

Elena's mouth falls open slightly before she snaps it shut. "He doesn't *allow* you to have social media? Are you serious?"

I stiffen. "It's not like that," I rush to explain, but my voice wavers with uncertainty. "I mean, I think he just… wants to keep me safe. Things can get dangerous, and he worries."

Elena doesn't look convinced, her eyes narrowing slightly. "What about school? You said you were going back to campus. Is that true, or did he shut that down too?"

The question hits a nerve. Frustration and embarrassment bubble up, tangled together.

"I asked him about it," I admit, my voice quieter now. "He said I *could…* but he's not really comfortable with the idea. I might just stick to online classes for now."

Elena's eyes flash with something between disbelief and concern. She opens her mouth, then shuts it again, exhaling a slow sigh.

"Were you forced into this?" Her voice is softer now, laced with real concern.

I freeze for a moment, caught off guard. "What do you mean?" I turn to finally face her fully.

Elena holds my gaze, her brows furrowed. "I mean, I know it was an arranged marriage… but were you forced? Are you *truly* happy?"

A strange sense of relief washes over me. She's not scrutinizing me. She's *worried* about me.

I let out a small chuckle, shaking my head. "Yes, I'm happy. And I love Santo. Whether our marriage was arranged or not… it's a good match."

Elena studies my face for a moment, her eyes analyzing every expression before she rises from the chair.

"Is that just what you tell yourself?" she asks slowly. "Or do you really believe it?"

My heart races at her question, but I hold her gaze steadily.

"I believe it," I answer firmly. "Santo is a wonderful husband, and I wouldn't have it any other way."

For a brief moment, something like surprise flashes in Elena's eyes before it's quickly replaced by a genuine smile.

"I'm glad to hear it," she says sincerely. "I only ask because I dread the day when Angelo decides to ship me off to marry some stranger. How did you handle it?"

A wave of empathy and understanding washes over me, and I answer honestly.

"I always knew my marriage would be arranged, but I wanted to have hope that it would grow into love."

Elena nods in understanding, her long strides taking her back to her chair with a heavy huff. I can feel the weight of her thoughts as she sits down.

"Yours did," she states with a small smile.

"It did," I reply, offering her a genuine smile. "And if Angelo were to arrange a marriage for you, I have no doubt he'd choose someone who would treat you with love and respect."

Elena lets out a heavy sigh. "My brother... did he let you in?"

Confused, I set down my brush and look at her closely. "Let me in *how?*"

Her eyes meet mine, and for a long moment, we just stare at each other, as if weighing something unspoken. Finally, we both say it at the same time.

"Scythe."

Elena's eyes widen in surprise. "He told you about that?"

I nod. "I know it's a part of him, I understand and respect that."

Elena lets out a slow breath, as if she's been holding something in. "That's not an easy thing to accept."

She pushes up from her chair, walking toward the bookshelf, her fingers trailing along the spines before stopping on a large lilac-colored one. She pulls it free, turning it over in her hands as she strides back to the chaise, motioning for me to join her.

As she opens it, I realize it's an album. The first page reveals a photo of two young boys and a woman who bears a striking resemblance to an older version of Elena.

"When she was... murdered," Elena begins hesitantly, her voice softer now. "I was young. My memories are nothing compared to what my brothers have."

I reach for her hand, squeezing gently. She meets my gaze, offering a sad smile.

"She was truly beautiful. You resemble her greatly," I tell her honestly.

Tears glisten in her eyes, but she whispers, "Thank you... I remember what Santo was like before."

"Before?" I prompt, curiosity sparking.

She flips the page. A young Santo sits at a table, a toaster completely dismantled in front of him.

"He liked to take things apart, to see what made them work. He was always tinkering," she murmurs, sliding her hand over another photo. This one shows Santo, nose buried in a book, reading beside their mother.

"If he wasn't tinkering, he was lost in the pages of a book."

"I can relate to that," I murmur, taking in the fragments of memories captured in the photographs.

Elena's voice drops to something almost wistful. "He didn't want to be who he is now. He had other dreams."

I glance at her, drawn in by this rare glimpse into his past. "What kind of dreams?"

She exhales slowly. "He wanted to own his own business—like he does with ZEUS. But if he had a choice, he would have stayed in California, gone to university, and left Cosa Nostra behind."

My breath catches. "I don't have that choice," I admit quietly.

Elena's smile is rueful. "Neither do I."

She flips through more pages filled with photos of Santo, Angelo, their mother, and baby Elena.

I reach out, brushing my fingertips over a picture of Santo, smiling brightly at the camera. Before I can linger, Elena's fingers skim over my ring.

I look up, catching the shadows lurking behind her eyes. My stomach tightens. I quickly withdraw my hand, but before I can say anything, she murmurs, "Sorry."

"It's alright," I assure her. "I know it's your mother's."

Her expression flickers. "You know the story then?"

Before I can answer, she shakes her head. "Never mind." She shuts the book abruptly.

"No, please tell me," I urge before she can get up.

Elena hesitates, a shadow passing over her face. For a moment, I think she might refuse—but then, she exhales and begins.

"My grandmother, Regina, and my grandfather, Antonio, were arranged," she says quietly. "Antonio felt blessed to be paired with Regina, and he wanted to give her a ring fit for a queen—since that's what Regina means."

She lets out a soft chuckle, the sound light, but tinged with sadness.

"So, he used his connections to acquire the biggest diamond he could find and proposed."

I glance down at the ring, my fingers brushing over the cool surface of the diamond. A generational heirloom. A symbol of devotion.

But when I lift my gaze, Elena isn't looking at it with admiration. Her eyes linger on it with something closer to sadness. Distance.

A realization settles in my chest. "Oh," I murmur. "Did you want it?"

Elena's eyes widen in surprise. "No, never!" she exclaims, her voice sharp, almost too quick.

Confused, I study her expression. "Why not?"

She grimaces, her shoulders tensing before she finally explains.

"My grandmother was shot while wearing that ring. The bullet was meant for my grandfather."

I stiffen.

Her voice softens, but the weight of her words lingers in the space between us. "And then my mother…" Her voice trails off, but she doesn't need to finish. The unspoken truth is enough.

A chill runs down my spine. "Do you think the ring is bad luck?"

Elena exhales, shrugging helplessly. "Or even cursed."

Her gaze flickers to mine, uncertain. "I don't know why Santo would give it to you… when it was returned to him with *her*."

The unsaid words hang heavy in the air between us. Understanding crashes over me like a tidal wave.

I connect the dots—Lucia Amato was sent back to her sons in pieces. And this ring… I gasp, my breath catching in my throat.

Next to me, Elena bites her bottom lip, eyes flicking to mine, nervously.

"You're not going to tell him, are you?" she asks, anxiety lacing her voice.

Flabbergasted, I glance around the room, my gaze landing on the cameras, their dark lenses watching. Recording. My stomach twists.

"As if he doesn't already know," I reply bitterly, gesturing toward them.

Elena follows my gaze, and the moment her eyes land on the cameras, she curses under her breath.

As if on cue, Santo enters the library. His expression is dark, his brow furrowed, his presence suffocating.

"Out," he commands, his gaze locked onto Elena.

She rolls her eyes but turns to me, mouthing a silent apology before exhaling a resigned sigh. She gets up, leaving without another word. The door closes behind her, leaving me alone with Santo.

CHAPTER 50

SANTO

I was almost home when I *needed* to see my wife.

One day apart was too much. *Far too much.*

Spending a month with her, having her in my arms, in my space, *mine*; only to be separated for even a single day feels unbearable. I miss her terribly.

Vasilisa reminds me of before. Of a time when rebuilding computers, making honor roll, and losing myself in books were my biggest worries. She's my light. The one thing that keeps the shadows at bay—the shadows that come with the blood on my hands.

But then I pulled up the security footage and I watched as my sister tried to destroy my light.

I raced home, phone in hand, my pulse hammering as I stormed through the doors. I made it to the library just in time to hear Elena tell my wife that her ring was cursed.

That ring.

The same ring that haunted me for years. The one that sat on my mother's hand; lifeless, in a box. The one that buried itself into my nightmares, a reminder of how we lost her. The one worn by two women in my family who lost their lives to the darkness of our world, but now, it's on the hand of the woman I would sacrifice my life to protect. That ring no longer carries death. It's not a curse. It's something else entirely.

A harbinger of redemption.

And my sister is trying to sully all my hopes.

I stand in the doorway as Elena leaves, my jaw clenched, my breath controlled, but barely.

The moment the door shuts, my eyes lock onto Vasilisa. She's sitting alone on the chaise longue, looking so much smaller than usual. Her expressive eyes, the ones that always shine so brilliantly, are now filled with something else. Doubt? Fear?

I can't tell. The emotions swirl so quickly across her face, I can't keep up.

"Vasilisa," I start, but she lifts a hand, stopping me.

"This ring," she says, pointing to her left hand. "Was it?"

I know exactly what she's asking. And I won't lie to her.

"It was."

"Oh, Santo…" she exhales, her body deflating. She shakes her head, her expression solemn. "That's incredibly morbid."

I grimace, holding my hands up in surrender. "I know. I know it is. But hear me out."

I stride over, settling next to her, taking her hand in mine.

"This ring belonged to two incredibly strong women who loved fiercely and sacrificed everything for their family. They were victims, yes. But they were so much more than that."

She looks up at me, her eyes brimming with unshed tears. She's listening.

I press forward, my voice low, earnest. "It's *not* a curse, Vasilisa. I thought it was—I let it haunt me for years. I didn't even look at it again until I found out about our arrangement."

Her brows furrow, pain creeping into her voice. "But why?" she interrupts, her voice breaking. "Why give it to me?"

Her eyes search mine, like she's looking for an answer buried in the depths of my gaze.

I don't hesitate. "Because I lost the only woman in this world who had hope for my life to be more than what it is. I lost her while she wore this ring."

Her breath hitches. Silent tears slip down her cheeks, but she says nothing. She just waits.

My hand tightens softly around hers. "And it wasn't until I saw *you* that hope returned.

She blinks, her lips parting. "You… you see me as your hope?" Her voice stammers, breath catching at the end.

I nod slowly, bringing her hand to my lips, brushing a kiss over her knuckles.

"You, Vasilisa," I affirm, my voice steady, "*are* my hope. You're the one who chases away every inch of my darkness and leaves nothing but your light. And I want to bathe in it."

Her eyes widen, her body trembling under our shared warmth.

I brush my thumb over her ring, locking my gaze with hers. "This ring… it's meant to be a symbol of my redemption. Because you will *never* face what the women before you have. I will never allow you to be in danger."

She stares at me for a long moment, tears glistening in her eyes. And for a second, I think she'll nod. Accept it. Let my words be enough. But instead, her lips part, and her voice soft, but edged with steel, cuts through the silence.

"Santo… I trust that you'll protect me. That you'll keep me safe. But do you have *any* trust in me?"

Her question strikes like a blow I didn't see coming.

My brows furrow, confusion and guilt twisting in my chest. "What are you talking about?"

She sits up straighter, her shoulders squaring, the flicker of fire returning to her voice. "I'm talking about the fact that you don't even let me have basic things like social media. Or that you gave me a new phone, but wiped all my friends' numbers. That you make me feel like… like I can't be *trusted* to make my own decisions."

I open my mouth to respond, but she presses on, her words spilling out faster now. "Elena asked me about my socials today. She wanted to share hers, and I had to tell her I don't have any because you *took* them away. She wanted to know why I don't go to campus, and I had to explain how you think it's too *dangerous* for me to leave the house. Do you have any idea how humiliating that was? How it made me feel?"

"Vasilisa…" I begin, my voice low, but she cuts me off.

"No," she says, her voice trembling but steady. "I love you, Santo. I trust you with my life. But if I'm going to trust you, then I need you to trust me too. I'm not some fragile doll you have to keep locked away. I need to be *me*, not just your wife, not just someone you're protecting. I *need* trust."

I stare at her, the weight of her words settling heavily on my chest. She's right. As much as I hate to admit it, she's right. I've wrapped her in so many layers of protection that I've stripped her of her freedom, her autonomy.

My hand runs down my face as I let out a slow breath, the guilt and frustration clawing at my insides. "I didn't… I didn't mean to make you feel like that," I say, my voice quieter now. "I just…" I glance at her, the tears in her eyes cutting deeper than any wound. "I don't want to lose you. I've lost too much already, Vasilisa. I can't—"

"You won't lose me," she interrupts, her voice softer this time. "But you have to trust me, Santo. You have to let me live my life *with* you, not just as a footnote in your story."

I reluctantly nod, "I promise you are not a footnote in my story Dea, you're the center of it."

Her lips part, a flicker of surprise crossing her face before she nods.

A moment passes before she exhales softly, like she's been carrying the weight of this moment for far too long.

"Okay," she murmurs, not just in acceptance, but in understanding.

For a moment, the room is silent, the weight of her words still hanging between us. My chest feels heavy, like I've been cracked open in a way I wasn't prepared for. But as her hand rests lightly on mine, that heaviness shifts, replaced by something softer.

She looks down at the ring on her finger, her voice quieter now. "And the ring? You really see this as redemption?"

I take her hand in both of mine, holding it gently. "I do. Because it means I've found what I needed. It means I have hope again. You'll have your freedom, but nothing and no one will ever harm you, Vasilisa. I won't *allow* it."

Her lips tremble, and this time when the tears fall, they carry something brighter than pain. Slowly, she nods, a small smile tugging at the corners of her lips.

"Santo," she whispers, leaning toward me, her arms sliding around my neck. "I'll wear it proudly."

Her hold on me tightens, and I let myself sink into the moment, her light chasing away the shadows that have followed me for far too long.

I press a lingering kiss to her temple before murmuring, "I have something for you." She pulls back just enough to meet my gaze, curiosity sparking in her eyes. "But first," I continue, "you have to allow me to take you to dinner."

Her brows lift slightly, amusement flickering in her expression. "*Allow* you?" she echoes, tilting her head.

I smirk. "Yes, allow me, Dea. This is me wanting to spoil my wife."

Her lips curl into a small, knowing smile. "In that case… I accept."

★★★

The ride through the city is quiet, a rare moment of peace as I take Vasilisa to a small Russian bistro. The second we pull up in front of the quaint establishment, her eyes light up, a spark of recognition dancing in their depths.

She leans forward, taking in the warm glow of the windows, the hand-painted Cyrillic sign above the entrance, the scent of butter, herbs, and fresh bread drifting through the night air.

"Is this…?" she starts, trailing off, her voice barely above a whisper.

I nod, a small grin tugging at my lips. "Thought you might like a taste of home."

Her gaze snaps to mine, and for a moment, I see something unguarded in her expression—something raw, grateful. Then, she smiles. Not just any smile. *That smile.* The one that tightens my chest, makes my world feel right.

"Thank you, Santo," she says softly.

Inside, the bistro is cozy, intimate. Wooden beams stretch across the ceiling, the scent of dill and slow-cooked meats filling the space. A waitress greets us in Russian, and the moment Vasilisa responds, something shifts.

She comes alive.

I watch, captivated, as she effortlessly slips into her native tongue, her words fluid and bright. The waitress laughs, nodding along, and Vasilisa's laughter follows—soft, warm, like music filling the room.

I don't understand a word they're saying.

I hate that.

I *want* to.

I want to know what she's saying, what makes her smile like that, what makes her eyes shine so brightly. I want to exist fully in her world, not just as her husband, but as someone who understands every part of her.

I sit there, silent, listening. *Memorizing.*

And in that moment, I decide—I'm going to learn Russian.

She just doesn't know it yet.

When the food arrives, Vasilisa wastes no time, picking up a forkful of pelmeni dumplings and taking a bite. The second she does, her eyes flutter shut, a soft moan of delight escaping her lips.

"Pelmeni is one of my favorites," she sighs, pure bliss in her voice.

I smirk. "Good to know. I'll be sure to tell Julian."

Her eyes snap open. "He could make this?" she asks, practically vibrating with excitement.

"If I ask, yes. He'll make it happen."

Her face lights up, and she takes another bite, savoring the moment. "This is quite honestly the best gift ever. Thank you."

I shake my head, leaning in slightly. "This isn't the gift."

She pauses mid-chew, hand covering her mouth as she swallows. "It isn't?"

I smirk. *My girl is adorable.*

"Definitely not, Mia Dea. I have more in store for you tonight."

Her eyes widen slightly, curiosity flickering across her face, but she doesn't press me for details. Instead, the evening flows naturally—easy conversation, shared laughter, the warmth of something unspoken passing between us.

She finishes her meal with a slice of chocolate pie, the final indulgence that makes her sigh with pure satisfaction.

When we step outside, the city greets us with a cool breeze, alive with golden streetlights and the hum of distant traffic. Vasilisa nestles into her seat as I start the car, her gaze drifting out the window, lost in thought. I glance at her every few moments, admiring the way the city lights play across her features, turning her into a living work of art.

And she has no idea what's coming next.

Eventually, we reach our destination—a small, private observatory on the outskirts of town, nestled far from the city lights. I purchased it long ago, for nights when I craved solitude, silence, and the infinite clarity of the stars above.

Vasilisa steps out of the car, her head tilting back as she takes in the domed building.

"An observatory?" she questions, curiosity laced in her voice.

I shrug lightly, leading her toward the entrance. "There's something about looking at the stars that makes everything else seem… smaller somehow."

The moment we step inside, her breath catches. Above us, the sky unfolds like a masterpiece, the velvety black expanse of night pierced by thousands of shimmering stars. She gasps, her eyes wide with wonder, the reflection of the cosmos dancing in her gaze.

I wrap an arm around her shoulders, drawing her close as we stand beneath the endless sky.

"I wanted you to see this," I murmur, my voice low, intimate. "Because there's a story I read when I was younger… about a sun god who fell in love with a beautiful goddess. And because he loved her so much, he placed her among the stars so she could shine brightly forever."

She turns her face toward me, her blue eyes reflecting the starlight.

"Like my magical tree?" she whispers, recounting the fairytale she once told me.

I nod, adjusting the telescope to the exact coordinates I need. "Yes. You see, I used to believe in things like that too."

I position her in front of the lens, guiding her gently. "Look," I tell her. "Do you see that star?"

She leans forward, peering through the scope, and nods.

"That one, I had named *Vasilisa*."

She freezes. Her breath shudders as she pulls back, staring up at me in disbelief. "You what?"

A slow smile tugs at my lips. "That way, you can shine brightly forever."

Her lips part, her expression softening as the weight of my words sinks in.

"Really?" she breathes, wide-eyed and incredulous.

I nod solemnly, tucking a strand of hair behind her ear.

"Truly. Just like the goddess in the story, you deserve to shine forever, my beautiful Dea." I cup her cheek, my thumb brushing against her skin.

"You've brought light and warmth into my world—just like the sun. And nothing could ever dim it."

A single tear slips down her cheek, catching the light of the stars. She throws herself into my arms, holding me so tightly it's as if she's trying to become a part of me. I feel the tremble in her body, the emotion thick in her silence.

I press a kiss to the top of her head. "One more thing," I say, reaching into my pocket.

She pulls back slightly, wiping at her damp cheeks as I pull out a small velvet box.

Her breath hitches. "You're spoiling me at this point, Santo!"

I smirk, popping the lid open to reveal a delicate silver necklace, a star-shaped pendant hanging at its center. A blue opal gleams in its heart—the exact shade of her eyes.

"This," I murmur, "is so you can always carry your star with you."

She stares at it, stunned, her fingers trembling slightly as she touches the pendant. Then, before I can say anything else, she throws herself into my arms again, burying her face against my neck.

"Thank you," she whispers, her voice choked with emotion.

I wrap my arms around her, holding her tightly, protectively, *endlessly.*

The drive home is quiet, the kind of quiet that's full of meaning, full of love.

Vasilisa's hand stays locked with mine, my thumb brushing her knuckles. With her other hand, she lightly plays with the necklace resting at her throat, turning the star over between her fingertips as if grounding herself in this moment.

I glance at her between turns, catching the soft glow of the pendant against her skin, the peaceful expression on her face.

This night couldn't have gone any better.

And I can barely contain the boyish excitement stirring in my chest, because there's still one last surprise waiting for her at home.

I pull into the garage, avoiding the staff as we take the elevator straight to our bedroom. The moment we step inside, Vasilisa kicks off her shoes, stripping off her blouse and jeans.

I smirk, watching her move so freely, so unburdened.

A month ago, she was shy about her body, hesitant under my gaze. But now, she can't stand a second inside our bedroom with clothes on.

I dim the bedroom lights, and when I turn back to her, I pause.

Her silk red lingerie gleams under the soft glow, hugging her body perfectly. She is a masterpiece to me. Oblivious to my gaze, she reaches up, pulling the pins from her hair, and I watch as golden waves tumble down her bare shoulders.

"Ugh," she sighs, rubbing her stomach. "I should have thought to bring a snack cake."

I chuckle, and she immediately narrows her eyes at me.

"What?"

I take a slow step toward her, my voice low, sincere. "You're just… breathtaking."

The flush that spreads across her cheeks is everything.

"Breathtaking when I'm dying for a snack cake?" she challenges, a smirk playing at her lips.

I nod, taking another step closer.

Her smirk falters as I advance, a spark of anticipation flashing in her eyes. She backs up slowly, until her spine meets the wall.

I corner her, my hands resting on either side of her, trapping her in place. My gaze trails over her, claiming every inch with just my eyes.

She inhales sharply as I lean in, my fingers ghosting down her arm. She shudders at the contact, her breath hitching.

Her arms snake around my neck, pulling me closer.

"Yes," I murmur against her lips, our breaths mingling, the heat between us crackling like fire. "Even when you're dying for a snack cake."

A soft giggle escapes her, but I swallow it with a kiss.

And just like that, we fall.

The stars we admired minutes ago are now reflected in her eyes, in the way we explore each other like we're discovering something new; like every touch, every kiss is the first.

The heat rises between us, the air growing heavier, thicker.

I scoop her up, her laughter muffled against my neck as I lay her on the bed. I strip quickly, joining her again, my hands tracing the lines of her body removing the last scraps of fabric between us as I map out every inch of her skin with my lips.

Under the dim bedroom light, her skin glows, shimmering, like the star I named after her.

I kiss her deeply as she parts her legs, and I thrust inside.

Hours later, when our bodies have entwined and unraveled countless times, we lay side by side, our breaths finally steadying.

She turns to face me, her fingers lazily trailing down my chest. Her eyes shine—full of love, full of something unsaid.

I brush a wisp of hair from her face, my voice a whisper in the quiet room.

"I have another surprise."

Her smile widens as she groans dramatically, covering her face with her hands. "What in the world could it be *now*, Santo?" she giggles.

I smirk, sitting up as I open the nightstand drawer.

I pull out the stacked papers, setting them on the bed beside her. She blinks at them, confused, before picking them up.

As she reads the front page, her entire body freezes.

Her hand flies to her mouth as she gasps. "Santo!"

She looks at me, then back at the manuscript, eyes wide with pure disbelief. "Is this… the unreleased S. J. Nandez manuscript?"

I nod, watching pride and awe flood her expression.

Her fingers tremble slightly as she holds the pages as if they're sacred. "Santo, how did you—" Her voice breaks off, her breath shaky.

Then suddenly, she throws herself at me, arms wrapping around my neck, pressing frantic, grateful kisses to my face.

"I'm so happy!" she exclaims, her words muffled between kisses until I can't help but laugh.

"I called in a favor," I confess, still grinning. "She was happy to gift it to you, as long as you *tell* no one."

Vasilisa immediately sits up, cradling the manuscript to her chest, her expression deadly serious. "I would never."

I chuckle, pulling her back into me. I kiss those beautiful lips again.

"Read to me."

CHAPTER 51

VASILISA

When I wake up, Santo is already gone. I half-expected to feel the warmth of his body beside me, but instead, I find only the soft imprint of where he was. His absence lingers, but his text is waiting for me.

Santo

Be home early

The house is alive again, filled with staff bustling in and out, the air thick with the weight of too many armed men. I know why they're here; Angelo, Maksim, and my husband are planning something, and whatever it is, it requires an army.

I should probably be paying more attention to the rising tension in the house, but instead, I decide to spend the morning in the library, painting.

It's a gift for Santo. A small thank you for yesterday, for all the surprises, for making me feel like something precious. I want it to be perfect.

I angle my easel carefully, just out of view of the security cameras. I know Santo watches them constantly, and I don't want him to see the painting until it's finished. Just as I lift my brush, Elena flings herself onto the chaise like a starlet in distress.

"I'm bored, and the house is filled with men who ignore me," she announces with a dramatic sigh, throwing her head back like she might faint. "Let's go out for lunch."

I put down my brush and wipe my fingers on my smock. I don't particularly *want* to leave since Santo will be home soon, but the pleading look on Elena's face makes me cave.

"Alright, just let me text Santo."

Elena immediately perks up, flashing a triumphant grin. But when I pull out my phone, there's already a message waiting for me.

Take Romeo and Riot with you, only go to La Serenata and back home.

I frown. A second later, another text pops up.

Please.

I give a knowing look at one of the cameras and blow a kiss before relaying Santo's instructions to Elena.

★★★

Lunch at La Serenata is wonderful.

I indulge on an extra helping of tiramisu. I take my time savoring it, ignoring Elena's teasing look as I scrape the last of it onto my spoon.

"It's a crime how much you love that dessert," she comments.

"A crime would be leaving any behind," I reply smoothly, washing it down with my third glass of water.

A mistake.

My bladder is now achingly full. I stand, excusing myself from Elena's chatter.

Romeo gives me a pointed look, but I shake my head before he can insist on escorting me.

"I think I can survive the ladies' room alone," I tease.

He doesn't look convinced, but after a tense second, he lets it go.

I slip inside, sighing at the quiet. The cool air is a relief, a break from the warmth of the crowded restaurant. By the time I finish washing my hands, my body is more relaxed, the pleasant heaviness of a good meal settling over me. The door swings open; I glance up in the mirror, expecting some stranger, but instead, I freeze.

Jude.

The name screams through my mind, but my lips don't move. His blond hair is unkempt, dirtied and tangled in a way that speaks of neglect. His once sharp, piercing blue eyes are sunken, hollow, filled with something dark and wild. The patchy stubble along his jaw makes him look like a man who's been running for far too long.

My heart slams against my ribs.

The Bratva and Cosa Nostra are hunting him.

My husband is hunting him.

I can't be in here with him. There's nowhere to run, except past him, and he knows it. I can't stay here either. I can't be trapped with him.

Jude's eyes follow me, predatory and cruel, as I take slow, measured steps backward toward the wall.

A sick grin spreads across his face as he steps forward.

"Stay away from me, Jude," I say, my voice shaky but strong. "Whatever it is you *think* you want… you don't want to do this."

I brace for him to lunge, but he doesn't. Instead, he leans against the door, his grin widening. The color drains from my face as his hand dips into his pocket and pulls out a syringe. The light from the fluorescents above catches the needle, and I blink back the sharp sting of fear.

"You're right, Vasilisa," he murmurs, his voice low and rough. "I don't want to do this. But sometimes in life, we don't get a choice."

My breath shudders. I should scream, but I know no one will hear me over the chatter outside.

Think.

I reach for the calm demeanor Angelo drilled into me. Control under pressure, never letting an enemy see fear.

"But Jude," I manage, keeping my voice even, "you do have a choice. You can walk away now, and no one would ever know."

For a second, something flickers across his face. Uncertainty.

I take my chance.

I lunge, my fist colliding with the syringe, knocking it from his grip. It skids across the bathroom floor. Jude lunges, wrapping an arm around my waist as I scramble for the door.

His hold is tighter than Angelo's when we spar, but I remember my training. I drive my elbow up, aiming for his nose. It lands hard. His head snaps back, his grip loosens, and I twist free, sprinting for the door.

Before I reach it, pain explodes at my scalp. Jude yanks me back by my hair. I cry out, tears springing to my eyes as he spins me and slams me against the wall.

"I *told* you," he snarls, rage distorting his face. "You *don't* have a choice."

His backhand cracks across my cheek, and sharp pain snaps through my skull. The iron taste of blood fills my mouth as I bite down on my tongue.

My head swims, but I fight to stay upright. Jude grips my arm and wrenches me toward the door. Before he can make another move, the restaurant erupts. Screams. Shattering glass.

Gunfire.

Jude's grip is ripped from me, and I barely catch a glimpse of Romeo slamming his fist into Jude's face before the room fills with smoke.

Gunfire rings out, rapid pops cutting through the chaos.

Jude lunges toward me. I drop to the floor. Another shot fires—closer this time. Jude staggers, clutching his shoulder before collapsing.

The gunfire ceases.

The sharp screech of tires peels into the distance. Hands clamp around me and then I'm lifted; panic flares. I scream, my limbs swinging, disoriented by the smoke and the ringing in my ears.

"Shh." A voice, warm and steady. His scent—spicy vanilla and something deeper, something safe.

Santo.

I cling to him, my hands fisting into his shirt as I blink through the haze, my eyes locking onto his face.

"I have you, Dea."

Santo's stormy gray eyes pierce into mine, grounding me. I bury my face against his chest, inhaling deeply, desperate to reclaim even the smallest semblance of calm.

I wrap my legs around him, clinging tightly as he carries me out of the restaurant. Blood and glass stain the floor, and I shut my eyes.

I don't want to know who's been hurt. Or worse—who's been…

I can't stomach it.

Santo lowers me into the backseat of an SUV, and as my eyes flutter open, I meet Luca's gaze in the rearview mirror. His eyes widen before his brows knit together in anger.

Santo slides in next to me, then he lifts me onto his lap.

"You should probably let her—" Luca starts.

"She stays on my lap. You'll have to drive slow," he grits out, his arms locking around me like a shield. His fingers brush over my cheek, circling gently.

I wince. The fury in his eyes is instantaneous. When he swipes his thumb over my lip, I see what's upset them both.

Blood.

My blood.

As the adrenaline wears off, the pain sets in. My face throbs, my arm aches, and exhaustion pulls at my bones. I just want to go home, sink into a warm bath, and forget.

"We're almost there, Dea," Santo murmurs, his lips brushing my temple. As if he can hear my thoughts. As if he knows exactly what I need. The low rumble of his voice is a comfort, a steady hum beneath the sharp, pulsing ache that follows every beat of my heart.

Luca takes a sharp turn, and my breath hitches. But Santo's grip tightens, anchoring me. His hand finds my cheek again, his thumb gliding back and forth in slow, soothing strokes.

Out of nowhere, the tears come. Hot and heavy, they spill down my cheeks, disappearing into the fabric of Santo's shirt. His body stiffens beneath me at the first splash of them.

"Hey," he murmurs, softer now. "Don't cry, Dea."

But it's too late. The dam has already broken.

My sobs come fast and violent, shaking my body so hard that Santo has to tighten his hold just to keep me from falling apart.

"We're here," Luca announces gruffly as the car jerks to a stop. He shuts off the engine, then exits, slamming the door behind him without another word.

Santo doesn't move. He stays there, holding me, letting me unravel against him, soaking his collar with my grief, my fear, my pain.

"I'm sorry," I hiccup between sobs. "I shouldn't have told Romeo not to come with me, I—"

"It's not your fault." Santo says sharply.

He grips my chin, tilting my face until our eyes meet. His stare is raw, burning, filled with something so intense it sends a shiver down my spine.

"You have nothing to apologize for. No matter what you *do*, no matter *where* you are, no one is *allowed* to touch you."

I cling to him as he carries me inside, as if letting go might send me spiraling. Maybe it would.

Maybe Santo knows it, too.

Because he doesn't put me down. Not as he strides up the stairs. Not as he carries me into our bedroom. Not even as he draws a bath, placing me on the counter for only a moment before stripping off his clothes, then mine.

Then he settles into the water with me, pulling me against his chest.

He doesn't speak. He doesn't have to.

He just worships.

A warm, sudsy washcloth glides over my skin, slow and careful, as if I'm something fragile. His lips find the back of my neck, pressing soft, lingering kisses between each stroke.

His fingers trace the bruises on my arm, heat radiating from his body as if his very anger might burn them away.

He kisses me then, a quiet press of lips that tastes like devotion, like rage barely restrained, like the silent promise of mine.

And then, as if I'm made of glass, he lifts me from the tub.

He dries me, slow and gentle. Dresses me in my favorite pink cotton shorts and tank.

Then places me in bed, tucking me beneath the covers before pressing a kiss to my forehead.

I watch as he dresses as if he's going for a ride sans jacket.

"Where are you going?" My voice comes out dry, my throat raw from hours of silence.

Santo tightens the laces of his boots, his movements precise, deliberate. *Lethal.*

"We have work to do," he says simply. "We're assembling our men. This attack was a warning and we're not waiting for another."

My stomach twists. "Elena?" I ask, fear creeping into my voice.

"Safe."

I hesitate. "Vincenzo?"

"Safe."

Relief floods through me, loosening the tight coil in my chest. *They're okay.*

I swallow hard, then whisper, "Will you please be careful?"

Santo finishes tying his boot and stands, striding toward me. His hand slips into my hair, fingers threading through the strands in a gesture so tender, so at odds with the storm brewing behind his eyes.

"I'll be careful." His lips brush against mine, soft, fleeting, before he steps back. Then he reaches for something on the nightstand. "Here. For the pain"

I blink as he hands me a pill and a glass of water I hadn't even noticed was there. I take the pill, washing it down with a slow sip, my eyes never leaving him, before I can say anything else; he's gone.

★★★

When I wake, the room is pitch black.

The last time I checked, it was four in the afternoon. I reach blindly for my phone, the screen glowing harshly in the dark.

2:00 AM.

There's no way I slept for ten hours.

My body feels heavy, sluggish, my stomach twisting with hunger. I need to use the bathroom. Maybe even grab a snack cake, something simple to ease the weight of the day pressing down on me. I slip out of bed, padding toward the bathroom. When I flick the light on, I freeze.

I gasp.

The mirror reflects someone I barely recognize.

A shadow of a bruise blooms high on my cheekbone, the faint mark of a backhand that shouldn't have landed. My arm is marred with deep, purple fingerprints.

His fingerprints.

I lift a trembling hand, brushing my fingers over the bruises. The moment I press against my skin, a sharp sting shoots through me. I hiss in pain.

My breath comes shallow, uneven.

Jude.

Jude did this to me.

CHAPTER 52

SANTO

Drugging my wife is not something I ever thought I would have to do, but it's a necessary evil. She needs to rest, and I need to keep Scythe far away from her.

Finding her on the ground, bleeding and bruised, almost made me kill Jude Olsen right there, but I *couldn't*. I had to focus on her. I had to take her home, hold her in my arms. I had to make sure she was calm, safe, *clean*.

Clean from that motherfucker's hands on her.

I thought about what I'd do to him—each step, every excruciating moment—while I held my wife in the tub and washed her. Her scent was the only thing keeping me from completely losing control.

I didn't lie to her when I said we had work to do. I met up with Angelo and Maksim—Jude's story is that Miroslav sent him to get Vasilisa, to bring her to him, to "keep her safe." I didn't believe that shit for a second.

I had the syringe that fucker dropped in the bathroom tested. When Luca came to give me the results, I could tell from the fury in his eyes that it wasn't just a sedative.

Potassium fucking chloride.

That bastard was going to kill my wife.

The taste of rage is venom in my mouth. I nearly crushed the report in Luca's hands when I snatched it from him.

Jude Olsen dies tonight.

Miroslav has a meeting with the Armenians at the dock the day after tomorrow, and we'll be there. Wesley figured out that a code word *'Kingdom'* will be used that night. The second that word is sent, we rush them.

We take them all down.

Maksim is setting up his snipers. I've called our Capo in Chicago—he's sending us a small army. Everything is handled.

No one comes for my family and gets away with it.

After finalizing our plans, I had Romeo and Luca bring me Jude. Luca cauterized the gunshot wound Romeo gave Jude at La Serenata.

They strapped him to the bolted chair in the basement, in the space, my brother likes to call the *"Guy's Night"* room.

Scythe hasn't killed in that room for a long time.

But I want the man who dared to touch my wife dead—on my turf, by *my* hands.

I stride in, shutting the door and flooding the room with fluorescent light.

Luca stands by the instrument table, a variety of my tools laid out in front of him. Romeo stands beside Jude, whose mouth is taped shut, his eyes narrowed on me as I enter.

I rip the tape from his lips. He spits, glares.

"Let me fucking go!" he shouts.

I chuckle darkly and punch him in the mouth. His teeth slam against my knuckles, pain shooting up my hand—but the sight of his split lip makes it worth it.

"Untie him," I command.

Luca and Romeo exchange a look.

"Santo—"

I cut Luca off with a glance.

They untie him. Jude's eyes flick to me, relieved for half a second.

I grab the seven-inch buck knife from the table. Jude watches me carefully as he stands, his gaze darting toward the door behind me.

I shake my head, a cruel smile curling my lips.

"That door won't open from the inside. Not without this." I extend my thumb toward the scanner.

His eyes narrow.

"Here," I say, flipping the knife in my grip before holding it out to him. "Take it."

Confusion flickers across his face. "What?"

"We're gonna spar." I cock my head. "To make it *fair*, you get the knife."

Jude shakes his head.

"Just let me go. I won't say anything."

"You think I'm afraid of you *talking?*"

I take a step closer.

"You touched my wife. Spilled her blood. Tried to *kill* her."

My jaw clenches. My fist itches to end this now, to skip the fight altogether.

"You hurt someone smaller than you. Defenseless. *Mine.*"

I thrust the knife into his hands.

"Fight."

I step back, taking my position in the middle of the room.

Romeo and Luca grab Jude by each arm and drag him forward.

They drop him at my feet.

His knuckles turn white around the handle of the knife.

"I-I don't want to," he stammers.

"Die like a man. Or die like a coward. Either way, you're dying tonight. Stand up."

Jude's hands tremble, but his eyes burn with fury. He rolls his injured shoulder, setting his stance.

"You're *so* upset," he drawls.

We begin to circle each other.

"You think she's yours. But she was *mine* first." His eyes stay locked on my hands.

Smart. Watching for movement. Trying to lure me in.

I shake my head. "She was never yours."

He smirks.

"Two years together. That's history she can't forget."

My teeth grind together, heat rising in my chest. "You were in Seattle for most of it. Now shut the fuck up and fight."

Jude shrugs, smirks.

"One year I had her to myself. Did she tell you that? Every. *Single.* Day. What do *you* think we did?"

I chuckle knowingly. "Nothing."

Jude's jaw ticks. Anger. Frustration.

"Just because you got her to bleed on your sheets," he sneers, "doesn't mean we didn't do *everything* but."

He lunges.

I see the knife coming too late. Steel slices through my arm, tearing fabric, spilling blood.

Jude grins, backing up a step, his blade streaked with red.

"She's a weak spot, huh?" He licks his lips. "Does she moan when you kiss her too?"

The thought of his hands on Vasilisa overrides everything.

His smug fucking face blurs. My control slips.

I see nothing but red.

He can't talk about my wife like that. Can't mention the sounds she makes. Can't compare the longevity of their relationship to the minuscule time she's spent with me.

She's *mine.* She'll *always* be mine.

I don't register that I'm on top of him. That my fists are breaking his face open. That the knife in his hand is swiping at me until it clatters to the ground—until hands are prying me off him.

When my vision returns, Romeo is strapping a bloodied, barely-conscious Jude to the chair.

His eye is swollen shut, bruises blooming across both cheeks. His lip—split wide open, drips blood down his chin. His teeth are stained red when he smirks at me like an idiot.

Luca releases my arms.

"He got you good. You're bleeding." Luca's voice is sharp, urgent.

I look down. My shirt is in tatters, blood trailing from wounds down to my hands.

I take a breath, mentally assessing the damage. Nothing feels fatal.

I shrug him off.

"I'm fine." I step toward Jude. I ask him which hand he used to hit my wife.

Then I shatter both anyway.

The meat tenderizer slams down. The crack echoes through the room.

The blood splatters onto his stupid, stunned face, and a surge of joy floods through me—sharper than I thought possible.

Jude shakes violently, his body convulsing from the pain.

"Please." His voice is wrecked, choking on his own suffering.

"I'm sorry," he coughs out.

I stare down at him. No remorse. No pity. Just cold, consuming rage.

"You will *never* touch her—or *anyone*—again."

I extend my hand. Luca places my next tool into my palm.

The metal bat.

Jude's breath shudders.

"You won't even think about her again."

I swing.

The bat slams into his leg.

His scream pierces the night, and I silently thank myself for giving my wife that sleeping pill.

I swing again.

A sickening crack.

Jude's body jerks violently, his breath choking out between screams. I toss the bat to the ground.

Romeo hands me the buck knife. I twirl it between my fingers.

Jude's eyes widen in pure, primal terror.

Good.

"No," he whines, "No, don't kill me, please, my father—"

"Your father?" I echo, tilting my head. "Your father thinks you're back home in Seattle. Like you told him you were."

"I didn't—"

Romeo holds up Jude's cellphone tauntingly.

He whimpers in pain before screaming in rage.

"No!" he shouts. "You motherfuckers don't get to do this. You don't get to win!"

He thrashes in his restraints, only aggravating his shattered bones.

"I've already won."

I drag the tip of the knife down the side of his face, splitting the skin open.

Blood trails down his jaw, staining his clothes. He grits his teeth through it, then spits in my face.

I wipe it away with the back of my hand, smearing my own blood across my cheek. The metallic scent fuels Scythe within me, a rush of pure fury ripping through my veins.

I stab him in the stomach.

Jude gasps, choking on the pain.

I release the handle, leaving the blade lodged deep in his gut. I know I didn't hit anything vital. And I won't. *Not yet.*

I'll him on the edge of begging for death before I grant it.

He coughs, breath ragged, before chuckling like the arrogant bastard he is.

"You find death funny?"

"No," he wheezes through the pain. "I find it funny that he's going to kill you."

"No one will kill me."

Jude smirks, eyes half-lidded with amusement. "Sarkisian will."

"So you *are* working for him?"

"No," Jude grins, "but I know he's going to kill you—by breaking *her.*"

Ice slides down my spine. "No one will ever get near her."

Jude's grin widens. "I did."

I punch him in the face. Hard. His head snaps back, a deep groan ripping from his throat.

I grab the pliers.

"Sarkisian is going to fuck your little whore," Jude sneers, "and pass her out to every single one of his men until she's nothing more than a broken shell of—"

Romeo grabs the back of his head, yanking it back hard. Luca forces his jaw open.

Jude chokes on his own breath, his body jerking violently.

I clamp the pliers around his lying, filth-ridden tongue. My mind is fire, *pure fire,* burning through my skull.

His words, disgusting, harrowing filth, about *my* wife, *my* Vasilisa.

No one. No man. Will ever touch her again.

A beep cuts through the air.

Jude goes still. His eyes lock onto something behind me.

A gasp.

I know that sound. It's soft, breathless, but it cuts through me like a blade. I *know* it because I've spent months *craving* it, *chasing* it, memorizing every way she breathes, speaks, sighs.

I know it because it's hers.

Dea.

My stomach drops. My pulse slams through my veins. I don't want to turn around. But I do.

And there she is.

Her eyes are wider than I've ever seen them. Her chest rises and falls in panicked, uneven breaths. Her mouth parts, trembling. Her body shakes. The snack cake in her hand drops.

She turns and runs.

CHAPTER 53

VASILISA

I don't know why I'm running, but I'm running.

I went down to the kitchen got my snackcake, heard some noise downstairs and thought it was Santo. So I went to the basement.

It was *not* Santo.

That monstrous thing, covered in blood was Scythe. Santo told me he didn't want me around Scythe.

So I ran.

I *know* Santo wouldn't hurt me. Even if he's in some kind of fugue state, even if he's lost in this violent, fractured version of himself—he wouldn't hurt me.

But my feet won't stop moving and my body won't stop shaking.

This is too much trauma for one person, right?

I should be logical about this. I was attacked earlier today and now Santo is hurting the person who hurt me.

No.

Scythe is *killing* the person who hurt me.

Santo hurts bad guys. But that person isn't just *any* bad guy. That person is Jude. My ex-boyfriend. Someone I knew.

Until he punched me in the face.

My brain can't rationalize it. So I run.

I slam my finger against the elevator button so hard I think it won't register, but it does. The doors glide open. I scramble inside, frantically jabbing the button to my room. My heart pounds as the doors start to close—

But just before they shut, Scythe steps in.

I scream, startled, as he looms inches away, his presence overwhelming.

I didn't think he'd follow.

I didn't think he'd dare.

But here he is, slipping into the confined space, the scent of blood and cedar clinging to him like a warning.

The silence is suffocating. The only sound is the low hum of the elevator.

His dark eyes pin me in place. Scythe steps closer. I shrink back instinctively, my spine pressing into the cold metal wall. He doesn't stop until he's caged me in, his body an inescapable force. His head dips low and he breathes me in.

The sound is deep and drawn out, like he's savoring me.

"Vasilisa," he murmurs, his voice a low growl, his breath warm against my ear.

He nuzzles into me, his face brushing against mine. I want to recoil—to pull away from the sting of his touch on my bruised cheek, from the blood smearing onto my skin.

But I freeze.

Then his lips press to the pulse at my throat, and he stills.

"Breathe," he commands, his voice like steel.

A shaky breath rattles through my chest just as the elevator doors slide open into our bedroom closet.

Now.

I duck out from under his arms and dart into the closet, rushing toward the bedroom.

But he's faster.

He catches me in an instant, scooping me up and pushing me against the bedroom wall.

Pinned.

A startled gasp escapes me as his strength holds me captive. My legs instinctively wrap around him, trying to anchor myself.

He grunts. A low, primal growl rumbles from deep in his chest as his lips claim my neck, each heated kiss sending a shiver through me.

His hands move with urgency, gripping the fabric of my shirt.

A sharp rip splits the air.

I bite down hard on my lip, trying to swallow a scream, but a shaky gasp betrays me.

His eyes flick to mine.

And I see it. *The void.*

His pupils have swallowed his irises, leaving behind nothing but a feral hunger that sends ice-cold fear down my spine.

There isn't even a little bit of Santo here.

This is pure Scythe.

His handsome face, smeared with blood, is a stark contrast to the savagery in his expression. His tattered, blood-soaked shirt clings to his frame. His hands, painted crimson, leave streaks across my skin.

His mouth is relentless, kissing, biting, licking, claiming me with a sharp carnal intensity.

He inhales me—deep. Like he needs it. Like he's been starving and I'm the only thing in this world that still makes him feel alive.

"Vasilisa," he growls against my skin, voice dragging across my throat like a blade.

My breath catches.

Then he bites.

Hard.

No warning.

His teeth sink into the curve of my shoulder, and the pain is instant; sharp, bright, real. A cry rips from my throat, more animal than human.

He freezes.

His eyes snap to mine, and for a fleeting second, the wildness falters. Something flickers there. A shadow of something human. Something like fear.

Like *guilt.*

As if my reaction, my pain, has betrayed him. Abruptly, he lets go.

I drop to the ground, stumbling, struggling to catch my breath.

I glance down at my torn shirt and blood-stained shorts, the crimson smearing across my chest from his clothes and hands.

The metallic, sickly smell lingers in the air. My skin crawls with the evidence of what just happened, but when I look up at him, I see it, the lost, confused look in his eyes.

He backs away, his movements slow, hesitant, like a predator suddenly unsure of its instincts. That wildness is still there, but now it's tangled with something else.

My breathing steadies and I focus. The smell of blood clings to me, suffocating, but the sight of him, lost, almost broken, pulls me back from my own panic.

He looks at me like he's waiting for rejection, bracing for it, as though he's sure I'll run.

I take a tentative step forward, ignoring the way my legs tremble beneath me. His eyes track my every move.

I reach out, my fingers brushing against his blood-smeared cheek. His breath hitches, and for a moment, he doesn't move.

Then he leans into my touch, his eyes closing as if he's grounding himself in it, desperate for something real to hold onto.

My voice is barely a whisper. "Santo…"

But he doesn't respond. Scythe still lingers in the way his body remains coiled, the predator barely beneath the surface. I see both of them—the man and the monster, and I refuse to look away.

I hold my breath, my fingers still gently tracing his jaw. His skin is warm beneath my touch, but the tremor running through his body tells me just how much control he's fighting to keep.

His eyes flicker, still full of that wild hunger, but now there's something else—something deeper, more vulnerable, almost broken. It makes my heart ache for him.

He leans into my hand, a silent plea for reassurance, as if he needs me to bring him back from whatever abyss he's fallen into. The silence stretches between us, heavy and thick, filled with the tension of two people on the brink of something they can't quite understand.

"I'm not going anywhere," I whisper, my voice a little steadier than I feel.

He doesn't say anything. Instead, his eyes stay locked on mine, as if searching for something—something only I can give him. His breath is slow now, as though he's trying to calm himself, and for the first time, I see the man behind the monster. The weight of everything he's carried, the darkness he's buried deep within, is all in his gaze.

"I'm here," I say again, firmer this time, my hand steady on his cheek. *"You're still you."*

Scythe's eyes flicker, a brief flash of the man he used to be before he closes them again, his cheek pressing lightly into my palm. He takes a deep breath, exhaling slowly, like he's trying to push the storm inside him into submission.

I watch him, my heart pounding, waiting for him to pull away, but he doesn't. He stays, his body still pressed close to mine, his skin warm and trembling beneath my fingers.

Then, finally, he speaks. His voice is rough.

"I don't know how to stop this...stop myself."

The words hit me like a punch, and I step closer, my hand now cupping the back of his neck, my thumb brushing over the tense muscles there.

"You don't have to stop," I whisper. "Just...don't do it alone."

His eyes snap to mine.

There's nothing controlled left in them. Nothing hidden.

Just need.

Then he's on me—pulling me in, mouth crashing down on mine in a kiss that's rough and desperate and starved. No softness. No restraint. Just everything he's been holding back breaking loose at once.

And I let him.

I jump into his arms and he takes. His mouth rough against my blood-streaked skin, teeth scraping, biting, claiming. Copper coats my tongue as his tongue forces into my mouth, wet and demanding. His hands are everywhere, rough and sure, dragging heat from my skin.

The pain sharpens everything. The blood. The breath. Him.

There's no room for anything else. I disappear into it.

He hauls me into the bathroom, the door slamming shut behind us. His shoes are kicked away somewhere. He kisses me hard, like he can't afford to stop, then drops me just long enough to tear his clothes off, his eyes never leaving me. I shove my shorts down my legs and let what's left of my tank top hits the floor.

I look up at him.

He's bleeding.

Wounded.

Blood slicks his chest, streaks down his arms, and my eyes drop. To his cock. Thick. *Hard.* Straining like he's barely holding himself back.

There's no time to think, no time to check the wounds. I don't even get a step before he spins me around and slams me into the full length mirror. The glass is cold against my cheek for half a second—then his hand closes around my arms, yanking them behind me in one brutal grip.

The blunt head of his cock nudges at my entrance—no teasing, no softness—just raw, demanding possession.

And then he's in.

One savage thrust and he fills me to the hilt, punching the air from my lungs. The glass shudders with the force of it, my breath fogging the reflection.

I cry out, the sound ragged and high.

His hand clamps around my throat.

His rhythm is brutal, each thrust slamming me against the mirror hard enough to rattle it.

My body shudders with every inch of him.

"Look at yourself," he grinds out, breathless.

I do.

And the reflection is obscene.

My mouth is open in a silent cry, my skin flushed and streaked with blood. His blood. My tears. The room smells like sex and violence and something unholy.

I look wrecked.

And I've never looked more like *his.*

But just when I think I might collapse under the weight of him—he wrenches me back.

He yanks me away from the mirror in one powerful pull and drops onto the ottoman behind him, dragging me with him so fast the room spins.

I land in his lap, still speared on his cock.

He doesn't stop.

He thrusts up into me hard, fast, wild.

My legs scramble to hook over his, but he locks me in—

One hand braced tight against my stomach, the other tightening around my throat as his mouth brushes my ear.

"Take it," he growls. *"Fucking take it."*

He exhales, a dark hum vibrating against my skin. His palm presses low.

"I can feel how deep I am," he murmurs, almost in awe.

Then he presses harder—right above my pussy.

"Right *here.*"

My breath catches. My whole body shudders, aching and stretched and completely undone.

His grip is brutal—like he's holding on for dear life or dragging me into hell. Every thrust slams me down harder, deeper, until my vision sparks and whites out in bursts of blinding stars.

I can't breathe.

I can't think.

I'm unraveling beneath him, coming apart one sharp, shuddering gasp at a time—and he won't let me go.

"You're mine," he hisses into my ear, his voice cracked and hoarse, wrecked with need.

Then—he bites again.

His teeth sink into my neck, rough and unyielding. The pain is electric. It shoots through me, raw and searing, setting fire to every nerve ending.

I cry out. Half gasp, half moan.

He doesn't let go.

The mark he leaves is brutal. Permanent. It feels like ownership carved in flesh.

And I need it.

Because I'm already his.

The mirror in front of us tells the truth I can't say. His blood-slick body crashes into mine again and again, every muscle taut and trembling.

Scythe isn't just fucking me. *He's devouring me.*

His tongue laps at my blood.

"Look at us," he growls into my neck, voice deep, wrecked, almost reverent.

I lift my eyes to the reflection.

What stares back is ruinous.

A nightmare. A masterpiece.

Our bodies, slick and bloodied, tangled in some twisted ballet of possession and surrender. His cock buried deep inside me, his hand wrapped around my throat like a collar.

It's grotesque. It's holy. *It's ours.*

My tears blur the edges of it. My body is trembling, open and stretched and too full, but I never want it to end.

"Scythe," I gasp, the name falling from my lips like a prayer I was never taught to say.

He growls in response, deep, guttural, *animal*—and tightens his grip on my throat, just enough to make the world blur at the edges.

My lungs stutter for air.

His thrusts turn wild, erratic, his entire body vibrating against mine. The restraint is gone. He's breaking.

And then, suddenly—

He's gone.

He pulls out in one ruthless motion, leaving me aching, empty, gasping for breath like I've been plunged underwater and abandoned there. I whimper, a ragged sound. The loss is a wound. My body clenches around nothing, aching for him; aching for more.

He doesn't speak.

Doesn't let me recover.

Just stands—arms banding tight around my waist, and lifts me.

My breath catches as my back collides with his chest. His cock, slick and hard, throbs against my thigh as he carries me across the room in silence, blood-slick skin against skin, his grip bruising with urgency.

He stops at the counter. Marble. Cold. Unforgiving.

Then he places me down.

My ass hits the edge of the sink, legs dangling, chest heaving.

Before I can blink, his hand fists in my hair and yanks my head back, forcing my gaze up to meet his.

"On your fucking knees," he growls.

The command cuts through the fog in my brain, blistering, undeniable.

I scramble to obey, shifting my body on the cold marble counter, turning to face the mirror. My knees slide beneath me, teetering on the edge, barely holding. There's no room. No leverage. Just enough space to brace my palms flat and arch my back as I try to keep steady.

My thighs tremble. My breath hitches.

I feel exposed. *Vulnerable.* Like one wrong shift and I'll slip straight off the edge.

And maybe that's the point.

He steps behind me; towering, feral, and lets out a low, rumbling sound at the sight of me trying to stay balanced.

"Look at you," he snarls. "So fucking helpless. Can't even hold yourself steady without me."

His hand slides down my spine, slow and possessive. Then he grabs my hip and yanks me back just enough for my knees to slide even closer to the edge.

"You gonna *fall?*" he murmurs darkly. "Better hold on."

His hand returns to my hair, curling tight and possessive. His other hand slides over my ass, gripping, kneading, owning. I gasp as he presses his cock to my entrance again, the tip nudging.

"Look," he commands.

I lift my gaze.

What I see in the mirror is devastating.

Blood and sweat streak my back. My lips are swollen, parted in a silent gasp. My eyes are glassy, ruined.

He's menacing behind me, like he's barely holding back from tearing me apart. His cock pulses, thick and angry and ready.

"This is what you wanted?" he hisses. "What you *allowed?* You want Scythe. *Me.* Beg for it."

"Please," I whisper, my voice shaking.

"Louder."

"Please," I moan, shameless, wrecked. "Please, Scythe."

His growl is a reward.

He drives into me.

I scream.

The sound ricochets off the tiles, echoes against the mirror as my body jerks forward from the force of it. He doesn't let me go. His hand fists tighter in my hair, dragging my head back until I'm looking only at him.

"That's it," he snarls, hips slamming into me. "That's how I want you. Bent over and begging. My cock so deep you'll feel me for days."

Each thrust is punishing, perfect.

"I can feel it," he growls. "Right *here—*" he thrusts hard, "You feel that?"

"Y-yes—God, yes," I cry out, my body trembling violently.

"Not God. *Say it.*"

"Scythe! I feel you," I gasp. "I feel *all* of you—"

"You'll never take another man again," he bites out. "No one else could ever touch this pussy. It's fucking mine."

"Yours," I pant, nodding frantically, tears streaking my cheeks. "I'm yours—only yours."

He grunts, feral, undone.

"Good girl. You take me so fucking well. So tight—*so fucking mine.*"

His rhythm breaks, just a little. His breath hitches, hips slamming harder, faster. My body rocks against the counter, the marble slick beneath me as he uses me, fucks me like he needs to destroy me to survive.

And I let him.

Because I want to be destroyed.

By him.

My eyes flutter closed—

"Don't you fucking dare," he snarls. "Open them."

I do.

And watch.

His expression twisted in something like pain, like worship.

"Say it again, scream it while you come, Vasilisa," he demands, voice breaking.

"I'm yours," I choke out, my orgasm building too fast, too wild.

"Louder!"

"I'm yours, Scythe! I'm yours!"

My climax detonates like a grenade behind my ribs—violent, all-consuming.

It tears through me with the force of a scream, my entire body convulsing, my spine bowing as pleasure crashes over me in brutal, electric waves. I seize around him, pulsing tight, refusing to let him go, like my body's trying to keep him inside forever.

I sob his name, wrecked and reverent, each cry laced with surrender.

His whole body goes taut.

"Fuck," he chokes out. "*Fuck* Vasilisa—"

A strangled, primal sound tears from his throat, half growl, half gasp, as he explodes inside me, cock twitching, pulsing deep. Heat floods me in hard, punishing waves, each spurt of release dragged out by the clench of my still-throbbing walls.

He doesn't pull out.

Doesn't move.

Just stays buried to the hilt, his chest pressed to my back, forehead resting between my shoulder blades as he shudders through the aftershocks. His breath stutters against my skin, ragged and broken, like he's come undone from the inside out.

One arm wraps around my waist, holding me up as my knees give out. The other snakes under my breasts, possessive, trembling with the intensity of what just tore through him.

The haze of pleasure dulls to a warm hum, leaving me wrapped in Scythe's arms. His lips ghost along my neck, whispering low, reverent things that make me shiver despite the exhaustion pulling at my limbs. I let out a breathless, dazed giggle—because for the first time tonight, the storm inside him has settled.

"You are my everything. *Mine*," he whispers. I nod, too spent to speak as I close my eyes, but the sentiment is clear. I am his and he is mine. Santo and Scythe in perfect harmony.

Chapter 54

SANTO

Finally. I am finally myself; I can be both monster and man and still have her love. In my arms I look down at my wife, bloody smears are all over her beautiful body. I cradle her gently and her eyes flutter open, her perfect face marred by my blood, her neck and shoulders bruised by the bites I left on her skin, she's bathed in my blood as if in a ritualistic binding, the possession I feel for her... at having her filled and covered completely with me is *overwhelming.*

The need to take her again coils low in my gut.

I don't.

She needs rest.

I turn on the shower and feel for the warmth of the water before bringing her under the rainfall with me. I place her on her feet and watch as the blood washes away from both of us as if clearing our souls from everything that once tainted our love.

I kiss her—soft, reverent, worshipful. Her eyelids. Her nose. Her cheeks. Her forehead. Her lips. Each touch a vow, each breath a prayer.

She sighs against me, her hands gliding down my back, soothing, accepting, embracing every part of me. The *man,* the monster, the reaper, the *husband.*

I'll spend the rest of my days thanking her. Worshiping her in every breath, every touch, until there is nothing left of me that isn't hers. The water continues to rain down on our bare bodies each touch from her, washing away my past mistakes and every kiss echoing promises of forgiveness and a shared future.

I am reborn in her love.

She takes refuge in my darkness, and I bask in her light.

★★★

The bedroom is dimly lit, the air thick with the scent of us, residual blood, and something deeper, something unchanging. Vasilisa sits cross-legged on the bed in my button-down, the fabric draping over her bare thighs. The sleeves are too long, swallowing her delicate wrists as she rolls them up, preparing to tend to me.

She looks soft, ethereal, even with the bruises from the bites I left blooming along her neck, that mark on her cheek from that bastards hands.

I'm glad I shattered them.

I sit on the edge of the bed in nothing but sweatpants, watching her work.

She doesn't hesitate, doesn't flinch as she takes my arm and dabs at the slashes along my skin.

"You've done this before." It's not a question.

She nods, focused, her fingers steady as she presses gauze to a deeper wound on my chest. "Maksim made sure I knew how to handle wounds. I had to be prepared for anything."

I exhale through my nose, my eyes tracing her features. "He made you a soldier."

She finally glances up, her expression unreadable. Then, with a small smile, she says softly, "No, he made sure I was the perfect, dutiful wife."

I scoff, shaking my head. "You're never going to let me live that down, are you?"

Her lips twitch. "Why would I? It was the most *ridiculous* thing you've ever said to me."

She's right.

"I take it back," I murmur, my fingers brushing her thigh. "You're not perfect."

She raises an eyebrow, waiting.

I smirk. "You're *mine.* That's what matters."

She hums, satisfied as she continues working. "Still perfect though, you say it every time you touch me."

I chuckle.

Her expression shifts, her brows drawing together. "You need stitches."

She's right. "I'll do it."

"No." Her voice is firm but soft. "I will."

I arch a brow. "Since when do you stitch wounds?"

She sighs, shaking her head.

"Since always. You think Maksim wouldn't have trained me to do that too? He was always injured, always up to something,"

She reaches for the suture kit, already threading the needle like it's second nature.

"Of course he is." I exhale, bitterness washing over me. But then I watch her. "I learn something new about you everyday."

She smirks. "And here I thought you already knew everything about me from watching me twenty four-seven."

The sharp pinch of the first stitch barely registers. She watches me, waiting for a reaction, but I don't give her one.

"You don't even flinch."

"I've been through worse."

Her hands hesitate for half a second, but then she keeps going.

"You don't have to do this," I say, quieter now.

"I do."

There's no hesitation in her voice. She keeps her focus on my skin, finishing the last stitch with a deft, practiced movement before tying it off.

"Santo," she says softly.

I tilt my head down, meeting her gaze.

"Are you going to *finish* it?"

I already know what she's asking.

"Of course I am."

Her throat bobs as she swallows. "I don't think Jude is worth it."

I study her, my expression blank. "Why?"

"Because you already won. Because he's nothing. And because I don't want blood on your hands for something so insignificant."

My jaw tightens.

"He touched you, Vasilisa. Left a mark. That makes him *very* significant."

She shakes her head. "I don't want anyone dying because of *me*."

I exhale slowly, my fingers grazing her knee before I tilt her chin up.

"Dea, you don't seem to understand." My voice is low, steady. "Anyone who touches you dies; and I relish having that kind of blood on my hands."

She holds my gaze, searching. She knows me. She knows I am not a good man. That I will never be merciful. But still, she asks.

Still, she tries.

Because she is light.

Kindness.

Love.

"*You* are everything," I murmur, my grip firm against her jaw. "The way I love you, the way I *belong* to you—it's far more dangerous than simple obsession or devotion."

Her breath catches.

I brush my thumb over her bottom lip.

"Remember, I don't just devote my life to you, Dea." My smirk darkens, slow and possessive. "I own you. And you own me, *both* sides of me."

Her lips part, her pulse fluttering against my fingers.

"You still don't understand Dea," my voice drops, my thumb pressing lightly against her throat, feeling the soft, rapid beat of her pulse. "If I *ever* let someone live after touching you... it wouldn't be for them, it would be for you."

She shudders slightly exhaling, "Santo—"

I shake my head, silencing her with a kiss, her soft lips part, but I pull away. Her eyes flutter open meeting mine.

"But I can't do that this time, not even for you, Mia Dea. No one is allowed to take *my* light."

I pull back, watching the way her lips part, her breath uneven.

She blinks up at me, searching my face, her fingers tightening against my forearm as if trying to hold onto something—onto me.

My final words hang between us, thick and unchallenged.

Her brows furrow slightly, and for the first time tonight, there's something different in her expression—not fear, not hesitation, but determination.

Slowly, she moves, shifting forward on her knees, her weight pressing against my thighs.

"Vasilisa—"

I don't stop her.

Her small hands press against my chest, her nails lightly dragging over my skin as she moves deliberately, pushing me back until my spine hits the mattress.

I let her.

Because after *everything,* after being struck, after almost being taken, after being made to feel powerless—she deserves this.

She deserves to reclaim herself.

Her thighs settle on either side of my hips, her knees pressing into the mattress, straddling me.

And for the first time since she touched me tonight, *she* is the one in control.

I exhale through my nose, watching her. My hands settle against her waist—not guiding, not taking, just grounding her, letting her breathe in her own power.

Her fingers slide up my jaw, her touch delicate but firm, as if tracing every shadowed part of me, reminding herself that she owns *all* of me.

"Santo," she murmurs, her voice barely a breath.

I tilt my head back slightly, allowing her touch, letting her take whatever she needs.

"You have me, Dea," I murmur, my grip tightening on her waist. "Take what you want."

***

Spending my day with Wesley Beaumont was the last thing I wanted, not when Vasilisa was home waiting for me.

Last night, with my wife, was everything. And now, the ache of not being with her is a constant throb at the back of my skull.

I can still taste her on my lips, feel the warmth of her body pressed against mine. Wesley prattles on about code words and the dock deal, but my mind is somewhere else—with her, always with *her*.

I want to be home. With my Dea.

Her asking for mercy on that bastards life weighs on me. *My kind girl,* always filled with compassion and light. But I couldn't give her that mercy on his behalf, and I won't. She doesn't understand—she is *everything*.

If she wanted to leave this all behind, I'd pack up and go. No hesitation. No second thoughts.

I meant it when I said she was my world.

Nothing matters but her.

Wesley's voice breaks my thoughts and I grimace.

He advises that so far, no one has gone after Vasilisa's sister at Andras we still don't know what Miroslav is dropping off at the docks, but Wesley has figured out how to intercept Sarkisian's messages with Miroslav. Wesley is nothing like his brothers—less arrogant, more methodical. We wouldn't have gotten this far without him. I may just have to give the son of a bitch the collaboration he's been after.

Everything for tomorrow night is set, from how many men will be at the dock to who we leave with Vasilisa, Katya and Elena, instead of keeping the women together, we decided it's better to keep them apart. There's less risk of the Armenians attacking three separate places, plus maintaining their army at the dock. They have to have an inclination that we are on their trail. If they're smart, they'll plan for it, but with Wesley intercepting messages, we are one step ahead.

The day stretches on—*long*, tedious, but productive. Every piece is falling into place. We have the upper hand now.

Tomorrow, this war ends.

After Wesley leaves to prepare, and our men disperse with their orders, I'm left with a weary Angelo and an aloof Maksim. He leans back, feet kicked up on my conference table, his posture relaxed, but I know him better than that. For a man accused of starting this war, he's keeping his usual cool, calm, collected demeanor.

But his eyes betray him.

They flick toward Angelo in passing glances, but nothing more. Angelo, on the other hand, is easier to read. His tension is obvious, jaw tight, shoulders locked. Something unspoken lingers between them, a weight neither of them wants to acknowledge.

I feel it too.

"What is it you two aren't telling me?" I ask.

Angelo meets my eyes for a fraction of a second before smirking and shrugging.

"Nothing little brother. Just preparing for the take down tomorrow."

He lies through his teeth.

My gaze snaps to Maksim, who meets me head on, unflinching.

"We have this, Amato, the Armenians will be another name on the list of enemies who dared to cross us and failed by tomorrow night."

He chuckles, "Why don't you get home to my cousin and send her my love."

I glance between them. My instincts scream at me.

Liars.

"If I find out there's more to this… if my wife's life was put on the line because of something you're keeping from me—I will kill *both* of you."

"Santo—" Angelo starts.

"Big words for a man with so much to lose," Maksim sneers smirking.

I lean back in my seat, holding his gaze. "I dare you to harm my wife, Korsakov."

His eyes flicker—fear, just for a second before he covers it up with a tight smile.

"Never, Santo. Family is important to me," he replies, an edge to his voice that wasn't there before.

I let the silence stretch, watching Maksim shift in his seat.

Angelo clasps his hand on Maksim's shoulder, his grip firm, grounding. A warning, or reassurance… I can't tell.

I'll find out what they're hiding for Vasilisa's sake.
I push back from my seat. "I'm going home."
I level them both with a final, cold stare.
"I have a fucker in my basement to kill, and a wife to tend to."

***

A clean shot between the eyes. That's what Jude Olsen got after a full day of rotting in his own filth and blood, writhing in pain from his shattered bones.
A quick death—the closest thing to mercy I could give.
A mercy that wasn't mine, but my beautiful wife's request.
I call Luca and Romeo to handle the body and take the stairs to my goddess.
I find her in the library, paint smudged on her nose, an adorable contrast to the ethereal beauty of her face. She startles when I step inside, immediately covering her easel from my view.
I prowl toward her, smirking. "You shouldn't hide things from me, Dea."
She scrunches up her nose, shaking her head.
"It's a surprise, Santo."
She presses her tiny hands against my chest, trying to push me back. I let her.
"Please let me show you when it's done."
"Alright," I cave, holding my hands up in surrender before stealing a quick kiss from her lips.
"You're home early. Everything ready for tomorrow?"
"Yes. But the less you know, the better."
She scoffs. "Santo, I'm not made of glass, remember?"
"I know, Dea. But I want you safe in every way—" I step closer, tapping her heart. "Especially here."
She wraps her arms around me in a tight embrace.
"I love you," she whispers.
"And I love you," I press a kiss to the top of her head. "Have you had dinner?"
She buries her face against my chest, mumbling, "I had snack cakes."
I step back, tucking my finger under her chin until her eyes meet mine. "That's not dinner Vasilisa."
She huffs, but gives in. "Let's have dinner then, I'm sure Julian made something delectable."

Rubbing her palms together in excitement, she removes her paint-smudged smock and tosses it on the chaise. I grasp her hand, leading my wife downstairs.

When we reach the bottom step, I take a moment to drink her in.

Her golden waves cascades over her shoulders, her favorite short skirt hugging her hips with those damn pantyhose-the ones that only serve to get in my way. But instead of her usual button-down blouse, she's wearing what I can only describe as a corseted bra.

It accentuates every delicate curve, her silhouette more sinful than I have any right to handle.

I stop in my tracks. "You can't wear a bra around Julian."

She blinks up at me. "I've been wearing this all day and its a *bustier!*" She shakes her head. "You and your brother know nothing about women's fashion."

My brows lift. "My brother has *seen* you in that?"

She giggles, scurrying into the dining room before I can react. That sound forces the love to well up within me and it is as powerful as ever, if not more so.

In one swift motion, I grab her and turn her to face me, her giggles die at the look on my face.

Her mischievous eyes narrow playfully. "Something on your mind?"

I consider that question sincerely, grasping her hand in mine,

"Just thinking about how lucky I am," I murmur, squeezing her fingers.

A soft smile plays around her lips as we enter the dining room together.

Julian has prepared a feast, roast chicken, perfectly seasoned, sautéed vegetables, and for dessert, snack cakes with ice cream. Vasilisa's favorite.

We sit down to eat, and the weight of the day slowly ebbs away. For a little while, there's no war, no threats, *just us.* She talks about her new paints, her next piece, always brimming with creativity. We plan vacations, books to read together, ideas I want to bring to life once my latest innovations at ZEUS, Athena, and Artemis roll out. It's natural, peaceful, *real.*

As we finish our meal, a rare calm settles over me.

This is what it's all about—coming home to Vasilisa after a long day of work and strife. The thought of losing this. Losing *her* because of Miroslav and the Armenians stirs up a quiet fury deep inside me.

Before the darkness can take hold, Vasilisa reaches across the table, her fingers wrapping around mine, grounding me. "Where'd you go just now? What's wrong?"

I squeeze her hand, shaking my head at her concern. "Nothing, Dea. Just tired from today."

She lets go of my hand, reluctant, hesitant, but changes the subject to the manuscript I gave her, giving my raging thoughts a moment of respite.

I watch her talk—about stories, about art, about futures she assumes are guaranteed, and I let her believe in that world a little longer.

Tomorrow, it all ends.

CHAPTER 55

VASILISA

The house is quiet in the morning. Santo and I have breakfast together, the silence stretching between us, thick but not uncomfortable. Later, he trails beside me in the garden as I pick flowers for the vases around the house, his movements slow, almost hesitant. In the library, he lounges on the chaise, watching as I paint. His eyes never leave me—not once, not even when I glance at him.

It would be romantic if it didn't feel like goodbye. As if he were committing me to memory.

The afternoon leads us to our bedroom. I sit cross-legged on the bed, scrolling through my laptop, looking up the classes I'll have to retake and the new ones I'll need to add to my roster. Across the room, Santo lingers in the closet, pretending to busy himself with something, but I can feel his gaze, searing into me.

Burning a hole right through me. I snap the laptop shut. My eyes meet his. He doesn't even bother to look away. Doesn't pretend.

He just stares.

"What is it?" I huff, frustration creeping into my voice. "I know tonight is big, but you're acting like you're going to die, Santo."

He strides toward me, his expression masked, but I don't stop.

"Are you not confident in the plan you guys made?"

Instead of answering, Santo takes the laptop from my lap and sets it on the nightstand with careful precision. Then, without hesitation, he climbs onto the bed, pressing forward until I'm forced to fall back.

He moves over me, his body settling between my legs, caging me in. The weight of him, the heat, the way his forearms press into the mattress on either side of my head—it should feel suffocating, but it doesn't. It feels inevitable.

His eyes rake over my face, scanning, memorizing, before his hands cradle my cheeks, his touch almost reverent. My fingers trail along his back in soft, soothing strokes, but the tension in his muscles remains rigid beneath my touch.

"Santo, what is it?" My voice is softer now, pleading. "What aren't you telling me?"

His only answer is his lips.

He crashes into me, his mouth urgent, devouring mine with a desperation that sends a shiver down my spine. His tongue slips past my lips effortlessly, taking, claiming, as if salvation lies in my kiss and he's desperate to steal it from me.

"Santo," I gasp when his lips break away, trailing hot, open-mouthed kisses down my neck. I arch beneath him, my breath uneven. "*Please*, tell me."

But he doesn't.

He doesn't speak. Doesn't hesitate. He only moves, pressing his lips, his tongue against my skin, setting fire to the need pooling low in my stomach. His fingers slip beneath my blouse, pushing it up and over my head with quiet efficiency. My own hands reach for him, tugging at the hem of his shirt, desperate to feel him, to take from him as much as he's taking from me.

If he won't talk, I suppose I'll just have to give in.

And satiate us both.

SANTO

Something about tonight doesn't feel right. There are too many missing pieces to this puzzle, too many unanswered questions, and a creeping fear gnawing at my chest—the fear that I won't see her again. I can't shake it. I need to immerse myself in her, to feel her, touch her, take her.

It's *her*.

It will always be her and I cannot—I *will* not leave this earth without once more being a part of her. I remove our clothes in a rush, desperate to feel her skin against mine. Her breath hitches, sending a wave of heat through my body. Every sound, every movement she makes, is amplified.

Her hands find their way through my hair, urging me closer. I trace the curve of her collarbone with my lips, savoring the feel of her. She moans softly, sending a rush of adrenaline mixed with an insatiable desire through me.

I pull back for a moment, looking into her eyes. They're filled with love and a hint of confusion, and it pulls at my heart because I can't answer her questions right now. The love I have for this woman is so fierce it's sometimes overwhelming. I kiss her softly, feeling the tremor in her body beneath mine. Her eyes flutter shut, and I drink in the sight of her—the woman who has etched herself into my soul, the woman whose eyes, those eyes that I adore, remain closed as if savoring the moment.

"Vasilisa," I whisper into her ear, my voice a soft rasp.

Her eyes open wide, filled with that innocent curiosity that pulls me deeper.

"I need you."

The desperation in my voice is unmistakable, and she understands. Her hands cradle my face, pulling me down to her, pressing her lips to mine once more.

Her hands trail down to my back, her fingers tracing patterns as if memorizing every inch of me—just as I am doing with her. It's like we're saying a silent goodbye, but the words never leave our lips. We're afraid that if we speak them aloud, they'll become a self-fulfilling prophecy.

For now, this is all I have—Vasilisa beneath me, her warmth seeping into me, chasing away the cold dread that has settled deep in my bones. Her love wraps around me, a blanket against the harsh realities of the world outside these four walls. I kiss her urgently, pushing inside her, swallowing the gasp that escapes her lips. The feel of her, the connection, is like nothing I've ever known. Her body responds to mine in ways that make every second of this moment feel eternal. Her legs wrap around me, pulling me deeper, and I groan at the sensation. The world narrows down to her. Just for a while, all my fears about tonight slip away, and all that remains is Vasilisa.

Her breath hitches as I deepen our connection, my movements slow, deliberate, savoring every inch of her. I want to remember her like this—beautiful, glowing, beneath me, offering herself to me without reservation.

I feel a sting behind my eyes for the first time in over a decade, but I blink it away, refusing to let it form. Not now. Not here.

A knot tightens in my chest as the realization hits - everything after this moment is uncertain; a nebulous void of possibilities that could lead me away from her.

"Santo," she says urgently. Her hands clutch at my back, nails leaving half-moon imprints on my skin, her body arches beneath me, a silent plea for more and I willingly oblige. My movements become more deliberate, driven by an insatiable need to connect with her, to tether our souls together indelibly, so that no matter what may come, I will forever be a part of her. I kiss her intensely as I continue to lose myself in her.

"Santo," she whispers against my lips, her voice trembling. "I love you."

I pull back slightly, enough to gaze down at her face and see the euphoria mirrored in her eyes. Her cheeks flushed a rosy hue, a thin sheen of sweat covers her body making her glow under the lights. She looks at me with those achingly beautiful eyes that give up the secrets of her soul, filled with longing and unwavering love for me.

Everything inside me shatters. The last remnants of restraint dissolve, leaving nothing, but raw, aching devotion. I can see it in her face—her eyes tell me it's okay, that even if this is our last night together, it's worth every moment of pain that may follow. I hold on to that thought while I surrender myself completely to her - body, mind and soul intertwined with hers.

I would die for you.

I want to say, but the words get stuck in my throat. Fear and regret prevent them from leaving my lips. Instead, I pour all the love, all the pain, all the unsaid words into every kiss, every touch, every movement, hoping she understands what language fails to convey.

As I reach my peak, Vasilisa trembles beneath me, her climax shaking through her body. Her eyes meet mine, and in that moment, I see it—a flicker of fear in her gaze.

I pull her close against me. Our hearts beat erratically in rhythm, a symphony of love played out on the canvas of our bodies. If this is the last moment we have – this, right here, then I hope she will remember it for eternity.

Tonight may bring uncertainty, but right now, in this moment, all that matters is Vasilisa and the bond we share. I pull her against me, our breaths still mingling, our bodies still entwined, as if holding on tight enough can stop the inevitable.

Wrapping her in my arms, I hold onto what feels like the last semblance of peace before the impending storm.

★★★

The drive to the dock is suffocating, silent. The air thick with tension. Even the rumble of the car's engine feels muted beneath it. Armored SUVs flank us on either side, our men ready for war. Maksim grips the steering wheel so tightly his knuckles go white, jaw locked, eyes fixed ahead. Angelo sits in the passenger seat, just as quiet, just as tense. His gaze stays glued to the darkened city streets, watching them slip by like shadows.

I lean my head back, closing my eyes, letting my mind drift—to her.

Vasilisa.

I can still feel her, the warmth of her skin beneath my fingertips, the softness of her lips, the way she clung to me like I was her only tether. The scent of her perfume lingers on me, a cruel reminder of everything I've left behind and everything at stake tonight.

My heart clenches in my chest.

the dock looms—a grotesque silhouette against the moonless sky. Maksim kills the lights, parking far enough to stay unseen, close enough to see our men flood in like a silent storm.

One of Maksim's men steps forward. "Dock's clear, except for one. Miroslav."

Miroslav.

They drag him forward, and he doesn't fight.

That's the first thing that feels wrong.

Maksim, Angelo, and I approach as they force Miroslav to his knees, binding his hands behind his back. Maksim doesn't hesitate.

His fist collides with his uncle's face, the sickening crack echoing through the air.

"Where are the Armenians?" Maksim demands.

Miroslav doesn't feign innocence. He spits blood, smirks, then starts talking.

He spills what we already know—how he embezzled money from NovaRael, sold out to the Armenians, then ran when they demanded more.

Another punch to the ribs. A kick to his stomach. He grunts, coughs and then the bastard laughs.

His eyes find mine.

"Did she tell you?" he asks, voice drenched in amusement.

Something in his tone makes my blood run cold.

"Did she tell you she was taken?"

The world narrows.

"Yes," I snap. "And you paid them off like a coward. We know more than you think. It's pathetic that you offered your other daughter afterward and sent Jude after my wife."

Miroslav grins through bloodstained teeth.

"My *other* daughter?" he scoffs. Then he laughs, full-bodied, like this is all some fucking joke.

"You shit stains think you know everything."

I don't like this.

The unease claws its way up my spine.

"Jude went rogue," Miroslav continues. "Had a conversation with Sarkisian, thought he could take Vasilisa for himself. But *my* deal? That was set in stone."

"What deal?"

Miroslav shakes his head.

Maksim doesn't wait. He delivers another vicious blow, sending Miroslav's head snapping to the side.

"You're dead either way, old man." Maksim's voice is like ice. "Might as well spill it all."

Miroslav groans, spits more blood. Then, finally, he mutters the words that shatter everything.

"I offered Vasilisa."

The words don't register at first.

They can't.

There's no way he just said what I think he did.

He *offered* my wife

Miroslav spits blood onto the ground, shaking his head like we're all fools. "I offered her when she came of age, but then you," he glares at Maksim, "Married her off to the Italians and I was back on the hook. It was *her* or me, and I don't plan on dying."

Something about the way he says it—the casual finality of it—snaps something inside me.

"You spineless bastard," I seethe. "You gave up your own daughter just to save your miserable fucking life?"

Miroslav chuckles, coughing up blood. "You think this world cares about sentiment? About *family*?" He tilts his head mockingly. "You're not that naïve."

Rage claws at my throat, threatening to consume me whole.

Angelo slaps a hard hand against my shoulder.

"Your phone," he says, the vibration of my phone bringing me back.

I tear it out of my pocket, Wesley's name flashing across the screen. I put him on speaker.

"Go for Santo."

"The code word went out, and a response came in." Wesley's voice is clipped, urgent. "The Armenians sent back 'The Queen is in the Castle.' Does that make sense to you?"

Miroslav smiles a bloody smirk. Something heavy settles in my stomach. I turn to Maksim, but he's already staring at Miroslav, realization dawning in his expression.

Maksim goes still.

Then he moves. *Fast.* He grabs Miroslav by the collar, yanking him forward. "You have got to be fucking stupid," Maksim growls. "Tell me you didn't do it!"

Miroslav laughs, low and knowing.

Something inside me fractures. "Maksim?" My own voice barely chokes out.

He meets my gaze, and for the first time all night, there's fear in his eyes.

"Vasilisa's name," he mutters. "Her name *means* Queen."

The weight of it drops like a guillotine.

"This whole thing was a bait and switch." Maksim's voice is sharp, furious. "They're going after her."

The world stops.

Then it detonates.

I turn and run.

I don't remember hanging up on Wesley, but I do. I don't remember dialing Romeo's number, but it goes straight to fucking voicemail.

Angelo calls Luca—he's with Elena—"Get to Vasilisa. Now."

I hear Maksim barking orders, telling Vaska to leave Katya and head to my estate.

The panic is searing, suffocating. This is my worst fear come to life. I can't relive this nightmare.

They're going to take her. Torture her. Send her back to me in pieces.

Her delicate hand in a box with that *damn* ring on her finger.

The same fucking ring my mother had when they sent her back to me. The same ring my grandmother died in. The curse, real or not, has found her too.

If they take her, I will burn every city to the ground until I find her.

VASILISA

Santo left with an army of men. He left me here, safe with a group of guards at the gate and Romeo to keep me company. My nerves are frayed.

I could feel my heart racing as he walked away.

I longed to plead with him, to make him promise that he would return to me.

Promise that we would take countless vacations together, read endless books side by side, and make a family of giant babies. But I swallowed back the words and instead pressed my lips against his, silently conveying my love and trust as I watched him leave.

Romeo distracts me with stories and jokes about his family in Chicago. We sit in the library, and I continue my painting for Santo. I paint with hope—hope that when he comes home, I can gift it to him. I just have to keep positive thoughts.

Santo will come home.

"That's how I ended up here," Romeo says, and I realize I haven't been paying attention. Guilt prickles at me, but I smile politely and decide to ask questions—anything to keep my mind occupied.

"Will you be a Capo someday, then?" I ask, continuing to paint. A drop of red splatters onto my shirt, blending into the fabric. I now regret wearing a white sweater over my leggings.

"I won't. I'm the third son—not the heir or the spare," he chuckles. "It's why I was easy to send away."

"Would you rather be in Chicago?"

"Honestly, no. I like it here. Plus, I have Lila."

"Wait, you and Lila are—"

The deafening crack of gunfire erupts outside, shattering the fragile peace of the mansion.

I whip my head toward the windows, my breath catching as three cars barrel onto the property. Santo's guards open fire, bullets flashing in the night. Romeo jumps to his feet beside me, every trace of humor gone.

"Vasilisa, we have to get you somewhere safe," he says, snapping me from my frozen panic. He grips my arm, dragging me down the stairs to the master bedroom. We burst inside, and he slams the door shut, locking it behind us.

"Romeo, we need to call Santo, or Angelo, or Luca," I gasp out, panic setting in.

"Vasi, calm down," he urges, his voice low, but sharp.

He crouches, gripping my shoulders so I'm forced to meet his eyes. "You're going to lock yourself in the elevator and wait for Santo to come get you."

I shake my head frantically. I can't leave him.

"Romeo, you have to come with me. We could both—"

"No," he cuts me off firmly.

"You go alone and *stay there*. Only you, Santo, and Angelo have access to that elevator. If it opens, it will be one of them."

Tears blur my vision as the gravity of the situation slams into me.

"Romeo," I whisper, pleading.

Before he can respond a loud banging echoes through the mansion's front door followed by the sound of boots stamping inside.

Chills run up my back and arms.

They've broken in.

"Go, Vasilisa," Romeo rasps, his voice harsh with urgency.

My feet move on instinct, my hands trembling as I snatch the box with the gun from my window nook. I rush into the closet, slamming the button for the elevator just as another wave of gunfire erupts outside.

The doors slide shut, sealing me in steel and silence.

I lean against the cold metal walls, my breath ragged, my pulse hammering.

Dawning realization hits. *My phone.* I don't have it.

I left it in the library.

Panic rises, ice-cold and suffocating. I have no way to call Santo. No way to warn him.

And if these men are here... does that mean Santo is—

I can't finish the thought.

Pressing my back against the smooth metal, I try to steady my quivering body. I wait.

For rescue.

Or worse.

For the Armenians to find me.

And all the while, I wonder if Romeo will survive.

CHAPTER 56

SANTO

I'm driving faster than I ever have.

And it's still not fast enough. The road stretches out before me—endless, swallowing the distance between me and her in an ominous black void. I push the accelerator down, harder, my knuckles bone-white on the wheel.

My heart slams against my ribs, a relentless war drum, every beat screaming…

Vasilisa. Vasilisa. Vasilisa.

The city lights blur to the left. The dark waters roar to the right. The road ahead is nothing but shadows. Beside me, Angelo is speaking—watching the surveillance feed of my home on my phone. But his words barely register.

"They got in."

His voice is like a sledgehammer to my ribs.

Everything inside me shatters.

The car skids around a corner, tires screaming against the pavement as I push it beyond its limit. Fear and rage fuel my reckless speed.

"And her?" My voice is sharp, every muscle wound tighter than a bowstring. "Where is she?"

"She went to the elevator," Angelo says tightly. His voice is dark, clipped—punctuated by the gunfire crackling through the phone's speaker.

The sound makes my blood run cold. My jaw clenches so hard it aches. If they dare lay a finger on her— I will kill them.

And then I will take her.

Steal her away, far from Cosa Nostra.

And I will *never* return.

"Fuck," Angelo breathes suddenly. "Romeo's down."

"Shit."

"Damn it! The cameras are down!"

No.

My heart plummets. That means—they cut the surveillance.

"It's fine." Angelo's voice is tight, trying to keep me steady. "We're practically there. We'll get her, Santo."

No.

Ice grips my spine. My fingers strangle the steering wheel.

"Athena is a prototype," I say, my voice hollow. "I had to connect it to the lock system. If they cut off Athena—"

The realization slams into me like a wrecking ball.

"Then anything biometric will override."

"So what?" Angelo demands. "The elevator freezes? Goes dark? She'll be safe."

No.

My stomach twists. My breath is shallow.

"The elevator will descend to the basement."

I barely recognize my own voice—numb, disbelieving. My foot slams harder on the gas pedal.

Hoping.

Praying.

"The only way to shut down Athena is from the control panel." My voice is hoarse. "*In* the basement."

Vasilisa is descending right to them. She's a sitting duck.

CHAPTER 57

VASILISA

The deafening boom of gunshots echoes through my home, each one sending a jolt of fear and anguish through me. The sound of glass shattering pierces my heart, as I imagine the destruction. Romeo is out there, outnumbered by a relentless onslaught of attackers. My only relief is that the staff is gone, sent away by Santo to protect them from possible harm. My hands tremble as I open the box Angelo gave me, revealing a loaded gun - a violation of our safety rules, but now my only lifeline. A loud bang shakes the room and the elevator lights flicker as it begins to move.

My heart races with hope - Santo must be here to save us. But then a cold chill seeps into my bones as doubt creeps in - what if it's not him? I steel myself and stand up straight, gripping the gun tightly as memories of every training session with Angelo flood my mind. *I got this.*

I press back against the shuddering wall of the elevator, my breath shallow. The floor beneath me quakes, a constant reminder that every tick downward is pushing me closer— closer to whatever waits for me below. My hands, slick with sweat, tighten around the gun. It had been a mere tool before—just a weight in my grip during training, under Angelo's watchful eye.

Now, it feels alien.

Cold.

Unwelcome.

But it's my only chance.

I squeeze my eyes shut, going over the instructions Angelo drilled into me.

Grip.

Stance.

Sight alignment.

The mechanics are etched into my mind. But what terrifies me isn't the act of pulling the trigger. It's what comes after. The life I might take. The blood I might spill. The elevator keeps descending. And with it, so does my hope.

It feels like I'm being lowered into an abyss, an endless void with no rope to pull me back up. The distant echo of gunfire above grows fainter, drowned beneath the ragged sound of my own breath and the thunder of my racing heartbeat.

"Vasilisa, you have to do this," I mutter to myself, my jaw clenched, every muscle in my body wound tight with dread and resolve.

The elevator slows, and I know, just *know*, that in a few seconds, the doors will slide open to reveal my fate. The cold steel of the gun feels heavier in my hand now, yet somehow empowering, grounding me in the only reality I have left. I take a deep breath, steadying myself.

The doors slide open.

And what used to be beautiful—the open floor plan I once adored—now feels like a cage.

My heart sinks as my eyes lock onto the two figures standing about ten feet away. Their grins are sinister, gleaming under the harsh fluorescent lights.

My breath catches in my throat, and for a moment, the world seems to slow.

Time slows.

They start moving toward me, but instead of retreating further into the elevator, like my instincts scream at me to do, I force myself to stand straighter.

I lift the gun, pointing it directly at the closest figure.

"Back off," I warn, my voice shaking but steady.

Any hint of fear will only push them closer.

And just as the first figure lunges forward, I squeeze the trigger.

The shot rings out, a brutal crack that shatters the silence.

He drops.

The force of it—the finality, is instantaneous. A violent jerk of his body before he crumples to the floor like a puppet with its strings cut.

Right between the eyes.

My stomach lurches.

I stare, frozen, my breath strangled in my throat as a dark bloom of red spreads beneath his skull. His body twitches, just once, before going unnervingly still.

The smell of gunpowder lingers, burning my nose, mixing with the metallic tang of blood. I feel like I'm floating, like my mind has ripped from my body, hovering somewhere above me, watching in numb disbelief. I just—just shot someone in the head.

A blur of movement.

The second man lunges.

The gleam of steel catches my eye. I barely register the knife in his hand before his body slams into me, knocking the air from my lungs.

The gun slips from my grip, skidding across the floor.

I thrash, but his hands clamp down on me, his weight crushing. I react on instinct.

My elbow crashes into his jaw, the sharp clack of his teeth slamming together echoing in my ears as the impact reverberates through my arm.

He grunts, staggering back, his grip loosening just enough—

His knife slips from his hand, clattering to the floor. I twist free, reaching for my gun, but he shoves me down, his full weight slamming on top of me.

The glint in his eye sends a frigid wave of ice through my veins. Before I can react, his hands are on me.

Possessive.

Revolting.

Claiming.

I thrash, my body recoiling instinctively, every nerve in me screaming, but he doesn't stop. His fingers clamp down on my inner thigh, rough and invasive. A cold, nauseating dread fills my veins as his hand reaches the waistband of my leggings.

I freeze.

This is it.

I can't stop him.

Inevitable.

I shut my eyes, swallowing a sob.

After he's done with me, he'll take me or kill me or send me back to Santo in pieces.

Santo's face flashes behind my eyelids.

I *can't* be another person Santo loses.

I won't.

The second his fingers dip beneath my waistband, I snap.

My hand shoots up, palm slamming into his nose just like Angelo taught me.

Make the fucker regret breathing.

Blood gushes. His face contorts—not in pain, but rage.

Then his hands move.

Not to his face.

To my *throat.*

His fingers tighten like a vice, cutting off air, squeezing the fight out of me.

Stars begin to blur at the edges of my vision. I can feel it—death slithering closer, curling around me like a noose.

But I'm not done. I won't let him win. Through the fog of fading breaths, something sharp cuts through the panic—

That thought again.

Santo.

What if they got to him first? What if he's already—

No.

The thought ignites something inside me; a last, desperate ember refusing to be snuffed out.

Suddenly I see it.

A flicker of steel. His knife. Lying within my reach.

My fingers scrabble against the cold, unyielding floor, grasping, clawing—but I'm running out of time. My lungs are screaming, my vision darkening, my body betraying me.

One last stretch, one last agonizing inch. My hand closes around the handle.

I don't hesitate.

I rip the blade upward, dragging it in a jagged line across his throat.

His grip loosens. His eyes widen in shock.

Blood. Hot, thick, endless spurts from his neck, drenching my hands, my face, my lips.

My stomach lurches, every instinct screaming at me to not inhale, not swallow, to keep my mouth sealed against the flood of him.

His body convulses above me, his breath coming in shallow, wet gasps, his fingers still twitching, but I crawl out from under him.

I scramble away, coughing, heaving, dragging in ragged, burning gulps of air. The floor tilts, my mind spinning, my hands shaking.

But I'm *alive.*

I stagger to my feet, barely registering the mess around me, barely feeling anything beyond the raw, aching reality of survival.

My gun.

I spot it and snatch it up. Without a second thought, I fire one last shot into his twitching body.

Then, I run.

CHAPTER 58

SANTO

The mansion comes into view, its once-grand facade now scarred—bullet holes riddling the walls, windows shattered, the entrance marred by violence.

A wave of nauseating anger builds inside me, coiling tight in my chest.

Beyond the danger to my wife, beyond the bodies littering the driveway, beyond the thick, acrid stench of gunpowder and blood—

It's this.

Our home.

Her sanctuary.

Defiled.

I barely register the corpses, the men swarming my property, my own soldiers flooding in. My focus is singular.

Vasilisa.

I stop the car and bolt, my gun already in my grip.

Behind me, Vaska's tires screech against the pavement. Then Maksim. Then four more SUVs.

Armed men spill out, a swarm of reinforcements descending onto my home. Gunfire erupts, but I only hear my pounding heart.

"Santo!" Angelo's voice snaps from behind me. Urgent.

But I don't stop.

I can't stop.

Not now.

Not when she needs me.

I sprint for the garage, breath sharp, lungs burning, I reach the broken garage door.

My stomach free-falls. I raise my gun and barrel forward.

I rush past my vehicles, my nerves blazing at the deafening silence.

Swallowing hard, I keep my gun ready as I step into the glow of the basement.

My heart pounds against my ribs, every pulse a countdown to whatever waits for me.

And then I see them. Two lifeless bodies. Both Armenian. My eyes sweep over the scene.

A bloodstained knife.

Dark, wet pools of crimson seeping into the concrete.

The squelch of my shoes pressing into the blood makes my stomach tighten.

Where is she?

My eyes scan the basement, frantic, searching for any trace of her, of what happened here.

A flicker of silver amidst the crimson splatters catches my eye.

My breath catches.

I crouch, my fingers closing around the delicate chain.

Her necklace.

My grip tightens around the tiny charm, a surge of panic roaring through me. If they've taken her. They couldn't have gone far. There's no way. Desperation claws at me, my lungs burning with the urge to shout her name, to demand she answer.

But I hold back.

If those bastards still have her, they must be close. I turn toward the elevator, and—

A sound.

A faint, shattered whimper.

A sniffle.

My pulse stalls.

The elevator doors are open, but from this angle, I can't see anyone inside. I exhale slowly, tucking her necklace into my pocket, my gun raised, my body coiled. I creep forward towards the lift. I turn swiftly inside and she screams.

The gun slips from her hand, clattering to the floor, but she doesn't move to retrieve it.

She's curled up in the corner of the elevator, knees to her chest, hands raised in surrender.

Covered in blood.

Tears carve rivers down her pale cheeks, her eyes shut tight, as if she's trying to disappear.

She's shaking.

So violently that I fear she might break apart right in front of me.

"Vasilisa," I gasp, securing my gun and lunging for her.

Then stop short and crouch down toward her, terrified that any sudden movement might shatter her completely.

"Dea, it's me."

Her body jerks at the sound of my voice.

Her eyes snap open.

Wide, frightened.

For a second, I see nothing but panic, until it ebbs away to recognition. Her body reacts before her mind does. She throws herself at me, crashing into my chest with enough force to knock the breath out of me.

I catch her, my arms wrapping around her trembling body, holding her so tightly that I feel the way her ribs shudder with every ragged sob.

"Shh," I murmur into her hair, pressing my lips against her temple. "It's okay. You're safe now."

My relief is short-lived. The blood.

So much blood.

A fresh wave of dread floods my veins. I jerk back, frantic, my hands moving over her arms, her waist, her throat, searching, hoping that it isn't hers.

No wounds.

Nothing.

And then the realization slams into me. The blood isn't hers.

It's *theirs.*

The men *she* killed.

My courageous, unstoppable wife defeated them herself.

She fought them off.

I hold her closer. Her trembling lessens as she clutches onto me, burying herself into the crook of my neck, as if she can disappear into me.

"Come on, let's get out of here," I murmur hoarsely, lifting her into my arms.

She doesn't resist. She just wraps her legs around me, tucking herself closer as I step out of the elevator.

I cast a sweeping glance around the room, taking in the carnage—the bodies, the blood, the absolute violation of our home.

A fresh wave of anger coils inside me. She had to fight for her life tonight. She's no stranger to danger, but this... this is something else entirely.

"You did good," I whisper into her hair. I'm proud. Terrified. Both at once.

Footsteps.

Angelo rushes in, his sharp gaze flicking to Vasilisa's blood-soaked clothes. His brows lift—

But I shake my head.

"There were about twenty of them," Angelo says, voice clipped. "Most were injured or killed at the gate. Romeo took out nine before he got shot."

Vasilisa gasps in my arms, her head jerking up.

"Romeo is—"

"No," Angelo cuts in quickly. "Vaska's taking him to the hospital, but he's okay."

He shifts his gaze to the two dead men on the floor.

"You did this, Tiny?"

A small, shattered whisper. "Yeah." She buries her face against me again.

Angelo smirks. "Nice job, Piccola."

I feel her body shudder at his words.

My grip on her tightens.

"Any alive?" I ask.

"One," Angelo responds. "Nico's bringing him to the warehouse. He can marinate for a few days."

Vasilisa pulls away from me, her eyes frantic. "It's over?" Her gaze locks onto mine, searching for reassurance, for something I can't give her.

Before I can answer, Angelo speaks the truth. "No. Sarkisian wasn't here, just his men which means he will send more."

Vasilisa sobs, the sound breaking apart in her throat. Her breaths ragged, her voice shaking. "For me?" she whispers.

Her fear slices through me.

"No," I tell her, voice unshakable. "No one will come for you, because I'm never leaving you alone. Ever again."

Angelo gives me a look. A silent disapproval. A knowing gaze that tells me I just fed her a half-truth. Because she may still be a target. Until we end this, until we take down Arsen Sarkisian, this isn't over.

But I refuse to let her live in fear. I refuse to let her spend a single moment without me by her side. She trembles, her eyes fluttering, her body giving out as the adrenaline vanishes from her bloodstream.

Her legs go limp as she faints in my arms. I adjust her, cradling her against me. "I won't let her live in fear," I say firmly.

Angelo nods. But he won't meet my eyes.

"What is it?" I press.

"Nothing." A small shrug. "We just need to find this piece of shit and end this once and for all."

He turns, leaving the basement, and I follow.

I don't buy it.

"That's not just it," I say as we step through the ruins of my destroyed estate. "I get that you're the Don, that Maksim is the Pahkan. You have to keep things close to the vest. But I'm your *brother*. Eventually, I'll find out."

Angelo just nods, his silence weighing heavy.

Luca emerges from the broken shards of my front door, his sharp gaze immediately falling on Vasilisa in my arms.

His face darkens. "Is she—"

"She's okay," I cut in. "Just fainted."

Luca's worry is written all over him, his eyes flicking from her limp form in my arms to me. "What do you want to do?" he asks, his voice steady but edged with concern.

I hesitate. My eyes trail over her—the bruises already darkening on her skin, the smears of blood.

Some of it *could* be hers.

I don't know and that not knowing makes my chest tighten, a swell of rage rising with the fear gnawing at me. I need to know she's okay.

I need to be sure. "Take us to the hospital," I say, my voice firm, leaving no room for argument. I don't want to waste a single second. "I want her checked for injuries. *Every damn inch.*"

Luca nods, already moving to the car.

I adjust Vasilisa's weight in my arms, cradling her closer, feeling the rise and fall of her breath against my chest—a faint, fragile rhythm. I grit my teeth, my rage simmering just beneath the surface.

I need answers.

I need to know if they laid a hand on her in any way I *can't* see.

Luca pulls open the car door, and I slide into the backseat, never letting her go. The drive is silent. Tense. The city blurs by, unnoticed. All I can see is her. Every bruise. Every mark. I reach out, brushing a strand of hair from her face. My own hands are shaking.

Fury.

Fear.

Both coiling tightly inside me, suffocating.

They tried to snuff out my light.

I'll make sure they *never* get the chance again.

When we reach the hospital, the staff is already waiting, alerted by Luca. As they approach, I tighten my hold on her, barely restraining myself.

"Full exam," I growl to the lead doctor. "Every possible test. I want to know if she's hurt—*anywhere.*"

The doctor nods, keeping his eyes low, sensing the edge in my tone. I finally let them take her, my hand lingering on hers until they take her away, and I'm left in the hallway, fists clenched, every muscle tense, waiting. If they *touched* her, if she's hurt, I swear on everything I'll make them pay tenfold.

As the hours tick by, I remain in the cold, sterile hallway, my mind reeling with torturous thoughts. Every few minutes, I replay the scene of Vasilisa fainting in my arms, her body going limp with exhaustion and fear. Her fear. *My failure.*

I keep pacing, my steps echoing on the linoleum floors, each one tightening the coil of anger and worry wound up inside me. Every minute feels like a lifetime, every second I'm not by her side grates on my nerves like sandpaper. A voice breaks through my thoughts.

"Santo."

I glance up to see Luca striding toward me, a plastic hospital bag in his hand. His gaze flicks over me, and his expression darkens.

It's only then that I register it.

The blood.

It's on my hands, my clothes, dried in dark streaks across my shirt, my arms, my knuckles.

Their blood. *On my wife.* On me.

Luca exhales sharply, shaking his head as he hands me the bag. "Change. You look like you just walked out of a damn war zone."

Because I did.

I take the bag from him without a word, my jaw tight, my hands clenching around the fabric.

"I don't care how I look," I mutter.

"I know," Luca says evenly. "But she's gonna wake up, and you're the first thing she's gonna see. You want her to wake up to *this?*"

His words hit like a fist to the gut.

No. The last thing she needs is to see me like this, covered in blood, in the evidence of what she just survived.

Without another word, I step into the nearest bathroom, stripping out of the ruined shirt, the stiff, dried fabric sticking to my skin.

I scrub my hands, my neck, everywhere she touched with her blood stained hands, watching the blood swirl down the drain, but no matter how much I wash, I still feel tainted.

Like I didn't do enough.

Like I *failed* her.

Because I *did.*

I pull on the clean shirt Luca brought, rolling my shoulders, forcing my breath to steady.

Then, I walk back out, still restless.

Finally, The doors swing open. The doctor steps out, his expression steady as he approaches.

"She's okay," he says. And those two words ease something deep in my chest. "She's just dehydrated, and there's significant bruising around her neck, but no internal damage."

I bite back the questions still swirling in my head, forcing myself to focus.

But there's one thing I need to know. The question lodges in my throat, burning like acid.

"And…" I struggle to say it, my fury sharpening at the mere thought. "Did they…?"

The doctor meets my gaze, understanding the weight of what I'm asking.

"No signs of forced sexual assault, Mr. Amato." His voice is calm, carefully controlled. "She's physically unharmed in that regard."

A quiet, cold relief rushes through me, settling deep in my bones. I nod, trying to keep my composure, feeling the weight lift, even as the anger remains.

The doctor hesitates. "We had to give her a mild sedative," he says, shifting uneasily. "She woke up looking for you, and she… she wouldn't allow us to continue the exam until she saw you."

His eyes flick to mine, wary of my reaction.

"We did as you requested, but she was… understandably shaken."

A fresh wave of fury burns through me, my jaw tightening.

She fought for her life—*alone*—and then she had to wake up to this? Without me there?

I exhale, forcing myself to stay in control, even as my blood boils beneath my skin.

"You can see her now," the doctor says quickly, gesturing to the door.

I nod, then push past him without another word because nothing else matters.

Not the wreckage.

Not the war still looming.

Not the men I still have to hunt down.

Only her.

Inside the room, she lies beneath a blanket, her face soft, her breathing even in sleep.

The blood has been washed away, her bruises cleaned and tended to. For a moment, I just stand there, absorbing the sight of her like she's my lifeline.

She's safe.

I still have her.

She's here, but it's not enough.

I step closer, lowering myself onto the bed beside her, moving carefully. I don't care about the machines, the wires, the IV drip at her side.

I can't be away from her.

Not after seeing her like that. Not after knowing what could have happened. I brush a hand over her cheek, my fingers ghosting over her skin, needing to touch her to remind myself she's real.

That she's *here*.

That I didn't lose her.

Her breathing is steady, her presence soothing—a faint, fragile rhythm against my chest as I pull her closer.

I grit my teeth. Rage still simmers beneath the surface.

No one will ever come near her again. *Not while I breathe.*

CHAPTER 59

VASILISA

My eyes flutter open to the soft morning light filtering through tall windows, casting a warm glow across the room. The sheets beneath me are smooth, cool, not the sterile cotton of a hospital bed. I blink, my mind still foggy, trying to make sense of where I am. There's a faint scent of lilies in the air, familiar, comforting. I push myself up slowly, wincing as I feel the tenderness along my neck, the memory of hands around my throat surfacing before I push it down.

Scanning the room, this definitely *isn't* the hospital. It's… it's beautiful, warm, and somehow it feels like *him.*

Santo.

The mattress shifts slightly, pulling me from my haze, and my breath catches. There he is, sitting on the edge of the bed, watching me with that fierce, protective intensity that never wavers, never weakens. His hand reaches out to brush a stray hair from my face, his touch so gentle it nearly undoes me.

"You're awake," he murmurs. His voice is soft, but there's relief there. Maybe even something like guilt, shadowing his expression.

My gaze drifts around the room again, struggling to place where I am. "Where?"

"Our home," he says, a hint of a smile tugging at the corner of his mouth.

Our home.

I swallow, my throat tight, my voice rasping as I manage to ask "Our home?"

His gaze never leaves my face. "Our *other* home. Our penthouse," he clarifies. "It was supposed to be a surprise for you, to have you close to me when I worked."

His voice is steady, but there's a flicker of regret in his eyes. "I had it all prepared. I wanted to lead you here with your eyes closed, just to see the surprise on your face when you opened them."

His voice trails off and, his jaw tightens. I reach out, tracing my fingertips along the stubble on his cheek.

"You didn't have to do this, Santo."

His fingers twine with mine, holding my hand against his face. "It was more for me Dea, you get a nice new home and I get you."

A smile tugs at my lips, "It's for both of us then, because I love being close to you."

He presses a kiss to my hand before letting it go and sighing deeply.

"Is everyone okay?" I ask quietly.

"There were some casualties, we lost some guards," he admits, his gaze darkening at the memory. "But everyone else is safe."

"Romeo?"

"Vaska sent word that his wound was a clean shot through the shoulder, he'll be fine."

I breathe a sigh of relief. "I remember Angelo was there, is he alright?"

His eyes narrow slightly, a flicker of discontentment flashes in his eyes. "Angelo... well, if I'm going to tell you this Dea then I need to tell you everything, but I don't want to put any more on you then you already have."

"Please," I beg him, "I want to know."

He shakes his head, and I want to protest, but my eyes start to flutter shut, my body demanding rest. I fight it, suddenly afraid of the nightmares that will come.

Santo seems to understand. He doesn't ask. He doesn't hesitate. He just lays beside me, pulling me in, his arms wrapping around me, holding me together.

"Sleep, Dea," he murmurs, his voice a low rumble against my ear. "You're safe. I'm not leaving you."

His promise is the last thing I hear before exhaustion finally claims me, and everything goes dark.

★★★

I wake up alone.

Disoriented, my body feels heavy, my mind sluggish. Santo's side of the bed is cold. *Empty.*

For a moment, panic gnaws at me.

Pushing off the covers, I scan the room, searching. The bathroom door is slightly ajar, and I step inside—only to stop in my tracks.

The mirror.

I freeze.

I'm clean, but it's the marks on my skin that steal my breath. Angry purple bruises, scattered across my body like abstract art.

Tears bloom in my eyes as the memories hit, sharp and merciless.

Hands—grabbing me, touching me.

Soulless, dark eyes.

The lives I took.

Blood. So much blood.

I squeeze my eyes shut, shaking my head, trying to force the images away. *Not now. Not now.*

Reentering the bedroom, my chest still tight, I find Santo standing by the door. He's dressed in nothing but sweatpants, his broad frame shadowed in the dim morning light.

His eyes find me—and I *know*. His eyes reflect raw pain as they skate over me, falling on each bruise with a quiet fury.

"I should have been there," he says quietly, his voice heavy with guilt.

"No," I whisper hoarsely.

I cross the space between us without thinking, my arms wrapping around his waist. My fingers grip him, as if testing the reality of him, before I let them relax—my touch now soft against the tension in his body.

I tilt my head up, my voice steady even as my heart aches.

"You found me."

He takes a deep breath, his chest heaving. His arms encircle me, pulling me closer as he buries his face in my hair.

"What did they do to you?" He whispers desperately into my hair.

My body tenses.

Forcing my eyes to meet his, I change the subject. "I'm hungry."

His brows furrow. Reluctance… hurt maybe reflects softly on his features before he nods. "I had food delivered, let's feed you," he says, attempting a tone of casualness that doesn't quite reach his eyes. He leads me to the kitchen, a simple yet modern space with all the essentials. Breakfast is laid out on the table; eggs, bacon, and fresh fruit.

I take a seat at the table while Santo serves me, his movements stiff, almost jerky—a stark contrast to his usual composed self.

He's lost in his own thoughts, drowning in the guilt that's eating away at him.

I watch him in silence, my heart aching for him.

"I promise you, Vasilisa," he says suddenly, setting a plate in front of me, his voice low but firm. "This will *never* happen again."

I flash him a small, grateful smile, but I don't respond. Not because I don't believe him—I do—but because words feel empty right now.

Instead, I pick up my fork and start eating. The food is delicious, but my mind isn't on it.

It's still there, lingering in the darkness of last night.

Santo takes a seat across from me, his gaze heavy, burning into me. His intensity is both comforting and unsettling, like he's waiting for something.

Once I'm done, he clears the dishes without a word.

But when he returns, reclaiming the seat across from me, his presence feels even heavier.

His jaw is tight. His fingers curl into fists on the table before he exhales sharply, his eyes locking onto mine.

"Tell me what they did."

His words hang between us like a fragile thread, stretched thin, ready to snap.

With that request, he's asking for more than just a recounting of events. He's asking for my pain. My fear. My courage. *Everything.*

"I—" I start, but the words falter, catching in my throat as memories claw their way to the surface.

"So much blood," I whisper.

Tears slip down my face, dripping onto my trembling hands. My hands—the ones that carry the weight of the lives I took.

"I have blood on my hands."

Santo moves before I even process it, rounding the table, kneeling beside me. His hands find my face, cradling me like I might break.

"No, Dea," he murmurs. "This is *not* your fault. I wasn't there. I should have been."

His thumb brushes away my tears. "The blood is on *my* hands."

I look at him through my tear-blurred vision, wanting to believe him. But the shadows of guilt and horror still dance behind my eyes.

"I—"

He shakes his head, firm. "The blood is on *my* hands, not yours, say it."

My throat tightens. My voice cracks.

"The blood is on your hands, not mine."

He nods, pressing a kiss to my hands.

"If I were there, I would have killed them." His voice is rough with conviction. "I failed you. The blood is on *my* hands Say it again."

"The blood is on your hands, not mine."

"Good," he whispers.

His lips brush my hands again, reverent, sealing his promise.

And that's when I break. I crumble into him, letting the sobs tear through me, no longer able to hold them back. Santo doesn't say anything. He just holds me—silent, steady, unshakable.

My anchor.

My gravity.

The only thing keeping me from drowning.

And when my tears finally fade, when silence settles between us once more, Santo pulls away just enough to look into my eyes.

"I want to know what happened. *Why* did this happen?" My voice is steady, but inside, I'm splintering.

"I don't want to be in the dark anymore," I tell him.

Santo hesitates. I can see the war in his eyes, the battle between protecting me and telling me the truth.

Finally, he nods.

"All right," he concedes, his voice low. His dark eyes lock onto mine, the intensity leaving me breathless. "I'll tell you everything."

We move to the couch, and Santo pulls me close, wrapping me in the warmth of his body before he begins.

His voice is calm but deadly as he tells me how he knows Angelo is hiding something with Maksim. His suspicions. His unspoken rage.

And then he tells me about my father's role in my planned abduction.

The words shatter me.

A sob rips from my throat, raw and broken, my body folding in on itself. Santo tightens his arms around me, but it doesn't stop the way my chest contracts under the weight of betrayal.

"No more," he whispers against my hair, his grip firm, as if he's trying to hold me together. "I won't tell you more."

But I can't stop now. I *need* to know.

I force myself to breathe, to steady the ache inside me. My voice is small, pleading. "*Please*, Santo. Tell me everything."

He hesitates. And then, reluctantly, he does.

He tells me my mother was complicit—but ignorant to the deeper details. That her life is spared, but she's being sent to Russia to live with her sister. That she'll never set foot in our world again.

He tells me about the QUEEN file and how Vartan Sarkisian indeed had sent the order to have me taken as a child. A cold, creeping dread seeps into my bones.

"They've had me on their radar since I was young."

My stomach twists. The realization; how deep this goes, how long I've unknowingly been hunted, brings a kind of fear I wasn't prepared for.

"What if—" My voice falters. I swallow the knot in my throat. "What will we do if they keep coming for me?"

Santo doesn't even pause.

"I thought about this since the moment I knew your father was involved," he says, his voice hard, resolute, the voice of a man ready to wage war for what he loves. "I'll take you away. We have safe houses in Alaska. I'd bring you there."

Alaska. Far. *Cold.* Lonely.

The thought of being alone in an unfamiliar place fills me with dread. I shake my head. "No, I don't want to be alone."

His expression softens. But his resolve doesn't.

"Then I'll go with you."

My breath catches.

"I would leave Cosa Nostra in a heartbeat if it meant keeping you safe."

His words floor me.

"But it's a part of you," I whisper. "Your family—"

"Vasilisa," he interrupts, firm. His eyes bore into mine, unflinching. "*You* are a part of me. You are the only family I need."

His voice carries no doubt. No hesitation. Just love. Pure, unwavering devotion.

With a small smile, I suggest, "Then maybe we should stay."

Santo studies my face, searching for any hesitation. Any doubt. When he finds none, he nods.

"If you want to stay, then we will stay," he says, firm. "But I am *never* leaving your side again."

A small giggle escapes me at the thought of us being together at all times. "Santo, we can't be together every moment of every day. I have courses to complete and you have work."

He doesn't even blink. "You can work for me."

I stare at him.

"You can take your classes. We 'll set up a desk in my office, just for you."

I arch a brow. "I guess you've thought this through then."

His smirk is low and lazy, despite the exhaustion in his eyes "I've given it a thought or two."

He watches me with that same quiet reverence, the look that makes my heart ache in a way I'll never quite get used to. I exhale softly.

"Okay, then that's our plan," I whisper into the quiet room.

"That's our plan."

Chapter 60

SANTO

Four Months Later

The renovations on our estate are finally complete, but my wife prefers the penthouse now.

I've spoiled her—and *myself,* far too much, taking her to work at NovaRael every day. Having Vasilisa there has slowed my work and wrecked her grades, though I can't bring myself to care when she's sprawled out for me on my desk, moaning my name. I've taken every opportunity to have her—against bookshelves, over conference tables mere minutes before a meeting, and my personal favorite, in the elevator.

Vasilisa used to tremble with nerves every time we stepped inside one. Now, she trembles for entirely different reasons. One morning before work, I dropped to my knees, tasted her until she begged, and now? Now she gets wet the second those doors close.

When we aren't at work, we indulge. Dinners at the freshly restored La Serenata, lunches at the Russian bistro she loves. But no matter where we go, she always ends up in my lap, my hands under her skirt, my mouth pressed to her ear, reminding her *exactly* who she belongs to.

Romeo and Luca have taken to different sectors of our family business since Vasilisa has been with me full time, choosing to continue online classes instead of in person.

They still steal her away for the occasional poker game.

My father is doing well in rehabilitative therapy, for an old man he's well on his way to healing, his next venture is to retire in Italy.

As for my brother, I have yet to speak to him, it's the longest we've gone and the fact that he hasn't *demanded* I speak to him, further proves my suspicions that he has been hiding something.

At the penthouse, I watch Vasilisa paint as I go over details about Artemis and Athena for Zeus. Wesley Beaumont has a flagship on all things AI, and combining WesTech with NovaRael on this new endeavor is proving more difficult than we previously anticipated. I grab my notepad and flip the page where I sketch the design for my next gadget when the soft swish of her brush against the canvas pulls my attention.

She hums softly, lost in her own world, the sunlight catching in her hair as she tilts her head. There's a small crease between her brows—the same one she gets when she's focused, the one that makes her impossibly beautiful. I steal a glance before returning to my notes, but I don't miss the moment when she turns to me, her hands on her hips.

"You're not listening to me," she complains.

I set my pen down, letting my gaze drift over her. That yellow sundress, the one that makes her look like the first day of spring, only makes her pout more devastating.

Gorgeous.

"Yes, Dea. What do you need, my love?"

"Someone is requesting access," she says, hesitation flickering in her eyes.

Her fingers twitch slightly, a small tell I've come to recognize. Concern, but not fear. Still, I take her hand in mine, my thumb brushing over the faint streak of blue paint near her wrist before bringing it to my lips.

"I'm expecting someone," I reassure her, pressing a kiss to her skin. "It's okay, Dea. Why don't you let them up?"

She huffs, clearly unimpressed with my calm demeanor. Pulling her hand away, she tugs off the smock she's been wearing over that gorgeous sundress and tosses it into my lap, her lips pressed together in that way that tells me she's trying not to smile.

I watch as she strides to the elevator, her movements full of reluctant curiosity. I hear her push the button and wait, anticipating the gasp or squeal of joy that will more than likely follow.

VASILISA

I know Santo wants me answering doors to boost the confidence I lost when our home was destroyed. He thinks this will help me feel in control again, but I've told him time and time again—I'm *not* glass. Still, I sigh, pressing the access button on the elevator, waiting for it to arrive.

When the doors slide open, I expect Luca or Romeo, but instead, a woman stands there, her brown hair pulled into two playful space buns. She's wearing a crop top and ripped jeans, a grin already tugging at her lips.

It takes a second for my brain to catch up. I blink, my mind struggling to place her in this moment—then it clicks.

"Luna!" I squeal, throwing my arms around her.

We jump in unison like two kids reunited after a long summer apart. I can hear Santo chuckling behind me, his deep voice a warm reminder of his constant presence.

When we part, Luna's bright smile feels like a burst of sunshine on a cloudy day. "I've missed you so much," I say, squeezing her once more.

"I missed you too," she replies, her eyes sweeping across the penthouse. Her jaw drops slightly. "Damn, that husband of yours doesn't *miss.* This place is gorgeous!"

I giggle, taking her hand and leading her toward the living room where Santo stands with his notepad in hand. "I know," I reply, glancing back at her with a grin.

"Welcome, Luna," Santo says kindly, striding toward me. He presses a chaste kiss to my lips, his hand lingering briefly on my waist before stepping back. "Why don't you take her to the kitchen? If you need me, I'll be in the study."

He disappears down the hall, and I guide Luna to the kitchen, my heart still buzzing from the joy of her arrival.

The moment we step into the kitchen, my heart warms. The table is set with pastries, snacks, and a carafe of freshly brewed coffee, steam curling into the air like an invitation.

"Santo must have done all this," I say, gesturing toward the spread as I watch Luna's eyes widen in disbelief.

"He's a keeper, isn't he?" she says with a wide grin, taking a seat and immediately reaching for a muffin.

"He is," I reply with a giggle, sitting down beside her.

Our laughter fills the kitchen as we dive into stories of old and new, moments shared and moments missed. We talk about Mimi and her reluctance to return home, her newfound popularity at Andras, and everything in between. For the first time in what feels like forever, I feel a sense of normalcy returning to my life.

With Luna here, it's as if nothing has changed.

Eventually, the conversation takes a more serious turn. Luna's gaze lingers on me a moment longer than usual, her smile fading slightly. She reaches across the table, her hand warm as it covers mine.

"How are you *really* doing?" she asks, her voice soft but insistent.

"I'm good," I reassure her. "We're good."

"I mean with what you had to do," she says quietly. "Santo told me."

I nod, understanding now why my husband set this up. I won't speak to him about the lives I took.

"I know I did what I had to in order to survive, but I hated it," my eyes well with tears and Luna wraps her arms around my shoulders. "I hated it."

The sob that wretches out of me is cleansing as my friend holds me,

"We don't have to talk about it anymore," she whispers softly. "We can let it fall in the back recesses of our mind, okay?"

I sniffle and nod. "Santo says I'll never have to do that again."

She nods seriously, "With a husband like that, I believe it."

I giggle at that, and she chuckles wiping the tears from her eyes that haven't fallen. "Want to hear something weird?" she asks, letting me go.

"Of course," I say, grabbing a napkin and wiping my tear-stained cheeks.

"Nico's downstairs," she says, her lips tucked between her teeth.

"What?!"

She shrugs, "He's circling the block, he doesn't realize that I know he's there, but the man's been following me for *months*."

"Why?" I ask and Luna's face turns mauve, she shrugs again.

"I don't know, but having a *beastly* stalker isn't the worst thing that's happened to me."

We laugh and continue our conversation; I can't help but feel grateful for this moment of respite from outside worries. As hours pass by and evening bathes the city in its soft glow, Luna finally takes her leave. I walk her to the elevator, promising to see her again soon.

I find Santo still in his study, drowning in stacks of blueprints, his laptop blinking with unread emails. His sleeves are pushed up, his fingers tangled in his hair, the weight of the world sitting heavy on his shoulders.

"You're working too hard," I say quietly, leaning down to press a soft kiss to his forehead.

He looks up at me with tired eyes, but there's a smile—small, lingering, the kind that always makes my heart skip a beat.

"And you're distracting me too much," he counters, his voice edged with amusement as his hands find my waist, pulling me onto his lap.

"Then I guess I should leave," I tease, feigning an attempt to get up.

But Santo is quicker. His arms lock around me, pulling me back down, his lips chasing mine in an onslaught of kisses—cheeks, jaw, the corner of my mouth—until I'm gasping with laughter, unable to catch my breath.

Then, something shifts. His kisses slow, turning deliberate. His teeth graze my neck, his hands dragging up my thigh, fingers slipping beneath the hem of my dress.

"Santo," I sigh, threading my fingers through his dark hair.

His gray eyes smolder as he gazes up at me—not just with desire, but with something deeper. Something that always tugs at my heart.

"Just one more minute," he whispers against my skin, his lips sending a tremor down my spine.

Then his fingers slip past lace and silk, slipping inside me, parting me with ease. My head tips back as a soft moan escapes me, pleasure sparking through my veins.

"Alright," I breathe, surrendering.

The rest of the world blurs as Santo expertly unravels me with just his touch, his mouth, his whispered devotion. And even as my body hums with pleasure, my thoughts drift—to his promise.

That I will never have to experience what happened again. That he will protect me. Always.

He anchors me with that vow. And now, that same certainty is the fire burning through my veins, pushing me closer, higher, until I can barely breathe.

"I love you, Santo," I murmur against his ear, my heart swelling with something almost too big to hold.

A low growl rumbles from his chest—deep, possessive—before he captures my lips, stealing my breath.

"I love you more, Dea," he murmurs, his hands gliding over my body, leaving fire in their wake.

I whimper at the gentle scrape of his teeth, at the way his fingers trace lazy, devastating curls inside me, pulling pleasure from me like it belongs to him.

The space feels too confined, too warm—I want *more.*

I pull away slightly, breathless, watching the flicker of concern in his eyes, but he doesn't protest when I stand up and reach out for his hand.

"Let's take this somewhere more comfortable," I suggest with a sultry grin.

Santo's gaze darkens, anticipation sharpening the edges of his features as he rises, his fingers curling possessively around mine as he follows me.

The setting sun filters through the windows, casting him in gold, illuminating the sharp planes of his face, the hunger in his eyes.

By the time we step inside our room, I barely have a moment to turn before he presses me against the wall, his mouth claiming mine, his hands sliding beneath my dress, peeling away the last barriers between us.

His lips taste of mint and coffee, of warmth and home.

His hands deftly unbutton my dress, while mine fumble with his belt. He chuckles, pulling away to help me, his gaze never leaving mine. His touch is like a balm to my soul, erasing the haunting memories of the past and replacing them with joy and pleasure.

We shed our clothes like we're shedding layers of ourselves, revealing more than just our bodies. We're unveiling our hearts; all of our fears, hopes, dreams, everything that makes us who we are. And as I collapse onto the bed under Santo's weight, I know that this is where I belong.

With him.

To *him.*

Always.

SANTO

She grips the covered canvas like it's the last thing in the world and she can't bear to part with it, her knuckles white, she still won't let me see it, not until we get back to the estate. Lucky as I am that she's agreed to go back, at least to see Mrs. Keen, she's insisted we bring the painting she's been holding as a surprise for me. I suggested she put it in the trunk, but she refused, so now I drive my wife back to our newly renovated home canvas snugly in hand.

Her phone rings and I try to feign confusion as to who could be calling when I already know who it is. She scrambles to hold on to the canvas while she digs her phone out of her purse one handed, she hands it to me to answer.

"Put it on speaker please," she asks, her hands going right back to the canvas. I answer the phone and put it on speaker.

"Vasi?" Pietro's voice comes through and my wife all put tosses the canvas between her legs and reaches for the phone. Normally this would cause a ping of jealousy, but my Vasilisa has lost so much, she needs as much family as she can get.

"Pietro, how are you?" she asks concern etched on her perfect face.

"I'm well. Santo told me about what happened, and I wanted to apologize I wasn't there," his voice apologetic through the phone.

"It's okay, I'm okay," she says softly.

"No, you're like my sister Vasilisa, I owe you an explanation. After guarding Elena, I went to see the sister of my friend I told you about."

"Oh," Vasilisa breathes, "Is she okay?"

"She's doing alright, I'll be here with her for a bit and check in on my family, I'll be back in a few months' time."

"Okay, you be safe."

"Of course, you, too."

She ends the call her eyes flicking toward me, a soft smile tugging at her lips. "Thank you."

She slips her phone back in her purse, so I take her hand and intertwine our fingers before she can death grip the canvas again.

The rest of the drive is silent, save for the occasional hum of some passing vehicle or the wind rustling the leaves along the road. Vasilisa stares out the window, deep in thought.

As we pull up to our estate, she finally lifts her gaze from the scenery and looks at me. Her blue eyes swim with unshed tears, and I give her hand a gentle squeeze.

"Are you ready?" I ask her softly. She nods and takes a deep breath that sounds dangerously shaky but gets out of the car, nonetheless.

Our home looms over us as we walk towards the front door. It's been a while since we've last been here–too busy running from our memories and horrors of the past.

Mrs. Keen, opens the door before we even get to the first step. She looks tired, but her eyes still hold that same warmth they always did as she beams at me, my heart softens.

"Welcome back," Mrs. Keen greets us the moment we step inside.

Vasilisa rushes forward, throwing herself into the woman's arms, her small frame trembling with emotion. Mrs. Keen holds her just as fiercely, her eyes damp as she strokes my wife's hair.

We retreat to the kitchen, settling into the warmth of familiarity—hot tea, quiet laughter, the comfort of home. Mrs. Keen and Vasilisa clutch onto each other like family, and for a brief, bittersweet moment that makes me wonder how my wife and mother would have been if they had the chance to meet.

When we finish catching up, we move toward the pantry. Vasilisa clutches the canvas tightly between her trembling hands, her nervous gaze darting to the elevator. Her body shakes slightly, and anger rises—that something so simple has become a fear she has to conquer.

I wrap my arms around her shoulders, my grip firm but gentle. "It's just like the one at work," I remind her, rubbing slow circles into her back, trying to soothe her.

She shakes her head, tears brimming in those beautiful eyes that still undo me every damn time.

"I can't go in there, Santo," she whispers, voice raw, breaking something inside of me.

I can't have that.

Determined to help her overcome this hurdle, I hold her face gently between my hands, forcing her to look into my eyes. "Will you do this for me Dea?" I ask, pleading with her.

She tucks her lower lip between her teeth, her eyes filled with both weariness and love as she shakily nods her head.

I release her face and press my thumb on the call button, the elevator doors slide open. I take the covered canvas from her trembling hands and place it against the wall inside. Standing between the doors, I wait for her to enter. She looks at the elevator hesitantly before taking a tentative step inside. I nod encouragingly at her and feel anger boiling inside me at the thought that she has to overcome something so simple because of those bastards.

Feeling Vasilisa's warm hand grasps mine, I catch her gaze and notice the concern in her furrowed brow.

"Are you okay?" she asks, now standing in between the doors of the elevator with me.

I smirk at her small success and nod, squeezing her hand and pulling her the rest of the way in. The doors slide closed behind us and her hand shakes slightly in mine. I glance at her, noticing the paleness of her face and the wide-eyed look she gives to the floor.

I push the button for our bedroom before pressing Vasilisa against the elevator wall. A gasp escapes her lips, confusion flashing through her eyes before I kiss her—hard, deep, taking everything she gives me and demanding more. She melts into me instantly, moaning softly as her body relaxes, arms wrapping around my neck. I lift her up, and her legs wrap around my waist, where she belongs.

I swallow every breathless sound she makes, my hands already skimming up her thighs, pushing her dress higher and higher, impatient.

I groan as my fingers find thin silk; the only barrier between me and what's mine. My girl always makes it so easy for me. Hooking my fingers beneath the fabric, I push it aside.

Vasilisa gasps against my mouth at the first stroke of my fingers over her clit, her body arching into mine.

She tries to stifle her moans, but she's never been good at that, her lips latching onto my neck instead, biting down to contain the sounds.

"Is this what you wanted?" I murmur, voice low against her ear as I press a finger inside her, feeling her pussy tighten around me immediately. "For me to touch you?"

She muffles another gasp, her teeth grazing my throat, and it only makes me hungrier.

"Answer me," I command, my voice dark, even as my fingers keep teasing, stroking, pushing her further.

She nods frantically. "Yes," she gasps, voice shaky. "Yes, Santo."

"That's my girl."

I slide a second finger inside her, stretching, stroking, working her into a frenzy. Her hips roll, desperate, chasing what only I can give her.

The elevator jolts slightly as it stops, and her eyes fly open in surprise. I don't stop.

Instead, I press my thumb against her clit, rubbing in tight, precise circles that have her clutching onto me, nails biting into my shoulders.

"You're close," I whisper against her ear, watching every flicker of pleasure play across her face. "Let it happen."

As the doors slide open, her pussy clenches around my fingers, pleasure rippling through her in waves.

She gasps against my throat, soft, breathless, so fucking perfect as she shatters in my arms.

I stroke her through it, dragging out every last tremor until she sags against me, boneless, *spent*.

Slowly, I slide my fingers out of her and set her down on shaky legs.

She leans against me, catching her breath, and I take my time—licking the taste of her from my fingers, savoring every last trace of her pleasure.

She watches me, flushed and dazed, strands of hair clinging to the dampness on her forehead. I reach up, brushing them away, smoothing my thumb along her temple.

She's so fucking beautiful, I smirk. "Welcome home."

I grab the canvas, pressing it into her hands before leading her toward our bedroom.

She smiles at me following behind, I watch as she stands the canvas on the dresser and turns to me expectantly.

"Now?" I ask softly.

She nods and unveils the painting with bated breath.

My heart drops to my stomach, and a lump grows in my throat as I take in what my wife has created. It's a portrait of my mother. Vasilisa has captured the light in my mother's eyes so well, it's as if I'm face to face with her right now.

"I... I..." I stutter, struggling to find the words. The room feels like it's spinning around me.

"Do you like it, Santo?" Vasilisa looks up at me through thick lashes, her eyes wide and filled with concern. Her hands fidget together.

"Like it?" I echo, my voice hoarse. "Vasilisa... this... I don't know what to say..."

"I wanted to do something nice," she tells me in hushed tones, "A gift. I wanted to give you something that would mean a lot to you."

I take in another deep breath, forcing down the lump in my throat. My hands reach out for the painting gently, tracing over my mother's portrait reverently.

My wife has somehow managed to bring life back to a woman who is no longer with us. Every curve of my mother's face, every crinkle at the corner of her eyes, every strand of her hair - it's all there on the canvas.

"It's perfect," I whisper, my heart swelling with love for this incredible woman before me. "You've brought her back to me."

Vasilisa looks relieved at my words and allows herself a soft smile. She moves closer towards me and slips an arm around my waist while resting her head against my chest.

"Thank you," I tell her sincerely, wrapping an arm around her and pulling her closer into me. "Thank you for this and for coming back home."

Her fingers trace over the fabric of my shirt as she says quietly, "This is our home, Santo. No matter where we go or what happens, this will always be our home."

I press a tender kiss on top of her head, my other hand still holding onto the portrait of my mother. "I know the perfect place for it."

***

I hang my mother's portrait in the dining room, its presence a quiet reminder of the past, of everything that shaped me into the man I am. But when I turn, my gaze lands on the present—on my *future.*

Vasilisa stands beside the table, her delicate hands adjusting the final details, ensuring everything is perfect. The table is beautifully adorned, not just with the meal she and Mrs. Keen worked on with Julian, but with the subtle touches of her love woven into every piece. Fresh flowers in a delicate vase, folded napkins with precise creases, a warmth in the setting that never existed here before her.

She beams at me, proud of her display, her expression expectant—seeking my approval, my appreciation. But she should know, she has it. She *always* has it.

I take a long look at my mother's portrait, and for the first time in years, a sense of peace washes over me. A peace I never thought I'd find. A peace that exists only because of the woman before me.

I look at my Vasilisa, truly look at her, and awe anchors deep in my chest. At the love she shows me so effortlessly, so openly. She is my light, my peace, my salvation.

The constellation of my entire existence.

A love like this should be celebrated—not just today, but every single day for the rest of my life. And I will. I will honor her. Protect her. Worship her.

For now, I take a seat beside my wife and do what I do best—

I watch her.

Because there is no world worth living in where she is not beside me.

EPILOGUE ONE

TWO MONTHS LATER

Visiting my brother was the worst mistake I could have done. Vasilisa insisted I hear him out and *for what?* To find out he had *footage* of what happened to my wife.

The bastard put cameras in *my* basement and now I *know.*

I watched it.

How she fought.

What they did to my wife.

What I was inept to prevent…

The sound of her humming reaches me before I step into the room. It's soft, almost airy, and I know without looking that she's painting. She always hums now when she paints, like the brush and the melody are tied together, creating something I don't deserve.

I stop in the doorway, leaning against the frame as I watch her.

Vasilisa. My wife.

My light.

She's standing near the window, her hair catching the late afternoon sun, the streaks of it falling across her like a halo. She's happy. I can see it in the curve of her lips, the relaxed way she moves as her brush sweeps across the canvas.

And I'm about to *ruin* it.

I don't deserve this moment, this peace, not after what I've done—what I've *allowed* to happen. The weight of my failure has been clawing at me, suffocating me, ever since that night. Ever since I broke the one promise I swore I'd keep.

My chest tightens as I take a step inside. She turns when she hears me, her smile widening, her eyes lighting up like they always do when she sees me. *Fuck, how can she still look at me like that?*

"Santo," she greets softly, setting the brush down and wiping her hands on a rag. "You're home. How did it go with Angelo?"

"Vasilisa." Her name catches in my throat, and I see her smile falter, her brows knitting in concern.

"What's wrong?" she asks, taking a step toward me. "Did something happen?"

I hold up a hand, stopping her in her tracks. "Stay there," I say, my voice rougher than I mean for it to be. She freezes, her head tilting slightly, her confusion evident.

"Santo?"

I run a hand down my face, forcing myself to meet her gaze. "I broke my promise to you," I say, the words coming out like gravel.

Her face falls. She blinks, her lips parting as her breath hitches. "What... what do you mean?" Her voice trembles, and I see it in her eyes—the *fear*, the doubt creeping in.

I take a step closer, but she takes one back, her hand clutching the rag tightly. "Santo, what are you saying? Did you—" Her voice breaks.

"Did you cheat on me?"

"No!" The word bursts out of me, sharp and immediate. I cross the distance between us in two strides, my hands reaching for her shoulders, but I stop myself just short of touching her.

"No, never. *Never* that. Don't even think it."

Her shoulders relax slightly, but her eyes stay locked on mine, searching, unsure.

"Then what is it?"

I swallow hard, the guilt twisting in my gut. "I promised I'd never let anything or anyone harm you. And I failed. I let you get hurt."

Her breath catches, and for a moment, she just stares at me. Then, slowly, she sets the rag down on the table and steps closer, her hands lifting to cup my face.

"You didn't fail me," she says softly, her voice steady despite the tears glistening in her eyes.

"Yes, I did." My voice is hoarse, raw. "I swore to you that nothing would touch you, and it did. You were *hurt*, Vasilisa. And it's my fault. *I wasn't there. I didn't stop it.*"

Her fingers tighten slightly, grounding me, forcing me to focus on her. "I survived because of you," she says, her voice thick with emotion. "There was *no way* you were going to lose me, Santo. You've lost too much already, and I knew I couldn't be another piece of that pain. So I fought for you. I fought because I couldn't bear the thought of you in pain."

Her words slam into me, and my knees weaken. Before I know it, I'm sinking to the floor, wrapping my arms around her middle, pressing my head against her chest.

"I should have been there," I murmur, my voice cracking as her warmth envelops me. "I should have stopped it. I should have—"

"Stop," she whispers, her fingers threading through my hair as she holds me close. "You did everything you could, Santo. You've given me all I need and everything I want. I love you. *I'm here.* I'm not going anywhere."

I squeeze my eyes shut, the guilt and anguish pouring out of me as I cling to her. "I don't deserve you," I rasp, my voice breaking.

"Yes, you do," she says firmly, her hands cradling my head. "You do, Santo. You're my home, just like I'm yours. And *nothing* can take that from us. Not even this."

Her words wrap around me like a balm, soothing the raw edges of my guilt. I stay there for a moment, kneeling at her feet, holding onto her like the lifeline she's always been.

When I finally lift my head, her eyes meet mine, soft and steady.

"Dea," I whisper, my voice hoarse.

She smiles gently, brushing a tear from my cheek with her thumb. "You don't have to be perfect, Santo."

And in that moment, I know she's right.

She always is.

EPILOGUE TWO

SANTO

TWO YEARS LATER

The beeping of my phone wakes up my wife before it wakes me.

I hear her grumble as she reaches over me to grab it. I clasp her wrist before she can fling it across the room as she's done a couple of times before.

This is my *third* replacement phone this month.

"Make it stop," she whines, her voice still heavy with sleep. I gently pry the phone from her small fingers and answer it, bringing it to my ear.

"You couldn't have called in the morning?" I seethe, my tone sharp.

"No, Valentina is missing," Luciano Castillo, head of the cartel, says urgently on the other end.

His voice cuts through my irritation like a knife. I sit up abruptly, causing Vasilisa to slip off of me and onto the bed with a huff.

"What do you need?" I ask, now fully awake and ready to handle whatever trouble has arisen.

"Any resources you have. Maksim and Angelo are already on their way here. Can you get back tonight?"

I glance at Vasilisa, who has turned on the lamp and is squinting sleepily at me with one hand protectively cradling her swollen belly. "I can make it work."

Luciano ends the call, and Vasilisa sighs, pushing herself upright. "I know that look. Where are we going?"

"To Luciano's. His sister is missing," I say, getting out of bed and reaching for my clothes.

"Scarlet?!" Vasilisa asks fearfully, both hands moving instinctively around her belly.

"No, the *other* one, Valentina," I clarify, pulling on a pair of pants.

Vasilisa slips out of bed, waddling toward the bathroom, her petite frame struggling under the weight of her heavily pregnant belly.

"I think maybe you should stay here, Dea."

Vasilisa stops mid-stride turning abruptly to face me, her icy eyes locking onto mine as I button up my shirt.

"I go where *you* go." Her tone leaving no room for argument.

"But the baby—"

"The baby is safe inside me where you left her."

"Her?" I ask, freezing mid-movement. My heart skips a beat as her words register. "You said we couldn't look at the envelope. *You* said the gender would be a surprise!"

Vasilisa's face turns a shade of crimson, and she bites her lip guiltily. "I might have… *peeked,*" she admits softly, avoiding my eyes.

"You peeked?" I ask incredulously, stepping closer to her. "After you made such a big deal about us waiting?"

She fidgets under my gaze, her hands resting on her belly. "I wanted to buy some baby clothes," she says, her voice barely above a whisper. "And I wanted to know if we should pick pink or blue. I'm sorry, Santo."

My irritation vanishes in an instant, replaced by a surge of joy that feels like it might burst out of me.

A girl.

We're having a daughter.

"A daughter," I murmur, my voice thick with emotion. I reach out, placing both hands gently on her belly. "We're having a little girl?"

Vasilisa nods, her lips curving into a soft smile. "Yes. A little girl."

For a moment, the world stops. The chaos of Luciano's call, the worry about Valentina, all of it fades into the background. All I can think about is the tiny life growing inside my wife—the little girl who's already stolen my heart.

"We're having a daughter," I repeat, my voice filled with awe. I drop to my knees in front of Vasilisa, pressing a kiss to her belly. "Dea, you've given me the greatest gift I could ever ask for."

She laughs softly, her fingers threading through my hair. "You're not upset that I peeked?"

I look up at her, my eyes shining with love. "Upset? Dea, I'm over the moon." I stand, cupping her face in my hands. "You've made me the happiest man alive."

Vasilisa chuckles softly. "Good," she says, her tone light but commanding. "Now, can you please grab my hospital bag, just in case, and a couple of snack cakes to go?"

She smiles sweetly, mischief sparkling in her eyes as she waddles toward the bathroom.

"Thank you, Santo," she adds over her shoulder, disappearing behind the door, likely already delighted by the thought of indulging in another one of her tasty treats.

My chest still tight with emotion. A daughter. *My* daughter. The idea fills me with a sense of pride and purpose I've never felt before. I glance at the hospital bag sitting in the corner of our room, already packed with all her essentials—snack cakes included.

A small smile tugs at my lips as I lift it.

Of course, she'd want more. My Vasilisa always plans for contingencies, but her cravings for her favorite cakes are the only indulgence she never tries to resist.

As I head to the kitchen to add a few more to the bag, my thoughts drift to the tiny life growing inside her.

My daughter. I've haven't met her, but I already know I'd die for her. For *both* of them.

I will protect them with everything I am—every ounce of strength, every resource, every piece of myself. *Nothing* and no one will ever harm them while I'm alive.

I tuck the extra snack cakes into the bag, my hand lingering for a moment on the zipper. This impromptu trip is just another reminder of the dark world we live in, but it doesn't matter.

As long as I have Vasilisa and now our little girl, I'll always have the light.

ACKNOWLEDGEMENTS

Writing can often feel like a solitary journey, but I have been incredibly blessed with the most amazing support system.

To my mother – who is, without a doubt, absolutely *not allowed* to read this book – thank you for never giving up on my dream. Your faith in me, even when the path was uncertain, has been a light in the darkest moments. I am forever grateful for the love and strength you've shown me, and for reminding me, *always*, to keep going.

To my cousins, Destiny and Tianna, you both were the sparks that restarted this journey for me. Your belief in me throughout writing this first book meant everything to me.

My ARC readers, Amber, Ashli, Britnie, Cassandra, Chandra, Che, Frances, Natalie and Shan, Thank you from the bottom of my heart for taking a chance on this book, for being open to reading it, giving me feedback and being such wonderful humans!

To my fellow authors:

Julia Eichenlaub, I don't even know where to start because thank you will never feel like enough. You have been the best author bestie through this book journey—always supporting my posts, sharing them, and lifting me up when I doubted myself. I could text you anytime, about the smallest, most confused questions, and you were always there with advice, wisdom, and the reassurance I needed. You've *been there, done that*, and having you as a friend who truly *gets* it has been the biggest gift. I don't know what I would have done without your kindness, patience, and honesty. You have been an insurmountable support, and I am endlessly grateful to have you in my life.

Julia Andern, thank you for your unwavering support of my work, for your kind words, and for being one of my very first author friends. Having you by my side through this journey has meant more to me than I can express. Your encouragement, your excitement for every step I took, and the way you always cheered me on have been truly special. I can't wait to return the favor and hype you up just as much when your debut arrives—I'll be your biggest cheerleader!

Aurora Steinhart, thank you for always keeping your DMs open for my endless questions—even when neither of us had the answers. You are the most *unhinged*, beautiful soul I've ever met, a true rockstar in your own right while still lifting up everyone around you. Your support, your energy, and your friendship mean so much to me, and I'm so grateful to have you in my corner. Thank you for believing in my work and for being *you*!

And finally to every reader who has picked up this book, thank you for allowing these characters and stories to become a part of your world.

ABOUT THE AUTHOR

A lover of storytelling in all its forms, Amanda is known for building intricate, interconnected worlds, leaving behind hidden easter eggs for books years in advance. Her stories are intense, beautiful, and emotional, often featuring yearning men and women with quiet, unwavering strength.

Writing has always been a part of Amanda's world. As a child, she lived inside her imagination, and now, she pours that same magic into every book she writes. She believes destiny is real—but only for those *meant* to shape it. When inspiration strikes, she writes the scene immediately, whether it's for her next release or book thirteen.

When she's not writing, Amanda loves baking, creating book covers inspired by song titles, and indulging in tarot and natal chart readings (but don't expect her to reveal *all* your secrets).

She hopes that when readers reach the last page of her books, they experience a sense of longing—missing the characters, feeling happy for them, but always wanting just one more glimpse into their world. (*And she might just give it.*)

Amanda is currently working on her next novel, crafting another love story filled with depth, desire, and legacy.

www.ingramcontent.com/pod-product-compliance
Lightning Source LLC
Chambersburg PA
CBHW070151310726

48976CB00001B/68